SOLIPSUM

A Novel by Daniel Couto

Strategic Book Group

Strategic Book Group
P.O. Box 333
Durham CT 06422
www.StrategicBookClub.com

ISBN: 978-1-61204-722-5

Design: Dedicated Business Solutions, Inc. (www.netdbs.com)

Solipsum is dedicated to my parents.

And to Charlie.
I miss you.

Acknowledgements

This book took awhile (quite a while) to write and it couldn't have happened without the loving support of a number of people. I would like to thank the following: Ayres and Irmelind Couto, my parents, for their boundless love and support, and who never even blinked when I said I wanted to write, James Town, for providing invaluable feedback I didn't listen to the first time, and for the "Platinum Pussy," Brian Dawson, for his unchanging friendship over the years and invaluable advice, Leila Courey for her comments and enthusiasm and especially for her faith, Peter Mensah, who was a friend in some dark times and who's professionalism, sage advice and laughter have impoved my life immeasureably, Glen Hanson with whom I have done some of my best work and whom I will always love, Linda Gardiner, my NY roomie who read Solipsum and made some great suggestions, Kari Lakomski for her love, friendship, patience and spirituality, Oliver Couto, Natalie Couto and her hubby Keith Pace-Asiak, Rita Poole, the second subscriber, Henrietta Haniskova, for always being there and catching that Polaroid "girl-response-thing" and making a bunch of other valuable suggestions, Jonathan Boorstein for concise and powerful feedback that helped the story immeasurably, Betty Sze, Sabumnim David Herbert for technical help and being an astonishing and eye opening inspiration, Tony Chaar, a great artist and an even greater friend, Alisa Krost, stylist extraordinaire and great friend too, Kelly Meredith for her professionalism, artistry and great company, Michael Currie, who is Solipsum, Amber Noelle, Victor Tavares, Arash, Julie Miller (who never forgets), Willi, Drake, Anne Bock, Ilde DeMarco, Cory Mann and Lorraine Bird from NEXT, Cathy LeDrew and Cynthia, Mark Askwith, Michael Stevenson, Mark Terry, Walter Pacifico, Sifu Rupert Harvey, Sifu Simon, Bob Noorduin, Salem, Elle (you thought I'd forgotten you, didn't you), Vicki Sander, Lydia Pannicia, Gerry Turnbull, Wayne Barlowe and his book Barlowe's Inferno for its incredible depictions of Hell, and Sandy Tritt for her fine editing and suggestions, and Anna LeMay, aka Bunnie.

I would especially like to thank Donna Locke, my muse, for her love, friendship, beauty, intelligence and all those lessons about living in the Now (not to mention her great edits). You are the first reader and my best friend without whom none of this would have been possible. I will always love you. Hyuh!

A Note

Solipsum is set in a parallel universe where film is still revered. Digital photography as well as much more advanced technology also exist but it is film that is most respected as a shooting medium.

www.solipsum.com

SOLIPSUM

Prologue

I remember her kerchief, fluttering in the breeze, nails lightly trailing along my arm as she laughed that musical feline laugh.

The Italian Alps seemed especially beautiful on that perfect summer's day, and I didn't have a care in the world. I was with the best friend I'd ever had, the girl of my secret dreams.

"Come sit on my lap," she said, her voice strong and clear as it came to me over the wind, "I'm cold." Then she flashed that goofy grin, the one that drove every photographer crazy. Of course I came, nearly putting a knee through the picnic hamper, our rented sportster was so small.

A moving vehicle, a winding road, sure it was crazy. But we were all more than a little crazy back then. And when you're that young and beautiful, and I don't mean beautiful like you know beautiful, I mean anything-you-want-in-the-world-is-yours beautiful, well, you think you'll live forever.

You really do.

Then something—happened. I saw something I shouldn't have been allowed to see. And next thing I knew this huge dump truck was bearing down on us, horn blaring, brakes screaming. All of it happened so fast! And it was over the cliff or into the rocks.

I was thrown past the windshield; otherwise my neck would have snapped. That's what they told me later, anyway. They were amazed that I was even able to move, never mind find her.

She was so—bashed up—lying there on her back with that glorious face tilted up towards the sky. A face that was mysteriously unhurt—pristine. I'd never seen her look so sublime.

I fell crying to my knees and cradled her head. She looked asleep, her hair so soft and sun-warm as I touched it. Then I felt the blood, hot and sticky, its scent like sheared metal. My tears on her face must have brought her back because she opened her eyes, those blue, blue eyes, guileless and child-like and infinite as the vault of the sky above us. They found mine and her lips slowly parted, the tiniest trickle of blood meandering from her mouth.

"You—you do know that I love you, don't you?"

"M—me?"

"You, Spud. Not him. You."

1

Her eyes grew wide and held something in them I'd never seen. "My God," she whispered, ". . . what are you?"
Then she died.

Book 1

10 Years just past Now . . .

30,000 feet somewhere above the North Atlantic, London to New York. First Class.

Solipsum loved to fly. He leaned back in the wide seat, legs outstretched, comfortable in a black turtleneck and black slacks. On his index finger he wore a ruby ring that had once belonged to a king. He gazed out the window and noticed how much the clouds at this altitude resembled the fields of Heaven. It was the closest he came to the human emotion of wonder. He then settled back and closed his eyes, going deep into his mind exploring . . . potentialities. What would this world be like if all he had planned came to pass? He had almost finished constructing a consonance to his thoughts; the album Jim Morrison would have made had he not died so inconveniently. It would have taken the music of the next fifty years in such a completely new and impossibly fresh direction as to defy description. He was having trouble bridging the last chords. Like a broken record, one tone seemed . . . stuck.

His eyes snapped open, surroundings reassimilated, his crystalline awareness searching for and finding that which had disturbed him: the tinny jar of rap music leaking from someone's headphones next to him.

"Excuse me."

A man with a face like chocolate suet looked up from the fashion magazine he had been reading. He larded a shirt almost architectural in cut, dazzling leathers and colorful synthetics bitch-slapping each other, neither giving ground. He was also draped in what appeared to be a small rap label's entire gold reserve. Solipsum's eyes traveled to the man's face, where he saw his own meatsleeve reflected back at him in designer lenses.

A broad hole broke in the suet's surface. "The fuck, man, can't choo see I'm busy here?"

"Your music."

"What about it?"

"I find it disturbing. Please turn it down."

Suet's chubby hand knuckled with gold raised the magazine, his chin jutting to its cover. "This you?"

3

For the second time Solipsum saw himself as if in a mirror, this time photographically. "Yes."

Suet lowered his sunglasses to reveal fried eye whites the yellow of old crack. "Well, now that we know who you are, Mr. Pretty Boy *Versace* Dick Sniffer, you know who *I* am?"

"Yes, I do. Your name is Rufus Jelton, now known as ShitMou', one half of the multi-platinum rap duo ShitMou' and Vanilla-X. Formerly known as 'Jell-O' by the class of '09 because of your unfortunate tendency to jiggle, fat-like, no matter what you wore. That name carried over to your brief stint in Raiford. It was a term of endearment used by seven foot Billy Ray McGruder whenever he referred to his bitch. You."

"That's it! You *dead,* muthafucka! You hear—"

Solipsum raised his hand, thumb and index finger gently closing on nothing—and ShitMou' felt his breath stop. He began to shake, fighting for air. Solipsum grabbed the rapper's hand, almost crushing it as he placed it between his legs. ShitMou' pulled back hard, putting his weight into it. For all the good it did. Then his earpiece was removed with a lover's delicacy, the other man's voice filling his world with an intimacy that smothered all thought. "I am your worst nightmare. Nothing would please me more than to give you ten times what you received from Mr. McGruder. At once." Solipsum's fabric-covered genitals bulged suddenly, writhing and twisting like a sack of snakes. "Then watch your liquefied innards run out of the only orifice that has never lied to you. You will remain silent for the duration of this trip. Do I make myself clear, Jell-O?"

ShitMou's hand struggled feebly, pain-glaze dulling his eyes. He finally managed a nod.

Solipsum smiled, displaying a beautiful set of razored white teeth. Not pointed exactly, just very thin. Like razor blades.

His eyes cut to the aisle to see the first class stewardess approaching. The one he knew had been wondering all flight if he tasted as good as he looked. He released ShitMou's hand, but not the rapper's voice. The girl arrived and leaned over them just a little farther than was necessary. "May I bring you something to drink, Mr. Solipsum?"

"No. Thank you."

She gave the sweating ShitMou' a puzzled glance. "What about—?"

"I believe Mr. Mou' will be sleeping for the duration of the flight."

As he watched the girl go, he heard tiny rap obscenities still bleeding into the air around ShitMou's head. His fingers reached over, flicking off a switch.

Click.

New York City, SplashLight Studios

The most glorious ambient electronica was playing and she had never felt more alive. This feeling that she got whenever she was in front of the camera, this simple joy, was the one aspect of her life that never changed.

Ahhh, the dance, the give and take, the movement through her lovers, the light and the shadow as they concealed and revealed, revealed and concealed.

The clothes were the lens that filtered her essence.

Sometimes she was hard and shiny,

sometimes she was smooth and plastic,

cable knit and textured mossy,

synthetic android, super glossy.

Sometimes she was drenched in color,

saturated and fantastic,

sometimes she was raw emotion,

black and white, monochromatic.

Temptress, seductress, innocence, unconditional love. She was all these things and more. And like the infinite whose essence she embodied, she was never the same twice.

She was fully aware of her power, but what elevated her from the merely beautiful to the realm of the sublime was her knowledge that beauty fades. This awareness allowed her to be in the only place that has ever mattered in front of the camera—the *Now*.

As she moved and turned, the light faceted the jewel of her beauty into film-sized shimmerings of capture. Each was exactly 6cm by 7cm, the chosen format of the day. Moving effortlessly between poses, she marveled and reveled in the life she had been given. She suspected, but did not realize, she was one of history's greatest beauties. In her unique combination of line, grace, energy, and finally, humility, she rivaled Helen of Troy.

Whom she once was.

She made a thousand dollars a minute on a good day, and this was one of those days. She was now and would be for the foreseeable future the most stunning creature on the planet. Her name was Phoena, and she was a model.

She had just spun into a turn, extending the line, the Clothing mannequined to best advantage when the vision burst upon her mind, thrusting past her defenses. Her breath caught, the rhythm broken, body slamming to a stop flash-frozen by strobe burst. "Are you all right?" someone shouted but she barely heard, the drum-sound pounding in her ears, the pain a molten blade as it slid into her brain. She cried out, then screamed, fists jammed to her eyes, the blade sliding deeper, twisting as the face, that *face*, loomed larger and larger, the room spiraling, floor rushing up, the face now vast, Solipsum's face.

Before oblivion took her.

On a dusty road, somewhere in the Dominican Republic.

He was royally pissed. The location was too hot, make-up sucked, his first assistant was not working out and the models (except for one) couldn't ride and were thus completely wrong for the job. To top it off, the art director had taken to touching his ass (again) whenever she needed to make a point (which was often). He was shooting a campaign for *Repubic Jeans*. His name was Joshua Stone and he was the highest paid photographer on the planet. He was also one of its most talented. If someone were to mention these two facts to him, he would have assumed the bored expression he got when presented with irrelevancies. Because for Joshua Stone, it had always been about pushing the envelope, and everything was a tool in the service of that ideal.

Stone now stood in the burning sun, khakis and t-shirt already sticky, a hand shielding slitted eyes as he surveyed the scene before him. Motorcycles, shooting truck and jean-clad models all stood at the ready. He quickly ran through a mental checklist as the sweat began to bead his shaven skull. He noticed, not for the first time, that the silver halide black of his skin absorbed even more heat than it did light. Perhaps that was simply because at 6'6", he stood closer to the sun than most—a sun which he noted was finally at the perfect angle. He cupped his hands and shouted, "Okay, let's roll!"

Three bike engines roared to life as Stone clambered aboard the mobile shooting platform. The wide wooden ledge was spot-welded to the driver's side of the battered old pick-up, barely a foot above ground. Simple and solid, it was where he needed to be to get that special angle critical to his vision.

The convoy began moving along the narrow dirt road, trees and tropical foliage a solid wall of green almost close enough to touch. There was little room to maneuver, and even less for error.

He gave the signal and the massive prototype racing machines throttle-screamed with the power of burning high-test. The girls jockeyed furiously for position, fat grooved tires spitting up plumes of dirt and gravel. In an instant, a magnificent hurricane of grit, sound and streaking color filled his world. The hurricane's eye was Joshua's eye, the calm at the center, projected through his viewfinder.

He fired away, barely pausing to change backs on the 220 motor wind camera he held in his hands like a toy. Images that would later appear on billboards, bus shelters and in-store posters were chosen/frozen instantly, instinctively.

Jimmy, the first assistant, turned to look down the road ahead and felt his stomach drop. *Jesus H., I thought this road was closed!* An old junk truck had suddenly appeared in the road ahead of them, piled high with God knows what and taking up way too much room.

He hammered on the truck's side but fucking Pedro had the radio up too loud again and couldn't hear shit. Jimmy turned to his boss. "Josh! We got trouble!"

Stone was lost in the Now, eyes painted to the action. Jimmy saw the junk truck and quickly figured out there would be none of that ships passing in the night thing. *Unless we're talking Titanic. That old junker is gonna scrape our rig off like—fuck! No time!*

He jumped the rail into the truck bed just as Stone handed his camera back to be reloaded. The photographer twisted sharply when no one took it, to see his first assistant where he should not have been. Before he could yell "What the fuck?", they both heard the honking horn. Jimmy's skinny arm pointed up the road but Stone had already spun to look. His eyes widened with shock. The junk truck was almost upon them.

He glanced back at Jimmy who shrugged as if to say, "I told ya." Knowing he had no chance, Stone's leg muscles bunched as he reached high for the safety rail. Out of the chaos a voice screamed, "JOSHUA! GET ON!"

His head snapped around to see his best rider racing alongside. He crouched lower, preparing to jump, his eyes for an instant pulled to the motorcycle's wheels, spinning, spinning, close, so close, and time . . . s t r e t c h e d   .   .   .

He found himself falling into a Vortex of images, images, billions of images, like tumbling cards from God's tarot deck, tumbling, fumbling, stumbling—

—towards the edge of the shooting platform, Death rushing towards him, reflex taking over and he was suddenly in the air, camera thrown to Jimmy, landing on the bike's seat with teeth-jarring impact. His arms grabbed the rider's waist just as throttle torque almost threw him backwards to dust and doom.

Too late! Too LATE! his mind screamed as the bike accelerated and swerved between the two rushing vehicles toward a quantum gap that should not . . . have. . . been. And Stone knew they were dead.

Then they were through, rushing down the clear dirt road, wind in his face and it had never felt so good, the rig-wreck crash-sound already fading behind them.

By the time they returned, the ad agency's art director and the junk truck driver were face to face, screaming obscenities over the incredible pile of wreckage. The shooting rig was a write-off and Pedro had had the shit scared out of him, but other than that, no one had been hurt. Money would change hands, but that was not Stone's problem. Not today.

He dismounted and felt the tension-quiver jelly his legs. *Fuck,* he thought, *I can't believe I'm still alive.* It got better as he took the first few steps to the craft table already laden with lunch. The bike rider shut the engine down and sauntered over to join him in the shade. Joshua inclined his head, leaning back against a tree as he popped a cold one. "Thanks, you saved my life. I owe you. Big time."

The bike rider slowly removed her helmet, then shook out a tumbling mane of scarlet hair. She flipped it back from a face that was dirty, sweat-streaked and absolutely stunning. Joshua drank her in, seeing freckles, lashes, simple detail with a clarity he had never experienced.

She grinned at him as though she knew and her green eyes blazed with life. "Does this mean I get danger pay?"

Stone almost choked on his beer, laughing. He wiped the froth from his lips and turned to his first assistant. "Jimmy?"

A sheepish Jimmy looked up from the broken camera he had managed not to catch. "Yes sir?"

"You're fired."

New York City, lower TriBeCa

Sunlight gleamed from molten gold, from silky tufts and strands of blond that swayed and played and intertwined, breeze-coaxed for the briefest instant into something like a window. To look through it would reveal a timeless, swirling Vortex, a thing so beautifully vastly fractal in the backward origami of its complexity it could only be held in God-Mind. And it would seem that if you could look at it just a tiny bit longer, the Universe would be laid bare. And you would never have to ask another question.

Ever.

Then it was gone, as if it had never been. And you thought you must have imagined it. For really, what else could it be, but the breeze? Playing in someone's hair . . .

. . . a girl's hair that framed a striking face with the most intensely violet eyes. She stood amidst her clothes that had been strewn all over the alley, chin thrust forward as she glared defiantly at the window three stories up. "Fuck you, you creep!"

Her ex-boyfriend braced himself in the window's frame, brave with the safety of distance. "No, bitch, fuck you! Find yer own place to stay, ya fuckin' tease!"

"But it's my apartment!"

"Too bad it's my name on the lease!"

The new girlfriend joined him, dangling a bra over the window's edge. "Yeah, Charlie Brown, ya little fuckin' dyke, hit the road!" She snapped her gum with satisfaction, then skinned her teeth as she let the little piece of lingerie flutter to the ground. A pair of glasses were next.

The girl in the alley followed the progress of her favorite bra as it fell directly into a puddle and felt the hot tears come. She wore a cropped black baby-t with the logo for the grrlband *Three Hole Punch* in cracked and faded glitter. The sheared waistline of her baggy cargo pants revealed a thin crescent of thigh cut men's jockeys. Her arms were clenched around her portfolio, making the dragon tattooed on one shoulder puff with ferocity. *Fuck, I'm already late! What am I going to do? I can't just leave this stuff here!*

A change rippled through her like a cool wind, the tears replaced by thousand-folded steel as she remembered who she was, and how she came to be.

"To hell with it. I'm outta here!"

She grabbed her glasses and left the rest.

It was one of those beautiful New York days, an unusual late-October day when Fall forgot she wasn't Summer, so she could see all the bare arms and legs one last time. As the young girl moved through the crowd on her way to what would be the most important appointment of her life, she was completely oblivious to the effect she had on passers-by.

Her name was Charlie, and she was the Future.

She emerged from the subway's depths, still blocks away when she saw it, rising in the distance. It was arguably one of the world's most famous buildings, and now she knew why. She stopped and stared at her destination, peopleflow eddying around her.

Will you look at it! It's like someone made a playland for the Light! All those angles and textures, I don't think I'd ever get tired of shooting there. She shook her head in wonder. *I can't believe I got an interview with this guy, and me just out of photo school too.*

Soaring one hundred stories above the City on a slender stalk of cement and steel, Stone Studios looked like an offering to the sun. It was one of the strangest and most beautiful buildings Charlie had ever seen. It paid but passing homage to gravity and none at all to convention. Old and new combined in ways that surprised and delighted her eyes. She had an impression of massive rusted arches, glassy plasma hemispheres, walls that curved and ran like ridges in thick cream, slowly poured over the rusted crenellations of some long forgotten machine. Then she remembered how late she was and hurried on.

Arrival. And a glass lozenge that took her to the top, ears popping as its doors opened. She found herself in the wide, illuminated corridor formed by two walls that curved and recurved before ending in a large exhalation of stone: a reception desk, some distance away. Recognition flickered at the edges of her memory. The architecture reminded her of something, something so fundamental . . . then it was gone. She shrugged and continued on, marveling at the subtlety of the lighting. It was almost like being in some sort of backlit

(birth canal)

shirt sleeve. Then she saw the first framed photograph. After a quick check to make sure no one was looking, she put her glasses on. *Much better.* It was black and white, tiny, no larger than a 4x5 Polaroid. Which it was. Noon sun, desert, children, three of them, dressed in rags, but with the most beatific smiles on their faces. Such characters! They had obviously known each other forever. One held a hubcap as they laughed at the camera, pushing and shoving like puppies, slightly blurry, just goofing, and each had only one leg, and it wasn't a hubcap, it was a landmine—a dud?—all of this registering in a nanosecond.

She went to the next. There in original was an iconographic image she had seen before only in reproduction, on the cover of the world's leading news magazine. She was astonished at the original's subtle shadings of gray, the depths of emotion they created in the dead soldier's face. The . . . clarity. Very soon, she completely forgot why she had come as she zigzagged from photograph to photograph, wall to wall, lost.

Images assailed her, startling juxta/compositions of stupid rag doll bravery and petalled grenade blossoms, bloody linen trenches and tank tread suppression, symmetries of protruding limb and shrapnels of humility and life, life, everywhere Life. It was almost more than she could bear. What prevented her from feeling bludgeoned by the photographic gauntlet was the astonishing beauty the photographer had made her see in all these situations. Simple human situations that far transcended any artificial boundary of language, skin, border or birth. Slowly she understood that what she was seeing was Joshua Stone's photography.

Before.

The final picture in the series was unusual in that it featured the man himself, sitting in the cargo bay of some army helicopter festooned with gear, feet dangling, a small Canadian flag on his breast pocket. The look on his face was indescribable—Virgil at the Gates.

Then like a curtain dropping, the photographs abruptly changed. Bright flowers of saturated color exploded on white backgrounds and Charlie recognized several images that formed the core of fashion's recent history. Some featured a young and beautiful Harlow Bleake, and Charlie was momentarily saddened as she remembered what had happened to her.

A spread followed the cover, and then came a series of covers, more spreads, ads, nudes and personal work in a creative riot so boundless and exuberant it could only be the work of a child never grown except to mastery.

The last picture was a large 20″ x 24″ blow-up of a magazine cover that Charlie instantly recognized. Simple, just the model, nude, cropped above the waist, hair tousled, looking out at her as if she were right there. Charlie stared in disbelief. *My God, her presence!* It was one of the most famous fashion images in the world.

Phoena's first cover for *Vogue*.

The shot was magnificent but it was the model's eyes that held her, large and green and so compelling she felt she would fall into them. Then she heard a voice behind her.

" 'For her eyes are like armies,

And where her glances fall, there cities burn,

Until the dust of their ashes

is blown away by her sighs.' "

Charlie spun and found herself looking up into one of the most striking faces she had ever seen. "Who—"

"Euripides," said Joshua Stone. "Talking about that woman whose face launched all those ships."

"I've never heard words like that." She quickly removed her glasses.

"You've never met a woman like that." He stepped back a bit. "Who are you?"

"Charlie. My name is Charlie. And I'm—"

"Late," he finished. "You must be the last. Get over to wardrobe. Russ will tell you what to do. And hurry. You almost didn't make it." With that he disappeared around a corner, leaving Charlie staring.

She heard footsteps behind her.

"Hi, I'm Trish, Joshua's receptionist," said a red-haired woman as she approached.

"God, I took way too long to look at this stuff. Now I'm totally late."

Trish smiled in sympathy at this cutie who was so obviously a model. "No worries, frisky creature. They're running behind." She pointed. "First door on your left."

"Thanks!" Charlie smiled over her shoulder as she hurried down the hall.

Trish waved. "Good luck!"

The young girl entered what looked like some sort of model's change room, eyes and armies still reverberating in her head. She saw someone standing with a clipboard, tall and surfer-blond, with glasses and the sort of compact and fibrous musculature Charlie knew quite well. It wasn't the kind that came from the gym. It was the other kind you hardly ever saw. The kind that evolved naturally after thousands of hours of—

"Okay, we need to see you in your underwear."

"W—what?"

"You heard me. Your underwear. Change in there." He pointed.

Charlie hesitated. *This must be some kind of test or something.* She held up her portfolio. "What about my book?"

"Bring it with you."

In the main studio, Joshua Stone stood talking with a silver-haired art director, half his mind still on the strange and striking blond girl he'd seen in the corridor. Their backs were turned when Charlie snuck past in her *Calvin's*, clutching her portfolio to her bosom. She took one look, then quickly averted her gaze. *Oh God, there he is! And I'm nearly naked!* She made a conscious effort to relax. *A test, a test, this is just a test.*

The art director sighed and looked up at Stone. "I know we're a cosmetics company but this has to be the biggest casting *Narcissia's Hope* has ever done. What did we see today, a hundred girls?"

"Probably closer to two. But I think it's Phoena."

"I would have to agree." She glanced at the set. "But this last girl does look rather interesting, even though she's far too tiny."

Charlie watched them from the little black tape X Clipboard Guy had told her to stand on. Stone barely glanced at her as he stepped behind his camera but she still felt her heart do a funny little flip. Then she noticed the rather large crowd of onlookers all staring at her, like they were waiting for something. *Narcissia's* art director crossed her arms and nibbled on her lower lip as Clipboard Guy, Trish and two other assistants lingered a bit farther back. She caught a funny look on Clipboard's face, like he hoped she'd drop her book or something, the oily dog. A strange and powerful tension filled the air, out of all proportion to the events that were unfolding. Everyone seemed to be holding their breath. *This is one hell of a test*, Charlie thought, but after what she'd seen in that corridor, she knew she would do anything to learn from this man.

She pressed her portfolio a little tighter to her breasts as she watched him bring his face to the viewfinder and focus. Then he lifted his head and his eyes met hers. "Uh, we need to see your body."

"Okay, Cherry Co-ra," she whispered. "This is it."

Charlie placed her portfolio on the ground and slowly rose, flowing with only the slightest hesitation into a pose. Feet spread apart as toes gripped the floor, hands resting in tiny fists on either side of her canted hips. Line of leg flowed through tautness of belly to breasts high and shapely, capped with pink translucence. Clean limbed and beautifully proportioned, Charlie was simply exquisite. And completely unaware of her effect. She could have been carved from living marble, were it not for the two bruises, one large and purple-black on her rib cage, the other, fading to yellow, on her forearm. The small dragon tattooed on her shoulder seemed somehow perfect. She stood with an easy grace and sunny confidence, radiating what once we had when the world was young.

It was Charlie's first time in front of the camera.

When Joshua said "Okay!" she looked straight into the lens, past glass, past film plane, directly into his eye.

And smiled.

At that instant, the camera for Stone disappeared and he was back in the hallway. He distantly heard the shutter click, unaware he had shot the Polaroid that would change their lives forever.

Time seemed to lengthen and then it was as if everyone remembered to breathe again. Two assistants began whispering and Stone finally stepped out from behind the lens. "Let's see your book. And you can put your top back on. What agency are you with?"

Charlie blinked. "Agency?"

"Yes, you know, Agency. *BORD, ELITIST, P.M.P.,* what?"

"Uh, I'm not a model, Mr. Stone." Charlie was getting a bad feeling.

"You're not a model?"

"No, I—I had an appointment for an assistant's position." She tried to smile, the feeling worsening.

"Uh—that was two hours ago. I'm sorry, but that position has already been filled."

Charlie jammed her book against her breasts, the smile sliding off her face. "Oh it has, has it? Let me tell you something. I've had one hell of a morning. I've been kicked out of my own apartment and my clothes are scattered over half of New York. Now I come here to see the man who's been my shining idol all through photo school and I'm made to stand in front of him practically naked! And he won't even look at my book? Fine! Fuck it! I'm outta here. I hope you got a thrill." She whirled about, strides long and angry, her tears making the studio blurry. "God, why did I ever come here?"

Stone caught up, a hand tentatively reaching out to touch her shoulder. "Hold on a minute. I've obviously made some sort of mistake."

Charlie kept her back to him and wiped a tear away with a small fist, not sure if she'd heard him correctly.

"I—shouldn't have cut you off in the hallway. I made an assumption because of how you looked."

She turned at these words, still very aware of her nakedness. "Does that happen often?"

"No. Never." Something moved in his eyes before his client-face snapped back into place. "Please. Get dressed. Then we'll schedule an appointment for first thing tomorrow."

She noticed his hand was still on her shoulder at the same time he did. But there was no awkwardness, even when he left it there, gently guiding her in the direction of the change room.

New York City, Stone Studios

A sleeping cat with silver fur lay under a couch in Joshua's main studio. At least he appeared to be sleeping, until his paw streaked down, pinning prey.

Time does not exist when you have endless patience, for all things come to he who waits. Even redemption, he hoped. This he had learned over hundreds of lifetimes. He had learned it so well that for his final incarnation on this plane, he had earned that most special of gifts, the physicality of a cat. His true name was unpronounceable but humans called him Bruun. And he was nine lives in one away from Enlightenment.

Bruun thought that now would be a great time to show the pleasant burden that was his human pet what he had been up to for the past three hours. Perhaps the poor creature would finally learn something. He crept past furniture, seeing the world as most animals did, low to the ground with wide perspective. He nudged Stone's shin, then looked up. *Here, Tall One! See its blood? See the symbol?*

He had brought the dead mouse to show Stone. Were the man to look closely at the pool of blood that had spilled from the tiny creature's mouth, he would see something familiar. Something he had last glimpsed in a spinning motorcycle's wheel . . .

See what comes? How you must prepare? No, NO!

Stone picked up the cat and cooed to it.

Idiot! Did I make the pick-me-up sound? No! Are you deaf as well as stupid? Ah, the One preserve me, how am I to communicate with something so closed? Let me look into the creature's mind while I make the contented sound.

As Bruun purred, he saw a collage of images, sex, money and shoot details, all blending and overlapping like transparencies spilled on a light table.

Ahhh, the usual. Even the mouse-thing is more ordered in its thinkings. I will sleep now. But beware, Jo-shua, something comes that will change your world forever. And I do not know if even I can save you.

Book 2

"Beauty. . .must be served. . ." —William Sharp

New York City, Midtown

Solipsum stood on the sidewalk outside the sleek and priapic edifice that fronted on Fifth Avenue, glad to be back home. He paused to adjust a cuff of the vintage cashmere suit he wore, its buttery cinnamon color in perfect contrast to the clear Fall sky. Something flashed and he looked up at the top floor to see sunlight glinting from the windows of P.M.P., the Agency. He then entered the lobby and walked towards the elevators of the building he secretly owned.

As the doors opened at the penthouse floor, he paused for a moment to gaze about, to see and enjoy the massy light. It poured through curved and arching skylights, cascading down walls to warm wooden floors, flowing and spilling through a layout clean and modern, sculpting of it distance, space, serenity. He entered the Agency proper, the strains of Alphaville's *Forever Young* subtly audible. It was insulated from the waiting area by giant faces debossed onto white substrates as thousands of tiny lozenges, washed of all color unless seen obliquely. All else was white, white, everywhere white. The only color permitted was in people's clothes and, of course, the ubiquitous photos.

He sauntered past the Wall, the white expanse racked with model composites, a sea of faces all staring back—the Beauty Pool—then finally entered the circular desk area that formed the heart of the Agency.

Magma Frost, the Agency's head, looked up from her flat screen monitor, her face suffused with joy. She was possessed of a particular beauty, Nordic in structure and regal in bearing. She wore white today, as she did most days, except during Collections and Open Call. The thick sheaf of her ice gold hair was carelessly tied back, a few tendrils spilling just so, to frame her cheekbones and pale gray eyes. These were guarded by dark lashes and imbued with ancient tragedy, like some Valkyrie failed on mythic quest, now bound to earthly form forever. Yet for all that she stood aloof, when she smiled you knew that spring lay banked beneath her frosty shell, heat emanating like the borealis glimpsed on distant horizon.

She stood and smiled like she hadn't in months. "Trey! Darling! You're back! Was Italy fabulous? Did you have a good flight?"

Solipsum laughed, palms raised. "Whoa, whoa, Magma! Yes to both."

He joined her and they kissed as everyone else looked on, pretending they were not. Two bookers smirked at one another knowingly. Nothing remained secret for long at a modelling agency.

As Magma cheerfully burbled on, she looked into his eyes and—remembered. She remembered how he had found her, a burned out also-ran at twenty-seven, third string booker at a Z-list agency specializing in "real people." How he'd promised her head position at what would be the top agency in the world in five years. Prestige, wealth, even notoriety, but most of all—Power. The only thing she had to do was what she did best—run an agency. That, and quit heroin. It was surprisingly easy. All it took was one look into his eyes the first and only time they'd ever made love.

What she saw there had burned all desire for drugs from her being.

And he had delivered, oh, how he had delivered. Not only did she book the highest paid male model in the world, she also booked nine of the other top twenty men and women. All models the mysterious Trey Solipsum had brought her over the years. His eye for not simply beauty, but commercial, marketable, *manageable* beauty, was simply unparalleled. She sometimes felt guilty that it was all so easy, but then her mind would flash back to that night. She would remember what he had said as he looked into her eyes and she felt her drug-whipped synapses scream their last of want.

"Beauty must be served."

And he had been right. She was utterly helpless before it.

Magma made a come-along gesture. "Let's go to my office, Trey. Penelope," she sang, "hold all my calls." He followed her to the large transparent cube at the center of the Agency.

Once inside she touched a switch, causing an opacity to rise in the glass walls like silk sliding up a woman's leg. Magma kept her office like the rest of the Agency, predominantly white, the entire space clean, with no personal mementos. One wall was covered in fashion tears from the latest magazines, all featuring their models. Her life was the Agency and it was always lived in the present.

She gracefully sank into a chair behind a desk of palest marble and held out her hand, fingers long and tapered. "Trey, let's see your book. Three months! It's too long, even if you were in Italy."

She began flipping through the leather portfolio he handed her, marveling again at his sheer photogenic presence. Each page was a work of art. He had done every major ad campaign, editorial and magazine cover.

He had worked with some of the most beautiful men and women in the world, yet he always stood out. There was just something about him.

Solipsum watched her face as he made himself comfortable in the molded temperfoam chair that fronted her desk, legs outstretched, hands tented, smiling. As Magma went through his portfolio, he reflected on how comfortable he was with her, how she was so totally his creature, and he knew she would never betray him. He also knew that in the place she kept hidden even from herself, she suspected what he truly was but would never admit this to anyone, least of all herself.

"So, Magma dear, how's business?"

"Fabulous, Trey. Our best year ever." There was a small 'spack' as she closed the portfolio. "The money we're seeing from the residuals in the commercial division is utterly mind boggling. To use your phrase, it's 'sick cash'. And the new talent is doing quite nicely as far as editorial placement goes. Barbitua just landed a major cosmetics account and it looks like Alabasta Twigg is going to be optioned for another year by *Drevlon*. Oh Trey, I—I really think she could be the next Harlow."

"Harlow Bleake is dead, Magma. Please don't mention her name again in my presence."

"I—I'm sorry, Trey . . . I didn't mean . . ." Magma cursed herself for a fool, nerves jangly as she tucked an errant wisp behind her ear. *He just came back from Italy! Did you think he wouldn't be reminded of her everywhere he went?*

"What else?" His lips barely moved.

She came around the desk and perched on its edge. "I've set up a dinner for you tomorrow night at *PreVom*, the hottest new restaurant in the city. They have a binge and purge tapas that is out of this world. It'll be just us plus some boys and girls from the Agency."

"Good. I always seem to come back from Europe with an insatiable appetite for—fresh meat." Solipsum's teeth became briefly visible.

She blinked, eyes darting, her laughter quick and nervous. "Oh, and a writer from that new magazine *PRY* has been asking to interview you. I've told him you don't—"

"Call him back. He can come to the restaurant and interview me there."

"Trey, you never do interviews."

"Times are changing, Magma. I've decided to make myself a little more—accessible. Any luck luring Phoena over here?"

"No. I've offered her everything you authorized." The words left her mouth like curdled milk spit back down the straw. "I even met her personally over lunch. That cost me more favors than I wanted to call in. And for nothing. She absolutely refuses to budge."

"Hmmm." Solipsum's gaze turned inward as his head tilted back. "This may require a more—personal intervention."

The sun crept past the skylight's edge, briefly illuminating the model's face, and Magma found herself in that rarest of moments, to see a thing so very few had seen.

Solipsum unguarded.

His blue eyes glittered like the facets of some precious alien gem in the exquisite setting of his face, the planes of bone a sheered symmetry that led to lips the color of cruelty, full and ripe, the fleshy fruit of kiss, his wild beauty a seduction that rendered you powerless, luscious as it sang of dark delight and pleasures beyond imagining, of your soul's own slick surrender delivered up in laughter and screams, the heat from his core so strong you knew if you stood too close you would burn.

Beholding him like this, she felt again that icy fire racing through her body. How naked and exposed she'd felt that night as her entire essence had been laid bare. She shivered at the memory and thought again how strange it was to feel such equal parts of love and fear for the same man. Then he sat forward, the moment broken, and she continued as if nothing had happened. Nothing at all.

"One more thing. There's a rumor going around about a new advertising campaign unlike anything that's ever been attempted. And it's big, possibly the biggest I've ever encountered. Certainly the money is staggering."

"It will be all print. And *Fa-Shin, Inc.* is paying for it."

Magma's eyes widened. "Trey. You never cease to amaze me. I just got this an hour ago. How did you find out about it so fast?"

"Your sources are very good, Magma. Mine are simply—better." He smiled. "I must leave now. I can be reached at the apartment."

New York City, Stone Studios

Joshua Stone felt his muscles loosen as he relaxed into the large semi-circular couch, enjoying the day and the beautiful play of light in this, the studio he had designed. He let his mind wander for a moment, back over the years and what it had taken to reach this place in time, this tiny moment, to savor the special stillness that only came from being so high above the city's teeming pandemonium. He saw the parade of a billion images, each a step, a single stone that had finally built a tower to touch the sky. *And where will it all go now?* he wondered.

Trish's intercom voice interrupted him. "Charlie's here, Joshua."

"Thanks. Send her up."

The elevator doors opened to frame a somewhat cleaned up Charlie, clutching her portfolio. In this light her face was even more striking than when he had first seen it, her hair today spikier, though he liked how she was still so scrappy-looking. She wore a white t-shirt and black leather jacket, black vinyl stretch pants snug at the juncture of her legs that billowed until they ended, jammed into oversized black combat boots. Fat white thong straps hiked above the low cut waistline bracketed her slender hips, completing a picture he was surprised to find himself framing.

Jesus, she really could model. She's electric . . .

As she walked towards him, Joshua found himself focusing on Charlie's carriage, her effortless grace. She moved, it seemed, with a complete lack of friction, the deliberate placement of each step precise yet unconscious—a perfect runway walk. But there was something else, something more that he couldn't quite put his finger on, as though he was seeing the manifestation of some deep and special training.

Charlie was aware of his attention, then felt herself becoming somewhat overwhelmed as the size and splendor of the main studio made itself apparent.

So that's what those girders look like up close! They're huge, like rusted dinosaur ribs. Her head tilted up and she found herself doing a slow turn. *And this dome is unbelievable! It must go up a hundred feet.*

Her eyes traveled back to Joshua, reclining on the couch. He was dressed casually in black jeans and a frayed black flannel shirt, his arms stretched to either side, legs extended and crossed at the ankles, his face partially in shadow. A tiny smile played at the corners of his mouth. *He looks like some dark and ebon god,* she thought, *timeless and implacable.* Charlie remembered what she had seen in the hallway, struck by how much Joshua Stone embodied his own photography.

He sat forward into the sunlight and she found herself staring.

Oh my God, he really has got the most amazing face. Like some jungle panther evolved. It all depends on how the light hits him—sometimes he's almost beautiful, and other times, he's like a darker version of himself—a negative.

Joshua rose to greet her and she found herself walking into his shadow.

"Hello, Charlie. I didn't know if you'd come back." His voice was deep and liquid, a succulence of vowel and thinly sliced consonant that gave her a slight shiver.

"There was never any doubt, Mr. Stone."

They shook and she found her hand engulfed by something not unlike a catcher's mitt. She wondered what her hand felt like to Joshua, sure for an instant he could feel her heart beat.

Stone studied the girl before him. Her face was almost perfectly symmetrical, its elliptical contours offering up her violet eyes, marquised and brilliant. Her nose was strong and simple, a tiny spray of freckles across the bridge, its sleek line leading down to lips so plush and full they seemed designed for only kissing. His eyes were drawn again to hers, to their astonishing and iridescent depths, and all the while he could feel her hand, nestled in his. The moment elongated and he felt himself staring as she looked back at him expectantly, guilelessly.

Then she blinked and the spell broke.

"Call me Joshua." He slowly relinquished her hand. "Please, sit down. Let's take a look at your book."

He started flipping through her portfolio, and immediately saw that Charlie had enormous raw talent and potential. She was unafraid of any subject or technique, but more importantly, she seemed unafraid of making a mistake, her intuition powerful. The almost Asian discipline coupled with a lack of compositional inhibition was bracing. He came upon a series of flowers done in black and white with selective focus and drew a sharp breath. Effortlessly casual yet geometrically precise, each bud, each leaf subtly framed a draping stem or spill of shadow. They were the work, he reflected, of a master photographer. They were by far her best pieces, yet she seemed unaware of this, judging by what filled the rest of her book— work that was comfortably jumpy, with strong style but no central theme.

I haven't seen a book like this in I don't know how long—maybe never.

He took his time looking at the images. Charlie sat across from him, a large oval table of inch-thick glass separating them. Her elbows rested on her knees, chin propped in cupped hands, occasionally stroking the purring silver mammal that had somehow found its way onto her lap. She felt him squirm as he flipped onto his back. "Oh," she murmured, "you want your belly rubbed, do you?"

Bruun squinted as if to say, "*That is obvious.*" She stroked and rubbed, careful not to miss his little paw pits, the purring becoming louder.

Joshua looked up for a moment and gave her a small smile. "He likes you." Then he continued turning pages.

Bruun fluttered his head and Charlie saw that half of one ear looked as though it had been torn off in a fight. She gently rubbed the velvety thinness, the sensation triggering a tactile memory of another cat's ear, a cat she had shared with someone what seemed like a lifetime ago . . . in Japan. She pushed the memory away and focused on Joshua's face instead, looking neither for approval nor disapproval, only reaction. She instinctively understood even at this early stage that there was only one person she need ever please. Herself.

"Very impressive." He closed her book and carefully placed it on the table between them. "Besides a job, what are you looking for?"

Charlie lowered Bruun, then sat forward, her face shining like a newly minted coin. "I want to be the best. To go to the very top. To play by the rules, make it by the rules, then break the rules."

A corner of Joshua's mouth lifted. "Easier said than done. But your heart is in the right place. Now, I really only have one test. Come with me."

She followed him past a massive curve of girder, ready for almost anything when he stopped abruptly and pointed down. All she could see was a piece of floor that was dirty and stained, boxed by black tape. Leaning on a wall nearby were a broom, mop and bucket.

"Okay. Here's the test. I want you to clean that piece of floor. You have as much time as you want."

Charlie's features crowded together. "That's it?"

"That's it. Starting now."

She grabbed the broom and began to sweep. Stone watched with arms crossed. There was an economy of motion in how she worked, sweeping in a practical pattern that cleaned the floor in the most efficient way. She mopped in the same way. All that remained was the large stain which wouldn't come out no matter how hard she scrubbed. She looked at Joshua, who remained implacable. The stain reminded her of a nautilus shell, or pictures she'd seen of distant nebulae, almost hypnotizing her as she scrubbed away to no avail. Suddenly, a clarity occurred in her mind and she just—stopped. She calmly decided that stain or no stain, she had done her best and was finished. She put the mop back where she'd found it, then turned to Joshua. "Well? Did I pass?"

"Before I answer that, let me show you something."

They walked to the edge of the glass dome where Joshua touched a panel. A section of plasma hemisphere dropped to floor level and they stepped outside onto a balcony that looked as old as the dinosaur girders. Charlie's mouth slowly opened.

"Wow!" She could feel the air on her pant cuffs, jetting up through the holes in the metal flooring as she walked to the railing.

Stone's eyes were ever cameras, and what they saw now made him long for film. But he surprised himself by letting go, knowing it was enough just to see her like this, standing before him, the wind at her back, hair rustley as the sun gilded her.

"How far up are we?" she asked.

"About a thousand feet."

Charlie leaned over the railing and saw the tops of many buildings. The clouds at this height seemed close enough to pet, the city visible to the horizon. She looked down, working her jaw and cheeks, then opened her mouth and gently . . . spat. She caught Joshua's eye and grinned, shrugging her shoulders as he began laughing helplessly.

"So? Are you going to tell me if I passed?"

He squinted at her through the laugh tears he was still knuckling. "As a matter of fact, you did. With flying colors."

Charlie crossed her arms under her breasts and leaned back against the cool metal. "I don't get it. What does sweeping and mopping a floor have to do with photography?"

Joshua raised his hands in a noncommittal gesture. "Nothing. And everything."

"But I thought there would be all these technical questions. About f-stops and power packs and equipment . . ." her voice faded.

"Didn't you learn all that in school?"

"Yeah . . . I guess."

"Your book tells me you learned enough to take those pictures. The rest you learn here. All that I can teach. And you learn by doing." He paused for a moment. "There's only one thing I can't teach, and that's a work ethic."

Charlie uncrossed her arms. "A work ethic? You mean working hard?"

"And working smart. And never thinking you're too good for any job, no matter how small or how mundane. It's the little things that help you keep your edge. They keep you in touch. Working hard means doing that shit job well. Working smart means doing it in a time-efficient manner. Sweeping and mopping a small piece of floor show me how good you are at both."

"And the stain that won't come out?"

"It represents the obstacle you have to go around, not through. There are times when the straight ahead method will not work. A smart assistant will recognize those times and find another solution."

"Hmmm . . . and they're such simple tools."

"That's also part of it. After all, at the end of the day, this is a business. If you can't handle ten bucks worth of mop and broom, how can I trust you with five million dollars worth of camera gear?"

"That's quite a test."

"And like I said, you passed. With flying colors. So I'm hiring you as my new first assistant."

"You're kidding! I'm in?"

"Yup." Hope and disbelief, fast as barn swallows, flew across her features and left a joy he could only smile before. "Now I want you to meet Russell Hernbauer. He was first, but that was only since yesterday. I'm putting him on as second because you're better." Stone pressed a button on the outdoor intercom. "Trish, page Russ and send him up."

"Sure thing, Josh."

The dome's warm air welcomed them back. Charlie wandered past the couch and spun to look at him as she continued walking backwards. "This is one of the most fantastic places I've ever seen. The light in here is so beautiful!"

She made her way over to the dome's curved wall and pressed both hands to the glass, the tip of her nose just touching it. Far below, past the tops of her boots, the city spread out before her like a magic carpet, twinkling with all the jewels of the world. Joshua joined her and they stood together in silence for a moment, simply enjoying what lay before them.

"That's just the beginning," he said quietly after a time.

Charlie glanced over to see him pull out a remote and thumb a switch. The city slowly passed before her as the floor began to rotate about the central turning shaft.

"Hey! We're moving! This is so cool!" She laughed like a child at Christmas.

The elevator doors opened and Russ Hernbauer ambled towards them. "Hey, Stone Man," he interrupted, "here I am."

Charlie spun and gaped, instantly recognizing the Clipboard Guy from the casting. The guy who couldn't stop staring at her boobs.

Russ stared back, wondering what she was doing here. Then it dawned on him that the Stone Man was "interviewing" her alone. His smile became wolfish, his glance dismissive as he turned back to his boss. "What can I do for ya?"

Charlie felt a sudden tension fill the air. She looked at Joshua to see his face had become a mask.

"First off, my name is Joshua, or Mr. Stone. Sometimes it's even Josh." She could almost hear the cleaver hit the cutting block. "That's it. I won't tell you again. You are now officially second assistant. Charlie is the new first assistant in this studio."

Russ looked as if he'd been slapped in the face with a soiled diaper. "The fuck? I thought I was first when you hired me yesterday! What happened?"

"I've changed my mind."

Russ was about to speak until he saw the thin ice in Joshua's eyes. Charlie saw it too.

"You can go back to prepping for tomorrow's shoot. Charlie will be here at 8:00 a.m. and that's when you can give her the tour."

Russ slunk back to the elevator, shoulders rigid, muttering to himself.

Stone shook his head, some part of him wondering why he hadn't fired the insolent fuck. He walked over to a small computer alcove and wrote something down on a piece of paper. Charlie watched him as he walked back, appreciating his smooth and easy grace, the interplay of muscle. She was thinking that she hadn't looked at a man that way in a long time, maybe ever, when he handed her the voucher for $10,000.

She held it in both hands, staring at the amount, then slowly tilted her head up to look into his eyes. "What's this?"

"A pay voucher for your first week. Take it to accounting. Trish will show you the way. They'll give you a check for this advance."

Charlie stared down again in shock, tears welling in the corners of her eyes. "But this is—"

"Not enough?"

"*No!* It's more than I ever made in my life! It's just—"

"Are you okay?"

"Something in my eye." She stood on her toes and kissed him on the cheek. "Thanks."

He watched her cross the studio to the elevator, resisting the urge to touch his cheek. She waved to him just as its doors closed.

"Hey, Charlie!"

The doors opened again.

"Yeah?"

"There's a night club called the Seventh Level. It's very special. I'm going there tonight with some friends. I hardly ever go out but this is— worth it. Would you like to come?" Stone wondered why he suddenly felt so prom-shy.

Charlie shrugged and smiled. "I'd love to. Do you want me to meet you here?"

"Sure. At eleven."

"I'll see you then."

The elevator doors closed.

New York City, Upper East Side

Phoena was balanced in *Padangushthanasana*, feet in the air, toes pointed, her hands the only part of her that touched the floor. Sunlight streamed through the windows of the high-ceilinged loft as her many plants silently breathed and purified the air. The serenity, the stillness, were like a world apart. She wore a white workout bodysleeve of her own design and was still except for the micro adjustments necessary to maintain her balance. Sweat streamed freely, a sensation intimate yet distant in the there/not there of her concentration. Gone even was the disturbing incident from the other day. The Breath was All.

Trembling slightly, she lowered herself to the ground and completed the *Ashtanga* set. But today she decided to indulge herself. *Shivasana* would take place in the bathtub.

She peeled off the soaking body sleeve as she walked to the kitchen, raiding the refrigerator for some organic oranges. Their color and texture seemed particularly vibrant and she ate, it seemed, with her whole body, the juice running down her front unheeded.

She savored the last of the fruit, wiping her mouth with the back of her hand, then padded off to the bathroom and the promise of the whirl-pool. The pre-filled tub was at the perfect temperature, a sticky orange seed floating away as she lowered herself into the water. She stretched out a leg, adjusting a dial with her toe, muscles loosening and lengthening, her features now bliss slack as the hot jets began to do their work.

Shivasana. Corpse pose.

She gradually sank lower in the tub until only her face remained un-submerged. Her eyes gently closed, head slipping under, the water enfolding her like a womb as she crossed the boundary into sleep. Then the dream began.

It began as it always did, with idyllic flashes of green woods and the rambling old house. The warm August night was like something from a storybook, colors vibrant and saturated, the air redolent with the smell of all things good. She found herself on the old dirt road, walking towards the house in the distance. Details emerged as she came nearer, the sprung porch with flowers crowding wild around it, the weathered gray wood lit by the buttery spill of light from the open door.

And of course, *him*.

He stood there, silhouetted in the doorway, shadow stretching out like some great black tongue. The stumps of three fingers on his right hand twitched spasmodically as his eyes crawled over her chest like stick bugs. Then it all started to twist, the smells going first, changing, changing, her eyes still deceived until the dream caught up to the rancid pork-reek of sizzling man-fat. Jagged splinters of image stabbed into her eyes, faster and faster, jolting pain as her mouth filled with blood from the first ringing slap, sheets of flame, screams, the bottle smashing, fire now roaring, *roaring,* God I never knew it could burn so *fast* and over it all, the voice, the voice, his face running like tallow as he screamed, "I'll kill you, you fuckin' BITCH!"

She exploded from the water, almost drowned, coughing up fluid, too choked to scream. It took her several seconds to realize that none of it had been real. She flopped out of the tub, limbs quivering, still gasping for air, regaining her bearings to find herself in front of the medicine cabinet. As she had so many times before. She opened its door and saw the bottle of *Prozac* sitting there, looming larger and larger, filling her vision, paralyzing her with want.

Fuck! How did that get in there? I thought I threw all that shit out! Just one oh that was a bad dream you fucking liked it didn't you when he finally—No! I HATED it! Just one . . .

She reached inside, grabbed the bottle, ripped off the lid and hurtled the pills into the toilet. She flushed it again and again, only then daring to look at the bowl. Her legs shook and she fell to her knees, skin beading with sweat, the long muscles of her back morraining.

I almost lost it. Jesus that was too close.

She lowered her head with infinite slowness, until her forehead touched the cool wet tiles.

Garbhaasana. Child's pose.

New York City, Lower East Side

Bentley Sween, the young journalist from *PRY,* knew he was lucky to be here. Very lucky. Asking for an interview from a man notoriously press shy, a man who guarded his privacy as a cult leader guards his past, well, he had been almost certain of rejection. Yet here he was inside *PreVom,* the most exclusive and expensive restaurant in the city—at least this month. The place had no phone number that he could find and a "CLOSED" sign hung perpetually on the frosted glass slabs that barred entry to the great unwashed. But once inside, he had to admit, it was a whole other story. The restaurant bustled now with activity, the air fragrant with aromas of fusion elevated to art form. The most coveted tables here were at the back because *PreVom,* he had learned, was as renowned for its privacy as it was for its cuisine.

He lounged now at the luxurious and exquisitely lit banquette that formed the centerpiece of the rear room. Sandy-haired and of average build, he sported horn rimmed glasses in black frames that made him look like a code breaker, secretly employed by Her Majesty's Government circa 1942. He wore a Savile Row suit that was slightly rumpled, as if he had been dressed in a hurry by his mother. His face shone and his eyes were alive as he looked about him and once again thanked his lucky stars. He could actually feel his elbow sink into the plush cream linen of the tablecloth as he leaned forward, eyes momentarily drawn to the gleaming *rondage* of Magma's breasts. She and a preen of models from the Agency sipped martinis as they awaited the last of their party. Everyone was dressed to thrill, plumage bright as stars and as exacting as diamonds, a calculated seduction of curve and limb, all carefully draped with the illusion of indifference.

The stunning confection known as Quinby Delicious, (rumored to be Jane Bond's paramour), was slightly bored and slightly drunk. She wore a vintage A-line dress, half white, half orange, bisected diagonally. It ended at mid-thigh, a single orange button floating like a flower on the white portion near her heart. Her make-up tonight was simple, only retro eyeliner and a bit of mascara needed to enhance eyes like diamond chips of sky, languid and blue as they looked out at the world from the heart-shaped setting of her face. The blonde bob she affected was ever-so-slightly bed-tousled, in perfect compliment to her tanned and golden skin. She lifted a knife, casually inspecting her reflection in its face, then tilted it a bit to notice Trabia Moore, deep in conversation with photographer-of-the-moment Guido Ponce. *I think I know where that's going to end up. Oh so boring, yes it is.* She carefully set the knife down, squaring it with the other cutlery. Her fingers then began to idly trace the base of her wine goblet, circling, circling, until the liquid sloshed over the rim, to make a satisfying stain on the immaculate white linen.

"Quinby, you brat."

She turned to Petula Stamen, *P.M.P.*'s latest acquisition. "Quiet, or I'll launch an oyster at the reporter over there."

"You wouldn't!"

Quinby's eyes sparkled. "Try me."

"Here." Petula poured more wine into the other girl's glass, then topped her own. "This should hold you until a certain Mr. Wonderful gets here."

"What's he like now?"

Petula giggled. "You'll find out soon enough, babe."

Quinby leaned closer, her breasts lightly brushing Petula's upper arm. "Where did he find you?"

"At a rave in Goa. What about you?"

"On a streetcar in Toronto."

Petula rested both elbows on the table and smiled dreamily." God, he has the biggest—"

"I know."

Quinby felt the other girl's nails dig into her arm.

"What?"

"I don't even know why I told you that."

"But I thought you were—"

"Gay?"

"Well . . . yes."

"Don't believe everything you hear."

She felt some disturbance in the ether she could not define and instantly knew Solipsum had arrived. A quick glance at the foyer confirmed it. She nudged the other model. "Here he comes."

Solipsum was dressed in viscous and lightly textured black, the crimson exclamation of his tie the only splash of color. Quinby watched as he walked towards them through the restaurant, his movements clean and muscularly concise, like a continuous signature on reality. As he passed the other diners, conversations ceased, as did laughter. Their heads slowly turned, like time-lapsed flowers tracking a dark and distant sun, the rustling of their lips his whispered name. Then everything resumed as it was.

Quinby felt the touch of something surreal, a ripple in the fabric of normalcy caused by that covenant of blindness. For no one wanted to acknowledge what their collective soul knew had passed.

Solipsum ascended the dais, his eyes sweeping the table, missing nothing. He laid his hand on Magma's shoulder and Quinby noticed for the first time the massive square-cut ruby adorning his index finger.

"Trey!" the booker exclaimed, setting down her martini, "You made it."

Solipsum leaned forward to kiss her cheek. "Sorry I'm late. You look stunning, as always." She blushed and they talked quietly for a moment before he sat down.

Bentley Sween watched the exchange and admitted to himself that he was impressed. Used to the crushing disappointment of celebrity reality, he was surprised by how magnetic Solipsum was in the flesh. Pictures actually did not do him justice, and that was saying something. The man crackled with an energy far greater than mere star power. He was almost godlike. And there was something else he felt

(ball-shriveling terror)

but its specificity eluded him.

A waitress appeared. "Cocktail, sir?"

Solipsum looked up. "Stolichnaya and cranberry, please."

"Right away, sir." She flounced off.

Magma lightly touched the model's arm. "Trey, you remember Quinby and Petula?"

"Of course. How could I forget?"

Petula blushed and looked away. Quinby did not.

"And this is Bentley Sween, the young reporter from *PRY* I was telling you about."

"Writer, ma'am."

"Excuse me?"

"I'm a writer, Ms. Frost, not a reporter."

"What's the difference?"

Solipsum took a delicate sip of the drink that had magically appeared at his elbow. "The one attempts meaning through truth, the other, truth through meaning."

Magma's gray eyes slivered in confusion. "Which does which?"

Solipsum smiled. "That would depend on what truth you are seeking."

She turned to Bentley. "And what truth are you seeking, Mr. Sween?"

"That all depends on how you define truth."

"'Beauty is Truth, Truth Beauty.' Coleridge." Solipsum sat back, a certain linguistic smugness settling on his features.

Bentley looked at this man who seemed so much more than human and realized with a start that he was not infallible. He began swirling the water in his glass, ice tinkling against its rim. "Actually, it was Keats who said that. John Keats. . ." suddenly becoming aware his voice was the only sound at the table. He looked up to see several glances sliding away. A fork clattered noisily and a model at the end giggled. Solipsum arched an eyebrow, his voice very still as his eyes found her. "Aren't you feeling a little—full, Tara?" His gaze was heavy with the lidded indifference of a reptile that has just eaten its own young.

The girl felt her stomach convulse and rushed from the table, gorge rising.

"Well." Solipsum's eyes met Bentley's. "I stand corrected."

The extraordinarily striking girl seated beside Solipsum finally decided to speak. "Wasn't it Anatoly France who thought 'Beauty more profound than Truth itself.'?" Her sea green eyes blinked rapidly, bee-stung lips a-pout, the skin of her face as clean and silky-smooth as undeveloped photo paper.

All eyes turned to this newest contributor, arrested as much by this observation as by her chirping delivery.

Quinby nudged Petula. "Who's Anchovy France?" she whispered.

"I don't know. I think it's some guy she fucked."

"She sounds like a budgie."

"Sssshhhhhh!"

Solipsum turned a lazy eye to the newcomer. "I don't believe I've had the pleasure. You are . . . ?"

"Oh Trey! Where are my manners?" said Magma. "This is one of our newest girls, Straenje Atrakta."

"Straenje." He rolled the syllable across his tongue, tasting it. "What an unusual appellation."

"My dad is a quantum physicist. He named me after his favorite particle."

"I'll just bet he did." Solipsum's attention was slowly becoming tumescent. "Have you found your name opening the doors to any—Hidden Universes—lately?"

He brought his face closer to hers, eyes lambent and intense, galaxies spiraling slowly in the depths of his irises. Straenje became mesmerized by what she saw there. She felt her motor control begin to slip.

"Uhhh . . . no . . . not yet . . . but . . ."

"All that is about to change?"

"I feel . . . strange . . ."

Solipsum's tongue made a brief appearance as it touched his lips. "It just goes on forever, doesn't it?"

Bentley felt the fine hairs at the nape of his neck rising. Even Petula noticed something amiss. She put an arm around Quinby and pulled her close. "This is getting way too heavy for me. I'm gonna go nose my powder. I—I—mean—powder my nose. Wanna come?"

Quinby nodded, already out of her chair, a Pavlovian response she wasn't even aware of.

Petula glanced at Straenje, then reached under the table and pinched the model's thigh. "Come on, babe," she said brightly, "we're going to freshen up." She dragged the reluctant girl away and the three of them went off to the washroom.

Magma barely registered what had just passed. Her brain was trying to tell her, again, but she had already filed the event away, in the bulging folder marked "Unexplained Solipsum Moments." She shrugged. "Why don't we get the bill and go to the Club?"

Solipsum watched the girls retreat. "Good idea, Magma."

He absently pulled out his wallet and dropped two ten thousand dollar bills on the table. "This should cover it. Would you all excuse me? I have to use the facilities."

The Washroom

Solipsum pushed open the door and entered the marbled room, his thoughts a black cloud. He walked through the modern-and-then-some pissoir, languid with buttressed sinks and erotic charcoals, past a row of stalls where someone was on his knees, vomiting or fellating, it was hard to tell. He approached the shaved thorn of a urinal and began to relieve himself, whistling "Strangers in the Night" as his stream splashed. He was not alone. The other man beside him casually looked over to equipment check, his eyes widening. Solipsum waited until the man looked up, then slowly winked and finished. He left without flushing.

Sighing with relief, the man shook himself and zipped up. As he walked past Solipsum's urinal, he glanced over to see it filled and spattered with a viscous blood-like substance. An emotion he had no name for, something so primal it impelled him physically to flee, *flee, FLEE!* came shrieking up from the depths of his reptile brain. He began to sweat. Coldly. Profusely. Then he rushed from the washroom, eyes darting everywhere but at the strange man in the black suit and crimson tie.

Solipsum scented his fear like a thing decanted, savoring it as he thought, *alas, poor Malcolm, I fear I've left a bit of you behind.*

He snickered as he walked down the hall back towards the dining room, his mood lifted. The door to the girls' washroom popped open and Quinby Delicious, Petula Stamen and Straenje Atrakta came tumbling out in peels of laughter. Solipsum watched the commotion and couldn't help but smile. He reminded himself in that moment that it was rather pointless to constantly exercise his power in frivolous ways. Life was too short. He joined the girls and put his arms around their shoulders.

"Ever been to the Seventh Level?"

New York City, an alley somewhere in the Meat Packing District

You'd never be able to tell, thought Quinby, *never in a million years just looking at it from the outside.* The scarlet door with the golden handle was the only incongruous thing on a street that was narrow and gray, empty storefronts and warehouse docks watching her with a vacant hunger that made her want to get inside.

A huge line lead from the scarlet door and snaked around the block. In it were some of the most stunning people she had ever seen. She recognized more than a few of them; people who would never have had to line up outside an ordinary Club. But this was no ordinary Club, this was The Seventh Level, the hottest Club in the City. What made it so hot? Quinby wasn't really sure. Perhaps it was the musky peppering of celebrities, perhaps the décor, which had to be seen to be believed. It could have been the five hundred dollar cover, which everyone (or nearly everyone) paid. The music definitely had something to do with it. Why, rumor even had it that the Club was owned by a Lord of Hell. But when all was said and done, Quinby decided, it was all of these things. This made The Seventh Level a place where anything could happen. And *that's* what made it hot. Because hot, like cool, cannot really be defined. Like Enlightenment, it can only be experienced.

Solipsum lightly rested his arm around her shoulders as their party proceeded directly to the front of the line.

"Hey!" A businessman thrust his fat face at them. "You can't cut in like that!"

The doorman quickly moved forward but was stopped by a glance from Solipsum. He looked at the irritant and seemed about to say something, to bequeath something

(*cancer*)

before he changed his mind. "Go home," he said. "Tonight is not your night."

Quinby watched as the crowd closed over the man, the skin of his face now white as mollusk flesh.

They approached the scarlet door with the golden handle and Quinby noticed again the strange disclaimer on the small sign at its center:

YOU RISK SERIOUS INJURY OR DEATH BY ATTENDING THIS VENUE.

The door was opened and in they went.

Their party proceeded down a carpeted hallway paneled in dark mahogany. Music with the primary beat of the human heart welcomed them into a place Quinby had almost come to think of as alive. She ignored the other girls who where lining up to get their wrists stamped with ultraviolet free drink ink and made her way forward. The Seventh Level had only two areas, the Anteroom (what she had come to think of as the staging area) and the Seventh Level itself. The entrance to the former was guarded by two enormous mastodon tusks that joined to form an archway. Quinby looked up as she walked beneath them, yellowed-cream and thicker at the base than she could get her arms around. The walls then changed from wood to mountainous rock, underlit as though by lava, soaring up so high the ceiling disappeared. Small chandeliers of scarlet glass descended on impossibly long chains to add their light to what looked less like man-made room and more some rocky alcove at the heart of the Himalayas. A circular bar was visible through the crowd, it's roof an onion dome of beaten metal, the spire at its tip like a spindle upon which slowly seemed to turn that which she could see beyond—something like the ruby core of a galaxy. The others had now joined her and they all walked around the bar, through the gap between the fissured walls, to see the Seventh Level spread before them like something from a dream.

She had an impression of a cathedral's shadowed intimacy, of couches, crowds and cloth-of-gold, of a vast space where bars and plush lounge areas rose for seven stories to cradle like cupped hands the thing that still took her breath away. They were on the third level and Quinby backed up from the transparent railing slightly, neck craned to better let her eyes drink in the spectacle before her. Floating in a slowly turning anti-gravitational mael-strom that extended from floor to unseen ceiling were thick slabs of scarlet glass. They floated at the horizontal, forming islands of leisure and pleasure that clubgoers alighted to from every level, sometimes to linger, sometimes to alight anew, all depending on what passed. And who was on it.

The largest was the size of an aircraft's wing, the smallest a chariot's wheel. Some had railings, tables and bar stools, some only cushions while others were bare but for a matchbook with a special phone number written on it, or some other strange gift. The technology that kept them afloat was, she knew, hideously expensive and the path of each slab (if left alone) purely random, collision detection always operative. They all had simple steering mechanisms, allowing them to dock at every bar, lounge and with each other. Each was lit by some inner point source that spread its glow softly, radiantly.

Crowning the floating glass were models and predators, agents and rock stars, drifters, gamblers and women of means, dealers, faded glo-ries and the Next Big Thing, killers, whores and celebrity dust-heads, straining-breasted wannabees in retail last-year, the Naked Cowboy, re-alized talents and wasted opportunities, queens, rent-boys, dream-boats and dregs, daddy's girls, photographers, ponces and touts, all dressed in their best, dressed to impress, in expensive jeans and tattered t's, in couture this and vintage that (just never tell them it's off the rack), in costume, plumage and ready-to-wear, in outfits red as rage, tinted the green of forgotten youth, candy flossed and party purple, yellow as accident tape on the cornflower blue of your sweetheart's eyes—carnivore colors and salty sparkles, pearls as black as homemade sin, neon racy rainbowed bling. She saw people dancing and cavorting, some kissing and drinking, some slab-skipping and others just sitting, feet dangling, body weight shifting in centrifugal accommodation to the ride they were so clearly enjoying. People and glass floated round and round, with the stately majesty of tiny scarlet schooners sailing into Eternity.

Their party broke up. Some to dance, some to get drinks and some to get drugs. The rocket needed fuel.

Quinby walked to the bar, the blond helmet of her hair gleaming as she passed beneath the spotlights. The crowd parted before her like cloth before the shears. All eyes tracked her as she walked across that room, wondering what she felt like, smelled like, fucked like, looked like naked, and she hardly felt a thing.

She reached her destination and perched on a stool, elbows resting on the velvety hardness of the sandblasted glass. The bar was an opulence of drapery and scarlet brocade, of muted illumination, the shimmering blood light pinpricked by luminosities of green. She could just make out in the smoked glass mirrors behind the bar the ghostly kanji impressions of the glassy maelstrom's movement.

She closed her eyes, then sighed and opened them. Tom the bartender stood before her, looking quite perfect in his crisp white shirt and crimson bowtie. He gazed into Quinby's eyes and she smiled at him as they both remembered the time it went a little further than it should have.

"What will it be, Miss Delicious?"

"Triple Vodka Q, please, Tom."

"Right away."

He made her drink and in no time at all, placed an enormous martini glass on the bar top. In it, a lathed toothpick skewered two very large pills.

Quinby handed over two folded hundreds. She always made it a point to pay for her own drinks. Tom still raised an eyebrow.

"Get one for yourself. And keep the change."

He grinned at her, his hands already busy.

She took a sip of the thick and icy vodka he set before her, then pulled out the toothpick and placed it into her mouth, slowly withdrawing it to crunch on the pill left behind. A look of ecstatic communion, gentle and inexorable, suffused her features and soon she felt like a giddy young blood cell jet-streaming back to the Center of it All.

She turned in her seat to face the crowd, the VQ now opening for her the room's secret heart. She could feel it, hear it, see all those thoughts and emotions swirling in the air like the breath of a dream; eternal youth that would last the night, promises broken before they were spoken and kisses of hope like liquor-filled chocolates, tongue-pushed and bursting, their sweet ichor flooding her mouth with only the slightest aftertaste of ash.

"What's that you're drinking?" asked Bentley, making himself comfortable on a bar stool.

Quinby continued to watch the room. "Try one and find out," she replied, her voice both warm and icy.

"I do believe I will."

He ordered and watched, fascinated, as Tom prepared the sweating martini. "How do I . . .?"

She leaned back slowly. "Just slide one into your mouth, like this, chew it up, then sip some vodka, sit back and enjoy."

Bentley followed her directions somewhat hesitantly. "What are these?" he asked around a mouthful of sweet and chalky tartness.

"A new designer drug called *Anything*. It only comes in pills and it's metabolically specific, whatever that means. All I know is that it gives you the best high you've ever had. Each experience is better than the last and there's no tolerance build-up."

"That's incredible! But the crash must be horrendous."

"There is no crash."

"Then what's the price?" He brought his lips to the rim of the glass.

Quinby finally faced him, her teeth almost blinding as she flashed a smile in perfect counterpoint to the touch of madness in her eyes. "Two weeks of your life."

Bentley sputtered and spewed the drink across the bar top as Quinby laughed and laughed. She left the choking writer and wandered closer to the Scarlet Maelstrom, hanging out by a rail, just watching the show unfold before her as her pupils began to dilate.

She saw someone who looked like the Creative Director of *Fa-Shin, Inc.* talking to some male models. Solipsum joined her and put his arm around her waist and she felt a twinge of jealousy as she remembered a rumor about this woman and that man. *And isn't that Phoena's agent over there? What's that in his hand? Oh! It is his hand!* A slab drifted by and she quickly averted her gaze from a former supermodel, now gone eel-faced with surgical skin carding, all beady eyes and shaved nasal cartilage, tiny nostrils flaring ceaselessly in anticipation of the next bump. Next she noticed someone truly famous, at the level of icon, rumored to dispense the most electrifying blow jobs in the men's washroom. She continued sipping, rushing, smiling. A movement caught her eye and she looked up to see someone plummeting from the seventh level, stroboscopically illuminated as his flailing form passed slab after slab. She thought again about the sign on the door. *What it didn't say was the reason you risked life and limb was because you were probably fucked up like you'd never been before.* The people around barely noticed, except to laugh and point as the unfortunate disappeared through the holographic floor, to impact the large gel-sack placed there for such eventualities. *That guy doesn't know how lucky he was, missing all that glass.* She remembered the graffiti she had seen once in the washroom: *This Club has gone 0 Days without an Accident.* She was about to board a nearing slab, Petula waving to her, when she saw Joshua Stone. *Omigod, he never comes out! And who's that with him? That must be the girl everyone's talking about. The girl who showed and told—off that is. This one I have to meet.*

She shook her head and waved Petula off, then made her way through the throng, the drug now singing in her body. "Hi! What's your name?"

The girl turned, a smile on her lips. "Charlie. What's yours?"

"Quinby," she answered, taking a sip of her drink. "Wanna take a ride?"

"Hell, yes!"

They climbed aboard a nearing slab that had slowed. The model touched a mark debossed onto its surface and their little platform rose higher like a leaf in a gentle updraft, then began its leisurely preprogrammed orbit.

Quinby noticed the other girl's studied nonchalance and knew she was more than a little star struck. "So, where are you from?" she asked, sitting on the slab's edge, careful not to spill her drink.

"Here, originally." Charlie sat down beside her, surprised at how stable the glass remained. "But I lived in Japan for a long time. I just got back a little while ago."

"Really? Where in Japan?"

"Tokyo. Shinjuku"

"That's a pretty wild place, especially if you spend any time there."

"You've been?"

"Yeah. I've modeled there." Quinby paused, then took a chance. "Did you develop a taste for anything exotic?"

She watched, fascinated, as the drug revealed things she didn't understand in the sudden brightness of Charlie's eyes, the floating slabs a scarlet corona as they drifted behind the young girl's head. It was as though the masks of their individual personas had been stripped away to reveal a psychic bond of shared experience as intensely dangerous as it was erotic. *Now why would I feel that? Unless she goes out with a sanctioned killer.* Quinby laughed at the absurdity of such a thing.

"What's so funny?" The girl's eyes were as large as moon globes and Quinby noticed their unusual color for the first time.

"Nothing, Charlie, nothing. Sometimes it just strikes me as funny, that's all. How we all seem to crave those peak experiences, even as we deny that part of ourselves."

"I—I'm not sure I understand."

"You will, Charlie, you will." Quinby then pointed down, the soul of discretion. "See that guy over there?"

"Mr. Solipsum? Mr. Stone said he owns this place."

"There's a lot of things Trey Solipsum has his snout in. But if there was ever a peak experience, it's him."

In that instant, as though he could somehow hear them, Solipsum's eyes met Charlie's and he winked. She suppressed a shiver, her gaze returning to Quinby as they passed him.

"What do you mean?"

The model's eyes glittered. "Why don't you find out for yourself?"

She reached into her purse, almost dropping it, then pulled out a card with cursive type etched on a perforated wafer of clear acrylic. "That's where he lives. And this will slot you in. Just say those words and the doorman will let you up."

Charlie squinted at the card, tilting it. She could just make out a phrase: 'Beauty must be served.'

"Is that what you're into? Peak experiences?"

Quinby studied the other girl in the slab's soft underlight. "Only a few of them, because really they're for junkies. But they're fun to have, once in awhile. And you have to go through them before you realize what you really want is

(love)

more than that. So now I look for plateau experiences."

"What's the difference?"

"You *stay* on the plateau, and it's a much smoother ride." Quinby grinned and stood as their floating shard neared a dock on the fourth level. "I'm off to get a refill. Want one?"

"No, thanks. I have to work tomorrow."

"Okay. Maybe I'll see you around. It's been a pleasure." Quinby hesitated, as though she wanted to say more, then shrugged and stepped off the scarlet edge, disappearing into the crowd.

Charlie turned to watch the slow ruby maelstrom, then touched one of the simple controls as she'd seen Quinby do. The slab drifted off to join its fellows and she leaned back, somehow glad to be alone now. Her elbow brushed something cool and she looked down to see a filigreed silver bowl filled with candied violet petals. She took a small pinch and placed it on her tongue, taste and scent now interchangeable, savoring as the little petals slowly dissolved. *I could get used to this,* she reflected, already aware of how much she loved this place, seeing all these people and the elegant spectacle they participated in. A wave of distance and perspective swept over her then and she was struck by the most powerful sense of déjà vu. She remembered that great line at the end of *Gatsby* and smiled.

Then she became aware of the music, tugging at the tides of her body like the gravity of some unseen moon . . . music that was nearly impossible to describe, like nothing you had ever heard, and it was available nowhere. It was akin to hearing the music of things normally experienced through other senses. Close your eyes and—hear—the fleshy sound of cherries, bitten right through to stone, a lodged numbness of rock cocaine, the depths of your lover's eyes as you/she/he are buried in each other like ice cream melting into pockets of brain, hot and cool, sweet and sticky, pooling and osmosing through mellifluous fibers you didn't even know you had—the sound at the meeting of lava and jungle, lush and fiery, yin and yang, give and take, shake and bake, wake me never because it just goes on and on and on forever, doesn't it? A backbeat of musical magma and shifting tectonics, flowing notes that bridge wire tense, pulsing, pulsing, in the synaptic gap that makes us all the same.

She looked down to see a great circular slab below her, pulsing with people. On that slab was Solipsum, having the time of his life.

Because Solipsum, she saw, could *dance.*

New York City, Stone Studios

There is a Place so beautiful that your words to describe, to grasp, to own, are stolen by awe and tumble away like the scales from your eyes when first you beheld it. It is a Place you have never seen but instantly recognize. And it is here that . . .

Joshua dreamed. He dreamed of the place that he would most like to shoot in, a Place he knew only as The Clouds. An endless Sky that was ever-changing, but where the light always remained the same. An eternal twilight of ochres and mauves that belonged to the hour before the sun set.

Here he was able to fly.

His camera shot 8x10 roll film in endless quantities and weighed nothing. He flew with an effortless grace, tracking a model, his muse of the moment. She soared, glided and floated through the monumental beauty and simplicity that was this Place. Time had no meaning here and he never tired of what he saw. Because when flight entered the model-photographer equation, the end result was infinite variation. Which for Joshua Stone meant just one thing.

Bliss.

Book 3

> *"All photographs are there to remind us of what we forget. In this—as in other ways— they are the opposite of paintings. Paintings record what the painter remembers. (But) because each one of us forgets different things, a photo more than a painting may change its meaning according to who is looking at it." —John Berger*

> *"A photograph is usually looked at, seldom looked into." —Ansel Adams*

> *"My job? It's like driving to work but you never get there." —Dick, an L.A. limo driver*

New York City, Central Park West

Solipsum lay in bed with Quinby, Straenje and another boy of a certain rude beauty whom they had found later. They lay in tableau, artfully draped and arranged, awaiting only a camera that would never come. Sleep had relaxed their features into an innocence that suited the white surroundings. Sex and drug paraphernalia abounded, all except for condoms—of these there were none. Only Solipsum lay awake, naked but for the small black key that hung about his neck. He was a remarkable physical specimen, with slabs and ridges of musculature geological in their contouring and formation. The picture of perfection—outwardly. Smoke curled lazily from the tip of the cigarette he had forgotten. He stared up at the shivering wreck of the barely alive creature that stared back at him from the mirrored ceiling. To see his own reflection. Meatsleeve. It was long overdue for replacement, especially in light of what was happening. There were forces building that would change his life irrevocably. A nexus approached, a major fork in the path of Reality. One branch would lead him back to where he had come from, forever. The other led to a place of permanence and invincibility on this plane unassailable by any of its current inhabitants. He knew all this and yet could not determine the final outcome. Able to foresee events of futures yet unborn, he also knew that what he saw was not really the future, only one of many possible futures. The distinction was one of life or death. His.

He levered himself from the bed, careful not to disturb his toys. He needed to get outside. To think.

New York City

Charlie felt the cool breeze on her arms and legs as she stood on the sidewalk outside her new apartment, wondering what her first day would bring. She was still scanning the street for a cab when one material-ized curbside. She jumped in and it pulled away, smooth acceleration belying its scratched and dented carapace. The cab's interior was grimy and worn, loud rap music spackled with gunshot distorting from ancient speakers. Something dangled from the rearview mirror that caused her mind to blank for an instant. *What the hell is that? It looks like*

(the stain in Joshua's studio)

some sort of voodoo fetish. She snapped back and noticed the absence of the usual polycarbon barrier. Then she saw why.

A large and magnificently ugly black man was driving. He was so enormous, it was as though someone had stuffed a sofa into the front seat. His hands on the wheel were massive and scarred, like hams sculpted from tarmac. All she could see of his face were his eyes, small and flinty as they pegged her in the rearview mirror. A voice like rusted ball bearings asked, "Where to?"

"23rd and 10th!" she yelled. "Can you turn that down a bit?"

Instead, the music became louder. The cab leapt forward, slamming Charlie into the seat back as it muscled its way into traffic.

Fuck, just my lucky day! The psycho cabby from Hell! What kind of system has he got in this thing? It sounds like a ShitMou' concert in here. Before he lost his voice.

They passed Solipsum as he walked the streets, and Charlie caught a glimpse of trench coat before her eyes were snatched back by the sway-ing, bobbing fetish. She shivered with sudden cold.

The music stopped. With one hand still steering, the cabby turned his head and peered at her. His face was like an old leather bag, worn and scraped and full of rocks. "Your name is Charlie," he rumbled.

He turned back and continued driving. Somehow he had managed not to hit anything or run over anyone. The music started again and she found herself staring at the loaf of his neck.

Oh my God, how does he know my name?

"Hey mister, how do you know my name?"

He ignored her.

Lotta good that's gonna do! Think, Charlie. Don't panic.

Her hand snuck towards the rusted handle to her right and jerked it sharply. Instead of opening the door, it simply snapped off. She stared at it in disgust, tossed it aside and reached for the other one. It was jammed and wouldn't open.

Fear coiled in her belly like a tiny eel. She felt the cab pick up speed, buildings and people flashing by before it began a series of sharp turns, flinging Charlie about its interior like a rag doll in a dryer.

Where did this guy learn to drive? Crack Pick-up and Delivery? And where the hell are we? I don't recognize this part of town. Shit, Charlie, what have you gotten yourself into this time? Her jaw began to clench, arms cording with tension. *No, Cherry Co-ra, breathe, that's it, use what she taught you . . . breathe, breathe, breathe . . .*

She closed her eyes and consciously willed each part of herself to relax. Taking the air deep into her body, she filled her lungs, then her *qi* center.

Suddenly, the cab stopped and the music shut off.

"Here we are, miss."

"Where? Where?" She pressed her face to the window, instantly recognizing the distinctive entrance to Stone Studios.

She fumbled for her wallet. "Uh, how much do I owe you?"

"Sixty-two fifty."

She pressed some bills into the Driver's outstretched palm. A small part of her noticed that it was even bigger than Joshua's.

"How did you know my name?" she asked.

He smiled, revealing a beautiful set of perfect white teeth. "My daughter's name is Charlie. I know *all* Charlies."

His hand closed over the money just as the broken door nearest Charlie magically popped open. Before she could stop it, the laughter came burbling up. She heard a musical thunder coming from the front seat and realized she wasn't laughing alone. *What a beautiful sound,* she thought. Her whole body felt wonderfully loose and she slumped back into the seat. The Driver hadn't stopped looking at her and now held something in his hand.

"Take this, Daughter." He handed her the small white card. "In case you ever need a—taxi."

New York City, Central Park West

Solipsum was glad to be outside. It was a windy day in New York City and the magnificent trench coat he wore billowed like a thing alive. He passed a couple, meandering and in love. They turned to stare, clearly affected by his unbelievable beauty. Then, for no reason the man would ever be able to discern, an argument erupted and the girl he had loved since high school left him standing there. He would see her again, years later, badly used and long past her memory of him.

The window cleaner who watched the model pass thought, *now there goes a guy who will never have women problems.* Then the carriage bolt exploded and he found himself dangling in the air from the safety harness he had almost forgotten to put on that morning.

Solipsum passed a group of school children who fell into a mass of accusation and crying. He hardly noticed any of it. His mind was occupied by far more important matters.

It had been a very long time since he had been put back in touch with his survival instincts. Like the great white shark, he was used to being at the top of the food chain. To realize he and everything he had worked so hard for were now threatened was extremely disquieting. Especially because this threat was internal, and he now had to deal with an issue that should have been dealt with years ago, when he was less vulnerable to outside forces. Six to eight months, nine at the outside, before the body he was using rotted into liquid and gristle. It was only his enormous willpower that allowed him to maintain this illusion.

He suddenly felt the deliberate brush of eyecrawl and whipped around to stare back. "It's a tight fit, isn't it?" he asked.

"What?" the businessman stammered.

"That *Weeping Orifice Love Doll* you purchased over the Internet last month. You remember, the one you spent your retirement savings on?"

"W—what?"

"Oh, come now." Solipsum made a small moue of disappointment. "You named him Kip. At least that's what you whisper in his little plastic ear when you—"

The man's face dissolved. "I'll—I'll—"

"Hurry home. If you catch a cab, you just might make it before your wife looks in that closet behind your suits."

Solipsum laughed and thought about what a wonderful place this world was, a banquet really. He watched the businessman run into traffic, screaming for a cab.

He felt a slight itch and looked down at his hand to see it had rotted through at the palm. This was something he had not seen before. He watched for a moment in mild fascination as the flesh slowly re-knit itself, then shook his wrist and continued on.

I am using this form far more quickly than I intended. Perhaps I am enjoying the pleasures of this plane too intensely. He smiled thinly. *Thus far I have found only one person whose body can withstand my presence. I have spent years searching for another but time has run out.*

He stopped across the street from a large billboard, shoulders hunched against the wind as he lit up. He took smoke deep into the meatsleeve's lungs and then looked up, Phoena's enormous billboard face filling his vision.

It must be her.

New York City, Stone Studios

Trish hung up the phone and saw Joshua's new assistant walking down the hall. *God, she's cute!* she thought as she stood and propped her elbows on the high reception counter top. "Charlie, I'm really sorry about the other day. I hope you weren't embarrassed."

Charlie smiled, still wondering how many other Charlies that cab driver must have met. "No harm done, Trish. I mean, it all worked out for the best, didn't it?"

"Yeah, I guess it did. Anyway, head on in, Russ's waiting for you. And Charlie?" Trish leaned forward and continued quietly. "Don't let him push you around."

Charlie's mouth tightened. "Don't worry. I won't."

She rode the small elevator to the main dome, noticing the sweep of city through its glass walls. The doors opened and she stood for an instant, struck once again by the epic grandeur of Joshua Stone's studio.

Russ watched her as she began walking towards him in her jean shorts, white t-shirt and treaded sneakers. He stifled an urge to lick his lips, reflecting instead on how good he felt. He'd had some time to think things over and figured a gig with Joshua Stone was way too good to pass up, even as second assistant. For now.

"Hey there, Goldilocks," He asked, his smile more like a leer. "How's life at the center of the Karma Deluxe Hamster Wheel?" He flexed lightly so she could scope the goods.

"What? Speak English."

Russ shrugged and gave her an extra greasy smirk, like he'd just licked a chop or something. "Hey babe, learn English. Just another name for the Big City, ya know?"

Charlie studied him, wondering if there was going to be trouble with this one. "Whatever." There was something about his face, something in the way he held it that made him less handsome than he really was. His eyes were long and narrow as they studied her, his mouth well-shaped but pinched slightly, as though it had been painted on and dried smaller.

"Well, come on, we haven't got all day to stand around." Russ turned and walked towards the studio's cyclorama. "We got a huge shoot for *Narcissia's Hope* tomorrow."

They stopped at the edge of an immaculate expanse of white floor and what appeared to be a flat white wall. As Charlie stared, detail reluctantly emerged until she saw the large curvature where ceiling, wall and floor all joined. The effort to resolve what was essentially nothing induced a slight vertigo.

"This here is the main studio," began Russ. "Floor to ceiling cove, sixty feet high by eighty feet long by fifty feet deep. Absolutely seamless. Joshua used space age construction materials in this place and that cove is one of the little things here he's proudest of. Watch this." He walked over to a wall, tapping a sequence into the small keypad. The cove changed color to a deep mauve.

"Wow!"

"'Wow' is right, little girl. This place is the shit. The whole cove is made of a special polycarbon that can electronically change its color. Not only that, but it can pick up any pattern you can scan in or digitally generate. That includes movies of reflections, ripples, fabric blowing, palm trees, you name it. It's also tougher than steel and never scratches."

"I've never seen anything like it."

Russ leaned against the wall. "You don't know how lucky you are, sugar cube. This is the only studio of its kind in the world. Nothing even comes close."

She placed a sneaker experimentally on the cove floor, then looked back at him over her shoulder. "How do you black it out?"

"Easy. Watch."

He tapped out another sequence and the dome enclosing the studio slowly turned inky. "Same technology. Only this time, you can program different levels of translucency as well as different colors. The light that comes through this dome, courtesy of the sun and the dome's fiber optics is so freakin' awesome, it blows even my mind."

Which would be like blowing a ten watt light bulb. She almost laughed but quickly smothered it. "I don't know what to say."

"How about—Jane Bond lives? Now close your jaw, Cool Whip, and follow me."

They continued touring the studio where Charlie saw the two darkrooms, a kitchen, the client lounge with its pool table, offices, the boardroom, computer rooms, the library, washrooms, the make-up and ward-robe rooms, even an outdoor swimming pool. All of it connected by passages and ramps, elevators and gear-tooth stairs. The whole studio had a minimalist aesthetic, composed of curves with very few straight lines, except where walls blended with some great cog or piston or huge wedge of cowling. Each time she turned a corner, there awaited another structural surprise. A tapered machine-organ wrapped in mirror like something dipped. A ten foot face constructed of tiny fiber optic rods. An industrial fridge, embedded in a sweep of knurl, dull steel pea in its labular pod, fold becoming wall becoming sink.

The way the light wrapped seemed unique to each area. Sometimes womb-like, other times cutting and defining, like it was mining shape. She gradually became aware that what Joshua had built was a lens, a prism, that focused not only the light but her awareness of it, of bath-ing in it even as it bathed. She stopped for an instant, stunned by this realization, the Light somehow brighter as it poured and poured, almost slowing, it seemed, to the point she could see the individual photons dance. She continued walking, looking at the architecture with this new awareness and instantly, she had it, why these lines had looked so haunt-ingly familiar, even from her first day. *It's the body. That's what he's do-ing. The body. Outside and in. And not just the physical one.*

Russ slowed his pace, allowing Charlie to take the lead, unaware of the effect the studio was having on her. He smiled as he checked out her bum, which he had to admit was pretty special. He thought again about his recent demotion and figured *What the fuck, they say that if you ain't the lead dog, the view don't change. Well, this is one view I could live with for quite a friggin' while, lemme tell you.* He paused in admiration. *Jesus wept, will you look at that?* He held his hands out to frame the bouncing bubble before him. *She's got an ass like a—*

"What's this?" Charlie turned, hooking a thumb over her shoulder to a set of elevator doors they hadn't seen yet. Russ quickly pocketed his hands.

"Uh—this takes you up to The Bossman's digs. Stay out. Unless, of course, he calls you up. Like maybe when he's cravin' a late night *chicken* sandwich—"

"Drop dead, pervo!"

Russ just grinned a toothy grin as he shouldered past.

They continued through the studio and down a long, curved stretch of hall until they arrived beside the unmarked door.

"This is the Image Room," said Russ, his voice hushed. "It's where the Stone Man does the work he does alone. No one, and I mean *no one* is allowed in here." Russ' eyes were strangely vacant as he said this. Before she could ask him what he'd meant, he had walked past her, back the way they had come. She had no choice but to follow.

"So," Russ said as they returned to the main shooting area, "just thought I'd clear the air about what Joshua was saying yesterday. You know, about me being second and you bein' the new first? Well, I think the best way to handle things is if we make it *look* like that's the case, but you an' me'll really know what's going on. I'll be top dog and you'll be second. Got that?"

Charlie stood with her hands on her hips, mind still back at that strange room. Then she realized what he had said. "No, I don't got that. We follow Mr. Stone's instructions or I'll let him know how you're trying to ooze around behind his back, bottom dweller."

"You wouldn't!"

She bared her teeth in a not-smile. "Try me."

A strange sound came from the floor. Charlie looked down and saw a rat-like Chihuahua with enormous eyes, balanced on its hind legs, forepaws clutching Russ's calf. It looked up at her, yip breathing in short bursts as it began humping Russ's leg. Vigorously.

He looked down, aghast. "Fucckkkk!!!" he bellowed, flicking his leg.

The dog went sailing across the studio like a fur-covered missile, trailed by a long yowl. A sudden squeal of anguish erupted from make-up artist Sindra Djarhm. "Roquefort!"

"You bastard!" cried Charlie. She stepped forward and did something she had been trained never to do—attack first. She launched a backfist, which was blocked so quickly and efficiently she barely had time to register what that meant before the counterstrikes came, one—two—three, and she was forced back a step—to almost have her jaw dislocated by the fourth percussive. Then a perfect roundhouse kick came from nowhere like a bullet to her head. She leaned back to evade and Russ left the kick hanging in the air, fully extended, to Charlie's utter disbelief. *The arrogance!* she thought as she dropped low to the floor, executing a spinning sweep that Russ easily avoided, jumping high, knees at his shoulders. He landed and the fabric of his pants snapped like a flag as he pistoned two sidekicks, one to her side, the other to her head. She felt a sharp pain in her ribs and almost eluded the last kick, backing away, a stinging wetness in her mouth, to rest in Mantis Stance, panting.

Russ smiled at her. He was not even breathing hard. "Some training, eh? Good. I'm going to enjoy this."

Charlie just wiped her mouth and waved him forward. Her mind weighed options, time lengthening/compressing as they circled and evaluated each other. She was slightly faster, though not by much, and she was definitely more flexible. But Russ was stronger, much stronger. Thus Spirit and Strategy would decide. As, she knew, they really always did.

Her focus tightened as they began the final dance, the world reduced to breathing, instinct and unconscious strategy—the mind too slow at this level. Sounds of cheering make-up artist and squealing dog faded as she entered the Void.

Instead of retreating, she moved in, raining a combination of punches, kicks and elbows, each hand a striking osprey, closer and closer, almost finding the targets, but Russ's body twisted and turned and she missed the vital nerve plexi. Her blows came so quickly though, he could not counter, only defend, yet still he managed to block everything she threw at him. He continued to backpedal, trying to gain leverage and distance. She decided to subtly break their rhythm. Feigning exhaustion, she let her breath become more ragged, her movements fractionally slower. Then suddenly planted her foot, power coming up from the ground, twisting her hip as she drove her left fist, middle knuckle extended like a tiny beak, right into Russ's sternum. He blocked and countered simultaneously, knowing he had won.

"You fucked up, girl. Came in too close."

And never saw the outside crescent kick that came looping over his shoulder, still in his blind spot as it clocked him upside the head. Smartly. He staggered back, dropping his guard. Charlie saw the death blow opening, hesitated, and then it was too late. Russ danced away, ear inflamed and bleeding slightly.

"You're good, Charlie."

She blinked in surprise. It was the first time he had called her by her name. "You had me there, but you didn't finish it. So now I will." His eyes glittered and he smiled, lips stretching tight in a rictus that sliced through her calm like a *katana*. With a conscious effort, he repressed his rage, using a *ki* breathing technique Charlie had never seen. She felt the first faint touch of fear.

They circled again, Russ predatory, scenting victory. A movement caught her eye and she turned her head minutely, surprised to see Joshua. Her concentration slipped—*tsuke*—the Lapse. It was more than enough for Russ. He struck with the speed of a cobra, palm heel perfectly angled to drive the nose cartilage into her brain. Charlie saw his hand blur, her own block far too late, bracing for the impact when at the last second, he shifted the death blow, just grazing her.

"Break it up!" Stone shouted as he rushed over.

It ended as suddenly as it had begun and they both stood before him, breathing heavily. He saw Charlie's face, the blood at her mouth. As he watched, a small drop fell onto her white shirt. She brought a fist up and carefully wiped her lips, eyes large and unreadable. Something in his chest shifted and he forced himself to look away from her.

"Are either of you hurt?"

"No, sir," from both. "We were just playing," Russ continued, "weren't we?" His foot nudged Charlie's as he muttered "Wanna keep your job?"

Stone's eyes returned to Charlie. "Is that right?"

"Yes, sir. We were just fooling around." She sent a warning look to Sindra, who stood behind Joshua. Roquefort whined softly.

Stone heard the dog. "Sindra," he snapped, "get some ice from the kitchen. Please."

"Right away, Joshua." The make-up artist fled, clutching his pet.

Russ watched him go, then gingerly checked his ear for damage. *Fuckin' great kick! That came outta nowhere.* He looked at the smear of blood on his hand. *And there's other shit she knows too. Things are about to get real interesting.* He glanced at his boss. *If we're still working here tomorrow.*

"I have no idea who started that and I don't want to know," Stone's voice scourged them. "But if I ever see it again, both of you will be out on your asses. Got that?"

"Yes sir!"

"Good. Russ, clean yourself up and do final studio prep. The clients will be here first thing tomorrow and I want the studio immaculate. Now go. Charlie, come with me."

He led her to one of the washrooms and closed the door, then helped her onto the counter. Her ribs shifted but she didn't make a sound, aware of how close he was. Joshua broke out the first aid kit and started to clean her up, working quietly and diligently. He finally spoke. "Are you okay?"

She nodded. Tears brimmed in her eyes, but not of pain. Rather, shame.

"Let me see those ribs."

Charlie winced as he peeled her shirt up. He saw two areas of skin already purpling, near to the bruise he'd seen the other day. *So that's how she got it.*

"Those look pretty serious." He reached for the large roll of bandage.

She gently pushed his hand away, not really wanting to, and started to lower her shirt. "I'll be okay."

"You sure?"

She smiled wearily. "I've had worse. Way worse."

Joshua was about to say something, then stopped himself. Instead he began cleaning the blood around her mouth.

Charlie kept waiting for it to hurt but it didn't, at least not much. *He's got great hands. He could have been a surgeon. I don't think I've ever felt anyone touch me quite . . . Whoa, Charlie. Don't even think of going there. Grit your teeth and focus on the pain.*

Joshua daubed the last bit of antiseptic on the cut near her lips, strangely sad he no longer had an excuse to touch her.

"There. That should do it." He caught her peeking at him and noticed for the first time the tiny flecks of green in the violet near her pupils.

"Thanks, Mr. Stone." Then the words came tumbling out. "I just want to apologize for what you saw back there. I am so grateful for the opportunity you've given me and—"

"Joshua."

"Pardon?"

"Call me Joshua. And don't worry about it. No harm done. Now go home and rest. Tomorrow's a big day."

She was about to jump off the counter when the pain hit, freezing her. She caught Joshua looking into her eyes, and found herself looking back. And looking back. And looking back.

Book 4

"Photographs have a kind of authority over the imagination today which the printed word had yesterday, and the spoken word before that. They seem utterly real. They come, we imagine, directly to us without human meddling and they are the most effortless food for the mind conceivable." —Walter Lippman

"A great photograph is made, not taken."
—Ansel Adams

New York City, Stone Studios

Roquefort skittered into Joshua's main studio, eyes bright, head held high, yesterday's bootflight but a fading memory. He spied Bruun dozing in a patch of sun near the couch, and instantly quieted his panting. He crept over, closer and closer, almost upon the sleeping mammal when Bruun opened one eye and froze him with a look.

Don't even think about it.

Think about what, oh Exalted One?

Barking loudly, so as to startle me from a particularly sound sleep. Or quietly farting near me, doubtless a far more vicious awakening.

The dog looked rather sheepish. *I would never do such a thing!*

Bruun stood and arched his back, stretching his legs, claws extruding through the ridged spread of his toes.

I will see you later, ΘφϽΓϾφXΗσʃʃδ, Bruun projected, using the dog's real name. *Try not to eat my food.* His ears flattened as a voice began screeching in queen, "Roqueffffooorrrtttttt, oh Roqueffffffffooooooorrrrrrrrrrrtttttttttttttt!" Bruun eyed the dog. *Your pet is calling.* He licked a paw and rubbed his face.

Sindra saw his dog with Joshua's cat, and for an instant swore the two were having some sort of conversation. He was dressed simply today, in burgundy harem pants, buckled shoes and a vintage designer top a bit too small for him. He was of medium height, about thirty happy pounds overweight, and could not possibly have cared less. He spoke with the lilting cadences of the small Caribbean island that had been his home, back when. What many in the industry found so fascinating about Sindra was not that he had turned himself into one of the best make-up artists in the world, but that he continued to operate at this level with an almost complete lack of ego. The dog and Sindra had been together as long as anyone could remember, and it was possibly the only thing he loved more than Joshua.

"There you are!" Sindra cooed, as if to his first born.

Roquefort leapt from side to side, small driblets of joy-urine speckling the floor. This sometimes happened when Sindra came near and he really should know better but oh, oh, oh, he just couldn't help it! Besides, his bladder was the size of a vitamin.

The dog was scooped up and instantly took this as a signal—the game had begun. His little head darted hither and thither, tongue lapping and flapping like a small wet pennant as he licked the make-up artist's face. Soon they were practically French kissing, Sindra's hand glistening with residual urine that he did not seem to notice.

"Come with Dadee, Precious."

He set the dog down and they walked to the make-up room. Sindra began thinking about the day ahead and the numerous and precise make-up changes that would be required of him. Luckily, there were only two girls, both drop-dead, and the clothes were fierce. He saw Charlie and stopped, making a little bow. "My Maid in Shining Armor," he said, liking the way she looked in her faded jeans and cropped white t-shirt. Then he noticed her face. "Oh my, look what that bastard done to you!" He cupped her chin and lightly touched her lips.

"Ouch."

"Still a bit tender, eh? Well come to the make-up room and we'll see what Sindra can do for you."

He soon had the young assistant seated and began skillfully applying eye make-up and concealer to cover the bruise on her cheek. "I want to thank you for standing up to that jerk-boy the other day. I owe you one for that. And Sindra never forgets a favor."

"God, Sindra, don't worry about it. I'm just glad that Roquefort wasn't hurt." Charlie watched him in the mirror, enjoying the way his hands moved, how he smelled of cardamon and the way he was unaware that the small pink tip of his tongue protruded.

He had almost finished when he stopped for a moment and studied her. "You are very pretty, Charlie. I want you to promise me something."

"What?"

"That you will let me create your look for Joshua's big party."

"Sindra! I couldn't ask you to do that."

"Nonsense, Charlie. I am doing it." He delicately kissed her forehead. "I will hear no more." His hands then gently angled her face from side to side. "I am done," he finally pronounced. "You are all ready for the big day."

Charlie stood and leaned into the mirror. "Wow. What an amazing job. I can't see a thing. Thanks, Sindra, you're the best."

She kissed him on the cheek and hurried out of the make-up room.

"Joshua, Prissy Kin on line one."

He grabbed the wall phone and leaned against a counter, looking out at the city. "Stone here."

"Hello, Joshua! You're going to have an amazing shoot today with a very special model. Unfortunately, it won't take place until ten thirty because she's missed her flight. Sorry, babe!" He heard a sniffle.

"Missed your flight, eh? Got a cold, Priss?"

"No, Stoney, just my allergies. Oh! Here comes my cab!"

More like your dealer.

"See ya soon," she finished brightly.

Stone hung up, smiling despite himself. He took a sip of coffee, burned his mouth, cursed, and happened to look over just as the elevator doors opened to admit Phoena into the main studio. The pain of his scorched tongue was instantly forgotten as he gazed upon her. She wore a red fall coat and green sweater thickly woven and wild with texture over moleskin breeches a deep moss in color. Her appearance was striking as always, but for some reason, as she walked towards him today, he noticed her as if for the first time. Her huge green eyes with those crazy long lashes, feline and sensuous even in repose, the sculpted elegance of her face, the lips just a bit too full and the deep black tousle of her hair. He remembered her body, how the Light so loved to wrap around it, how endless his joy in exploring it photographically and later, physically. Suddenly, gratitude came over him like a wave. To have been blessed with such a muse. And then the years flew away like windswept leaves as he remembered the day they had first shot. The transformation that had taken place when she'd emerged from make-up in the designer's dress. How young she'd been and awkward too, yet with the hand of Grace already so firmly upon her, guiding that willowy walk on those long, long legs. And how, in the stunned silence that had greeted her, she'd thought she'd made some huge mistake and ran crying back to the change room. The make-up had been ruined and they'd decided to call it a day. It was only as an afterthought, when he'd seen her clear and shining face cosmetic–free, that he decided to shoot some film. When he'd seen the first Polaroid, it had fluttered from his fingers as he stared at her in awe. And he knew what Givenchy must have felt when he first saw Audrey Hepburn.

Phoena could barely grab her own wrists behind his back as she squeezed him. "Hi, babe!"

He hugged her back, inhaling her scent, feeling the warmth of her. "Wow, Phoena, you look amazing, as always."

"Flatterer."

They embraced again, both remembering what it had been like. Even Russ turned away to give them some privacy.

"I brought you something." she said, her voice shy as she gently disengaged from the circle of his arms. She reached into her purse and handed him the small box wrapped in silver linen.

"What's this?"

"Open it. A little surprise for your Party."

Stone unwrapped the textured cloth and opened the thin leather box. Nestled inside were a pair of admantium alloy clear lens glasses. He carefully set them on his face, noting without surprise how perfectly they suited him.

"Thank you, Phoena."

"Don't leave them in a drawer somewhere. A little sparrow told me you'll be needing them. Soon."

He slipped the glasses off. "Did he tell you anything else?"

"Yes." She took a sip of his coffee, completely unaffected by its heat. "We're going to have a great shoot today."

He laughed. "I just heard that from someone else."

Phoena peered at him over the rim of the cup.

"Prissy called to say she'd missed her flight. Her allergies were acting up. She won't be here 'til ten thirty."

Phoena set the coffee down and unbuttoned her coat. "Wow. Only an hour and a half late. That's pretty good for her. And her allergies," she rolled her eyes. "Great excuse."

They both laughed.

"Hey, what's the best one you ever heard?" asked Joshua.

"Male model blew in three hours late once. The clients were freaking, the photographer was climbing the walls and we were up to six hundred grand in overtime. He walks in, totally calm, and goes over to the make-up table as if nothing was wrong. Everyone is staring at him and there's dead silence in the room. The photographer finally can't stand it any more. He marches up and starts peeling the paint off the walls. 'Why the fuck are you so late?' he screams. The model looked him dead in the eye and said, 'I was bathing my mother.'"

"Wow. What do you say to that?"

"Exactly."

"And the client ate it? The whole six hundred?"

"Yup."

Stone shook his head, amazed.

"Joshua, who's that girl over there?"

"My new first assistant. Let me introduce you. Charlie? Can you come over here for a sec?"

The young assistant walked over to join them, trying very hard to appear casual, like she hadn't noticed Phoena the second she'd come into the studio. She tripped over the cord before she'd even seen it, catching herself before she crashed into the model but still ending up way too close. She found herself staring. *Oh my God! Her eyes!* She barely heard Joshua's introduction.

Phoena stepped back slightly and extended her hand. "Hi, Charlie. Joshua's been telling me a lot about you. He says you have tremendous potential." She smiled.

Charlie flushed as she felt Phoena's cool fingers touch her own and found herself looking at the tops of her shoes.

"Coming from him, that's some praise."

The young assistant looked up again into the green depths of Phoena's eyes and almost asked her if cities really did burn.

"I better head over to Sindra," the model continued. "Looks like we'll have to shoot some solo stuff earlier than we planned."

"Thanks, Phoena. You're the best," Stone tried and failed to hide his relief. He and Charlie watched her walk to the make-up room just as another page was heard. "Joshua, the people from *Narcissia* are here."

"Thanks, Trish, send them up."

Stone turned to Charlie and spread his arms. "Well, let the Games begin."

What followed next was textbook big money fashion advertising, perfectly run, perfectly shot. Joshua Stone was the consummate professional, expertly orchestrating everything from clients and models to lights and lunch. And though he listened carefully to everyone's concerns and opinions, he somehow always managed to get his way. At one point Charlie realized there was a complete lack of friction—she had never seen this many people all working together towards a common goal. It was an eye-opening realization that made her understand there was far more to photography than just taking pictures.

She noticed how Phoena, Sindra and even Russ integrated so seamlessly even Prissy Kin's late arrival was barely noticed. Lunch consisted of a double-seared Atlantic salmon in a coconut pear sauce with glass noodles and cherries. It tasted like nothing she had ever experienced. The clients seemed so happy with the food that their approval of the Polaroids went even more quickly. And Charlie wondered if everything, even the food, was all geared towards creating this level of smoothness.

Just as lunch finished, she noticed Phoena staring at a magazine cover, her face expressing such a powerful mixture of hatred and distaste, Charlie was stunned. The model closed her eyes and put the magazine back on the coffee table, then stood and walked away. Charlie waited until she was almost to the make-up room, then snuck over and picked it up.

Solipsum stared out at her from the cover.

The day progressed and Charlie realized that what had initially seemed like chaos was in fact very carefully planned. She began to understand how the Polaroids related to Joshua's lighting, and how the subtleties of that lighting combined with the color of the clothes, the make-up, the models and their movement, everything in service to the client's mandate. Which, it dawned on her, was to sell clothing, not to make art. Their job, it seemed, was to make the garments as seductive and attractive as possible, and the fact they were creating a beautiful image was simply a byproduct. She watched how carefully Phoena and Prissy posed, yet they moved so effortlessly it was easy to see how she had missed it at first. She also saw why certain angles she'd thought were great had been completely ignored by Joshua. To be sure, she stepped behind him as he was shooting and soon enough Phoena hit a pose, lasering the camera with a look that Joshua refused because the clothes, the presentation of the Cloth, was not perfect. Then she understood why she'd missed this earlier. It seemed the gap between a great fashion photograph and a great photograph was so small it as to be virtually nonexistent.

Joshua shot a Polaroid and they both relaxed while they waited for it to develop. There were many now who brought retouching into this phase of the creative process, shooting then scanning 8x10 Polaroids to get themselves as close as possible to the finished ad, but Stone was not one of them. It was simply not the way he had been taught. The day his photography required digital crutches at this early stage was the day he would lay down his camera.

"These are almost ready for ads," Charlie said, as though reading his mind. "They're so carefully lit, they'll hardly need any retouch."

Joshua peeled the backing, his eyes like polished optics as they found hers. "That's the idea."

They looked at the Polaroid together and were, for a moment, transported.

"It's—art," breathed Charlie.

"No. It's *commercial* art." Joshua's voice was cool. "That's what I do, Charlie. As will you some day. And the word 'commercial' comes before the word 'art'. Art and Commerce. Two sides of the same coin. Because at the end of the day? *That's* what makes the world go round. *That spinning coin.* On whose edge we balance."

"How?"

"Art induces by seducing. Commerce satisfies by gratifying. But it's only temporary. And a material thing, like a dress? It can never satisfy a yearning of the soul, which would be to . . . ?"

" . . . look like Phoena?"

"Close. To *be* Phoena."

"But they don't even know what she's like!"

"They don't need to. Don't want to. And we don't want that either. What we want is for them to *imagine* what such an existence is like. So the picture isn't only a window, it's also a trap—it makes them chase something they'll never catch. Because not only is the message contrived, the messenger is made-up, lit, photographed and retouched so she's four generations removed from reality."

"But—but that means were not just selling the dress, we're secretly telling them that if they buy it, they'll somehow have all the things they imagine Phoena has."

"Yes."

"Which isn't true."

"Yes."

"Isn't that—cheating?"

Joshua gave her that strange and ineffable look she'd seen Phoena give the camera. Then he returned to the set to leave her standing there, implication like a fire coursing unchecked through the forest of her assumptions. Her face betrayed everything, and Joshua knew he had gone too far, too soon, before he'd even revealed the whole house of cards. So far it had only been the two Red Queens—Hearts and Diamonds—Art and Commerce. She would have been devastated had he shown her the two Black Queens, who reigned over Clothing's manufacture.

The day continued and Charlie found herself becoming more and more depressed. She felt like she was doing something that had not only revealed itself to be substance-free, but secretly hurtful as well. She felt, in a word, soiled.

She was handing Joshua another film back when he looked at her. "Charlie, you have to put in perspective what I said earlier. We live in the time we do, and do the things we must. Always remember that."

He returned to directing Phoena and Prissy, the two models moving through sets of double poses as if they had been doing this their whole lives. Which, Charlie supposed, they had.

The day was almost done when Stone said, "Last roll!" but ended up needing more. He called for a five minute break while Charlie dashed off to the film fridge. Prissy joined Sindra to get her make-up retouched as the gaggle of clients from *Narcissia* indulged in the chocolates Russ was serving.

Phoena found Joshua by the film cart. "Watch it with that one. She's the real thing."

"I know. She's smart as a whip."

"That's not what I'm talking about. Don't you see the way she looks at you? No, of course not. You are probably the most enlightened man I know, but at times I swear I've never seen anyone so unobservant! Can't you tell that Charlie's totally infatuated with you?" Phoena plucked a chocolate from the passing tray, catching Russ's eyes on her breasts.

"You're dreaming."

"No. I'm not. But the future will tell us whose right about this one." She was about to turn away, then changed her mind, some secret knowledge pulling up the corners of her mouth.

"Oh, oh. I know that smile. What's up? Out with it, girl."

Phoena leaned against the counter and set the chocolate down. She pushed it around a little before looking at Joshua with an unreadable expression. "There's something in the air. Something big."

"What?"

"I'm not quite sure, but I did have an unusual lunch the other day. With Magma Frost. Know her?"

"Do I ever. One hell of a negotiator. She's probably the best booker in the city. Outside of your booker, Rothman, of course." Joshua tried to grab the tiny treat but she was too quick.

"Rothman Cartilage is an agent, not a booker. There's a difference." She bit off half the chocolate as if to illustrate her point. "To make a long story short, she wanted me to leave him and join *P.M.P.*"

"Solipsum's Agency."

"Yes. She offered me a lot. Frankly, more than I'm worth."

"What happened?"

Phoena laughed. "I politely told her to fuck off." She held the chocolate out to him, its viscous center slowly running. "I could tell that—he—had put her up to it. She hid it very well but I'm sure she didn't just suddenly decide she wanted me over there."

Joshua took her hand, guiding the sweet into his mouth, his lips lightly brushing her fingertips. She felt the slightest tingle and knew that all they'd had was still there, just beneath the surface. As it probably always would be.

"Besides," she continued, licking her fingers in a gesture as unconscious as it was sensual, "we both know how dangerous it can be to lock horns with Mr. Cartilage over something."

"Or someone," he said around a mouthful of chocolate.

"Point."

"You know something, Phoena? This may tie in with that rumor that's all over town."

"The one about some sort of huge experimental ad campaign?"

"Yes. Elora Gorj called me this morning and asked me what I knew about it. I told her not much more than everybody else. 'Joshua,' she said, 'I'm finally going to offer you something that will challenge you fully.'"

"Her vagina?"

He laughed. "I think she was serious, Phoena. I tried to press her but all she said was, 'I'll tell you all about it. At your Party.'"

"That's showing remarkable restraint. For her."

"Let it rest," he said, exasperation creeping into his voice.

"You know how I feel about that grasping bitch. She's a dangerous woman because her ambition has no limits. And from what I've heard, neither does her libido." Phoena looked for the chocolate tray.

"If it wasn't for her, I wouldn't have this studio."

"I know, Joshua, I know. But that doesn't make her any less a cun—"

"Here's the film," he said a little too loudly as Charlie joined them, brandishing two ProPacks.

Phoena squeezed his shoulder as she walked past. "We'll continue this discussion later."

The shoot went on without further incident and ended with a stunning double of Phoena and Prissy. Joshua passed his camera to Charlie, clapped his hands and yelled, "That's a wrap!" to cheers and applause. Lights were then struck, film bagged and logged, kits closed and cameras put away, the clothes all carefully re-skinned in their shiny plastic sleeves.

What have we just done? thought Charlie as she watched Joshua herd the happy clients to the elevator. They seemed so ordinary, once she got to know them, these people who influenced the lives of so many. *Do they ever wonder about what they do?*

Phoena looked at herself in the change room mirror, her thoughts turning to Joshua's new assistant. She was about to remove her shoot make-up when the inspiration blossomed. She smiled and instead touched up what had looked so good all day. *I wonder where we'll go first*, she thought as she strode across the studio, her smile loosening a little when she noticed the strange expression on Charlie's face. She dropped her bag by the camera cart and touched the young girl's arm. "What are you doing right now?"

Charlie looked away from the elevator and snapped the clasps on the Pelican case. "Packing the gear, why?"

Phoena turned to Joshua, a gleam in her eye. "Are you done with Charlie? Can I have her for the rest of the day?"

"I can handle the rest," said Russ, lowering the last of the lights. "Take off."

Charlie's eyes narrowed and she opened her mouth to speak.

"In that case, she's all yours," said Joshua.

"Thanks, Josh."

"Thanks, Mr. St—uh, Joshua."

The elevator had begun its easy fall and both took a moment to enjoy the city, bathed in the warmth of the setting sun. The tall buildings were edged in mauves and oranges and looked like some petrified forest, a fire frozen in its desiccated limbs. Charlie watched the dying rays caress Phoena's profile and felt just a little awed.

"Where are we going?" she asked.

Phoena smirked. "Why, shopping, of course! I mean, really, what did you think you were going to wear to Joshua's big party? Your work clothes?"

Charlie smiled and looked back at the city, the buildings growing taller with their descent. She remembered Joshua's words and thought she understood what he'd meant about living in the age we do and doing the things we must. *Sometimes stuff doesn't change overnight, much as I might want it to. So why not enjoy life and just do the best I can?* The doors opened and she suddenly remembered where they were going. "Phoena, I—I can't afford—"

"Charlie, don't even go there." The model strode to the curb, pulling the young assistant in her wake, arm already raised as she yelled, "Taxi!"

New York City, Upper East Side

Very close to Stone Studios was one of the city's most exclusive luxury apartment complexes. Available units were never advertised conventionally, because they were available only to those with staying power.

This was usually evidenced by a massive fall from grace, then a return, Lazarus-like, to smote all those responsible for their initial downfall. And if an innocent or two were caught in that vengeful sweep, well, what of it? It was all omelets and eggs. Such at least were the thoughts of the person who owned the only two penthouse suites: Rothman Cartilage, Super Agent.

A sunset Roman in spectacle was just commencing and the illumination in Rothman's massive living room was magnificent in its subtlety and palette. A sixty foot wall of glass provided a view of the city second only to Stone's. The furnishings were sparse but exquisite, each piece carefully selected as much for function as for effect.

Along the far wall ran a fifteen foot glass tank, empty except for water and nine piranhas. Rumor had it that he sometimes fed these creatures during one of his rare and exclusive parties. Gold fish, usually, the large and expensive ones from Japan. Perhaps the odd mammal. And just before the wriggling sacrifice was tanked, he markered onto it the name of some partygoer unlucky enough to be the night's object lesson.

Among the scattering of magazines on a low glass coffee table was the same magazine Phoena had been affected by so strongly. For all her distaste, there was no denying the sheer magnetic power of its cover. On it, Solipsum stood resplendent, pinstriped suit and silken tie immaculate, a raw cut ruby in a twist of gold adorning his index finger.

The horizon's sandy edge drank the last red seep of sun and the shadows in the room deepened and pooled. A new shadow slowly joined them. A shadow where none should have been. It was cast by the image of Solipsum
unfolding
from the flat plane of the magazine's cover
until it was no longer a photograph of
but simply
Solipsum himself
walking through the magazine's cover
as if through a door.

He stood and brushed off an errant serif as he gained his bearings. Then he leaned against the glass wall and gazed out at the city, the dying blood-light on his face exquisite. A bathrobed figure entered the room to see a silhouetted form where none should be.

"Who the fuck?" snarled Rothman.

A cigarette lighter snapped. Its glow illuminated a face as a *Gitane Red* was lit. Rothman instantly recognized his unexpected guest. "Solipsum?"

"In the flesh."

"How did you get in here?"

The model languidly exhaled. "A door was left open."

Rothman turned his face to mask his surprise and made his way to the bar. "Cocktail?"

"No. Thank you."

"You don't mind if I indulge? It's so rare I get the pleasure of unexpected company."

Solipsum inclined his head. "By all means."

The Agent glanced over his shoulder as he mixed something complex and very alcoholic. "That could be your motto, couldn't it? 'By all means.'"

"I'm not sure I understand."

"Let's just say that in this business, a certain ruthlessness can take a man very far."

"Are you suggesting I get a t-shirt made?" said the model, smiling.

Rothman barked a short laugh. "Perhaps in Italian?"

Solipsum's smile slowly faded, his lips compressing to a wire thinness. "Sometimes you go too far. And forget to whom you owe much of what you are."

"As you forget who helped you once. Out of a very messy situation."

"That was—unintended."

"Be that as it may. That girl was worth a great deal of—"

"Agent. I did not come here to discuss the past. Let us leave it where it belongs. Dead. Buried. Unless, of course, you have no interest in the future?"

Rothman knew when to be silent. He took his time crossing the room, his thoughts racing, finally seating himself on a lounger covered in the hide of some endangered exotic.

"To business then," said Solipsum. "There is a new advertising campaign coming up, a very large campaign. Possibly the biggest ever. It will involve only the best people at the very peak of their form. And they want Phoena. And I. Together."

Rothman laughed harshly. "That's impossible. It simply won't happen. Not for all the money in the world. I can't even mention your name in her presence, not after what she went through with you."

Solipsum's gaze turned inward, his voice tinged with a certain regret. "She never did care about the money." Then his eyes met the other man's. "But there is one thing she does care about. The one thing she desperately desires but can never have. Unless you choose to give it to her."

"Unless I choose to give it to her." The Agent did not flinch under a gaze most could not even meet. "Now why would I do that?"

"To fulfill your dream, Rothman."

"And what dream might that be?"

"Why, the dream of owning your own agency, of course."

"I already have an agency."

Solipsum waved a hand in dismissal, the stone in his ring glinting. "You have one girl and nine also-rans. I'm offering you far more than just an agency, Rothman. I'm offering you what you've always wanted. The chance to become a Player again. By becoming the majority shareholder in *P.M.P.*"

Rothman's glass clacked as it hit the table. "You can't be serious."

"On the contrary, I've never been more serious about anything in my life."

"So the rumors are true. *P.M.P.* is yours."

"Yes."

Rothman smelled the blood in the water. "Why are you offering me this? This—Campaign—you mentioned must be something very special."

"You cannot even begin to imagine."

"I'll let you know in the morning. I need time to think this over."

"No. You will decide now. I think we both know you have already made up your mind. So—" Solipsum's eyes seemed preternaturally bright. "Do we have a deal?"

"Yes. On one condition."

"Careful, Cartilage." Solipsum looked pointedly at Rothman's right hand. "Be sure your reach does not exceed your grasp."

The Agent pretended not to notice. "The Club. The Seventh Level. I want that too."

"In five years."

"One."

"Three. But if circumstance permits, I'll give it to you sooner. My final offer."

"Deal."

They shook hands, Solipsum enjoying the cool feel of plastic.

He was almost at the door when he turned. "I will see you at the Party on Saturday."

Rothman smiled. It was very disconcerting, like watching a shark attempt such a facial expression. "I wouldn't miss it for the world."

New York City, Soho

Charlie thought she had known the meaning of the word "whirlwind." That was until she'd seen Phoena shop. It was unbelievable. They would go into stores Charlie had never even heard of, let alone spent money in, and see the most incredible things. Fabrics that shimmered and gleamed like treasure from the stories her dad used to tell her, dresses and pants and "capri" this and "bias cut" that and "bell epoch" and "ep-au-lette" and God! it was all so bewildering! She figured she'd changed clothes more times in the past two hours than she had in the past two weeks. And somehow, what had started as a hunt for one special item had transformed into a shopping expedition to "spruce up" Charlie's non-existent wardrobe.

After the first few stores, she had stopped trying to make sense of all the eye candies fighting for her attention and watched Phoena instead. How she seemed to ignore nearly everything, walk to some display or rack and choose the perfect dress that was just—so.

Everywhere they went, Phoena was treated like the mega star she was. Charlie, by extension, was also pampered. Gild by association.

The next stop was the *La Perla* store and oh, what fun this place turned out to be! Phoena made certain choices, sending the salesgirls scurrying, and before Charlie knew it, she stood in front of three very tall mirrors in something silky, sheer and beautifully cut. She saw, as if for the first time, the lines and planes of her own body, her muscularity taut and sleek, her posture balanced. *My legs look like they go on forever! And God, this bra make my boobs look huge! I look . . .*

"Sexy, Charlie! You look soooo sexy!" said Phoena.

Charlie blushed.

Phoena touched Charlie's rather amazing dragon tattoo, noticing its exquisite workmanship for the first time. The scales almost shone and its tiny face was so expressive it seemed it would spring from myth to life at any moment. She met the other girl's eyes in the mirror. "Does she have a name?"

Charlie smiled, so very pleased that Phoena had guessed her dragon was a girl. "Yes. But it's a secret."

Then suddenly a dam burst in Charlie's mind, a flood of images and feelings rising inside her, feelings she had kept bottled up for so long, that she had thought to escape by crossing the ocean, came hurtling down the dark tunnel of memory like a mailed fist that simply would

not

be

denied.

Love and loss and Tokyo, and *oh how I miss that place and my parents and Haiku, and the birthday cake and the training* and how she had never seen a wound so great.

She began to shake, almost overcome, and before she could stop herself, she rushed back to the change room. She slammed the door, then broke down, shaking and bawling like a child, great wracking sobs, muscles spasming as the hot tears and snot ran down her face. It seemed like an eternity before Phoena quietly entered the room and took the shivering girl's shoulders in her hands. She slowly turned her around and looked at her, Charlie's face red and raw. She hid nothing and Phoena felt some part of her swept away by the enormity of what she saw in Charlie's eyes, those violet, violent eyes, where memory moved like the light behind bruised clouds.

Phoena did nothing, her gaze never wavering. She did not speak. She was simply there. Finally, Charlie moved a bit closer and allowed herself to be held. Her sobs subsided into sniffles and the odd hiccup as Phoena stroked her golden hair.

They left the store, even making a few purchases, and Phoena figured they were ready to call it a day. Charlie, however, strangely wasn't. She seemed like a person with a great weight lifted from her shoulders, as if she now knew past any doubt that life was meant to be lived. They walked down the street and Charlie turned to her friend, a friend she now felt a strange and powerful bond with. She said almost formally, "Thank you. Thank you so very much. One day I'll tell you. Soon. But not today. Okay?"

"Of course it's okay." Phoena squeezed her, then grabbed her hand. "Come on. We still have a dress to find." With that, the search continued.

They breezed through five more stores, picking up what Phoena called "daywear." They had still not found "the Dress," and Charlie had almost given up hope. Suddenly, something caught Phoena's eye and they were darting across the street, bags in tow, through the mysteriously open door of a very high-end boutique. Charlie just had time to see a small sign with the words "By Appointment Only" before they were whisked through its dramatically lit interior to a special room at the back. There they were greeted by the owner, with whom Phoena began speaking in French. The older lady looked Charlie over with a practiced eye and said something that caused Phoena to flush. They both burst out laughing. Before Charlie could figure out what was so funny, amidst much bustling of staff and rustling of tissue paper, a dress was brought forth that brought two simple words to Phoena's lips:

"It's perfect."

Charlie looked at it in shock. "But—but—I've never worn anything like that!"

"First time for everything, girlfriend!" Phoena's eyes danced with glee.

They left the store clutching a mass of bags. And one special box. Phoena stepped to the curb, raised a hand and said in an almost conversational tone, "Taxi."

A cab made an outrageous U-turn through three lanes of traffic and ran over a median. As they piled into the back, Charlie shook her head in wonder.

How does she do *that?*

New York City, Financial District

Elora Gorj's office was perhaps the thing of which she was most proud, the clearest indicator of her meteoric rise to the top. Very high up, it was, of course, a glass wrapped corner suite, bright with vaulted ceilings, chunky cravings of furniture and enormous photographs, all done in a tasteful and minimalist *moderne* style.

She sat at her desk, something weighty and dark, fashioned from an extinct Peruvian wood. It had been reverse-engineered from a picture she had seen in an old architectural magazine. When the designer had informed her she was really looking at an aerial view of a house, she'd corrected him.

She was, as always, smartly dressed in an outfit whose seasonal obsolescence hugged the curves of her machine-toned body, an outfit that cost what her three secretaries made in a month. Which was, she thought, befitting for the Creative Director of *Fa-Shin, Inc.*

It hadn't been easy coming into the upper echelon of one of the world's largest mega-corporations. Reaching its inner circle had been quite an eye opener. Because *Fa-Shin, Inc.* was HUGE. It controlled so much, under names the public still thought of as fiercely independent entities, it had actually achieved a cradle-to-grave ubiquity of every person on the planet. You could, were you so inclined, experience your entire life through nothing but *Fa-Shin, Inc.* products. Vodka, diapers, jeans, spaghetti, engine oil, tampons, kibble, guns, corporate jets, lingerie, sprin-

klers, fertilizer, yoga mats, blockbuster films, *Three Hole Punch* cd's, super tanker hulls, watches, cocaine, panties, barbeque-flavoured cashews,
prophylactics, Kobe beef, tricycles, waffles, banned AIDS7 meds, the list
just went on and on. There were literally tens of thousands of "things"
Fa-Shin, Inc. made. It's metastasization just there beneath the fiction of
everyday "freedom" was astonishing. And not a little frightening.

For there was no limit to its appetite.

That was, she supposed, why she was here in this office. Because
she'd learned that only one thing really mattered at the highest levels
of inter-corporate warfare: Market Share. And if you could deliver that,
in a way so radically new and dangerously different, in quantities that
caused open salivation in the boardroom, well, you could pretty much
write your own ticket, couldn't you?

The day was done except for one last meeting. Light streamed through
the windows, edging her as she waited, turning the invitation to Joshua's
party over and over in her hands.

Tonight's the night it really begins.

She slapped the invitation down.

*Good God, what have I gotten myself into? I am about to involve
Joshua Stone in something so over the top, even I'm still blown away.
And all of it started by a man I barely even know! I mean, yes, he's the
best fuck I've ever had, but is that any reason to believe him about this
idea?*

She laughed aloud.

*Why do I keep doing this to myself? The time to tell him no was three
years ago, when he first dropped this quantum mind bomb in my lap. But
then I wouldn't be where I am today, would I?*

"Ms. Gorj?" the intercom ventured, "Mr. Solipsum is here."

"Send him up."

She rose and smoothed the front of her dress before going over to a
small alcove where she checked her make-up. Her hand was surprisingly
steady as she poured a drink from the compact but well-stocked mini bar.

Calm down, Elora.

She looked in the mirror and saw for an instant the girl she used to be.
The girl who'd started very poor and was now very rich. The one about
to become richer still by far. She smiled, then slammed the drink back,
icy vodka fingers instantly numbing her throat like some sort of

(cryogenic demon sperm)

liquid nitrogen. She gasped and clicked the glass down, quickly refilling it, then poured one for Solipsum. She slowly lifted her face.

"Why am I always so nervous when he comes here?" she asked her reflection.

The door to the office swung open and Solipsum entered. The light glorified him and she almost had to look away, forcibly reminded of what a stunning creature he was. His beauty was elemental, like a force of nature.

"Not having second thoughts, are we?" He took his time walking towards her.

"Whatever gave you that idea?"

"Good."

She could wait no longer, almost running to meet him in the center of the room. They kissed, slowly at first, then the passion began for her, unaware that she had taken his hand and crushed it to her breast, ruining her dress. She broke away for a moment, sucking shallow vodka-burned breaths as she gripped his arms. Her soul was screaming danger but the roar of loin-fire drowned it out.

Slowly.

Wetly.

Solipsum left her there, conflicted and shivering. He walked to the desk and flicked the intercom. "Maggie?"

"Yes, sir?"

"Please hold all calls."

"Yes, sir."

And they began what would be a very pleasant afternoon. The last thing Elora remembered seeing was the invitation to Joshua's party.

Then he took her.

Book 5

"Crowds have always undergone the influence of illusions. Whoever can supply them with illusions is easily
their master." —Gustav LeBon

"A man in his glass house, inside the heart of a bliz-
zard, harvests roses." —Susan Katz

New York City, Stone Studios

There are really only two ways to experience a mega party. From the
Gray. Or from the Red. It all comes down to which surface your shoes
are in contact with. Concrete? Or Carpet.

It was a crisp November evening and the limousines were arriving at
the ground floor entrance to Stone Studios. Twenty massive searchlights
ringed its base, all pointing skyward like the petals of a flower, opening
to reveal its fragile heart. The Red was rolled out like a lifeline to the
curb. It was early and the carpet was still pristine, as yet untrampled by a
thousand feet. Tall gas heaters stood at intervals, like sentinels warming
the way. All was in readiness for one of the most special nights of the
year—Joshua Stone's annual Studio Party.

If you were standing on the Red, you would see the massive crowds,
barely kept at bay by the rope barriers, their mingled breath a low lying
mist, the paparazzi corralled behind a separate barrier, flashes pulsing. If
you were on the right drug, you would even see their true piranha faces,
swimming just beneath the surface of their flesh. The first names they
screamed would be your only clue as to the mega-wattage of celebrity
turnout that was packing this event. But you were on the Red. You could
see those people for yourself.

Couldn't you?

Solipsum arrived with two beautiful girls, one on each arm. His smile
was dazzling, as was his red tuxedo. The girls' pupils were starry with
stimulants and they seemed impervious to the cold as they walked up
the Red. Solipsum saw the sheeple and decided to indulge them. He approached the barrier, allowing the mob to glimpse an icon in the flesh,
then did a slow turn, teeth flashing. As they strained against the rope cor-
don to touch him, he briefly wondered if electricity might not have been
a more effective form of crowd control than hemp. He and his dates then

70

proceeded down the carpet and disappeared through the ground floor doors.

In the main studio high above the city, the Party was slowly becoming crowded. Numerous guests were already in attendance when Solipsum and the girls stepped from the elevator.

Bruun watched their arrival. He had been sitting, quietly bemused by the whole human pageant, patiently awaiting this moment. It was as he had feared. One glance and he quickly vanished.

Just inside the studio doors downstairs, the two massive security guards, Kobe and Carpaccio, continued checking everyone's invites. Their biceps bulged in Super-Tight designer T-shirts and both were sporting headsets and odd facial hair stylings that substituted for personality. Carpaccio casually gripped a clear acrylic clipboard that was actually a wafer-thin monitor.

A huge roar came to them from outside. Kobe looked over at his buddy and mouthed the words, "Who is it?" Carpaccio shrugged his meaty shoulders and they both turned towards the doors. The barrage of flash-bulbs going off became so continuous, it provided a constant source of illumination. They could now hear the paparazzi screaming, "PHOENA! PHOENA! Look this way! Over here! One for me! Who's that with you? Is she the new 'it' girl? Who is that? PHOENA! PHOENA!"

Two girls gradually made their way up the ramp to the security guards, flash frozen all the way as they giggled and laughed together, arms linked. Kobe recognized Phoena, but not the other girl. Both wore winter coats, their cheeks flushed with cold.

"Yo, Carpach!" Kobe elbowed his staring partner, who suddenly remembered how jaded he was supposed to be. They both smiled, and Kobe waved the girls through without even bothering to check their invites. "Good evening," he flexed as they passed, expanding like a dehydrated sponge animal dropped into a glass. "Take the first elevator to reception, where you can check yer coats. Then the other one to the main studio. Have a great night."

Phoena graced him with a low watt smile. "I'm sure we will."

The girls walked past and waited for the elevator.

Phoena's guest looked at her, snowmelt beading her lashes. "Wow! I have *never* experienced anything like that before! It's like my—"

"—first orgasm?"

"Phoena! Jesus!"

The elevator arrived.

Phoena laughed and looked at her companion. "Come on, it only gets better."

They were about to go up when a commotion erupted at the doors. It appeared that Bentley Sween was having trouble gaining entry. Kobe stood before him like the Colossus of Rhodes, arms folded over his massive chest.

"Hey! What gives? My name's supposed to be there!" insisted Bentley. "Check under *PRY*. We're supposed to have a blanket invite."

Carpaccio looked at his monitor/clipboard with an extremely bored expression on his face, like he'd never heard *that* one before. He resisted a vague urge to pick his nose.

"Sorry, sir," sneered Kobe politely. "Doesn't seem to be anyone by *your* name on the list. I'm afraid you'll have to leave."

"Let him in, guys. He's with us."

Carpaccio looked at Phoena, brow creasing, his face strange and bovine in the monitor's underlight. "But Mr. Stone said—"

"Don't worry about Mr. Stone. I'll take full responsibility."

Carpaccio shrugged his shoulders and motioned to Kobe, who moved aside with the gravitas of his namesake.

Bentley joined the girls, thanking Phoena with his eyes, heart beating a little faster when he saw what she wore. "I owe you one."

"Anytime, Bentley, anytime."

He pretended to notice the other girl for the first time. "Who's this? Don't I get an intro?"

Phoena sighed. "Later. And only if you promise me you'll stop being a reporter for the rest of the night. Just enjoy yourself for once, okay? You never know what might happen."

"Okay," he quickly agreed.

The other girl was gazing at him.

"You look very—fetching in that outfit," he said, kicking himself, the line lame and him a writer.

She smiled as though she knew some secret. "Thanks."

"Come on." Phoena hurried them. "I don't want to miss a thing."

They all crowded into the lift and began their ascent.

In the main studio, Stone was checking his watch again, wondering where Phoena could possibly be, when the elevator doors opened. He could hardly believe his eyes. Phoena wore something filmy and negligent, a dress of an indigo hue so deep as to be almost black. It seemed a color plumbed from ocean depths as yet unreached by man, except by shipwreck. He noticed that the garment's fabric drank the light unless pinned by it, just so, then it gave of itself fully, in diamond glimmers of blue that exactly complemented the color of her eyes. Its cut left arms and shoulders bare, covering her body in a flowing sheath of finest silk that pooled at her feet like ink. As she walked towards him, the fabric clung and caressed, moving as if impelled by the caprice of some unseen breeze. A slit in its side traveled almost to her waist, revealing flashes of leg like moonlight through forest.

All this Stone saw in an instant, and it took his breath away.

Then he noticed the other girl and several thoughts arose almost simultaneously. She was obviously a veteran model, as was bespoken by her walk and carriage, but most of all by how she wore the clothes. A rare ability. Her make-up was exquisite, smoky and iridescent, picking up and complementing the gorgeous reds and oranges of what was obviously a vintage dress. And what a vintage dress! Highly experimental in cut and bursting color, silk of red and yellow blending with feather detail and crumpled organza. It shouldn't have worked, but it did. Completely. Because it was that rare garment whose perfection manifested only in symbiosis with the perfect wearer.

And it seemed it had found her.

The hem ended in a profusion of tiny plumes that brushed her thighs, his eye then drawn to her legs, coltish and long, emphasized by a stylish heel she wore without tottering. The lustrous blond helmet of her hair seemed burnished as it followed the delicate contours of her skull with a sleekness that reminded him of a sea otter emerging from an icy pool. She almost looked like—

They were standing in front of him. "Phoena!" He kissed her cheeks. "I was wondering when you were going to show up." His eyes drank of her friend. "And who is this stunning girl?"

The girl looked at him with mock indignation. "Joshua! It's me! Charlie!"

Recognition slammed into him, and he wondered how he could ever have mistaken her for someone not-Charlie. He brought a hand up, half-covering his face in embarrassment.

"Wow. I don't know what to say. I had no idea . . ."

Phoena smirked, enjoying herself immensely. The Dress was having its desired effect. It was not often Joshua Stone was caught off guard, especially not so completely. Definitely a moment to be savored. When Sindra had first seen Charlie in The Dress, he'd fallen into some sort of shrieking glee-fit. Phoena had almost thought they would need the smelling salts, but he'd recovered soon enough and applied one of the most thoughtful and beautiful make-ups she had ever seen him do. She left the memory and tuned back in to Charlie and Joshua, the photographer still reeling from the transformation her friend had undergone. Seeing the sparkle in Charlie's eyes, it seemed she too was enjoying how she looked tonight.

"What fragrance is that you're wearing?" Joshua asked her.

"I'm not. This would be my natural scent."

And because he'd had a few drinks, the words were out before he could stop them. "What happens when you exert yourself?"

"My scent becomes more intense," she answered without missing a beat, looking directly into his brown eyes as the corner of her mouth rose slightly, significantly. For it seemed she too had had a few drinks.

Phoena figured now would be a good time to let them both step back a bit. Reflect, as it were.

"Come on, Charlie." She grabbed her friend's hand and pulled her along. "We'll let Mr. Stone greet his other guests while we go mingle."

Just before they disappeared into the throng, Charlie looked back over her shoulder and gave him a smile, shrugging helplessly.

Bentley wished in that moment that he was Joshua. "Quite a pair, aren't they?"

"You have no idea," Stone breathed, smiling despite himself.

Bentley held out his hand. Stone looked at it briefly before taking it, then eyed the young man. "Let me guess. You're a reporter, right?"

Bruun moved through the never ending forest of feet and legs searching for fallen morsels. The crowd by the buffet table was still too thick to risk going in after the choicer bits so he contented himself with flopping on a small machine-ledge near the dome rim, front and rear paw dangling.

These creatures never seem to tire of talking to one another. Yet their thoughts and mouthings are often opposite. So many of them in one place, so loud their thoughts! If they only knew to communicate by scent. Much purer, much more direct.

He saw a girl gleefully sipping champagne as she told her friend that it's all about *altitude*, not *attitude*.

He turned his head to see a model introducing the new girl to photographer Rank Pedophite, who wore a large button that read "It's not Creepy if it's Love."

The furtive movements of a fashion editor then caught his eye. She paused to make sure no one was watching before vomiting into her handbag. After several fast and practiced retches, her head popped up like a marmot's. She spied Bruun and scowled. "Shoo! Shoo! Go away! Stop staring at me!"

The cat didn't move. She finally made a "humph!" noise and spun on her heel to disappear, the stench of stomach acid and shrimp lingering faintly in her wake.

Bruun wandered over to his favorite place under the couch. He was almost there when a hand reached down to rub something that looked suspiciously like coke snot on the couch's underside. Its owner was still wiping when he spied Bruun and thought perhaps the cat's fur would make a better tissue. He reached and Bruun slunk low to avoid.

"Here, kitty, kitty, kitty," Coke Mitt cooed, "Oh, I just love cats."

The hand reached again and Bruun swiped at it, drawing blood before he backed away, hissing.

Other guests turned to gape and Coke Mitt almost jammed his hand into his mouth before he remembered what was still stuck to it. He looked up at several faces in embarrassment, then shrugged and said, "Oh. I think he bit me. Maybe he hasn't been fed yet," as the thought *miserable fucking animal* went through his mind. Bruun saw it as clearly as if it had been spray-painted on a wall. As clearly as he saw most everyone's thoughts . . .

More like your b.o. drove him away.

Poor cat!

Watch it, kitty. This guy could be exploring a new species in his quest for the perfect O-ring.

The Agent stood on the machined curve of an upper tier directly above the main studio, watching the hundreds of guests press and gyrate to music he did not understand. Multicolored lights dissected his face as they swathed upwards through the tier's glass floor.

Rothman Cartilage had been part of the world of fashion his entire life, and he still didn't know if he loved it or hated it. He did know that the money at this level was often criminal and that the spice of the Game was something he was helpless before. And as in every Game, there were moments when great change occurred in seemingly ordinary circumstance.

This was one such moment.

He watched now as his greatest creation walked towards him. *My, my, my, how far you've come from that insignificant life and those insignificant people! And how completely unaware you are that once again your life has been altered. Irrevocably.*

His eyes made a practiced sweep over her dress and make-up, their effect instantly gauged and categorized. His evaluation was automatic, its smooth surface broken only by the briefest bubble of realization that this was the last time he would do this to her in a professional capacity. He smiled then with genuine pleasure, revealing his shark-like teeth. This model was one of the few he truly liked.

"Hello, Phoena. Great party, isn't it?"

"Yes, it is."

She noticed how his shark-skin suit shimmered in the light, how dangerous and predatory he appeared. But then, she thought, he always did. She looked more closely and saw how the lines bracketing his mouth seemed cut more deeply tonight, as though he had swallowed something tasty and chunky, only to discover it riddled with hooks.

"Are you feeling all right?"

His hands spread wide to encompass the dome. "I guess it's just this place. It's so—beyond reality. It kind of makes you feel closer to God, doesn't it?"

"Yes, I guess it does," she said uncertainly.

He smiled at her again and took a sip of a very red drink. A shaft of light prismed the glass, his face suddenly blood-washed. She stared at his meaty maw, distorted and huge in the tumbler's bottom, ice cubes clicking against his pointy teeth. Phoena shivered for a second, the long-buried memory of some nightmarish amusement park ride, the

(tunnel of rape)

thought of which caused bile to rise. With an effort, she swallowed once, her mind quickly snuffing that bleachy rancid memory.

Rothman lowered his drink and studied her curiously, finally speaking with a slow deliberation. "Phoena, I've got something I want to talk to you about. This will probably be the second most important conversation we will ever have. I'm sure you remember the first."

"How could I forget?" She was very much on her guard now.

"A job has come up. It is by far the biggest thing I have ever encountered. The money is certainly staggering. In fact, it is such an unusually large amount, it allows me to give you the one thing you have always wanted." He looked at her expectantly.

Phoena's head reeled. Her hand jumped to her breast, waiting for the words she had thought she would never hear.

"Your freedom."

"*What?*" She hardly noticed she'd dropped her glass.

"We'll go over all the details in the morning, but suffice to say, after this job is over, your contract with me will be terminated. I will no longer be your agent."

Her eyes became steely. "Is this some sort of joke?"

"No. Let me tell you what this is all about."

He put his right arm around her, the arm that was actually an unusual prosthetic—smooth gray carbon fiber with a pebbly texture. It was silent as powerful servos caused organic "fingers" to close lightly upon Phoena's shoulder.

Their touch feels almost human she reflected as they walked away. *Just like him.*

Bruun had come upon something very interesting: another predator stalking its prey. He stopped to watch as German photographer Arragon Schwein skillfully separated former top model Donatella Stack from a small herd of friends. Her thoughts were particularly loud.

God, he is talking such shit! He must be crowding sixty with that brillo-y mass of white hair, and those Kaiser glasses with the thick plastic frames look just plain weird. At least that crushed velvet jackety-thing is well tailored. It almost hides his gut. They say he goes to every party, whether he's invited or not. God, he'd probably go to the opening of an envelope. But, alas, he still has some power left which means I need to kiss his ass. Ick!

"Ahhh, my little gazelle. I remember when you were zo young und beautiful, just out of za jungles of Sous Amerika, nein?" Even with the lifts in his shoes, he looked up at her.

Donatella put on her "interested" face. *Jungles of South America? Where half your fucking family and their hordes of Nazi gold probably fled to, back when? Give me a break!*

"Heh, heh, heh." His laugh was dry and papery, like a sock drawer full of roach carcasses. "I mean, you are still very beautiful, but it is such a—youzful market, nein?"

"Oh, Arragon," she simpered, "you were always my favorite photographer. No one can hold a candle to your blazing talent."

God, Donna, don't lay it on too thick!

Arragon was getting that warm and fuzzy feeling at the base of his colon. "I know, I know, I am zoooo exiting, ya? Vell, perhaps there iss something I can use you in, my little Mädchen. Vy don't ve go upstairs to discuss this in sommore—privacy, ja?"

"Ja, ja . . ." *Fuck, now he's got me doing it!* "I mean yeah, sure." She looked about furtively, then quickly grabbed his hand. "Come on," she whispered, and dragged him up the stairs.

Russ Hernbauer was holding court among the four other assistants he'd invited. Each had brought a case of beer so it wasn't like they were going to run out any time soon. They had scored a great spot, up the ramp from the main studio, a perfect vantage point to check out all the amazing babes. A joint made the rounds as they traded war stories, pulling beers from the large bisected piston that served as a cooler.

They had all agreed to wear slogan T's tonight. Lozoratto, a gangly assistant with thick glasses, wore a t-shirt with the words, "PLANTS AND ANIMALS DISAPPEAR TO MAKE ROOM FOR YOUR FAT ASS." His buddy, Humber's, read, "I PHUCKED PHOENA." Russ had hacked the sleeves off his. It featured the words, "ACTION FIGURE SOLD SEPARATELY" in condensed Impacta. Ryerson was the smallest assistant any of them had ever seen. He was also the smartest. On his shirt was printed, "IT DOESN'T SUCK ITSELF."

They were all eyeing Molasses, who weighed close to three hundred pounds. He stood before them, proudly displaying a shirt on which were printed the words, "DON'T STARE, GROW YOUR OWN"

Ryerson gaped at the stretched lettering. "That's a girl's shirt, ya know."

Molasses snorted. "No, it ain't."

"Uh, dude, I think it is."

"It means 'Don't be jealous 'cause my unit's bigger than yours'." At least, that was what the salesman had told him.

They all started laughing.

Ryerson broke it down. "Cock breath, it means that if yer, like a girl? And a guy's like, staring at yer tits? He shouldn't stare but, like, grow his own? Get it?"

"Fuck," Molasses muttered, "your kidding."

Lozoratto then continued with the story he had been telling. "So me and Christie kind a segued into the back room . . ."

Russ coughed out a huge cloud of BC chemobud. "You and Christie? Gimme a fuckin' break! She wouldn't polish your chrome if you changed your last name to Demarchelier."

"Yeah, ya loser!" Molasses chimed.

Lozoratto turned on him, blinking furiously. "Shut up, ring worm!"

"Blow me, stool!"

Ryerson was getting bored. "Anyone got any nose dirt?"

"Who do we look like? Joshua 'Moneybags' Stone?" Russ shoved a cold one into his hand. "Have another beer."

Humber felt something rub against his leg. "Bruun! What's happenin'?" He took a hit from the cannoncracker they were smoking, then reached down to scratch the cat's head. "Want some?"

Russ watched the two disinterestedly, then turned to Ryerson. "So, how's your new girlfriend?"

"She's totally crazy, man. She'll do anything."

Russ sighed wistfully. "I had a girl like that once. She'd eat the chocolate rosebud, dirty or clean."

"Well, that's okay for a new girl. Hey, and speakin' of new, what's the story with Charlie, Russ? Are ya prongin' her yet?"

"Fuckin' A, Ry-High. I nailed her sweet ass Day Two."

"Really? I heard it through the grapevine that she nailed *your* ass right after you was dee-moted by the Man."

Russ's jaw dropped. "What? Who spun that ripe bullshit on you?"

Molasses saw a girl approaching. "Guys! Let's ask Charlie."

"*That's* Charlie?" Ryerson rubbed his eyes. Her dress was unbelievable.

"Hot fuck, what happened to her?" Lozoratto had grabbed the other assistant to steady himself.

"Wow, what a babe." Humber felt his heart do a slow somersault.

"Hi, fellas," said Charlie, who was just a little drunker than she'd planned. "Enjoying yourselves?"

She saw Humber's t-shirt and her eyes went wide. *Oh my God, if Phoena saw that she'd kill this guy!*

Humber didn't notice where she was staring, only that she was staring—at him—which suddenly made him a lady's man. His voice became a silky snot rag. "Charlie. You look amazing. Want some?" He flourished what was left of the burnt offering.

"No, thanks. But don't let me stop you."

"Cool." He began to test his lung capacity.

Lozoratto snapped his fingers impatiently. "Puff, puff, pass man, it ain't a fuckin' baton!"

Humber took another huge haul and blew a stream of smoke into the other assistant's face. "Who the fuck are you, the Joint Chief of Staff?"

"No," Lozoratto thrust his jaw forward, "The Minister of Defense!" He then farted loudly.

"Oh yeah?" Humber lifted his own leg to launch a rebuttal and a mighty sound like a sail ripping filled the alcove. It ended in a small squelch. The assistant's face suddenly turned bright red. "Oh fuck! I think I drew mud." He hobbled off to the washroom, sphincter clenched tighter than a submarine hatch.

The laughter began, loud and hysterical as Charlie looked on in astonishment. *Jeez, no wonder none of these guys gets laid.* Then she couldn't hold back any longer and found herself joining them, helpless.

The merriment finally subsided and Lozoratto gave her a lopsided grin. "So, how are you likin' it here?"

"It's the best job I've ever had. Lots of work, but I love it."

"Yeah, well, we'll see how long it lasts," muttered Russ from where he leaned against the wall. "It's still early days and the Stone Man, he's just getting started." He straightened a bit. "And Charlie, let's be honest. You look like the kind of girl who would probably—I don't know—" he lurched suddenly, "cry? When the going got tough?" He steadied himself and realized he was drunker than he'd thought.

Charlie glared at the besotted lout and figured, *both barrels*. She smiled sweetly. "Gee, Russ, while we're being honest, you look like the kind of guy who would—oh, I don't know—throw his back out, trying to blow his own horn?"

She smoothly tossed a parting grenade into the stunned silence. "I'm sure I'll be able to handle anything Mr. Stone throws at me, right *Hornblower*? Oh! I'm sorry. I meant *Hern-bauer*." And in a swirl of skirt, she marched down the hall towards the main studio, hootings of "Hornblower" and assistant laughsnort diminishing behind her.

Bruun padded about once more, the forest now a jungle. He was having trouble making sure his tail was not stepped on. The buffet, however, had become too tempting. A vision blossomed in his cat-brain, himself under the table, lying on his back with his paws in the air, mouth open as the food-rain descended. He could almost taste the goodness and so did not see Coke Mitt, who had not forgotten the source of his previous embarrassment.

"Hey fur ball! Let's see how ya like this!"

Coke Mitt took a deep drag, his cigarette glowing like a tail light, then dropped the butt onto Bruun's back. The cat jumped and screeched, paws flying, running, running, flashes of what they had done to him before he had come to Joshua exploding behind his eyes, fragments of Bruun-image in Man-mind, head partially shaved and covered with electrodes as current crackled again and again, the memory rending as another slashed through, a figure looming with a giant syringe, then another and another and another and another, animal screams, so loud, so LOUD, the death and pain, and *pain*, and *PAIN*!

Still he ran, faster and faster, trying to outrun the claws he could feel sinking into his back, spilled drinks and outrage marking his passage as he tore through the guests like ball-shot concertina.

Hands suddenly reached down and grabbed him. He clawed and bit, not even recognizing Phoena in his terror and pain as the smoke rose from his once immaculate silver coat. She rushed him to the sink, taps blasting, Bruun not even struggling as the water poured over him. He finally looked up at her, sodden and shivering, his eyes almost human in their gratitude. Phoena found herself staring into them and seeing something moving there, some strange intelligence, her mind letting go as a part of her she did not know reached out, almost touching—then he squirmed from her grasp and was gone.

She was still a bit dazed when she left the kitchen and decided to go upstairs, liberating a champagne flute from a passing tray. *Well that was an adventure,* she thought. *Joshua's strange cat. I still remember when Josh got him . . .* She climbed some stairs subtly inset into a sweep of wall, enjoying the cool and sensuous sweep of silk as the dress slid across her body. The small alcove was right where she remembered it. She leaned against the railing and brought the glass to her lips, savoring the chilled champagne, the tip of her tongue unconsciously touching her front tooth. She let her eyes wander over the main studio, transformed now into a glass-covered dance bubble. Seeing Charlie brought a smile to her face. *Just look at her go. I can't believe the splash she's made tonight.* She raised the glass and offered a silent toast to her new friend. *Here's to you, special girl.*

She was about to take a sip when she suddenly felt

(an ill wind blowing)

cold and knew she was not alone.

"Hello, Phoena."

"Hello, Trey." She glanced at Solipsum beside her. "I knew I would run into you sooner or later." Her mind flashed back to the day she'd collapsed on set, memories of what had passed between them flooding through her in a torrent violent and mercifully brief as she brought her will to bear. And though *she* knew what he really was, her body still responded to the man who stood before her, to the memories he embodied as he looked at her, as handsome and seductive as ever.

"You look very beautiful tonight."

"Stop it, Trey."

"Whatever do you mean?" he asked, the picture of innocence.

Her eyes flashed. "I'm not going to sleep with you. Not now. Not in the future. Never again."

"Never say never, Phoena." He smiled, idly looking at the long scratch on her forearm.

He is not going to get the best of me. He. Is. Not. With an effort she pulled her gaze free and turned away, gathering her thoughts. Images rose, a kaleidoscope unbidden, beautiful girl and beautiful day, the

Italian Alps in summer and the wind in her hair as she raced along the mountain roads with the objects of her desire. And Solipsum, Solipsum, always Solipsum. With an effort, she brought her eyes back to his.

"I swore I would never have anything to do with you after—what happened."

"Yet here we are."

"There's only one reason I'm doing this—Campaign."

"Oh?"

"To finally be free of all this bullshit. And you. Forever."

Solipsum laughed. It was a beautiful sound, sparkling and golden, stirring in her memories she'd never had of that lost summer of perfect youth.

"Come now, Phoena. Look at yourself. If you hated fashion so much you would have arrived in your old jeans and a t-shirt, instead of that . . . remarkable outfit. No. You love this business as much as I. Perhaps even more so. We are very similar, the two of us. Cut from the same cloth, you might say."

He suddenly seemed to be standing much closer to her. So close she could scent him.

"I'm nothing like you," she hissed. "I don't know what's going on but this time, I'm not going to stand by and let you get away with anything. This time, I'm going to . . ."

Solipsum's gaze intensified, his eyes, she swore, now somehow burning.

"Don't bother, Trey. Remember. I know what you are."

"And what is that?"

"A . . . a . . ."

"Come on. Sayyy it." His voice caressed her like a sibilant oil.

She slammed her hands onto the rail and broke her second glass that night. "God damn you!"

Solipsum laughed again. This time the sound was different, a rotted discordancy that mocked even as it reminded.

His full lips twisted cruelly as his voice dropped. "You will do nothing, besides your job. Or have you forgotten how weak you are? Be a good little girl, Phoena, because after this, you'll never see me again. I promise. And you'll walk away a very rich girl. But if you do decide to make things difficult, I might just take it out on a certain assistant we both know."

They turned to look at the room below, where Charlie was dancing with Sindra and what seemed like half the male models in the city.

"And what a spectacular little confection she is, no? She inspires a certain—sexual creativity, wouldn't you say?"

"Trey, you wouldn't! She's just an innocent!"

"And she'll stay one. If you behave." He finished his drink and set it carefully on the rail's edge. "Remember, Phoena. Her fate is in *your* hands."

And with that, he left her.

The man sat at a small wooden table, bare except for a deck of tarot cards, ancient and ornate. He was startlingly beautiful, blonde and so delicate of feature as to be almost feminine. He was also quite obviously blind. He waited at the table, telling the fortunes of the various partygoers bold or foolish enough to join him.

Damien Fortune had been blind since birth but he saw in ways few could comprehend, let alone encompass, were they gifted with his sensorium. The cards had found him when he was six, at his grandmother's cottage. When she'd caught him playing with them, he looked up at her with milky orbs and said, "They're all asleep. Under the shed. That's why no one can find them." The mass grave had been so extensive the site was still considered a live crime scene. How he was able to divine this, sightless, using a totally visual divination system, was something no one had thought to ask. Had they bothered, they would have encountered an expression on his face that spoke more to their own blindness than in answer to such an obvious question. That was the beginning. Since then, Damien had learned the hard way that ignorance truly *was* bliss. And that it was more curse than blessing to know so intimately the Tree of Probability, let alone to eat of its Fruit.

He sat and "watched" the crowd. The people who came and went represented as pulsing outlines carbonated with tiny multihued spheres of illumination. The veil of their passage shifted and shimmered, peaceful and serene, like melting celluloid speckled with odd pieces of telekinetic drift. Then a very bright and powerful aura entered his field of "view."

"Solipsum," he murmured.

"Who—? Ah, you."

"Would you like to have your Fortune told?"

"Of course." Solipsum drew up the chair that had suddenly become vacant. "How could I refuse an invitation from the most Prescient Man on Earth?"

"You mock me, but it matters not. Please." Damien pointed to the deck and made a sign indicating Solipsum should shuffle them.

The model riffled the cards, noticing the strange and hypnotic pattern that decorated their backs. It was as beautiful as it was complex, and it was somehow not—unfamiliar. He looked at Damien as if the latter could see him, then began speaking in French.

"I know this deck. But I have not seen it since—"

"It last foretold your Fortune. In 1790. At the Court of a King. In that time too you wore the skin of another."

"And if memory serves, you were as blind then as you are now."

"Touché. Now, please." Damien gestured again. *"Cut."*

Solipsum did as he was told, noticing with interest the bead of sweat that slowly rolled down the Fortune Teller's right temple.

"May we begin?" Without waiting for an answer, Damien laid three cards on the table. "What was, what is, and—"

Solipsum leaned forward. "What will be."

Damien turned the first card, indicative of the past.

"The Three of Cups. A card of birth, but a very special kind of birth. The birth of something very—large. A plan, with great potential, for Good—and Evil. That which was definitive has taken the final, irreversible step towards multiplicity."

Solipsum smiled.

Damien then turned the next card, indicative of the present. He laid it down carefully, fingers tracing its notched edge as he ordered the tempest of thought and impression that always accompanied a card of the Major Arcana.

"The Moon. It appears the plan you have initiated is about to become your path. A difficult path it can be, but only if you lose sight of the final goal and allow yourself to become—distracted. A juggernaut has been launched and it matters not whether you ride it, for it rides you. Many destinies have been linked by this action. Many. One in particular will act as lynchpin to all you have planned. But because you must so closely align your destiny with this one's, your perception will become dulled, divination useless, the waters cloudy. Intuition must needs be your guide, for without it you are lost."

Damien's voice became faint as the psychic winds that buffeted him began to howl and shriek. "I—I see so many faces, people, the entire world, all joined in something so powerful—so black—my God, Solipsum, what have you planned?"

"Finish it, Seer."

"The Gateway, here," he pointed to the crystalline doorway through which the Moon on the card was visible. "The Amethyst Gateway is the key to everything. It represents a person—female—unbloodied." Damien's chin then lifted as though his eyes could see the man who sat before him. "Solipsum, the Moon is the card of madness. This, in conjunction with the other card . . ."

Solipsum paused for a moment, things unanticipated rising in the symbols of the Moon card as he stared at it. Symbols he was not sure had been there before. "The last card. I must see the last card." He turned it before Damien could stop him.

"The Devil. But now reversed." A short laugh escaped the Fortune Teller's lips. "Patience was never your strong suit, was it?"

Solipsum seethed, the truth of Damien's words burning like acid.

"A reverse card inverts all meaning. And thus what was male has now become female. A counterpoint external, a mirror. And possibly detrimental."

Solipsum stared at the figure on the card, half man, half animal, the image beginning to swim and change before his eyes until it embodied the form of something—someone—he had known. Intimately. His eyes widened, the muscles in his back tensing, even as his groin stirred.

"Alas the power of this—adversary—is also reversed and what is external on the card yet rests inside, awaiting manifestation. This will be, I am reluctant to say, almost impossible. For the Gateway between Worlds must be crossed, and it is but the first of many trials."

"More. I must know more."

"I have already told you enough." The Fortune Teller gathered his cards. "Have a care, Solipsum. I am not your creature."

The man in the scarlet tuxedo shrugged his shoulders. "My apologies for being so brusque. Please, allow me to redress my lack of manners. With a gift."

Damien's heart began triphammering, his senses screaming danger as tendrils of Solipsum's aura reached out to him. He leaned back, palms raised.

"Wait! There are other Forces that exist on this Plane. I am under their protection. Perhaps it is best I do not to alert them to all you have planned, eh, demon?"

Solipsum paused for a second. But only a second. "Fuck them. They cannot begrudge what is merely payment for service rendered." The tendrils plunged into Damien. "I give you the gift of sight."

Solipsum got up and quickly left the table as Damien held back a scream. He frantically brought his hands to cover his eyes in an attempt to block out the sudden onslaught of sensory input. He seemed momentarily taken aback when this worked, the flow stopped. Until he realized that the other flow had stopped as well, and his gift for Divination had been stripped from him.

Bruun had wandered into the bathroom where he stopped to once again lick the small bald spot in his fur. He glanced up occasionally at Donatella Stack, sitting on the bathroom counter as she waited for Arragon, who had his pants around his ankles.

"Sit still, Donatella. Do not move. Do not make a sound. Prepare yourself. I will now grace you wis the Bounty of my Aryan Schperm."

Donatella tried to keep her face still after each utterance from Arragon, but it became harder and harder until she just said *fuck it!* and let the laughter come. Peals and peals of laughter as the tears streamed from her eyes and her belly *hurt* she was laughing so hard. Arragon tried to shush her but she pushed him away easily, then slid from the counter, wiping the wetness from her cheeks and eyes.

"Oh thank God I didn't fuck you, thank God! To think I was so in love with this business that I thought I had to do *that* to keep going."

"But—but, mein little Liebchen . . ." Arragon wrung his hands plaintively, the nubby protrusion in his underwear wilting.

"Shut up, Arragon." Her gaze lanced him like a boil. "You're a talented photographer but you're also a shameless old perv. Shame on you for pimping off your talent and position to ooze your way into a fuck. And shame on me for almost letting you. See you in the Fashion Pages."

She winked at him over her shoulder, a new and different woman as she exited the washroom, her mouth the cruel thin curve of a shroud needle. The door slammed behind her. Bruun watched Arragon hike his pants over his skinny legs, suddenly an old man, and thought that there was not very much to learn from this creature.

Symmington Brood casually palmed the bindle to Alabasta Twigg, a model who was probably too young, in human years, to be doing cocaine. In model years, she had already orbited the sun. She was as slender as her portfolio, all eyes and lips and hip bones, with a certain glazed quality, like a day-old donut.

"So, Alba, when am I going to see some cash, huh, babe?"

"Soon, Sym, soon." She tugged at his sleeve, quickly wiping her nose with the other hand. "As soon as I get my next check. It's supposed to be a big one for that *Drevlon* campaign I did."

"Listen, Alba, I'll give you this now, but that's it for tonight. And I expect to get paid by the end of the week. Come by anyway, even if you don't have the money." He brought his lips a tongue's breadth from her ear. "We'll figure out some other way to square your debt." He then spun her around and squeezed her small bum as though checking a baked good for freshness. "Now run along."

"Well, if it isn't my old friend Symmington Brood," Stone greeted the dealer. "What did you just give Alba?"

Brood turned to this interruption, top lip fish-hooking in a sneer. "Nothing I haven't given you a hundred times."

"So that makes it right?"

"Right, wrong, who gives a fuck? It's a business, man, it's her choice. All I do is supply my customers with what they need. Just like you."

"What are you talking about?"

Brood's contempt was withering. "Come on, Joshua *Stoned*. Those pretty pictures you pimp off are even worse than my shit. At least my drugs deliver before they leave you jonesing."

"How can you compare pictures and drugs?"

"How can I not! It takes a dealer to know a dealer and that's some fine shit you are selling there, my man. As you have been for years." He spread his arms. "And it's paid off, hasn't it?"

"My pictures give people hope, dreams—"

"Just like my shit. And for about as long."

Stone paused, suddenly defensive. "There's no crash after you see one of my ads."

"Ever look at your credit card statement?"

"Your shit kills people, it ruins lives. It almost ruined mine!"

"And your pictures don't? The effect may be slower but it's still the same. We're brothers, Mr. Stoned. Ain't you figured that out yet?"

They stood, eye to eye, both tensed and evenly matched.

"Get out," said Joshua.

Brood's eyes bulged with fury, the veins at his temples like blood worms. "Are you crazy? Do you have any idea who you're fucking with?"

"Yeah. A liar and a loser who'll do anything to be around the beautiful people."

"Time for your medicine, bitch!"

Brood planted his feet, the punch already vectored when something grabbed his fist. "Who the fuck?" He twisted sharply and Joshua watched, transfixed, as the dealer's rage melted into terror.

"What seems to be the problem here, Symmington?"

"Nothing, I—I was just leaving."

Solipsum looked over the dealer's shoulder and met Stone's eyes. And for the photographer, thought and impression were suddenly frozen as he found himself drawn by what he saw in the other man's gaze, to the infinitely swirling chaos, fractal, beautiful, beckoning, a spectacle so hypnotic and seductive he felt himself falling into its promise. And it was somehow strangely familiar.

Brood looked back and forth between the two men and realized he was in way over his head. Solipsum tightened his grip until the dealer's bones began to grind. "Not so fast, Symmington. Know this. Stone Studios are now off limits to you. Permanently. After all, there are plenty of other places to sell your wares, aren't there?" The dealer nodded quickly. "Now, get out."

Brood slunk away, his hand like a glove filled with thick chunks of glass. The pain when it came would be monstrous, yet he knew he had gotten off lightly.

"Nasty man," Stone commented.

Solipsum seemed surprised. "You know him?"

"I did. In another life." He extended his hand. "Joshua Stone."

"Trey Solipsum."

They shook and Stone instantly felt the other's surprising power.

"You seem so familiar to me," Solipsum confided. "I'm a great admirer of your work. It's a shame we've never done anything together."

"I know. It's strange, isn't it?" Stone felt an odd sense of displacement at hearing his own thoughts spoken aloud.

"Something tells me that's about to change. I think we'll be seeing a great deal of each other. Very soon."

Joshua raised an eyebrow. "You know something I don't?"

Solipsum smiled the Secret Smile. "Let's just say it's in the cards. I find myself thirsty. Perhaps it's time for some punch."

"Go ahead, I'm sure I'll see you around. Enjoy the rest of the evening."

Solipsum looked back at the photographer.

"Oh, I will."

It had turned out to be one of the better parties he had attended. There were so many people to encounter that it had almost become tiring after awhile. Almost. He was put to mind of what someone had said about the poet Byron, how the women would fall into his mouth like roasted larks.

Solipsum now found himself standing by the punch bowl, lips slightly parted, as though he were about to taste of something unexpected. All it would take was one drop of his blood, one tiny drop, and this party would take a decidedly different turn. The vision of a vortex filled his mind, a blurry swirling, a rise and fall that finally snapped into focus as a collection of bodies, writhing and twisting like

(a sack of snakes)

sybarites.

Some say demon's blood is the deadliest substance on the physical plane. Some say it is the most intoxicating. But Solipsum knew the truth. A demon's blood was capable of whatever its demon wished it capable of. It was all a matter of intent. And right now, Solipsum's intent was decidedly—sexual.

The nail on his index finger extruded and sharpened, then punctured the pad of his thumb. A bead of blood so scarlet it was almost black welled. Solipsum knew he should not be doing this, that it could destroy his entire future. But the smile on his lips became wider and wider, because sometimes,

he

just

couldn't

help

himself.

The drop fell to the punch bowl when suddenly he felt it, the furtive caress of telepathic trespass. His fist shot out and caught the fattened bead, vaporizing it instantly.

Who's that looking into my head? Ah, it's you, €ϖφƷƷεϖϭϭφΞ⌐φδ. *Would you really like to see what's in here? Then come.* Look.

Bruun felt his mind caught in an ectoplasmic vice, an immense hand which held him as he struggled, contemptuous. Then it began tightening into a fist, slowly squeezing, the pain far beyond anything he had ever experienced. The demon's voice filled his head with the crushing mass of a continent. "Do you now regret your decision, €ϖφƷƷεϖϭϭφΞ⌐φδ? Your betrayal of me? And what did you gain? A chance to make amends? As if that would somehow erase the debt of souls you brought to me. Foolish creature! I know not yet who it is you guard but it matters not. Your time here is done, and I will have you once again, but this time only as a thing to torment. Slowly. Endlessly."

Bruun felt the terrible weight of Solipsum's presence grow as he began to pluck and strip the lives from the cat's core essence. Bruun screamed as the eighth life fell, then he was suddenly—

—slammed back into his body. His paws skittered as he staggered, disoriented. He looked up and saw a girl apologizing to Solipsum, a stain slowly spreading on the demon's sleeve. Solipsum's eyes found him and Bruun realized the danger was not yet done. He bolted into the crowd, yowling as he ran, a tearing sensation in his ribs where none should have been, crashing into feet and furniture in his efforts to get as far away as possible.

Charlie watched the strange scene unfold before her, then turned to Solipsum. "I'm sorry. Here, let me wipe that—oh my God! You're—"

Her words were cut off as Solipsum grabbed her hand and reached with his eyes directly into her mind. Charlie felt something root around in her head with the delicacy of a convict raping a nun. Then it stopped. A terse confusion furrowed Solipsum's brow. Accustomed to being able to instantly penetrate another's psyche, he was stunned to discover that in this blond distraction he had come up against a featureless white wall. The disorientation lasted only an instant before it dawned on him why this was so. It seemed that Damien Fortune's prophesy was correct— his normal talents had been rendered useless by contact with someone whose future was inextricably linked with his own.

But how?

Before Charlie could comprehend what had happened to her, he released her hand. And mind. The entire episode had lasted less than a second.

"Don't worry about it—Charlie, isn't it?"

She nodded mutely.

"See? The stain is already disappearing."

She looked at the sleeve of his tuxedo. Sure enough, it was. Its shape tugged at her mind, then the pain in her wrist made itself known. She rubbed as she watched the stain become smaller and smaller.

What just happened? Jesus, he's strong. "How are you doing that?"

"Me? Silly girl. This garment is made from *Fa-Shin, Inc.*'s new Viral Cognizance Fabric. It eradicates anything not of itself. I guess you could say it has a very specific mandate. And if you aren't part of it . . ."

He winked at her and turned, leaving her to stare at his departing back, still rubbing the skin of her wrist.

Russell Hernbauer leaned against a curve of wall in the main studio, drunk and bitter, holding his last beer. *Hornblower! Great. That name's gonna follow me to the grave. Thanks, Charlie, you little fuckin' bitch.*

He stared at the two stunning models who were giggling by a dome-girder. They looked over at him and began a new round of whispering, one that quickly degenerated into another giggle-fit. He found his bitterness increasing.

"What I wouldn't give to fuck either one of those two bitches."

"Stunning, aren't they?"

Russ was somehow unsurprised to discover Solipsum standing next to him.

"Whatever," he muttered.

The model removed a speck of lint from his sleeve. "Do I detect a note of bitterness, my friend?"

Russ's stare became defiant. "It's easy for you. You're the best looking dude on the planet. The rest of us have to, you know, *work* for our pussy."

"Doesn't have to be that way. In fact, I can guarantee you could have just about any woman you want."

"Eh?" Russ's mouth hung slack. "How?"

"Let's just say I have that power." Solipsum's eyes seemed to glow briefly.

"What do I have to do?"

The model leaned closer. "Something is coming up. Something big. It involves you, me, Joshua Stone, Charlie, Phoena and a whole lot of other people. I'm going to need someone I can rely on, someone I can count on when push comes to shove. Someone who knows the meaning of the word . . . loyalty."

"A man on the inside?"

"I knew you would get it. After all, we're both men of the world, aren't we?" Solipsum looked at Russ with the expression of a man who had just seen a dog perform a simple trick—perhaps the licking of its own testicles.

"Uh, yeah—yeah, we are!"

"And Russ? You'll find me a far more—appreciative employer—than Mr. Stone. So, what do you say?"

"Deal!"

They shook hands.

Solipsum laid his arm across the assistant's shoulders and waved to the girls by the girder, inducing in them a sudden loin-smear. "Now go over there and say hi. Oh, by the way. Here's a little something to—enhance your evening."

He handed Russ a red foil bindle. "Use it sparingly. It's very—potent."

Russ pocketed the party favor, gave Solipsum a thumbs up and said "Later, dude!"

Solipsum was left by the wall, shaking his head in wonder.

Hornblower. How apt.

Elora finally found him by the small elevator, the one in which she had never ascended.

"It's time, isn't it?" he asked.

"Yes."

"Then let's go."

Stone placed a hand on her shoulder and palmed a small panel near the elevator doors, guiding her in when they silently parted. The two then rose to the very peak of Joshua Stone's studio, his sanctum sanctorum. They stepped out into what Elora immediately recognized as a miniature version of the main studio, complete with its own transparent dome.

They entered and a hush fell over them, for the glassy sphere seemed to have little more substance than a soap bubble. With the blaze of city lights below and the vault of the night sky above, Elora felt as though she were standing in the open air. An incredible sense of solitude and serenity permeated everything. It was as though she were standing inside her very own soul.

They walked over to a couch and chair separated by a simple floating coffee table. Stone picked up a remote and thumbed a stud. As Elora watched, the floor slowly became transparent. She had been ready for almost anything, but not this. It was one of the most disconcerting things she had ever experienced. Then, though her senses told her otherwise, she found herself simply letting go, as if dancing with a partner of years.

She stood and looked down at the party below, the blazing lights, the crowd of revelers.

"Can they see us?"

A bemused expression crossed Joshua's features.

"No." He held the remote up again. "But just to enhance things a bit . . ." He touched another button and the entire floor turned a deep aquamarine streaked with gold. Elora felt for an instant as though she were watching the dying of some distant and watery world, the light shafting up from its molten core to burst through fissured skin.

Stone settled into the couch and reflected for a moment on how nice it felt to simply sit down, to let this bliss wash over him. He put his feet up on the coffee table and stretched them out, finally turning to face her. "All right, Elora. Spill."

"First of all, I want to thank you for all the wonderful pictures you've taken over the years. For me and everyone else you've ever shot with. Money aside, I simply love your work."

"Why—thank you," Stone said, surprised. "That means something. If it wasn't for you, all this would still be just a dream."

Elora felt again the wave of guilt as his words hit her, their genuine appreciation wrenching, reminding her of the lie she was living and oh, how a part of her yearned to finally tell him the truth. It was not she who was responsible for all he had today, it was not she who had pushed and fostered a talent no one else would touch. In fact, years ago, when she had first been presented with Joshua Stone, an ex-patriot Canadian, as a likely candidate for a small assignment, she had laughed, pointing to his past and his complete lack of fashion experience. When she had realized she had no choice but to hire him, that he was in fact an essential part of someone else's plan, she'd gone along with it. What else could she have done? She'd been bought and paid for a long time ago.

The years had rolled by and the money had flowed and as she worked with him on campaigns of ever greater scope and magnitude, she had come to see what the other had seen, had come to see as justified the ever increasing sums that had found their way into Joshua Stone's bank account. These sums were injected subtly, massively, their Vatican-rumored origins still shrouded in mystery, the highly complex lattice of interlocking corporations impenetrable. All this money was destined not only to boost his career and every aspect of his talent, but also to finance the construction of a studio the likes of which the world had never seen.

It slowly became apparent that Joshua Stone was more than worth the investment, that he was in fact some kind of photographic prodigy. He had surprised them all with the effortless way he combined his exuberant talent and a genuine love of people, his remarkable physical presence and keen business savvy. But by far the most important thing that became evident was his obsessive and relentless pursuit of the perfect image. This had allowed the other's timetable to be greatly accelerated, to the point she could meet with Joshua tonight, to present what was really, finally, at the heart of everything.

Elora crossed her legs, wistful. "You know, Joshua, you are the only man who has ever said 'no' to me."

Stone took a deep breath. "But never photographically, Elora. Never creatively. The other you can get anywhere."

Elora paused for a moment before the rocky truth of his words, for Joshua Stone had become so much more to her than the sexual challenge he had initially presented. When she had found herself guarding so fiercely a young and angry photographer a hundred years ahead of his time, she finally admitted she had fallen in love. He had made her realize a truth about herself: she would rather be taken in someone's arms than simply taken. And this was why she sometimes felt so vulnerable and stormy when he was near.

She looked down at her hands, suddenly uncertain she had any right to do what she was about to do. For Elora knew that so much more was going on than even she had been made privy to, that she was as much a pawn as the man in front of her.

Then reality slammed into her with the impact of a high speed collision, one that effectively silenced the child in the back seat that had been trying to make itself heard, to warn and help her before it became too late.

"I promised I would tell you what this was all about," she said.

Stone looked at her face, seeing in her eyes something deep and unspoken, completely at odds with her innocuous words. He felt himself again in that cold and snowy clearing, when then, too, his life had changed forever. He almost took her in his arms but stopped himself, watching as the moment passed, some part of him still reaching, reaching backwards through the black sea of Infinity to touch, and this time clasp the pale and slender hand of an alternate possibility.

"I—I know you think this is about us, but it isn't. It's about the biggest print campaign of the century. Maybe of all time."

Stone took a moment to reorient his mind, to shift into the reality of what she had just said. "I've heard that before, but I'll bite. Before we go further, though, I have to ask. Why print? Why not TV or the Internet?"

"TV is extremely powerful. So is the Internet. But both require boxes that must be plugged in, turned on, tuned in and left on long enough for our images to register. And by extension, our message. On the other hand, a still image in a magazine or on a billboard requires only that you look at it. Your participation is, for all intents and purposes, free. It invites you in, *you* decide when to look away, when to leave the world your own mind and that image have co-created. A world born in the instant mind and image meet, when time stands still and utter vulnerability occurs. Vulnerability to a message, Joshua. Our message."

"And what message is that?"

"Buy."

Stone sighed, memories of his conversation with Charlie surfacing. *There's always a price, isn't there, Josh? But admit it. There's a huge part of you that gets off completely on the fact that it's* your *pictures that get people to buy,* your *pictures making them do something by some weird force of vision and will. And let's not forget ego. Maybe Symmington was right.*

"Buy, consume, eat, it never ends, does it?"

She gazed at him coolly. "Don't be a fool, Joshua. You've known that since the day we first worked together. It's what makes the world go round. You know it and I know it, and so does *Fa-Shin, Inc.* They want to make sure that the stuff you buy is theirs, and only theirs. By whatever means necessary. We both know that competition has reduced advertising effectiveness to a fraction of what it once was. We figured there was only one way to get around that competition. By eliminating it. All of it. At least temporarily."

"How?"

"The saturation campaign to end all saturation campaigns. We have orchestrated a media buy that will, less than a year from now, give us a three month fifty percent global coverage in *all* print-based media. That includes magazines, billboards, bus shelters, subway cars, telephone booths, you name it, we've bought it."

"That's impossible. Your talking billions in advertising."

"Fifty billion, to be precise."

"It'll never work. Besides, the nightmare of organizing all that space, people will get bored looking at the same images over and over. In fact, they'll probably get resentful as hell."

Elora shook her head. "No. They won't. Because they won't be looking at the same images. They'll be looking at a very loose, totally organic liquid visual narrative that changes each time it is looked at from a different perspective."

"You've lost me."

"Picture this. You get up in the morning and walk through the streets of New York or Paris or London. Any one of thirty major urban centers. You are on your way to work. You pass billboards, bus shelters, wall murals and phone booths. Each has a different image from our campaign on it. Just an image. And a small logo. You enter the subway system or board a bus. More of our images surround you. Maybe you buy a magazine or a newspaper. You open it as the train begins to move and there you see, in place of advertising, more of our images. As you flip through the magazine, you realize our images have replaced *all* the advertising. And all these images join together to form a story, a story that differs for each viewer and changes depending upon the order in which the images are viewed. It also changes depending on your mood, the weather, your clothes, what you had for breakfast. In other words, how you see our advertising is determined by your own life experience. Day to day, moment to moment. Even when viewed in the same order, the experience is different. Because it builds,

Joshua, cumulatively, subliminally, like a giant movie. You are the projector and your own pace determines the frame rate."

"Jesus. That's an incredible idea. The implications alone—you're talking about something so huge it would literally change human perception." A tiny voice inside him replayed all that Elora had just said, replacing the words "our images" with "my images." He tried to kill it but it only crept back further, into the darkness.

Elora smiled at him with satisfaction. "I knew you would get it."

Then something remarkable happened, a small miracle that has so often been taken for granted.

It began to snow.

Joshua watched Elora's face and knew she was thinking of a shake-up globe she'd had when she was a child, that this was what it must be like to live inside one. It was, he admitted, an effect that secretly pleased him more than anything else his studio had to offer.

He relaxed and let himself become absorbed by couch and falling snowflakes, to let them cleanse and purify, at least for now, that part of himself he had no control over. "It's beautiful, isn't it?"

"Yes, it is."

"I was referring to the snow."

Elora was watching the snowflakes, something child-like in her eyes, almost as though she could hear them. "So was I," she said absently. "I'm not completely soulless, Joshua." A small windstorm had spiraled the snow into a shape she almost recognized—a pattern of some sort. She turned and her eyes cut him. "You would find that out, if you ever took the time."

Words momentarily deserted him. So much had been put before him thus far that even the solidity of the Earth seemed cast in doubt. Now this. His face became very open then, and what looked out at her was the sheer and boundless child-master. "You're right, Elora. It's not fair that I never took the time. But I am what I am. And something inside me always said, 'Joshua, if you decide to go there, she'll eventually want to be the only one, to supplant even your Muse, because her jealousy would need that final sacrifice.'"

"I would never ask you to give up who you are," she said in a small voice.

"Never, Elora? Truly? We are both so very strong. Maybe that's why we stayed apart, only letting the best parts of ourselves interact and thereby elevate. Otherwise I think we might have destroyed each other."

Elora smiled at him, reminded of how much she loved to hear him speak, the way he sliced and served the language. "You're right, Joshua. But we still yearn, don't we?"

"Yes, we do. And we cause that yearning in others, too."

"What do you mean?"

"We induce their yearning artificially. With the tools of the Soul—Beauty, Youth, Freedom. That's what this is really all about, isn't it? Inducing that yearning on a massive scale. Doesn't that ever make you feel guilty?"

"Yes, it does. But at least we're not pushing—"

"Cigarettes? Vodka Q's?"

That caused them both to laugh.

"We live in the world we do—" said Joshua,

"—and do the things we must," she finished.

"But the scale you're talking about, Elora—this completely dwarfs anything that's ever been attempted."

"Yes."

"And this—Campaign. It all hinges on the images, doesn't it? And never becoming bored when this is all you see. I don't know if anyone could produce that kind of photography."

She leaned back again on the sofa and stretched her arms out. "Trust me, Joshua, it's all been tested. With the amount of money being spent on this, do you really think we wouldn't know what we were doing? The idea actually emerged as an anomaly that was reported when we did a massive focus group for a new campaign. Someone fucked up and showed the group the same images ten times, but in a different order each time. The response we got was off the charts. No one had ever seen anything like it. We tried to analyze how this was possible but it seems the entire process defies analysis. All we know is that it works. But only when you use the right images."

"Whose images were used for the focus group?"

She smiled, her face a mask of marbled turquoise in the underlight and he felt for an instant the beating of mighty wings, the movement of forces massive and implacable.

"Yours, Joshua. Just yours."

"You have got to be kidding," he murmured, but some part of him had already known what she was going to say.

His mind began racing, thoughts muscling and jostling one another as the enormity of what she had presented him with began to sink in. He took a deep breath and tried to slow it all down. "What's the mandate?"

"There isn't one."

"What?"

"There can't be one. It's part of the reason the whole thing works. It's almost completely random. It's your photographic soul, Joshua. Based purely on raw talent, on utterly letting go and shooting whatever captures your eye. The framework is photographing models. Male, female, whatever. And there are two stipulations. Beyond that, you've got carte blanche. We don't care what you do."

"Jesus."

"We need one thousand images. What they consist of is totally up to you. The stipulations are these: if you use clothes or products, they must be ours. And the two models that are to be the centerpieces of your creation must be Phoena and Solipsum."

"The two biggest models on the planet. And they've never appeared together in anything. How the hell did you manage that?"

"It's not important, Joshua. Let's just say that after this, neither of them will ever have to work again. Nor will their children's children."

"What's the timetable?"

"Six months from casting to the first finished images. Submitted in any form. Prints, transparencies, digital files, we don't care. From that point on, eight weeks until delivery of the final image. That way, some of your work is already out there as the rest is being created. Which means you too will be affected by the Campaign."

"Like a closed loop."

"Exactly."

"Perfect, Elora. Just perfect. I guess there's only one question left."

"Your fee."

"Yes."

She wrote something down on a cocktail napkin, then handed it to him. He slowly took it and opened it, to see the words "one billion" staring back at him.

"You're serious."

"Deadly serious."

He held out his hand.

"Deal."

They shook.

His eyes were drawn to the world outside the dome, to the snow so white and pure and driven. Then he looked back at her, the other decision made. "Only for one night," he told her. "Everything I have to give. But only for one night. This night."

She smiled.

"Deal."

Book 6

*"Things are in the saddle,
And ride mankind."*
—*Ralph Waldo Emerson*

New York City, Stone Studios

Elora Gorj still had her eyes closed, even though she was fully awake, just savoring the delicious soreness in her loins.

That was worth all the years I've waited. Thank you, Joshua, I thoroughly enjoyed that. And I think a part of you did too.

She felt the bed shift slightly and opened one eye as Joshua's back passed before her. She saw the deep nail furrows, still raw, and thought, *when did I do that?* She didn't yet have the distance to remember. He sat on the bed's edge and she noticed the many other scars that covered his body, scars that silently spoke of a lifetime's experience. She doubted her shallow contributions would even be noticed in the lattice. She had seen Joshua without a shirt on before, but he was now a whole new world to her after their intimacy, a world even deeper than she had initially suspected.

The circular bed they lay upon was like an iris, bracketed by the dome's glass wall on one side and a curved expanse of mirror on the other. Joshua sat on the mirrored side, face unguarded, looking past his reflection to that of the city beyond. The day was silvery, clouds and snow-dusted buildings forming a low contrast monochrome that never fully reached the far end of the grayscale— with the exception of Joshua's figure. Elora watched from beneath the quilt, composition and tonality slowly coalescing for her, and she was struck by the startling revelation that she was looking at a perfect black and white photograph. The urge to touch him then, to enter that photograph and feel the slight contusions of those scars, became almost overwhelming. But she did not. She remembered instead his words and how he had been more than true to them, for they played now a larger game, one that would require total trust. The Campaign of The Century would brook no less. That trust for her began when they shook hands and sealed the pact. It wasn't easy, in fact it was nearly impossible. She felt her hand move along the covers, almost of its own volition, inching, inching, and realized that Joshua had been right, that it was her bottomless capacity for more that in the end pushed everything else away. Before she could stop herself, to say "no" and finally touch that place in her own will, he reached for his briefs and the moment was taken from her.

99

He got up from the bed's edge, the sudden movement causing a small groan to escape his lips. She suppressed a smile and blinked back a tear, a little surprised by how that had snuck up on her.

Just before he left the room, he looked at the reflection of her head, just visible beneath the rumpled bedding. "Meet me downstairs for some breakfast when you get up. And Elora? Stay real. We have a long journey ahead of us." He gave her a small smile, then disappeared.

Descending to the main studio in the private elevator, he looked out at the city. The weak light and lack of color complimented his mood perfectly. He placed a hand against the glass and stretched experimentally. Even the stiffness of his muscles and the stinging in his back seemed somehow distant. He knew that in another universe, he had snuck back into the room and commenced tickling her mercilessly. Before fucking her again. Silly. And that the only person who would enjoy it more than Elora would be himself. He also knew that this one lapse would subtly erode his power base in a way that would eventually prove disastrous. He felt very sad for a moment, wishing that once, just once, he could behave like a normal person, agendas and consequences be damned. He had enjoyed making love to her more than he would have thought possible. She was far different in bed than her carefully molded exterior bespoke.

The doors opened and he wandered to the kitchen, still half asleep, popping the refrigerator door and pouring himself a large glass of orange juice. Then he perched on a stool by the kitchen counter and looked out at the city. Were Elora here, she would have seen another portrait, as stark and beautiful as the first, the orange of the juice the only hit of color.

He sighed and lit a cigarette, a rare indulgence.

I can't believe this. I have what is probably the coolest studio in the world, I've known some of its most beautiful women and I've just been handed The Campaign of The Century. Why do I feel so sickened? Stone, old man, what the hell is wrong with you?

He gulped some of the juice, barely tasting it.

I am just so utterly tired of selling people shit they don't really need. Day in, day out. And making it all so beautiful. Because dammit, pictures ARE like drugs and I AM the Pusherman. More in my own way than even Symmington Brood, because I reach so many more customers. Or consumers. But is that really a fair analysis, Josh?

He banged his fist down and the glass jumped.

Dammit! It's too much to think about right now.

He sat back and took a long pull from the cigarette, finally coming to a decision.

It ends after this one. No more. After this I'll be a free man. Free to go new places, try new things. Or maybe just relax and shoot some flowers, nature and the occasional nude. What else would I want besides that? Well, the one thing I've always wanted. To fall in love. Crazy, balls to the wall, fuck it all love. Once. Before I die.

He laughed quietly.

Yeah. Right. With who?

A picture of Charlie, not as she looked at the party, but as he saw her day to day, in all her scruffy glory, arose in his mind unbidden. He took a last drag from the cigarette, then crushed the butt, along with his hopes. He turned away from the sky beyond the dome, his sight wavery and wet.

New York City, Chelsea

The alarm clock went off. And went off. And went off. A hand finally slammed down the snooze button, then there was no activity. For awhile. Suddenly the covers were yanked down to nose level.

Fuck, where am I?

Two huge puffy eyes darted about in panic.

Oh my god! Where the hell am I? Oh God! Oh God! Oh God! Oh! Oh! Oh . . . I'm home . . .

Somewhat bewildered, the girl pulled the covers down further, then off the other side as well. *And there's no one here with me.* "Damn, what time is it?" She grabbed the clock, rubbing her eyes as she squinted at the numbers. "Shit! I've got twenty minutes to get to the studio!"

Alabasta Twigg got out of bed, ready to greet the day. Sort of.

She stumbled to the bathroom, face still smeared with last night's make-up, hair a rat's nest, loose-limbed and dopey. She felt a take-out container crunch under her foot and exude a smell like

(a dead animal farted)

something rotten, felt a warm squishiness between her toes, then began hopping about on one foot, screaming "Ewww! Eewwww! Eeeewwwww! How fucking grossss!"

She did a full turn, dimly registering the heaps of clothes, fashion magazines, full ash trays and empty wine bottles, all cheerfully irradiated by the TV. She jumped into the shower, slipped, grabbed the curtain and almost pulled it down before she steadied herself, then turned the taps, to discover that yet again, there was

"NO FUCKING HOT WATER!"

She emerged from the bathroom fully awake and dripping, almost through the living room when a glimpse of something stopped her. She reined up and turned to fully face her reflection in the big living room mirror. She dropped the towel and stood there, naked, staring at herself.

What are they seeing? Just what the hell are they seeing?

She was now at a stage where her professional photos and the picture she had always had of herself were colliding. Like a butterfly slowly emerging from the chrysalis of her own self-doubts, she was beginning to reevaluate her opinion of just how it was she looked, juxtaposing the fact that at seventeen she made more money in a day than all her friends made in a summer. *So maybe I'm not skinny. Maybe I'm willowy. Maybe my boobs are small but boy oh boy are they well-formed.* She stepped closer to the mirror to look at her face. She widened her eyes and laughed. *God, they are so huge. Like some great big owl's. Hooooo! Hooooo!*

She trailed a finger along the slope of her tiny nose, then lightly pressed it into her top lip and grudgingly acknowledged that though her lips were practically the size of an angelfish, they were exquisitely shaped. She puckered them together in a fish mouth, then blew a few experimental bubbles as she crossed her eyes and burst out laughing. *Hurry, hurry,* she thought, scooping up the towel and a handful of clothes. A short time later she was sitting in front of the mirror.

"Alabasta," she said in parent-voice, "you are getting way too old for this shit. Making owl noises at yourself is all fine and dandy but this is your *career*! Pull yourself together, you stupid hole! This can't go on for-ever! Look at those bags." She thumbed an eyelid. "*Luis Vuitton*, match-ing set. Here we have the steamer trunks and just below, the carry-on. Well, a little *Prep H* will fix that in a jiffy."

She grabbed the half-used tube of *Preparation H* and applied the oint-ment to the swollen tissue beneath her eyes, then lit a smoke and began what turned out to be a very good natural clean-up. She pulled her hair into a pony tail and was almost ready to head out the door when it hit her.

Fuck! Still frazzled around the edges! I haven't even had a coffee yet, never mind a morning dump.

She started rooting through her bag like a truffle-swine.

"Where is it? Come on, come on, where the fuck did I put it. There it is!" she squealed as she lifted the vial of something, probably coke, whatever it was that Symmington had given her last night. She tapped out a large heap into the thumb-distended hollow on the back of her hand, then hoovered it up.

Oh, that burns! I don't remember this coke burning like that.

Her eyes widened.

*Oh, fuck. That wasn't coke, that was "Special K." Run to the cab before—*she dashed from the apartment and ran to the elevator—which wasn't working—then it was—*too late! K-hole!*

She raced down the steps, vision progressively distorting as it assumed the extreme fisheye perspective typical of the K-hole. She managed to endure a severe case of vertigo as she rounded landings, clutching walls and banisters as though they were magnetized. She had made it to the front door when she saw her neighbor, seventy-five year-old Irene Dodder, creaking up the walk.

Mrs. Dodder peered at the young model, gripping the railing like a lifeline in her effort to negotiate three stairs. *Land sakes,* she thought, *children today—no spine.*

"Are you all right, dear?"

"Fine, Mrs. D. Totally fine. Just late for work."

"Better hurry. Oh look! There's a cab for you."

Alabasta ran to the curb and dove into the cab and just had time to think *What's that weird thing hanging from the mirror?* before the door slammed and it rocketed into traffic.

New York City, Chinatown

A naked Russell Hernbauer lay in bed, a bed not his own, in a luxury apartment that was definitely not his own, and thought *How sweet it is!*

He slowly turned his head from one side to the other, first admiring the redhead's milky curves and then the black girl's gorgeous face.

Russ old boy, you have really hit the big time here. I don't know what was in that package Solipsum gave me, but that was the best night I have ever had. I never imagined it could be like this. And all because of him. Well, Mr. Solipsum, wherever you are, you've found your man.

His eyes lingered for a moment on the small bloodstain near one of the girl's legs. Something about its shape was vaguely familiar, like he'd seen it

(on the studio floor)

somewhere before. Then the thought evaporated as his eyes continued on their journey to far more interesting sights.

New York City, Lower East Side

Charlie lay on her futon, the sheets wound around her sleeping form. She was all alone but for the company of the worn old doll she held so tightly. It was very dear to her, all she had left from the time before. That and her dragon. She knew anyone who saw it would laugh and laugh but she didn't care, for it had always been her friend, there to share the many tears. Who cared if it looked a little ratty?

The light coming through the window got a little brighter, edging the Dress as it rested across a chair back, carefully folded so it wouldn't wrinkle. It was the first thing she saw when she opened her eyes. Memories of the night before came flooding back and she smiled sleepily, then rose, head still fuzzy from too many martinis and too much attention. She sat on the edge of the bed, rubbing the sleep from her eyes before meandering to the kitchen, squinty with yawn. She opened the cupboard door, a hand absently hitching the bottoms of her flannel pj's as she reached for the coffee, mind running free. *What an unbelievable night! And to think, these people actually live this way.* She stopped for a moment and set the coffee down, rubbing her wrist unconsciously. *And Solipsum. I've never met anybody like him. Compelling as hell but scary too.* A vague and uncomfortable memory surfaced, of another—presence? *is that what it was?* in her mind. Then the sputter and hiss of the coffeemaker distracted her. Soon she was sitting at the kitchen table, lightly blowing on the steaming mug, all thoughts of Solipsum forgotten. The ghostly morning light made everything milky, and she found herself drifting, remembering her life before America. She set the cup down and unconsciously brought a hand inside her top, rubbing the shoulder where her dragon sat. They came to her then, the memories drowning her as she fought them, pulling and powerful, reminiscences of love and death and fear and lust and guilt and *oh god sometimes I wish I'd never made us take that shortcut.* Images, moods, tastes and textures, silken skin and liquid mouth and hot summer nights that seemed as though they would never end, the sensual tide so strong now she could barely breathe, responding physically to sight and sound and lingering touch, to scent and detail and the taste on her tongue when first it had touched the other's tattoo. She felt a delicious wave come over her, a familiar tingling, building, building, and then the final memories came crashing in, Haiku! Haiku! the blood and battle and *god, we fought them all, we beat them all, we're winning 'til the tenth one came, the masked one, good, so good, even you were scared and then I moved when I should have stayed, oh god! forgive me, I never wanted you to die!* And then the tears, the tears, so many tears. She buried her head in her arms, sobbing.

Minutes? An hour? She had no idea when she finally wiped her eyes, rising then to pace the little kitchen, opening a window to let the winter cold in. She gazed out at the city and the gray stillness beyond, purposefully leaving her top loose so the icy air could touch her skin.

God, will I ever be free of that time?

She laughed a teary laugh for asking such a stupid question.

Do I really want to be free of it?

No.

Never.

She closed the window and sat down again, taking a big gulp of the still-hot coffee. Her mind felt free now, the memories ebbing, thoughts turning to her new friend.

Phoena. She is so totally amazing! I've never met anyone like her. Does she really like me or is it because I'm part of "Rolling Stone"? Come on, Charlie, you were taught better than that. She's the real thing and you know it.

Joshua bloomed in her mind then, the dark and ebon photo god. *Who isn't really all that stony. In fact, he's just about the coolest, sexiest man I've ever seen. And I think he likes me. God, Cherry Cora, could he be the one? Whoa! Slow down girl! One day at a time. Let's maintain a certain degree of professionalism here.* She hugged herself. *Yeah, right, Charlie. Oh what a life I've lived! And something tells me it hasn't even begun.*

She leaned back in the chair, arms hanging at her side, unaware that she was smiling.

New York City, Upper East Side

Phoena knew she was dreaming but that didn't make it any easier. She felt like someone had strapped her to a wheelchair and had pushed it to the top of a very steep hill. The dream had come before and she hated it more each time. She tried to force herself awake but it was already too late, rolling forward now as the dreamtime took her to that place where once again her life had changed forever.

She found herself back in Italy, laughing with such delight, to finally meet someone and have a moment she'd only ever seen in films. And oh my God! The man her newfound friend was with! Phoena in her young life never even imagined such a man could exist. He wasn't just good-looking. Oh, no. There was something about the way his eyes met yours that made you melt, that made you cross your legs when you didn't need to, that somehow made you feel as though you stood before him naked. But you didn't mind. In fact, you loved it. The girl touched her elbow and said something that made Phoena laugh and next she knew they were on their way to yet another club. So the night went on, effortless entré into the most exclusive nightspots, terraces, and at the end the massive warehouse simply called *Verde*. Drinking, eating, dancing, bumping, and none of it seemed to do anything, none of it able to further enhance the incredible tide of lust that consumed her, a hunger she had never before experienced, a physical rapacity so compelling she thought at any moment she would rip off all her clothes and pounce on her two companions. And unless she was entirely stupid, she wasn't the only one who's control was slipping. It started with a little squeeze here, and a kiss for luck at the casino. Then the washroom stall at *Verde* when the other girl had touched her breasts, even as that kittenish tongue had found its way between her lips. *So that's what that feels like*, she'd thought, surprised that she'd rather enjoyed it. Enjoyed it a lot. Then it all became a blur, the night transforming into one long tingle of laughter and musky ambivalence that . . . the dream sped more quickly now, became almost painful as sensation piled on sensation, things she'd never felt before, the things their hands were doing to her body, the two of them together, their tongues honeyed and curious, waves of pleasure, barriers crashing, inhibition completely discarded, motion and hip thrust and *that's how that's done*, the subtle steering of her screaming sexuality until something happened, something flipped and she became the one in control, she became—her mind began to fight, clawing and darting as it sought to evade, to deny what had happened next, when her body—she screamed as the pain forced her rigid on the mattress, tendons stretched, the sweat slick upon her, unable to move as her muscles pulsed and quivered with memory repressed and so long denied, tighter and tighter the memory squeezing as her soul fought to breach the confines of her flesh. What happened, *what happened?* Then the final searing pain as she felt the skin of her legs splitting, bones stretching, the other now monstrous, magnificent—

—she bolted upright, eyes wide open, the sheets soaked and twisted around her, gasping in anguish as she brought her fists down again and again on the cramps that were seizing her legs.

New York City, Central Park West

Solipsum's bedroom was empty, but strange sounds were audible from the bathroom next to it. The sounds escalated into a series of wet gravelly screams, quickly muffled, followed by a throat-torn animal coughing. They were sounds that should never have to be heard, sounds no human body was designed to make. An arterial gout of brightest red splashed through the doorway to splatter the bed. A blood-drenched Solipsum then entered the bedroom and sat on the bed's edge. He propped his chin in his dripping hands, the whites of his eyes like beacons in a sea of crimson. He punched the mattress in frustration, almost putting his fist through it.

Damnation! It is too—close! We are already in it. And no matter how much blood I spill, I still can't—see. That fucking Fortune Teller was right.

Thus it begins.

The Campaign of The Century—Day 1

"*The Campaign of The Century really began soon after Joshua's party, but that was really just a time for logistics. It wasn't until the Spring that the search for talent actually got underway. The Casting itself took four weeks. Stone had decided that in addition to Solipsum and Phoena, he would need ten other models. He also decided that for added spice, he would use ten others who were definitely* not *models.*

I remember the first day of casting as very special because it was the first time any of us understood that what we had conceptualized was real. It was also then that everyone associated with what was now being called The Campaign of The Century understood that Joshua Stone was the man for the job. The only man. Watching him in action, organizing, planning, shooting, just plain delivering, it seemed he'd done this a thousand times before, even though he was making it up as he went along. Masterfully.

That first day, there must have been thousands of casting hopefuls in a line that stretched for blocks and blocks, as far as the eye could see. They came in all shapes and sizes, all dressed in their best. Some clutched portfolios, some headshots and glossies, some videotapes and DVD's. They smoked, they ate, they encouraged one another, they stood, they leaned, and some even sat on lawn chairs, as though attending a turn of the century drive-in.

But all, at one time or another, looked up towards the Studio, as if towards Heaven.

They had come from everywhere, all drawn by the illusive power of fame and fortune. It was the opportunity of a lifetime.

Each had been preselected, based on images submitted to a special web site. In this way, the tens of thousands who applied could be winnowed down to a size more manageable, then be individually photographed. It was still an incredibly lengthy process.

At times it seemed their hope and yearning were so strong, it exuded as if from some bottled elixir, wafting up to hang over the city like a dream . . ."

—from Poverty Whip—An Inside Look at The Campaign of The Century *by Maurice Vellum*

Stone sighed and lifted his face from the camera, waving and smiling as yet another hopeful left the casting set. He had already been offered more sex, drugs, money and power than one man could use in ten lifetimes. He had turned them all down easily, although not in some cases without a tinge of regret. It was a regret he had felt approximately fifty times so far.

"Next, please!"

He looked through the viewfinder and saw yet another stunning model looking back at him as though he were something good to eat.

Make that fifty-one.

It was a very busy day and the main studio dome was packed with casting hopefuls. It was also a jeans and t-shirt day, everyone at the casting dressed as casually as possible—anything to help diffuse the palpable tension, the hunger that seemed to permeate the very air they breathed.

Stone used a digital camera as well as a medium format *Mamiya* for Polaroids he wanted right away. Charlie was acting as Number One while other assistants worked to keep the casting herd moving. Behind her, on a flat screen monitor the size of a door, a huge mosaic of tiny squares scrolled past. They were the thousands of head shots that had already been taken. Some pulsed with a colored outline, different colors signifying how close they were to becoming a final choice.

"Hey, Charlie!"

She turned from the monitor to see a smiling Quinby Delicious strolling towards her across the studio. The model wore a simple summer dress with a frisky insouciance that seemed to be her trademark. Charlie watched, fascinated, as a random breeze brought the dress alive, to cling and lift and rill like softest milkwater over the curves of Quinby's moving body. It seemed the whole room held its breath, lifted in that perfect moment, the only sound the sunny splash of Quinby's girlish laughter. Too soon, too soon, the model stood before her, and Charlie was sure she'd felt the air warm just a bit with the collective release of all their sighs.

"God, Quinby, what an entrance. And that dress." She had sudden thought. "You aren't wearing any underwear, are you?"

"I haven't worn underwear in eight years."

"Really?"

"Would I lie to you about a thing like that?"

Charlie bent her hands in paw shapes like a small woodland creature. "You know, you're like my hero."

"Stick with me kid and I'll show you the world."

Both girls broke into laughter and hugged one another. Quinby then kissed the young assistant's cheeks, stepped back and held her at arm's length. "Look at you! With that headset and monitor, you look like you're ready to launch the Jupiter Probe."

Charlie grinned. "Sometimes it feels that way. This has to be the biggest casting ever."

"Tell me about it." Quinby rolled her eyes. "I had to show my passport three times just to get to the elevator. Hey," she brought her face close to the other girl's. "Did you use that card I gave you?"

Charlie pouted. "No! I'm a good girl. Besides, I'll be seeing more than enough of Trey Solipsum in the days ahead."

"I guess you will. And me too, if I'm lucky." Quinby hooked a thumb over her shoulder, careful to block the gesture. "Who's that guy over there? The one that keeps staring at us?"

"Lozoratto."

"Loza-who-zis?"

"Lozoratto. An assistant. I think you met him at the party."

"Jesus. From the way he's gawking, you'd think I was his personal brood mare."

"What's a brood mare?"

"It's like a brood sow, only you ride it more often."

"Quinby, you're weird."

The model sighed. "I know, I know. But underneath it all, I'm just a little girl from Edmonton, looking for Mr. Right."

Charlie cuffed her. "Whatever!" Then she said quietly, "Why don't we go over there and give him a thrill."

"Oh, yes."

Lozoratto remembered many of the casting girls from the party. But none, it seemed, remembered him. Then he heard the voices.

"Hi Loz!"

"How's it going?"

He turned around to see Charlie and *was that Quinby Delicious?*

"Uh, f—fine," he stammered.

"Who's your friend?" Quinby asked.

"Th—this is Harry Bender. From *Fa-shin, Inc.*"

Harry stepped forward and adjusted his glasses, the temperature in the room suddenly higher than it had seemed a moment ago. "Greetings."

"I hope we're not interrupting anything."

"Oh, no," said Harry breezily, "I was just telling Loz here about the best place in the city to get a massage."

"And where is that?"

"That Thai place over on—ooops!" Harry slammed his hands over his mouth as Quinby eyed him suspiciously.

"Isn't that the home of the twenty dollar 'Rub 'n Tug'?" she asked.

Harry and Lozoratto looked at one another, the denial already on their lips. Then they all heard the voice from on-set.

"Rub n' Tug?" asked Joshua Stone.

Quinby elbowed Charlie, her face red with suppressed laughter.

Lozarotto glanced at Stone, and quickly averted his eyes. "It's a little extra service they provide."

His boss nodded knowingly. "Uh huh." He turned back to the view-finder, already positioning the next hopeful.

"Does he ever go in for one?" Harry whispered to Lozoratto.

"Who, Joshua Stone? No way! Why would he? He gets the Platinum Pussy."

Quinby shot Joshua a look and said a little too loudly, "The Platinum Pussy, eh?"

Stone tilted his face from the camera and shrugged helplessly. Then he barked "Lozoratto! We're out of 'roid!"

The assistant almost wet himself and scrambled from the shooting area as Harry sat on the couch, taking sudden interest in a half-eaten muffin. Charlie and Quinby couldn't hold on to it any longer and collapsed into each other's arms, shrieking with laughter.

"Are we next?"

Both girls looked up, quieted by the sound of two female voices in sync. That's when they first saw the Twins.

New York City, East Village—The Campaign of The Century—Day 2

Phoena said goodbye to the two models she'd had breakfast with and started the short walk home. The day was unseasonably warm, the sunlight anvil hard and armor bright as it beat down from the cloudless blue. She caught a glimpse of gleaming domes and thanked her lucky stars she didn't have to attend what was probably the biggest cattle call in history.

On impulse, she decided to take a detour through the flea market in the rundown parking lot close to her home. She began threading her way aimlessly through the various displays, furniture groupings and racks of old clothes, taking her time, not really looking for anything. She lucked out when a small pair of boots and a raincoat presented themselves, perfect for her new friend. Then she had a thought. *I've never seen Charlie wear jewelry. Maybe there's something cool here.* But as soon as she started looking, the market closed to her, the cases, as her eyes passed over them, filled with the usual flea market orts and leavings, estate dreck and garage sale compost. She began to wonder if it wasn't just all the same scummy tide that floated from place to place, unchanged.

Then something stopped her, commanding her eyes. She found herself bending over a cloth-covered table, really no different from the others she had seen, searching, searching. Were her eyes playing tricks? *No, there it was!* It looked like some sort of medallion, very old, on a thin piece of darkened cord. She gently lifted it, a fleeting impression of cool sleek weight as she brought it close to her face. It was not a medallion at all, but a fragment of something. She ran a thumb over its jagged edges, surprisingly soft, as though they had been rubbed smooth by countless waves. It reminded her of coastlines she'd seen in pictures from space. There was something etched into it—some kind of character. A glyph? Whatever it was, she couldn't tear her eyes from it as it began to spin and branch, forming a vortex she found herself falling into—

"May I help you?"

She looked up into the creased face of an old woman with impossibly hennaed hair. She was dressed in some vintage garishness she seemed born to and peered at Phoena through pop bottle optics, watery eyes myopic and bulging. It seemed Phoena had found the stall's owner.

"Yes. What is this?"

"Now how did that get in there?" A hand, quick as a crab claw, snatched the necklace back. "That's not for sale." The old lady blinked at her. "You don't want that anyway." She forced a smile as she grabbed something else from a nearby bauble tree. "Not when there's this. Look, it even matches your eyes."

"No. That's what I want."

"Why?"

And before Phoena could stop them, the words had left her mouth. "Because it's mine."

The old lady blinked at her again, eyes huge behind her thick lenses, hands crabbing as they plucked at her biddy chain. "What'll you give me for it?"

Phoena felt something that was and was not her, looking out from behind her eyes at the frail creature before her. "Nothing. And you will gladly surrender it."

"Now why would I do that?"

"Because Beauty must be served."

"Oh my." The old woman took a step back. "This *is* yours, isn't it?" She held out her hand, the other clasping its wrist, the shard nestled in her palm like a hole in her flesh. She bowed her head and extended the offering.

Phoena took it from her, the thing becoming warm the instant it touched her flesh and her world

shifted

and she found herself at the portal of some dark and ancient stronghold. She felt different here, more powerful in a way she found it difficult to describe. And her legs . . . The shard sat in her palm, now river-cool and strangely light. As she listened, it began to sing to her a song of blood and steel and ritual in notes low-voiced and clear. The song built and she heard now the drumming, then voices, many voices, the one voice like mountains grinding as it chanted words of power not meant for human ears. She found herself on the verge of surrender, of letting herself be swept away, as though she were living her dream. Then it

stopped. And the shard became nothing more than a scrap of old red metal. She could feel its weight and heat as she began fastening the two ends of cord about her neck.

"There's something I haven't told you." The old lady's head was raised but her gaze remained lowered. "That chunk of metal, dearie? I got it from some kid. At Black Rock City. That's were I met him, but he said he'd been in the desert for a lot longer. He looked in a bad way—like he'd seen too much of solitude. I traded him a name day for it. Before he walked away he said there were two things that I should know about it. The first was that it was indestructible. I laughed in his face, but when I got home, my curiosity got the better of me. Know what? I think that kid was right. I tried melting it, scratching it. I even ran my diamond over it, the one my Harvey gave me, God rest his soul. Nothing. I swear sometimes I even heard it laughing at me." She looked about her small stall, momentarily confused.

Phoena finished tying the two ends together. "The other thing."

"Uh?"

"What was the second thing he said?"

The old lady's right hand began to shake. She quickly put it behind her back. "It—it's supposed to be from something that had done a lot of killing."

"What?"

Phoena heard the old lady's voice, as if from a great distance.

"An Angel's Sword."

> *"By the end of the Casting, Stone had found the ten additional models he would use with his centerpieces, Phoena and Solipsum. They were:*
> ***Sable Sweet** and her twin sister;*
> ***Safron**, both from Georgia;*

Jaroslav Grok, an extremely skinny ex-pizza delivery boy from the Balkans;

Nori, the Asian Superstar;

Straenje Atrakta, P.M.P.'s newest sensation;

Quinby Delicious, rumored to be Jane Bond's paramour;

Gaton Boeuf, the winner of the World Model Sweeps;

Heather Reejon, a bald Twiggy look-alike;

Alabasta Twigg, a model he saw at the Party;

and *Lance Boyko.*

Stone also decided that using only models would push the Campaign too far past ordinary people's believability threshold. Thus he expanded the casting—greatly—for he wanted and needed characters. The final Campaign model selection also included:

Vera Moon, a former porn star who had ballooned to enormous proportions;

Golfillo Gancho, a seedy-looking ex-pimp from Mexico;

Hank Steadman, an old and powerfully charismatic shaman from the Nevada desert;

the child *Constance Squall;*

a circus dwarf named *Hemo-goblin;*

another child, black, named *Loa;*

County Bumkin, a man with massive cranial deformities;

the double amputee, *di Milo;* and

the virtual model known only as *Mola.*

Why had he chosen these people? No one knew, not even, I suspect, the man himself. He seemed to have let his instincts take over completely. Which, I suppose, was the idea.

After the Casting came eight weeks of preproduction. Only a photographer of Stone's caliber, with arguably the finest production personnel in the business already in place, could have hoped to tackle a job of this immensity. It was during this time that locations were scouted, ideas bounced back and forth, sets built, flights booked, hotels organized, wardrobe chosen and support personnel decided upon. All of the make-up was to be either done or supervised by Sindra Djarhm and his gaggle of assistants. Hair was the department of Anthony Chaar and his team. Finally, the job of wardrobe stylist had gone to Janus Blank, a onetime stylist for the PAP. Fourteen more assistants were hired as well as numerous production and research assistants, net jockeys and location scouts.

Stone began demanding books that had been out of print for decades, volumes of art collections, fantasy illustrations, Renaissance masters, medical treatises, old issues of Scientific American, photo collections, prints and folios from every age since camera and film were invented. Nothing remained unexplored. His staff was pushed to their limits in the quest to fulfill the demands of a mind flowing like mercury on a skillet.

Many of these images, all chosen completely by instinct, were taped and stapled in a massive random collage to a cork-covered wall in Stone's "Wishing Wall" Room. This is where most of the brainstorming sessions took place and a course set for the days ahead.

No one had ever seen him work like this. He hardly slept at all. When questioned, he was reported to have answered tersely, "Plenty of time to sleep. In the grave."

Slowly, a plan emerged. As it unfolded it entranced everyone, myself included, with its beauty and simplicity. Even "The Stone Man" was surprised by the elegance of the solution he had devised for what had now become known as The Campaign of The Century.

What lay at the heart of Stone's plan? Simply this: Chaos . . . and the order that was imposed upon it when an instant was frozen, something that only occurred in a still photograph.

During this time, the first ad consisting of a montage of Polaroids from the casting was prepped. As well, other shots taken during down time and off hours allowed Stone a large head start on an impossible deadline.

Finally, all was in readiness for the twenty-four weeks of actual photography. It had been decided that all editing, digital work and printing would be done on the fly. This was because the creation of one thousand images in such a short span of time required as much simultaneous work as possible. There was also the added parameter that images would start to appear in print media before he had created them all. In this way, Joshua Stone and everyone involved in The Campaign of The Century would be part of the feedback loop created when they viewed the images they had made.

And as for those images? Anything went. From high-tech studio shots with millions spent on lighting and sets to Polaroids taken at castings. Candids fired off with point-and-shoots to wide angle cross-processed macro. No technique would remain unexplored and more than a few would be invented.

It was during this time that the romantic relationship with his first assistant, Charlie, began to blossom. It seems in retrospect that this, too, was one of the cornerstones of the Campaign's success. She brought out something in Stone that had either been long buried or had simply never been allowed to see the light. Everyone who saw them together during this time knew it was inevitable that they would become lovers. Everyone it seemed, except the two of them. Both were part of the marvelous exploration that the early days of the Campaign were. Each day brought with it something new; a new film, a new technique, a new way of using a familiar tool, often a new way of seeing. Charlie probably experienced more photographic creativity in three months than most photographers did in a lifetime. I think it was at this time she discovered Stone's greatest secret: his endless capacity to learn. He was a great photographer precisely because he was a perpetual student. Can you imagine what it must have been like, being with such a man at that stage in his life?"

from Poverty Whip—An Inside Look at The Campaign of The Century *by Maurice Vellum*

New York City, Astoria, Queens, The Campaign of The Century—Day 15

Charlie looked up as she heard the train rattling overhead and thought that they had found a great location. What with the subway trellis, the cracked old street and the iron support beams, it looked like some ossified girder yard by way of the Steam Age.

It was an unseasonably warm spring day and just the two of them were out, scouting. Joshua had said that if he didn't escape the confines of the studio he would scream. She had agreed. They hadn't even started shooting yet and things were already nuts. Logistics, plane tickets, hotels, gear, film and tons of desperate phone calls from all sorts of people who just didn't understand that the casting was *over*. Even celebrities wouldn't give up their cellular storming.

She watched Joshua as he walked ahead of her taking readings with his light meter, letting herself become slowly mesmerized by the easy grace of those moving muscles, the tapered line of his back and arms, the smooth and rounded shift of his denim-clad ass. She forced herself to look at the cracked street, the spell becoming just a little too strong.

"What do you think we'll need?" she asked.

"Probably twenty HMIs and three 12K's."

"The Silver Bullet times three? And twenty thousand-watters? That's a lot of light."

"Yup."

Charlie shrugged. "You're the boss." She continued writing everything down on her small clipboard. "That much power's gonna be a bitch. We'll definitely need help from the ConEd guys to gaffer. Close it off?"

"Yes. Where are we?" He glanced up at the street signs. "We'll need 30th all the way up to 36th, one block over on each side, same distance. And clean. No gawkers, no cars."

"That's gonna be hard, Josh."

"No." He rattled off a telephone number. "Use that. A little gift from Elora."

"What else?"

"Water truck. I want the street wet."

Charlie squinted up at the train bridge, which fully covered the road. "Won't it look funny?"

"It's not supposed to be rain. Just effect. You'll get it as soon as you see it."

Charlie tried to picture what he was talking about, making a frame with her small hands and peering through it critically. Joshua was watching her when something caught his eye across the street.

"Wait here."

He had been gone almost twenty minutes and Charlie was getting a little worried when she saw him coming back, carrying something. Two somethings.

"Sorry, these took awhile to fill."

He handed her a heavy plastic contrivance that took her a second to realize was the biggest squirtgun she'd ever seen.

"Jesus, Josh, this must hold a gallon."

"Gallon and a half." He looped the strap over one shoulder so that it crossed his chest, the gun hanging easily at his side. Then he pointed. "Now, let's say that here is where the camera will be. Go up about thirty feet, then slowly hose the road from this side, going back until you're at the camera. I'll do the other side."

They began wetting the road's surface, gentle arcs of water overlapping as they slowly stepped backwards.

"Oooops! Sorry!" Charlie said after getting a bit of water on Joshua's shoe.

"No problem," he replied as he angled his squirt gun and sprayed her directly in the face.

The shock of the water's wetness, the hardness of the stream like a solid thing caught her totally by surprise. "Fuck! Fuck!" she sputtered as she wiped the water from her eyes. By then it was too late, Joshua had disappeared.

She began stalking, the big gun's nozzle swinging from side to side, feeling like some sort of alien hunter. A very wet alien hunter.

Suddenly a thick jet of water hit her from behind, completely soaking her t-shirt and jeans. She ducked behind a rusted support girder, water puddling at her feet. Russ's words

(some training, eh?)

popped into her head. She crouched very low and poked her head around the beam. Another jet came rushing at her, but aimed to where she would have been had she still been standing.

There he is!

She ran out to give chase, but Joshua had already retreated and was just out of range. The next thing she knew, they were having a raging squirt gun battle up and down the road, laughing, screaming, hitting cars and the odd pedestrian. It was the most fun Charlie had had in an age. She vaulted over the hood of a small car, firing as she went, just missing Joshua again.

Damn, he's quick! Like he's dodging bullets or something.

Traffic had practically stopped and passersby were yelling encouragement. Joshua was like a child, totally giving himself over to the wet, wonderful moment.

The battle finally ended when she cornered him in a narrow alley. He had run out of water and a soaking Charlie showed him no mercy. He tried to rush her but was stopped short by a jet to the groin. He danced backwards, howling, hands low to protect himself. Which of course left his face wide open.

Her gun finally ran out of water and she let it hang at her side, gulping huge breaths of air, convulsing with laughter. Then she saw her reflection in a window and gave a startled yelp. It appeared that her white t-shirt was not only soaking wet, it was now almost completely transparent as well. The fabric had molded to her breasts, her nipples pushing forward, rigid with cold, on the day she had decided not to wear a bra.

Oh my God! I've been running around like this the whole time! No wonder those guys in the truck were screaming so loud!

She wondered if Joshua had noticed but no, he was too busy wringing out his own shirt. Then something happened. She watched, transfixed, as the sun poured down on him like the laughter of God, the water mercury, tiny droplets beading his skin like a cloak of seed pearls, the alley transformed into a faerie land with Joshua its Briar King, limned by the light of another age.

Charlie felt her armor split, her walls cast down, as she finally stopped fighting her feelings for him.

*New York City, Stone Studios, Darkroom A, The Campaign
of The Century—Day 21*

She pulled the last print from the wash and set it on the drying rack. Then the idea hit her. Before she could stop herself, she ran from the darkroom to return a short time later and tack something to the shelf that ran above the sink. Charlie had never felt this way, giddy, nervous, her hand almost shaking as she pulled out a marker and began to write.

Why I am doing this, I have no idea. Quinby would be proud.

She capped the pen and hurried from the room before she could change her mind, leaving something hanging in the dark, pinned above the sink where it could not help but be seen. It was her infamous casting Polaroid, taken on the day she'd first appeared in Joshua's studio.

She had written the word *"Platinum?"* on it.

Book 7

"In its pregnant stillness, photography (can) stroke the depths of longing, implying everything, signifying nothing." —Stuart Ewen

" . . . since the decline of the crown, church and social class, and the rise in egalitarianism, propaganda (advertising) . . . has become the principle method of social control." —Harold Lasswel

"How could it hurt you when it looks so good?" —from the song Hollywood by Madonna

"Everything considered, The Campaign of The Century was, at this point, going remarkably well. Two thirds of the images had been created and the Campaign itself had just been launched. It was already causing an unprecedented uproar, because Joshua Stone was producing some of the most astonishing images of his career. Images that seemed to combine digital effects and conventional photography in an organic seamlessness that could not be defined. He had evolved what could only be described as a new way of seeing, a way with such depth and resonance, it was like falling into the collective pool of the human Soul. And we know what effect that eventually had on the world.

If you had walked the streets at this time, you would have seen the images already on billboards, in subway cars and in bus shelters. You would also have seen them on telephone booths, on the sides of buildings, on pizza boxes, on taxis, on bicycle messenger t-shirts, on hub caps, in the sky and above urinals. In fact, any available surface that we could co-opt for one of our advertisements, we did. It was not yet a fully immersive experience though, as some of the photography was still not in place. Thus the liquid visual narrative had holes and lost plot threads.

The 25th shoot, also know as the "Station Series," was one of the most costly of the entire Campaign. But

*our desire for dominance was as deep as our pockets.
And this was where things first began to get strange."*
    from Poverty Whip—An Inside Look at The Cam-
paign of The Century *by Maurice Vellum*

*On Location in the Sewers of New York—The Campaign
of The Century—Day 180*

*God I never thought I'd end up working with him! In fact, I swore it to
myself, didn't I? Yet here I am, whoring for my freedom.* Phoena slammed
a fist into her thigh, the pain spreading yet somehow soothing, triggering for an instant a memory of the dream she could never recall. She
absently touched the shard that hung about her throat. *What a weak and
pathetic creature I've become, just as shallow as all my pictures.* She
remembered the cigarette she still held and took a deep pull, shifting a
bit on the old wooden crate that acted as a chair. Beads of sweat tickled
her brow though she'd wiped it only a moment before. The heat down
here was unlike anything in her experience. It was not just the temperature, there was something about the very quality of the air, as though she
were breathing inside someone's lungs. She thought again of Solipsum,
the power of her lust for him and the night they had first met, five years
past. She still didn't know what had happened, mind always blanking as
it came almost upon the point of remembrance. But though her mind had
forgotten, Lord knew her body had not. Sometimes keeping control of
her physical responses around the other model was almost impossible,
like trying to break a wild horse that wanted only to run and run and run.
It hadn't helped being so close to him for this whole Campaign thing.
Being so close yet keeping him distant, and never in her eyes when the
camera could see. It was just about the hardest thing she'd ever done. If
it hadn't been for Charlie . . . she smiled as she remembered all the times
they'd had, the quiet moments between shots when a glance and a smile
would sometimes save each other's day, the late night glasses of wine,
the play fights and *God! that time she pushed Trey into the pool! I almost
kissed him then. If she hadn't come, that would have been it for me.*

    She sighed and dropped her cigarette to the ground, crushing it out
in the greasy carpet of dirt, rubble and bits of metal. She stood and
stretched, adjusting a garter on the black vintage stocking, then turned to
catch a glimpse of herself in the mosaic of mirror shards that decorated

the Station wall behind her like a cracked and shimmering skin. She gazed at her fractured self, at the corset, stockings, heels and bowler, her dirty sweat-streaked face, the heavy black eye make-up already starting to run—slutty little Match Girl. She struck a pose and watched, amused, as hundreds of Phoena-facets mimicked her motions. She smiled, first with her mouth, then with her eyes, trying on all the different smiles in her collection. Then her pose became a dance, became something else, the smile stitched, her body caught in a jerking puppet nightmare that wrenched her faster and faster, eyes riveted to the image of herself in the radiating spider webs of punch-impacted glass. Reality, reflection, reality, reflection as she pirouetted and saw herself again and again, strangely amazed that the girl staring back at her never missed a step. Suddenly she stopped, frozen in mid-kick, leg quivering as she stared at herself and willed the leg to stay in place. Sweat popped from her pores, arm and leg creases slick with effort but slowly, slowly, though she fought with all she had, her leg dropped back to the ground.

She heard three hand claps and spun about, shocked, to see the massive silhouette of Joshua Stone subtract itself from the low ambient blue before her.

"Jesus! You scared the hell out of me!"

He stepped forward into a pool of light like a shadow come to life. "I'm sorry, Phoena." He smiled at her, the scene still so vivid, Phoena-marionette before her faded broken mirror. His gaze drew back to take in more of the wall, to see the carpet of shards extending further, higher, and to each side before twinkling out a hundred feet in the distance. Some remembrance flared in his mind, a connection spun, interwoven with what he saw before him. He felt as though he had stepped back and now saw an overview, but of what? The Campaign? Then for an instant, the briefest instants, he felt/saw/experienced it all up until this moment, the shoots, the bonds, the happy accidents, the dinners and breakfasts, sunsets and sunrises, as he and everyone involved was born anew each day, challenged and laughing, taking deepest satisfaction in a job well done. He couldn't even pinpoint when he'd known, known for sure that he could do it. Perhaps it was in the grain silos in Kansas, or at the Eiffel Tower, so high in the air, when he thought he saw Phoena and Solipsum fly. The thing that was so surprising for him was how easy it all was. Oh, not physically or mentally, and certainly not logistically. But creatively? He was never at a loss it seemed, never groping blindly, hands outstretched to catch ideas that laughing tried to slip his grasp, always aware of the only thing he had so little of—time.

He held out his hand to Phoena. "Come on, we have a shot to catch."

She laughed and they began to walk through the pools of light, holding hands as they passed the islands of clothing, craft and make-up, ever deeper towards the heart of the Station. Their heads turned in wonder as their eyes traveled over the architecture of the rotting ruin, its massive vaulted ceilings, stunning and eerie in their silent majesty. Intermittent flashes sparkled in the vastness, now green, now turquoise, now scarlet, as second unit shooting proceeded somewhere ahead of them. They afforded glimpses, slideshow strobings of decaying walls, archways chiseled with cryptic cuneiform, broken balustrades and huge chunks of masonry like crumbling concrete cheese. They walked past a row of black abandoned ticket booths, bits of broken glass still glittering in their frames, to come upon a hanging garden of thick black cable. The strobes glinted from shatterings of machine like strewn jewels, final accoutrement on this dowager empress, buried a mile beneath the Earth.

They finally came upon Vera Moon and Golfillo Gancho, enthroned on abandoned furniture in an alcove covered in cracked and broken tiles. Both were drenched in sweat. Golfillo, the ex-pimp, straddled an old kitchen chair someone had dragged down here in 1950. He wore a pair of tattered underwear, black socks with garters and black shoes. Bits of hair sprouted randomly from his shoulders, head and upper lip. He rested his chin on his forearms and slouched, pot belly causing his legs to separate. His watery eyes, strangely compelling, tracked Phoena as she approached. She could feel their creeping caress, casual and shameless as it stripped and violated, missing nothing.

"Hey, Golfillo. Put yer eyes back in yer head," Vera drawled as she fanned herself languidly with an old issue of *Vanity's Glare*, gleaming white flesh rippling as her arm moved. Naked and drenched in sweat, the former porn star sprawled on a discarded velvet couch, almost managing to drape it, a fantastic creature stepped to life from a Joel Peter Witkin photograph (albeit with limbs).

"It's okay, Vera." Phoena stood before him with her hands on her hips and let him get a good look. Then she made a completely unnecessary adjustment to her corset. "I'm sure it's just an occupational habit, right, Golfillo?"

"Whatever you say," he smirked, flashing a gold incisor.

Phoena had met men like this before. They had the same addictive quality as a cigarette, and after you quit, you wondered how you could ever have let that filth into your body.

"The old pimp-eye," Vera clarified. She then looked at Stone, a co-quettish gleam in her eye. "Are we ready to shoot?"

He was about to speak when Russ arrived with a phalanx of three burly assistants, each of whom backpacked a portable strobe unit and acted as a human light stand. Stone winked at Vera, then positioned his light-men as make-up and hair scurried in for last minute touch-ups.

"Where's Solipsum?" he demanded. "And Charlie?"

Solipsum gripped the girl's ripe buttocks, then gently broke from her eager lips. She pressed her loins to him, trembling as she felt the length and strength of him. Then she found his eyes, the clockwork eyelash so oddly sexy. Her fingers reached out to lightly brush the leather suspender straps that were all that adorned his naked chest. Then they slowly made there way lower, past the top of his scarlet pants and their iridescent shimmer, to rest upon the hard shell of his ribbed codpiece.

"My God, Trey, I feel like I'm turning to water. I wish we could—"

"So do I, Quinby, so do I." She heard the mocking undertone in his voice, that he knew she belonged to another and didn't care. "I am needed on set and nothing can interfere with Joshua's shoot. Do you understand?"

She nodded, mute, her eyes huge and blue, not really understanding at all. He touched her chin, then leaned forward to kiss her once more, his tongue sinuous and rough as it thrust past her teeth into the liquid welcome of her mouth. They broke, her breath ragged as she touched a hand to her kiss-bruised lips and licked it, tasting him.

"Later," she said. The fear rippled through her as she watched him toy with the key about his neck, the memories dark and powerful as an undertow, remembering what awaited her in that Room. She could feel the luscious tide rising higher and higher, her iris's darkening with insipient lust. Then she spun and left him, before she lost herself utterly.

Solipsum smiled as he watched her go, the thought of revealing Quinby's infidelity a brief and bright titillation. His mind idly lapped at the having of them both, Jane and Quinby, and he wondered at this. Then his eyes opened wide as he was brought up short, remembering the time he had tasted of the pleasure that had transformed him. The time that in his arrogance he had let himself go, his soul laid bare in all its monstrous glory, black as night-blood on a battlefield, hungry and deep and still she had looked, and he found himself reaching for her, completely surprised, the last of his control finally slipping away, slipping like sand from his tight, tight fingers as he discovered the greatest pleasure lay in surrender, utter surrender, for therein lay the greatest freedom. He had felt something that night, something he was never meant to feel, encountering as he had Another who was Unaware, a thing so singular he had thought it impossible. It took all his will to crush what had taken root in him then, born in the catalyst of that union. He remembered how it had ended, when he had done something foolish and impulsive. He could still see the other girl, lifeless and falling, the fluttering yellow pinions of her dress, her streaming hair, time standing still as she fell and fell forever.

He shook himself, cursing, knowing he was now late. He began striding through the Station, feet effortlessly finding a path through the rubble as he hurried toward the intermittent flash shimmer in the distance.

Jesus, I can't believe I just saw that!

Charlie quickly ducked behind the column, even as Solipsum passed, holding her breath as she watched his silhouette small. She wiped a hand across her brow, the movement unconscious now, pausing for a moment, knowing that even though she was already late, it was best to wait. If there was one thing she'd learned since the Campaign had begun, it was that Trey Solipsum didn't like people nosing about in his business. That and that there was some weird and incredibly powerful past that Solipsum and Phoena must have shared. It was something her new friend hadn't told her about yet and Charlie hadn't dared to ask, afraid that the fragile and fantastic bubble of their friendship, the dream her life had become since the day she'd first stepped into Joshua's studio, might burst and leave her once again alone.

She shifted the big *Mamiya* camera body to her other hand, cursing herself for getting caught this way. Now she would really be late. *But they can't start without him either. One more minute, just to be sure.* Her mind came back to the Campaign. She'd been very careful to keep a smooth and even balance but sometimes she was overwhelmed by all she was seeing, learning, being. She'd had no idea the level at which Joshua, Phoena, Solipsum and even Elora operated, how far and fast they pushed themselves, like it was the most natural thing in the world. *They're people of excellence, Charlie.* Then a tiny voice inside her said, *Just like you.*

She figured she'd given him enough time but kicked a rock, just to be sure, listening to it click-clack as it skipped and diminished. As she focused on the sound, all her thoughts slowly fell away, and she gazed at the Station as a newborn, feeling its life, alien and somehow warm, its soul comprised of the billion passings, the petals of soft emotion adrift on a current of decades, circling, intermingling, fusing as their resonances, still strong, slowly died and dissipated.

"Charlie, is that you?"

A figure carefully picked its way towards her through the rubble of Station slough. She watched as the slender form resolved, intermittent highlights gleaming along the length of the girl's pleather clad legs.

"So was that a peak experience?" Charlie asked.

Quinby's face was unreadable in the murky light. "You saw that?"

"Just the last bit."

Quinby tugged on the laces X-ing up the front of her low-hipped pants and Charlie could faintly see the small and helpless smile playing at the corners of the other girl's mouth. "What can I say? He's like a drug."

"I know it's none of my business but—"

"What about Jane?" Quinby sighed. "She'd kill him if she found out. Or at least try to. But that man and me go back to long before I ever met her. I thought I'd gotten him out of my system but I guess there are just some things you can never rid yourself of." She was silent for a moment, then asked "Have you been out on the streets yet? Seen our stuff?"

"No. Too busy."

Quinby smiled. "The shots are just about everywhere. They're the coolest thing ever."

"Maybe I'll go after we're done down here."

"Which with any luck will be soon." The model tossed her hair, the short blond bob matted and truculent, hating the heat. "Hey Charlie, remember that day we met? At the Club?"

"Of course."

"You've come a long way since then, haven't you?"

"Yeah, I guess."

"And you've been so much fun to work with."

"Thanks. You too."

"But he still doesn't really notice you yet, does he?"

"Who do you mean?"

Quinby's teeth flashed briefly in the dimness. "I think *that's* one person I would definitely describe as a plateau experience."

"I—I wouldn't know."

Quinby laughed. "Whatever." Then she pointed to the flicker of illumination in the distance. "Better hurry. I think they're starting."

Solipsum strode onto the set, resplendent and kingly, the only anom-aly that his large ribbed codpiece was slightly askew.

Stone's eyes were ice. "Go see Sindra in make-up. That fake lash is on the wrong eye. And get rid of that thing around your neck." He then looked at the people surrounding him. "Has anyone seen Charlie?"

"But I always wear this."

Joshua turned back to the model, surprised at the interruption. "It doesn't fit. Get rid of it. Please."

Solipsum tramped off, leather creaking.

Phoena covered a smirk. *Oh, Trey, bet you didn't like that.*

Then she remembered that she too wore something around her neck, something she also wore always. Even when she slept.

Over by the craft table, Molasses was busy guarding the food, a "dog fuck" job if ever there was one. He munched on a candy bar, dripping sweat, trying to look alert and failing miserably. The furtive rustling noises came again, closer this time. He chose to ignore them. It seemed the homeless were not yet hungry enough to risk a full frontal assault. He skinned another candy bar and wiped the sweat from his brow as he shoved the log of pseudo-chocolate into his mouth. He chewed away, idly inspecting the words on the wrapper.

HEROIN™
"just one taste!"

Ingredients: Hey, you, Fat Fuck! Know what's in here? Sugar! That's right, Sugar, Sugar and more Sugar! The most addictive substance in the Universe! The Fifth Food Group! Oh sure, there's fructose, glucose, dex-trose, and a bunch of other shit you can't pronounce in here but who's kidding who, this little nugget of good-ness is nothing more than a whopping cavity-causing wrapperful of Sugar! Colorfully packaged, of course, because, hey, you gotta get the dumb monkey's atten-tion somehow, don't cha? Because if you don't turn on the blinking light, the monkey just keeps jerking off, don't it? So enjoy, fat boy! I'll see you again in five minutes. When you're jonesin' for another hit!

He was still chewing when he heard the raised voice coming from behind a rack of clothes.

"Where did it go?"

Then the sounds of smashing bottles and tiny breakings as the top of a make-up table was swept clean.

Molasses instantly recognized Solipsum's voice and stepped closer to the wardrobe picket.

"Are you crazy?" Sindra squealed. "What do you think you are doing?"

"My key. I just left it here. Did you take it?"

"Me? Why would I want that thing?"

"Then I will rip this place apart until I—"

A walkie talkie crackled and all three heard Russ' voice. "Mr. Solipsum? We need you on set. Now."

"I will be there shortly."

"Please hur—" his voice was cut off.

"That radio is always supposed to be on! Joshua will hear about this," the make-up artist finished.

"Turn the radio back on. After I leave. And if you find that key, you will be rewarded. Amply." Molasses could hear the effort in the model's voice.

"I will look. That is all I can promise."

The sound of boot steps came closer and Molasses dashed back to the craft table, wheezing with the sudden effort. He just had time to notice the whole thing had been picked clean before homeless hands reached out of the black and grabbed him.

Charlie finally found them and handed Joshua his camera. He took it without a word, without even looking at her. *Fuck, he's pissed* she thought before backing away to watch him work. Joshua then fired through twenty rolls and three lens changes in less than half an hour. She could feel the awe rising and glanced over at Russ, to see by his expression that he was similarly affected. Joshua's shooting style was probably where it ended for him but Charlie herself was feeling more. Much more. *God,* she thought, *even though he's mad as hell he looks so sexy down here. That beautiful black and velvet skin, those gleaming muscles. I wonder if he's seen the "Platinum?" Polaroid yet? Whoa, Cherry Cora, don't go off the deep end. If he sees it, great, maybe things will go further. But there's just way too much stuff to deal with right now for you to be acting like some lovesick schoolgirl.*

She brought herself back to the Now, where the action continued fast and furious as Joshua nailed shot after shot. Phoena, Solipsum, Golfillo and Vera all moved as if choreographed, so smooth was their interaction, so fearless their willingness to inhabit the characters the Clothes asked them to be. Solipsum glanced at her briefly and Charlie was startled to find that she'd been so absorbed by his posing, she'd forgotten he was posing. *Damn, he's good! They all are. But him and Phoena especially. It's like watching the weirdest, coolest movie ever, with no idea how it's going to end.* She focused on the two models, on the almost palpable exchange of energy that crackled in the air between them. She watched the way their eyes locked, their hands gripped, the way their torsos touched and ground, finally realizing that Phoena was driven by a sexual hatred so powerful it was like a sun, the only thing keeping her in check the opposing black gravity of Solipsum's intensity. She noticed Joshua lift his face from the viewfinder for a second and rapidly blink his eyes. Then he began shooting again. Her awareness expanded to include the camera's click and whir, the flash in synch with that sound, the clean geometry and compositional perfection that presented every time the shutter dilated, line intersecting/becoming/extending into line and plane and highlight and shadow, finally realizing the defining element of the whole chaotic dance was Joshua, the firmament in which his stars shone, the dance so fluid it could only be understood through photographic vivisection, slices of Now as thin as theory, wide as the gateways to Other Worlds.

Joshua finally handed his camera back to her and took the ice tea she offered him. His eyes met hers and he hesitated, as though he were about to ask something and had thought better of it. His throat worked as he gulped before passing the bottle back to her. Then he reached for his camera, turning it every which way, inspecting it, the muscles in his arm rippling as he finally lifted it high, looking up into the viewfinder before lowering it to his side where it hung from his hand like a toy.

"Charlie, did you see anything—weird—when we were shooting?"

She glanced at Vera and Golfillo. "Define weird."

"Something that isn't . . ." He stopped himself. "Never mind. Do me a favor and check the glass on this viewfinder. I think it may be smudged or something. Then meet me at the next location. The Twins are already there." He strode away, the three lighting assistants scrambling to keep up.

Charlie and Russ found themselves alone by the equipment table.

"Hey, Charlie?"

"Yeah, Russ?"

"Not 'Hornblower'?"

Charlie felt herself flush. "I'm sorry about that."

"Yeah, well, at least they don't say it to my face. Not if they know what's good for them." He sighed and mopped his brow. "Hot as fuck down here."

Charlie nodded in agreement. The heat down here *was* incredible, breathing a chest motion that gave no sense of air actually coming in and out, only liquid being stirred. Without really thinking, she lifted the bottom of her shirt and toweled her face, much to Russ's surprised delight. He found himself so very aware of how the sweat highlighted the muscles of her abdomen, the lower curves of her breasts. Then she dropped her shirt and he saw the dragon tattooed on her shoulder. He was struck again by how familiar it seemed, as though he had seen it somewhere before. No, not seen . . . heard of.

Charlie pushed her hair back, watching Russ for a moment as he picked up a lens. He seemed very far away as he began cleaning it. She watched his hands working the cloth over the delicate optics, then went back to logging the film.

"Russ?"

"Yeah?"

"Can I ask you something?"

"Shoot."

"Why didn't you break my nose? Or worse?"

He glanced up from the camera body he was now cleaning and she saw for an instant what he must have looked like as a child.

"Two reasons." He set the body down. "One, 'cause it was enough to know I could have. And two? 'Cause you're good, Charlie. Really good. I've been doing this since I was a kid and I know a lot. But you fight in a style I've never seen." His eyes slid away, uncharacteristically shy. "I was hoping maybe you could show me—"

Charlie shook her head. "I'm sorry, Russ, but there's no way. I swore an oath when I started."

He felt the anger rising until he remembered his own oath. "You got a boyfriend, Charlie?" He gave the camera a short burst of compressed air.

"No. No one right now."

"Do you wanna go on a date?"

Her eyes went to the film log, then she forced herself to look at him. "Russ, I could tell you it's cause I just broke up with someone. But I won't lie. Y—you're just not my type. But I respect you. A lot. Can we maybe be friends?"

His shoulders slumped. "What's wrong with me? We'd make a great team."

"No," Charlie said with finality. "I'm sorry."

"It's Joshua, isn't it? *He's* your type."

"Russ—"

"I've seen the way you look at him. Very professional."

"As professional as the way you look at those models? The way you look at me?"

"Hey! That's just—appreciation."

"Bullshit, Russell! Bullshit! See? *That's* why we'll never go out. It's just so sad, you know? Someone with all your talents and abilities, you could have anyone, not just me. If only you learned to let go, it would all come to you."

"I don't get it." he said, completely baffled.

"And you probably never—"

"What's taking you two?" Joshua asked as he joined them. "We've got three more shots."

"Just cleaning this, sir." Russ held up the viewfinder. "You were right, it's real dirty down here and we want to make sure you've got clear optics."

"Good work. Is everything ready?"

"Yes, sir."

"Then let's go. And hey," he paused, "it's nice to see you two getting along." He turned and strode off, his lighting phalanx falling in behind him. Charlie and Russ looked at each other briefly, then grabbed the gear and quickly followed.

Safron and Sable huddled beneath a massive crumbling archway, dressed in vintage lingerie. Their raspberry red hair had been back-combed into frizzy explosions that framed their porcelain faces, doll-eyes huge and wide-spaced above their petal mouths. Charlie found them strangely compelling, so slender and pale and gangly limbed, their breasts like buds about to burst from slender branch, the intertwining of their bodies as instinctive and intimate as the secret movement of plants at night. They peered about at the opulent decay of the Station, at the slow weep of city body-fluids, the colored flashes washing their faces as lighting gels were tested. *My Life With Thrill Kill Kult* boomed from deeper within the Station like the heartbeat of a distant rave.

Stone was still determining angles and light placement. "Over there," he pointed, "closer to the wall." One of the lighting assistants moved to comply, gingerly stepping over an old typewriter. He was still looking back at Joshua when the cable snagged his foot. With a cry he collapsed, his power pack smashing to the ground, capacitors instantly discharging a huge and powerful burst. Joshua was caught in the sidelight, half his face flaring out to phosphorous white, the other side unaffected, his silhouette stark against the lucent rock face. A huge shadow, mutinous and warped, spilled from his body like blood to claw its way up the wall beside him. Charlie almost dropped the camera case as the image seared itself into her visual cortex like a negative burned onto glass.

"Let's get that fixed! We're running behind!" Stone's voice cut through the sudden blackness. And Charlie wondered if she was the only one who had just seen what she had just seen.

Russ pulled out a maglight and replaced the flash tube as someone ran for another pack. "Okay! Let's roll!" Stone yelled. The delay had lasted only ten minutes. Charlie handed him his favorite camera and he slowly approached the Twins. They watched him carefully, like does poised on the edge of flight. Safron whispered something in her sister's ear. Sable giggled, then touched Safron's belly and rubbed it, as if for luck. She found her sister's hand and both their arms slowly rose, palms pressed. A languid pirouette and Sable dropped backwards into Safron's waiting embrace, leg kicked to the vertical. And thus it began . . .

". . . move, strike a pose and cant that hip, slide a glance, don't let her slip, just kiss her cheek then spin and leer, be brazen, feel the Station, what's she whispering in your ear? is it love? is it death? is it dream? is it fear? let me see it, past the glass with those big blue eyes, that's it, push her close, let her body touch yours while you freeze! that's the shot! give me more, push it more, now break it and change, something totally new while I get more film, yes, black and white and switch this lens to the fifty no the eighty are we ready to go? let's roll! all right, do the reading first, from her skin, not the room, are we ready to go? then fix that hair, bigger hair 'cause she's crouching low, that's great Safron! leg up higher, thrust that hip, fix her bra strap, not her lips, leave her face, leave the make-up, let it do what it wants!"

It began to run, the heavy black liner and eye shadow streaming now in the heat as Sable and Safron played, played, played off each other in posturings strange and provocative, faster and faster, Joshua firing away, talking mostly by body now, thrusting his will through the optics of the lens.

Then through the viewfinder, the world
shifted
and he suddenly *saw* ghostly layerings of faces, solarized and elongated as time decelerated, sometimes behind, sometimes through the twins strange lingerie *pas de deux*. Their shadows detached and came alive, dancing and capering like spirits from the Pit as the three assistants moved their lights in strange and instinctive syncopation to Joshua and *Carmina Burana*, which played now deep and ominous. The operetta built to a thunderous crescendo, the girls' frenzied posing cresting higher and higher, tension mounting until they became entangled and

fell in a heap to the gritty floor. The music was pounding, Joshua stepping closer to their supine bodies, already switching film backs, dark
slide glinting as he tossed it aside. His eye came back like a hungry
mouth, quickly jammed to the viewfinder teat, not wanting to miss a
thing, not even aware how very like a drug this was. Then he felt it again,
the moth wing beating at the backs of his eyes, the tiny voice whispering
i'll show you, i'll show you but only if you let me . . .

He opened himself up to it.

The world blossomed into Sable Lee astraddle her sister, back arched,
a chunk of masonry in both hands, grinning at the camera, mouth a demon rictus as she brought the rock down on her sister's lolling head.

"STOP!" Joshua screamed as he ripped his face from the viewfinder.

Who would ever know if Sable would have done it? The rock fell
from her lifeless hands, and she stared at them all in a daze. Then she
gently took her sister's face and cupped it, murmuring softly.

Charlie watched, still too stunned to move as Joshua hurried over and
helped them both to their feet. The girls seemed shaken and hugged each
other tearfully. Charlie had almost convinced herself that what she had
just seen wasn't an act when they began laughing, even as their tears
streamed. Wardrobe personnel scooted over with robes and led the
two away as dim worklights flickered on. Just before they disappeared
she saw Solipsum looking at them as though they were food. Then he
glanced at Joshua and a shiver ran down her spine, for coiled in that gaze
was the pre-determined knowledge of what they had all just seen. That
and something of the way a pusher would look at a schoolyard. *What
the hell just happened?* But by then Joshua was already marshalling his
crew, his eyes bomb-blasted.

"That was simply—amazing. Let's all meet by the Fountain in fifteen
minutes."

Then he strode off to follow the Twins.

Charlie was reloading the last back when the hand grabbed her from
behind. She almost screamed, spinning about, back fist launched, pulling
it just in time. "Molasses! Godammit, don't do that!"

"Sorry, Charlie. I didn't mean to scare you." There was a strange light
in his eyes. "Here." He placed something in her hand.

"What's this?"

"Some homeless people gave it to me. They said it was important,
that I had to get it to you."

Charlie looked down at the small black key nestled in her palm like
a dead bird's foot. It was one of the weirdest things she'd ever seen. Her

eyes went to Molasses again and she noticed his shirt had been ripped, his watch was gone and that he looked like he'd been rolling in the filth everyone else was trying so hard to avoid. He was also terrified.

"Are you okay?"

"Yeah." He gazed down at himself, as if noticing his condition for the first time. "Yeah, I'm fine. In fact, I've never been better. I think." Then he raised his head, eyes shining with that same strange light. "They're not stupid, you know. They see everything. Everything." He wiped his hands on the sides of his legs. "I have to go now." With that, he turned and walked away.

She looked again at the weirdling key and knew immediately to whom it belonged.

New York City, Stone Studios, Darkroom A—The Campaign of The Century—Day 182

Charlie was in an old t-shirt and jeans, developing prints in the lo-tech darkroom. "Lo-Tek" had already become her favorite. Like most darkrooms, it was actually painted white, to maximize the bounce of the orange safeties. The dark part came because the room was light-tight, black as the inside of a camera when the lights did go out.

Not only was it homey and intimate, Joshua's Bruun Polaroid collection was taped to the back of the door. It still filled Charlie with delight. There were so many crazy, goofy portraits you could almost do a book. The poor animal looked so tolerant in some of them, it still made her laugh. Her eyes traveled over the door again, pausing to linger on a series of three Polaroids where huge cloth flowers sat on his little head like Easter bonnets, their ribbons tied beneath his chin. But the one that probably took the kibble showed him standing on his two hind legs, eyes aglow with reflected flash. Someone had cut holes in a stocking and pulled it up over his torso so all the fur was compressed and he looked like some sort of sausage-cat.

She saw her "Platinum?" Polaroid tacked above the sink and wondered if Joshua had seen it yet. *Probably not,* she thought. But just the idea that he may have gave her a strange and delicious shivery feeling. She glanced back at the timer to see a minute had almost elapsed. Her attention then returned to the sheet of fiberbase paper floating in the tray of developer as one of the aspects she loved most about photography began. She adjusted the glasses she wore for close work then watched as the slow gauzy curtain drew back, and whatever Joshua had seen through the window of his viewfinder emerged, distantly. Detail resolved as silver halide traceries branched and gapped like black frost, filling, shading, then interacting with her mind as pattern recognition set in.

Will you look at that!

She quickly moved the print to the stop bath, instantly freezing the developer's action. The orange safelights prevented her from seeing exactly what Joshua had done but there was definitely something in the image that was not there when he'd shot it.

She rocked the tray for thirty seconds, then moved the print to the final solution, the fix. She waited impatiently for the chemical to affect, then snapped the lights on. And gasped.

Oh my God! How the hell did he do this?

She lifted the print with a set of tongs and studied it in the now white room light. It was from the series of Solipsum, that skinny pimp from Mexico and the hefty girl, Vera. Behind them all was a face, barely visible and solarized. Wherever they touched it, a strange negative overlay occurred. It was simply stunning.

This—this must *be digital. There's no other explanation. And whose face is that? I know the whole cast and this isn't any of them.*

She absently cleaned her glasses, then studied the overlap of face and bodies, letting her eyes defocus. Slowly, the face began to emerge, changing even as her mind grasped at it, the face now one she almost recognized, the personification of some

(dowager empress)

thing and then her eyes refocused and the moment disappeared. She clutched her head as a wave of dizziness came, hands slamming down to grip the sink's edge and steady the room. She saw the print swimming before her and waited a moment before leaning closer to peer at its tight grain structure. To her disbelieving eyes, she could find no evidence of digital manipulation.

Still peering, she thumbed the intercom and was about to speak when a thought hit her. *Oh God, if I call him in here, I know he'll see the Platinum? Polaroid. And with me in here too, I'll die of embarrassment. Maybe I should take it down.* She shifted her eyes from print to Polaroid. *No, Cherry Cora, you promised yourself that it would stay up until he had seen it, and if that happens while you're in the room, that's just too bad. Call him. Because what you just saw in that print is way more important than your silly Polaroid.* She thumbed the switch again. "Joshua, can you come up here for a minute?"

"What is it?"

"There's something you have to see."

"On my way."

Charlie's eyes were drawn back to the mysterious image, the Polaroid momentarily forgotten. *How the hell did he do this?*

She had pulled two more prints from the series when Joshua stepped into the darkroom.

"What's up?"

Charlie leaned over the sink in a way he tried not to notice. "Take a look at this."

He joined her and she held the print out for him to see. He spread his feet a bit and took it in his hands, elbows on the sink's edge as he leaned forward. Charlie suddenly became aware of how close they stood to each other, so close she could scent him. She was just beginning to wonder what that scent would be like if he exerted himself when her thoughts were interrupted by Joshua's low whistle.

"This is unbelievable."

His eyes traveled over the print, mind reeling because what he was seeing was exactly what he had seen through the viewfinder. His heart began to pound so loudly he wondered if Charlie could hear.

"Joshua? That's one of the most stunning effects I've ever seen. How did you do it?"

Stone knew she was not playing a trick, and that as much as he refused to believe what was right there in front of him, it remained right there in front of him.

Charlie looked at him, waiting for his answer, wondering why he hesitated when suddenly it hit her. She had crossed a line, had asked for instead of waiting to be given.

"Joshua, I—I'm sorry. I didn't mean for you to show me one of your special secrets. It's just that—"

"I can't tell you how I did this yet. Soon, but not yet." He turned to her, his expression grave. "Charlie, no one is to know about this. And I mean no one."

"I won't tell a soul."

"Good. Get Sindra on the phone. And book the Twins. We'll need Constance and di Milo as well. I want everyone in the main shooting area in one hour. Do we still have clothes here?"

"Tons. What kind of film do you want?"

"No film. I want this all digital." *Let's see if this works by itself.* "Page me when you're done in here and I'll give you the lighting instructions."

Then he left without another word. Charlie closed the door and felt a lump in her throat, her eyes moistening. *Good work, Cherry Cora. Not only did he not see your Polaroid, now he probably thinks you're trying to steal his secrets. What a wonderful seduction this is turning out to be!* She sniffed and rubbed her eyes. *Okay. Back to work. I'm pretty sure I caught him looking at my bum so things can't be that bad.* She smiled a bit at that thought as she straightened the "Platinum?" Polaroid. Then she hung the last print up to dry, and with a mixture of dread and fascination, prepared the negatives of the Twins.

New York City, Midtown—The Campaign of The Century—Day 185

Phoena looked up at the sky for a moment as she and her friend walked the streets of New York. The day was brisk and overcast when Charlie had called her and she hadn't really felt like going out. But now, she reluctantly conceded, it had probably been a good idea. The cool fall air seemed to be working wonders for her clarity of mind.

What is wrong with me lately? Why do I feel so—not myself? She lightly touched the metal fragment that hung about her throat, barely aware that she had even done so. *With freedom and more money than I know what to do with just around the corner, I should be happy. As happy as the Chipper One over there.*

She glanced at Charlie and marveled for an instant at how circumstance and chemistry had forged in the crucible of the Campaign a friendship she never thought she would experience again. If truth be told, she now found it more comfortable to be with Charlie than to be alone, more than a little because the young girl helped distract her from Solipsum.

Charlie skipped along, living from one puddle to the next, just splashing through the streets. She wore her favorite skirt, parrot green and white plaid, with leggings and short white rubber booties. The little raincoat Phoena had given her fit perfectly and the cable-knit mohair sweater did a good job of keeping the cold at bay. She touched the collar of her coat and remembered when Phoena had told her that she looked "effortlessly fashionable," whatever *that* meant. She had to admit that she was starting to like clothes, and that it was okay to dress up. Sometimes. Getting a little dirty in the pursuit of fun, however, was way more important than running around like the Virgin of Immaculate Fashion.

She had rarely been so excited in her young life. To see all these amazing images everywhere and to have taken part in their creation, it was like the photo shoots had never ended, like all the fun, sexy energy was still there for her to grab onto every time she saw a billboard. Especially when Phoena was in one of them. She peeked over at her friend, who seemed a little tired today. Probably just drained from all the shooting. She watched Phoena's beautiful legs scissor as she walked, and with that limousine black raincoat, the ribbed black stretch pants, patent *Miu Miu* boots and black turtleneck of some mysterious fabric, she could be on a runway in Paris or something. Charlie then focused on Phoena's face, how her pulled back and ponytailed hair emphasized a bone structure she still couldn't quite believe. She'd had lots of time to study that face and had yet to tire of it. In fact, she didn't think such a thing was possible. It was strange for her to be with someone who so constantly made her aware of light and angle, especially someone whom she liked so much. *I have to ask her to shoot when all this is done.* She swung a leg and skimmed another puddle. *I wonder if I should ask her for some "Platinum" advice. But she looks so down today, maybe I should cheer her up first.*

The young assistant stopped and pointed. "Look, Phoena! There you are!"

They both stared at the enormous billboard on Broadway.

"Wow! It looks amazing! You look amazing! God, Phoena, don't you get a rush just seeing yourself up there?"

"Yes." Phoena's voice was low. She looked down, smiled a bit, then her eyes found Charlie's. "Yes, I do. It's still something pretty special. But . . ."

Charlie frowned, puzzled. "Are you okay?"

"I'm fine. Just a bit drained from all the shooting. Come on. Let's go get some lunch."

They turned to leave, surprised to see a small crowd had gathered, easing their way through the people as several stared in obvious recognition. Then it was up Broadway, Phoena and Campaign billboards everywhere, Charlie pointing them out like a child on safari. "Look, there's another one! And over there. God, they're everywhere!"

"Yes. Yes they are. That's—" Phoena never finished what she was about to say. They had reached Times Square and had stopped to stare as something slowly and miraculously unfolded. Its centerpiece was a massive forty story vertical billboard that dominated the sky before them: Phoena and Solipsum's faces staring out at the world and inviting the world in. It was nearly complete and workmen on a crane-lifted platform guided the insertion of the final piece. Pressing in on either side were tall buildings whose walls and windows had been LCD'd and fiber-optically linked so they behaved like giant slide projectors. A slow progression of images passed and bracketed the enormous face. Between these, twelve other cranes lifted panels into conventionally-sized horizontal billboard slots. On the sidewalk and street, hundreds of other campaign images suddenly burst into visual bloom, pedestrians in t-shirts, cabs with roof signs, bus shelters, telephone booths and bike messengers all seemed to wear some sort of Campaign image or a fragment of one. And no one was aware of how everyone else was similarly branded.

As they watched, the final Phoena corner piece clicked home. At that exact instant, something that defied belief moved to the surface of their perception. Like some enormous visual symphony reaching its crescendo, every image they saw suddenly, jarringly, coalesced perfectly

into one master photograph

that was gone as quickly as it had appeared. And you were left standing on the tanker's deck, knowing you were the only one who had glimpsed the leviathan, a thing not supposed to exist, beautiful and extraordinary, its enormity dwarfed by the implication of its existence. And it had just shown itself to you.

And only to you.

They stood in silence as the magical instant replayed over and over in their minds. Charlie could still see them, breaking apart like an ice flow. "Oh my God, that's the most incredible thing I've ever seen. Phoena, did you *see* that?"

"Yeah. Yeah, I did. And you're right, Charlie. It was incredible. But—" Phoena looked frustrated, and more than a little sad. "—that's the plan," she finished quietly.

"Phoena, pardon me for mentioning this but you are being such a wet blanket. You should be so proud of what you've done."

"Why?"

"What do you mean, 'why'?"

"Why, Charlie? Why should I be so proud of what I've done?"

"Well, because—"

"What have I done, really?"

Charlie was brought up short." I don't know how to describe it. You're—beautiful—and with these ads up everywhere, you—share that with people."

"And that's an achievement?"

"Yes, godammit, it is! There are people out there who would give their lives to be in your shoes! You should be—"

"Grateful?"

Charlie was almost crying. "I was going to say happy."

"Oh, come here." Phoena hugged her for a long moment. "Let me tell you a bit about this thing we call Beauty."

They continued walking.

"Take a look at some of these other billboards. See that guy there?"

Charlie saw a beautiful male body, prime beefcake with lots of digital gravey. "The hottie in the underwear?"

"Yeah. Beautiful, isn't he?"

"Hell, yes! I'd go there in a nanosecond!"

Phoena looked at her friend and said very carefully, "His name is Matt and since he shot that campaign, he's tried to kill himself twice."

Charlie stopped and stared. "What?"

"Seems he can't come to terms with the fact he had to blow four Italian playboys after losing a drinking competition."

A vivid picture popped into the young assistant's mind. "You've got to be kidding!"

Phoena was already pointing to another billboard. "See that girl? Her name's Fawn. She's not even twenty and already a heroin addict. Got sucked in to trying something all the adults seemed to be enjoying and now she's a junkie. Wonder what her mother thinks of her little superstar now?"

The model pointed again and again to various billboards and bus shelters as they walked.

"Klepto. Nympho. Sexually abused. Bulimic. Raped in a washroom by some fifty year-old Italian businessman when she was fourteen. Closet case. Crack head. Pimped-off by her wannabe mother. That one started in a small Russian town and is now up to the triple digits of people she's slept with. She picked up AIDS7 last year and is in total denial, still screwing away like it's the last day on Earth. And, oh! An anomaly! Someone normal. But back we go again. That one's had more cosmetic surgery than half of Beverly Hills. And her. She used to be a he."

"My God, Phoena, stop!" Charlie's hands flew up to cover her ears. "My head is reeling!"

Phoena gripped her friend's arms, feeling the muscles striate as she tried to pull them down.

"Listen, it's not as bad as I'm making it out to be, but in no way is our reality the fantasy everyone mistakes it for."

Charlie felt a rush of anger that made her want to lash out, a basic touchstone of her reality disappearing beneath some dirty floodwater of deception. "How can you all be so fucked up? It's not supposed to be that way!"

"Because we're beautiful?"

"Yes! No! God, I don't know."

Phoena let go of Charlie's arms. She slowed things down then, trying to compress a lifetime's experience into something her friend would understand.

"Let me ask you a question. Do you think that just because someone's beautiful, they have it easy? I'll tell you a truth. Everyone has problems. Everyone has issues. And Beautiful People? We often times have more than most. Way more. Why? 'Cause we're preyed upon. And 'cause nearly all of us are lazy, indolent creatures used to getting the cream."

They walked in silence for a block as Charlie thought about this. Phoena kept glancing at her, hoping she hadn't gone too far. She finally pulled the young girl into a restaurant where they were quickly seated at a table by the front window with a view of Times Square. They ordered a light lunch, occasionally looking at the massive Phoena/Solipsum Campaign of The Century billboard and the ever-increasing crowd gathering below it. Shoppers walked past, some clutching bags with Campaign images on them under a sky as gray as their lives.

Their food arrived and Charlie still hadn't said a word. Phoena sighed and laid her fork down beside the uneaten salad.

"The two kind of go hand in hand. It starts when you learn that people will give you things from a very young age, just because of how you look. They're always telling you how pretty you are, like it's an actual concrete achievement, not just the hand you've been dealt. But most want something in return. And it's usually a piece of you, be it in the form of your company, your time, or your body. Usually all three. You get to a point where the only inner strength you develop is based on your ability to barter. Your ability to give up the least of you while gaining the most money, prestige, fame, fun, whatever. You have to decide: how much of me am I going to give up to get what I want? How much of me am I going to let them own? And we own things by either killing them or fucking them."

"Or taking a picture of them." Charlie finally spoke.

Phoena sat back, startled.

"Point," she said thoughtfully.

A face suddenly pressed up against the glass, lighting up in recognition. A man waved his arms, trying to catch her eye.

Phoena ignored him.

"Look at that guy staring at us. What is he looking at? Me? What's me? How could he possibly know me? We've never met, yet because he's seen my image, my manipulated image in a context that has caused him to buy something, he feels we have a connection. He's bought, i.e. given, and now he wants something in return. And God help us if he's ever jerked off to one of my pictures because then there's a sexual connection."

The man had been getting progressively more frustrated. He finally gave her the finger, mouthed the word "bitch," and stormed off.

"Where did you learn all this?" Charlie asked, a piece of strawberry shortcake poised at her mouth.

"At the University of Phoena. My own life experience. The stories I could tell you . . ."

Before she could finish, an extremely striking man with close cropped hair of iron and a deep tan stopped abruptly at their table. He was dressed in a style evolved so far beyond the cutting edge it was like looking at a living magazine page.

"Phoena! I thought that was you."

She brought a hand to her face and rolled her eyes at Charlie.

"Wow, babe, you are all over town, aren't you? May I?"

He sat down and joined them so smoothly it was a second before either girl realized the other hadn't invited him. Then he looked the little blond slice of breakfast cake up and down and asked, "Who are you?"

"My name's Charlie."

"Oh! Joshua's new assistant. I had no idea you were so pretty. You could be a model."

Charlie tried to look polite. She had heard this before. "I don't think so . . . I like what I do."

A satisfied smile crept over Phoena's face. "Charlie, this is Swinington Marzoopiel, stylist extraordinaire."

"I prefer the term 'Image Consultant'."

"We are all so particular about what strata of whoredom we currently occupy, aren't we?" she replied sweetly.

"That's a bit harsh, isn't it?"

Phoena leaned forward. "Yes, Swinnie, it is. Sorry, but I'm all of a sudden so sensitive to the whole Beauty Machine of late."

"And what a powerful machine it is."

"Yes. But pressed into the service of what?"

"Why, Style, of course. What else?"

"Ah, Style. Mass Consumed Style, the plague of the 21st century. So much of what's fucked up with this world can be directly related to Style. And we're smack in the middle of it. We machine the Dream that's so unattainable. We lathe, knurl, extrude, chrome and buff it 'til it's so edible chewable you just want to bite down and see if it delivers. But for some reason it's always like biting into a piece of chocolate with the tinfoil still stuck to it, and what you thought you owned ends up owning *you*."

Swinington sat back and stretched out his legs. "That's pretty bleak, Phoena. We all know what's going on but what would you have us do? I love my job, I love new things. I never tire of them. I love everything about the world of Fashion, from the clothes to the make-up to the models to the glamour. The magic of it—the sheer—thing-i-ness of it."

"Jesus, Swinington, so do I. But there comes a time when you have to step back and just—stop."

"Why?"

"Because we're killing the planet! We're killing ourselves!"

"Fuck the planet. It's doomed anyway. We may as well enjoy what's left."

"No, Swinington, fuck you!" She waved a fork, having no idea how it got into her hand. "We created this mess. We have to find a way to make it right."

He thrust his face into hers, a powerful hand gripping her forearm. "Wake-up, you silly bitch! There's no right or wrong. There's just *this*. That's it. You can't change the world. It's impossible. Besides, who are you to talk, with your picture plastered all over New York? I think that Joshua has surpassed even his highest expectations with this Campaign. I've never seen anything like it. And you're one of its centerpieces. What message are you sending? Where is your personal responsibility? You want to talk about power? Take a look outside." He pointed to the massive billboard and the large crowd beneath it. "That's power. That's juju even I wouldn't fuck with. And power in the service of what? Elevating the human condition? Give me a break! It's power in the service of Style. Which is just another partymask worn by Mammon."

"Who's Mammon?" asked Charlie, looking away from the shard at Phoena's throat.

He smiled coldly. "The Money God, dear child. Before whose altar we *all* bow at the end of the day. Phoena . . ." His eyes softened. "There are billions of them out there. Billions. How are you going to change them all? Eh? How?"

"I—don't know. But there has to be a way," knowing even as she finished she wasn't sure if she believed this herself anymore.

Swinington rose to leave. "Well, good luck. I certainly wouldn't want to stand in your way. But for what it's worth, I've always liked you, even admired you." He paused for a moment, then sat back down. "Phoena, let me be honest. When it comes right down to it, I think you're the best that ever was. But after this one? I'd retire somewhere. Maybe by the sea. This business is tearing you apart. Maybe it's time to stop. Maybe that will be your individual contribution."

"Fuck," Phoena whispered, watching him go.

She glanced at Charlie, who didn't know what to say. She gave Phoena the last forkful of cake, then gently took her hand. They both looked out the window at the massive crowd that had now spilled out onto Broadway, blocking traffic in both directions as it stared up at Phoena's face.

Interlude One—New York

Connie Spencer was buying her way through *Barney's*, ordering everything that caught her eye. She had already been through four floors and had spent nearly $2.5 million. She had maxed out three *Visas*, four *Gold IamYourMasterCards* and her *American Impress Black Card*. She had purchased a Finnish kitchen suite, Italian furniture, a 72 *Sony* HDTV and more clothing than most people owned in a lifetime. She had also bought a couture dress worth one year's salary. If *Barnney's* had sold cars, she would have bought one of those too. Why was she doing this? She had no idea. She couldn't quite put a finger on what had caused this sudden urge to spend, spend, spend. Maybe it had something to do with those ads *Fa-Shin, Inc.* had put up all over town. You just couldn't get away from them, could you? Though she had to admit they were kind of neat. They seemed to be trying to tell her some kind of story, but dammit, they wouldn't tell her how it ended. To know that required her participation, which meant she somehow had to get—in. The only problem was, no one had told her *how* to get in. So she fell back on what she knew, what she had always done when faced with a problem of access. She *bought* her way in.

The department store sales woman looked at her, face the very picture of regret. "I'm sorry. ma'am. This card's been declined. Do you have another?"

New York City, the Financial District—The Campaign of The Century—Day 187

Elora Gorj stared at the disturbing image propped up on an easel. She was dressed to convince today, in black slacks and a tailored shirt of watered silk, minimal make-up, her honey-colored hair carefully tied back to appear casual. She sat in the boardroom of *Fa-Shin, Inc.*, awaiting the other board members. The photograph she was staring at was powerful, sexual and disquieting in a way that was difficult for her to define. What was certain was that it was almost impossible to look away from. It was Joshua's latest Campaign image and it filled Elora with deepest satisfaction. Her reverie was disturbed by something that smelled like the floor cleaner in a whorehouse, a cologne she immediately recognized. She turned her head to see Maurice Vellum, Head of Finance—or as she had secretly come to call him, Fashion Slag. Short, squat and ugly, he wore a very expensive suit that was, of course, rumpled. She stared at him and wondered how someone so deeply ensconced in the world of fashion could hate it so vehemently. He was, however, extremely intelligent and an integral part of the company. He had also made no secret of his hatred for the Campaign from its very inception. It was a hatred he disguised about as well as the fact that he wanted to sleep with her. He had done everything in his considerable power to have the Campaign derailed—to no avail—and represented for Elora the only possible hurdle in the rubber stamp approval of the Campaign's next phase.

"What *is* this?"

"Art, Maurice. Art."

He glared at her. "No. It. Is. Not." He leaned back like his eyes had smelled something bad. "I know art when I see it and this isn't even close. It's an abomination."

"Maurice, you wouldn't know great art if it came up and punch-fucked you in your office. I told you that the deeper we got into this, the further Joshua was going to push the envelope. Now please, sit down." She moved to cover the image. "The others are coming and it wouldn't do if they thought I'd let you see something before them, now would it?"

"You'll never sell them on this, Elora."

"That's where you're wrong, Maurice. You see, even if they wanted to cut this off right now, they couldn't. If they did, I'd simply show them the data from some focus groups I've had run. Experiments using the actual images that are now running in our Campaign."

"Why? What happens when we cut them off?"

The smug line of her mouth hung suspended between two dimples. "Ever take away a junkie's stash without telling him about it? Multiply that by a factor of a thousand and you begin to get some idea of what will happen if we pull the plug."

"Your crazy! What have you done?"

She smiled sweetly, leaning forward, one hand resting on his shoulder while the other gently patted his cheek. "Changed the world, Maurice. Changed the world." Her last pat almost turned into a slap. "Trust me.

Let the Campaign run it's course and we'll be sitting on top of it all. Besides, it's too late to change a thing." Her smile became like a dare.

He was shocked by how badly he had underestimated her, finally understanding she was no longer rational, had in fact passed beyond her obsession to a place of danger and power he could not possibly assail. The only humanity left in her seemed to express itself solely in her appreciation and defense of Stone's work. And for some reason, the attraction he felt for her became even stronger. But before he could follow that thought and its implications, the board members began shuffling in.

Elora stood and immediately became the picture of expansive confidence. "Ladies. Gentlemen. Thank you for joining me today. I think what I am about to show you will change forever your perceptions of art. And advertising. Maurice? If you would be so kind?"

He cursed her silently as he closed the doors.

Venice, The Campaign of The Century—Day 190

"So, how is it going?"

"Truly, Phoena? I couldn't be happier. It's the most amazing thing I've ever done. It's as though I were born to it."

Phoena smiled then looked away for a moment to watch the crowds in San Marco Square. It was a strange and beautiful day, the sun like a yellow ember pillowed between the clouds, the light diffuse, then shockingly golden when it pierced a wispy thinness to burnish some façade or monument. She took a delicate sip of her cappuccino.

"Have you heard anything about those persistent rumors?"

"What rumors?"

"That our pictures are making people riot over the clothes."

A dark cloud passed behind Joshua's eyes. "Yes, I heard about this from Elora."

"And?"

He looked down and played with the handle of his cup for a moment. "She says it's an unexpected by-product. That it's not our pictures causing that behavior but the fact there's nothing else to look at."

"What are they going to do about it?"

"Nothing."

"What?"

"There's nothing they *can* do. Elora says we're not to worry about it, that it will go away by itself."

Phoena slumped back in her chair. "Oh great. Elora says. We should all put our faith in what that creature tells us to." She looked out at the crowds. "Wouldn't it be funny if we all just shut down?"

"What do you mean?"

"If we, and I mean the creative people, photographers, models, designers, art directors, make-up artists, wardrobe stylists, all of us, what if we simply—stopped? What would happen?"

"I don't know. We'd probably all go broke and wind up on the street. Why do you ask?"

"No reason. I just think about it sometimes."

Joshua spread his hands. "Phoena? I think it's far too late to change anything now. We have to finish the Campaign, one way or the other."

"We have to finish it because of the disgusting amounts of money they're paying us."

"That has something to do with it, but not everything. And honestly? At this stage? I could walk away from all the money because the creative satisfaction is like nothing I've ever experienced."

She gave him a small smile because she believed him. He looked very striking in his black turtleneck and yellow windbreaker, his teeth gleaming and white in the structured planes of his remarkable face. She remembered the time they'd had together, how wonderful it had been, and how badly timed, too, willing as they both had been to try almost anything once. Each had forgotten how an experience also looks into you. That thought brought her back to Milan, what had happened to her there, the thing she could never remember. Joshua seemed to read her mind.

"Phoena, these pictures we're taking far surpass anything we've ever done. I've never seen you move like this. And when you and Solipsum are together, it's simply astonishing. It's like in your joining you create some sort of heart that beats in sympathy with my own, with everybody's when they see the pictures. Why have you never shot with him before?"

"Fate."

"I don't understand."

"Joshua, we know each other well. Too well, perhaps. That's probably why I never told you about what happened between Trey and I. How can I explain this? Remember when we were shooting in Paris and we saw that extraordinarily beautiful man walking the street? Do you remember what you said to me?"

"Wouldn't you want to spend the rest of your life with him?"

"And how did I respond?"

The corners of his eyes crinkled as he remembered. "You laughed and said 'Never in a million years! But I would spend a 'lost weekend' with him.'"

"That's sort of what Trey and I shared. An—extended 'lost weekend'. And that time colors everything between us. That, and how it ended." She took his hands in hers. "That's all I can tell you for now. But I promise, when all this is over, you'll know the whole story. Deal?"

Joshua hesitated for a moment, saw in her eyes that she was poised on the edge, wanting him to push her further, terrified of what she would re-live if she told this story now. Then he remembered The Campaign. He gently rubbed his thumbs over the backs of her hands, feeling their smoothness, memories brought back by the texture of her skin, even as he decided to betray his intuition, to betray them both and let the Campaign have its way.

"Let's let sleeping dogs lie. But I do want to know what happened, after this is all over. Promise?"

He saw uncertainty, then relief flash in her eyes. "Promise." She pulled him to his feet. "Come on! I want to take a gondola ride."

Joshua dropped some bills on the table, Phoena tugging on his arm. Then they hurried across the Square.

Interlude Two—London

Huge cubes were being erected in a massive indoor mall space at Canary Wharf. They featured a stunning array of images from the new campaign by *Fa-Shin, Inc.*

Nigel Bracken, head of Mall Security, stared on and wondered what the Yanks thought they were up to this time.

Crazy Bastards! Look at this stuff. Just when I think there's nothing original left to come out of that place, they come up with this. How those buggers got this by the Board, I'll never know.

He hitched his belt and watched as Langdon Gentry, Chief Custodian, approached. " 'ello, Nigel."

He raised a hand in greeting to the old man. "Gentry. How's by you?"

"Splendid, Squire, splendid. Except for that." He pointed to the massive cube display that was almost fully erected. "*That* spells trouble."

"Ahh, Gentry, it's just more Yank fluff."

Langdon shook his head in disagreement. "Don't count on it, Guv. This is different. I kin feel it."

Nigel's interest quickened. The last time "Landed" Gentry had a "feeling," Mall Security discovered a massive credit card scam involving £500 disposable *Gotta Have it Now!* cards. The subsequent arrests had made the front pages of five daily papers. His salary had as a conseuqence tripled.

"Do tell."

Langdon squinted at the cubes with distaste. "There's something about them . . ."

Nigel peered at them too, trying to figure out why they were so compelling. "Yes. They're quite powerful. I suspect we'll see a huge boost in sales. Christ, I almost feel like buying something just standing 'ere looking at them."

"That's it. That's what's bothering me. They push too bleeding hard."

Nigel turned to look at him. "Shite. You've hit it. Because if you're pushed to buy but you haven't got the means—"

Langdon Gentry finished the thought. "You steal."

Both men turn back to stare at the completed display.

New York City, Stone Studios, Darkroom A, The Campaign of The Century—Day 205

Charlie looked up at the single red bulb suspended over the trays and felt an overwhelming sense of belonging. And for some reason "Lo-Tek" felt even homier when two people were working in it.

Joshua squeegeed a print and laid it on the drying rack. He glanced at Charlie. "Isn't it about time you went home? I mean, really, it's past midnight and that cruddy old air conditioner isn't going to get fixed until tomorrow. There's no reason for both of us to work in this sauna."

She turned from the enlarging easel and wiped her brow. "Hey, it's no sweat off my back."

Joshua's eyes rolled to the ceiling.

"Ouch, bad one," she cringed.

"It *must* be getting late. Let's soak that print."

Charlie transferred a large piece of fiber-based paper limp and heavy with amniotic chemistry from fix to swirling water bath. "Can I ask you something?"

"Sure." He rested for a moment, watching Charlie work, loving how studious and wide-eyed she looked with her glasses on.

"If we're under such a deadline, why don't we use the high-tech wonder darkroom over yonder?"

"You know why."

Charlie paused. "Because there's something about doing it by hand that puts you closer to the soul of the pictures."

Joshua smiled with satisfaction. "You nailed it, Charlie. But there's also another reason. It lets me remember where I came from. It lets me remember the endless nights as a young assistant, pulling my first prints, chemical smells, safelights and sepia toner so strong, it practically peeled the paint off the walls. It makes me remember that everything has a beginning."

"I can't picture you as ever having been an assistant, Joshua."

"Can't picture me that far back in time?"

"No! It's not that. You're not that old—I mean, you're not, you just— it's like picturing your parents as teenagers. You know what I mean," she finished, looking away in embarrassment.

Joshua laughed. "Yeah, I do. Didn't mean to put you on the spot that way." He picked up one of the photographs from the wash and studied it for a moment. "Now let me ask you something. What's so magical about black and white, Charlie?"

"It evokes a mood in such a strong way. It's the visual language of emotion."

"Why?"

She tilted her head, the red bulb's reflections disappearing from her glasses. "I think it's because we live in a world of color. And a black and white image has a kind of iconography that's totally free of confusion. But it can still be ambiguous. Gray, for want of a better word. There just isn't all that visual noise in the way and you can see it emotionally."

"Nicely put." He leaned his thick forearms on the sink's edge. "But now I want to hear what your heart has to say, not your head. Why are black and whites so powerful?"

"Close your eyes and I'll tell you."

She stepped up on tiptoes and placed the most tantalizing of kisses on Joshua's lips. It was by no means a weak kiss. Instead, it held the promise of the fire, sensuality, depth and wonder that was her love. It was as delicate as a small bird's wing yet as powerful as a first experience. In short, it was all that she was.

Joshua opened his eyes to see hers, blazing like violet gems.

"That's what a black and white does to me. That's what makes it so powerful."

Joshua was speechless, stripped of all artifice by this simple act. He realized in that instant that he loved Charlie, had since the moment he'd first set eyes on her. And that he need not apologize for this love, not even to himself. He also realized that nothing had ever felt more true to him than this moment, right here, right now. He reached for her face and delicately cupped it, tilting her mouth up to meet his. They kissed, slowly and deeply, both feeling the fire that had suddenly tasted oxygen, caught up in a rising thermal of mutual passion that surprised them both with its intensity.

She pulled back and held his face, feeling his breath, feeling the bones and skin as though they were somehow a part of her.

"Joshua? I—I only have one rule."

"What is it?"

She leaned in and whispered in his ear. Joshua Stone, who thought he was beyond all capacity for surprise, found himself utterly blindsided by this one.

He nodded slowly, lifting her up so she sat on the sink's edge. His lips touched hers very softly, then he slowly removed her glasses, Charlie's eyes never leaving his, the gesture strangely intimate for both of them. They kissed again and his hands found her breasts through the thin material of her t-shirt, momentarily surprised by their fullness, her nipples stiffening into his palms. He felt Charlie's hands as they ran over his back and buttocks, how small they were, yet hot and strong. Then thought was washed away by sensation as slow caress became liquid press in ever-escalating explorations of demand. He rolled the sticky t-shirt over her head and sun-browned arms, tossing it aside even as she reached impatiently for his buckle. The red bulb was knocked to one side and swung back and forth, cascading highlights and shadows, painting their sweat soaked bodies in myriad shades of red until limb and body and face and breast flowed to and through and over one another, liquid and living, their bodies now a black and white photograph run riot.

A hand finally reached for the bulb's cord before the smaller hand covered it and pulled down.

Click.

Book 8

"Who covets more is evermore a slave." —Herrick

"The poverty of our century is unlike that of any other. It is not, as poverty was before, the result of natural scarcity, but of a set of priorities imposed upon the rest of the world by the rich. Consequently, the modern poor are not pitied . . . but written off as trash. The twentieth-century consumer economy has produced the first culture for which a beggar is a reminder of nothing." —John Berger

"The Campaign of The Century was now three quarters complete. Joshua Stone's images had been in the world's eye for almost two months and their effect was simply astonishing. Fa-Shin, Inc. was reaping (some would say raping) monetary rewards that far surpassed our wildest expectations.

Why was the Campaign so incredibly effective? To this day, it is still difficult to arrive at a definitive explanation, because there still exists no yardstick against which to measure such a massive psychological experiment.

There were, however, two factors that emerged as the cornerstones of the Campaign's success. The first was people's hunger to make the images come alive. Stone's photography and the choice of models had combined in pictures with such a remarkable degree of surface tension it seemed they truly would come to life if you just—kept—looking.

It was the denial of that hunger by the very nature of photography itself that made The Campaign of The Century so compelling. Because though people were denied, they could not look away. And the more they looked, the more our message penetrated.

Buy. Buy. Buy.

The second factor concerned closure. Because Stone really had created a totally organic liquid visual narrative that was unique to each person who participated in it. He thereby achieved what should frankly

151

have been impossible. His photography invited them into something, a story, and to see where that story ended, they had to buy. After buying they were somewhat satiated, until a new story presented itself, a new facet of the jewel. Then they had to buy more.

Fa-Shin, Inc.'s Buy It Now! cards were also a huge hit and it was I who was responsible for their creation. I knew that consumers would find something irresistible about having Phoena and Solipsum in their back pockets. The two-for-one deal on all Fa-Shin, Inc. merchandise probably had something to do with it as well. No one really paid attention to the fine print. No one ever does. That's why we were able to get away with the 35% interest rate on all the merchandise, paid or "free."

Some of this had been anticipated by us. Some of it had not. Like The Campaign of The Century's darker side. Because by this time, a linked chain of effect-cause-effect had started.

And no one knew how to stop it.

It began with a craze in Japan sparked by an image of Solipsum wearing, of all things, a watch. This "fashion cult" spread so quickly by teens using ketei (SMS text messaging) that demand for the item could not be filled. That's when the first of the riots started: over three hundred dead in a Tokyo department store. Because it seemed that something that would ordinarily have been waited for, or simply done without, suddenly became indispensable. As necessary as air.

Dr. Hans Kaufmann has blamed it on what he calls the "Jones Factor." For it seemed that whatever The Campaign induced consumers to buy, they had to have immediately. Even an hour was too long to wait. During this short period, at least eight other fashion cults sprang up, from Paris and London to New York and Miami.

Item shortages weren't the only problem, paycheck shortages were too. People were simply spending far beyond their means. Bulk-theft and shoplifting skyrocketed wherever our merchandise was available. But because sales were so high, no one said a word.

The massive poverty whip that our analysts warned us would descend once the Campaign ended was something else no one talked about. After all, if we turned a blind eye, it would doubtless go away.

In retrospect, this was our most unforgivable sin.

But the media, it must be said, played their part as well. Like a dog chasing its own tail, they could not get enough. Never mind that we had already purchased every page of ad space, editorial pages and headline copy were now shamelessly devoted to our content too. Something Elora had predicted. No, let me rephrase that. Something she had simply known.

By the time Stone and his crew flew to Egypt, The Campaign had already spun out of control.

It just hadn't manifested yet."

from Poverty Whip—An Inside Look at The Campaign of The Century *by Maurice Vellum*

Cairo, Egypt—The Campaign of The Century—Day 238

HUNDREDS MORE RIOT IN TOKYO!
FA-SHIN, INC.'S COUP TURNS NASTIER AS MORE STORES FAIL TO MEET RAMPANT CONSUMER DEMAND!
In a stunning advertising coup, Fa-Shin, Inc. has rocketed to the forefront of fashion with a campaign that has blindsided all of its competitors and left them in the dust. But at what price?

Joshua Stone stared at the headline, feeling again the massive wave of guilt wash over him, a guilt he had been trying to rationalize ever since he had first heard about this Campaign side-effect. *There's no getting around who shot those pictures,* he thought. *Just as there's no getting around that strange feeling you get knowing you induced something so powerful. Liquid organic whatever, the whole fucking thing works. Even better than Elora dreamed. And they're killing one another,* some distant part of his mind reminded him. *But it's over the merch, not the pictures.* Or so he kept telling himself. He thought again about the incredible amount of money he was being paid, money to create images, not to think about their effect. It was enough to silence those thoughts, enough even to silence the little voice, the one that kept asking what was happening when he looked through the viewfinder.

He idly scanned some of the other headlines, forcing a snappy and sarcastic response to the more idiotic ones.

NEW YORK TIMES—What is happening
with The Campaign of The Century?
Tell us and we'll both know.

VOGUE—Fa-Shin, Inc.'s Amazing Fashion Coup.
More like Amazing Fashion Force-Feed.

HARPER'S BAZAAR—The Wonder Couple
of the New Millennium.

He stared at the image of the two models holding each other and re-membered what Phoena had said to him in Venice. He wished for a mo-ment that he had made her tell him that story. But there was nothing he could do about it now. He let his gaze drift to the next magazine's cover.

FORBES—How Are They Doing It? Record
Profits predicted for Fa-Shin, Inc.'s 3rd Quarter.
No kidding. Best be buying that stock, people.

AMERICAN PHOTO—Joshua Stone—An Exclusive
Interview with The Man Behind The Campaign.

Here his mind was silent, because even though the magazine some-times bore more than a passing resemblance to a camera catalogue, it had always been sincere in its presentation of what it had determined as photographically relevant. They had deserved the only interview he had given because they had helped him when he was nobody.

TIME—The Buying Frenzy: Media or
Consumer, Who is Responsible?
Well the answer to that would be—both.

LE MONDE—Are We Spending Too Much?
Yes! Yes! And a million times YES!

STERN—DEATH ON THE AUTOBAHN!
Are Sexy Pictures to Blame?
No. How could they be? The whole world is being affected to the point people are killing one another, but the autobahn is special, right?

PARIS MATCH—It Must Stop! Or Must It?
Too late now. It's called Pandora's Box.

PEOPLE—Most Eligible Bachelor? Mystery
Man Solipsum is Most Controversial.
Here he simply laughed, the truth of that statement so self-evident.

Stone looked up from the barrage of words and pictures to see the *djaballa*-clad Egyptian news vendor, smoking, bored and sullen, oblivious to all the screaming headlines.

Well, that's a sight. If it isn't me, right in the eye of the Hurricane.

He shook his head, then made his way to the luggage area to watch as his huge cast and crew slowly collected their bags and gear. An entire 747 had been chartered to bring everyone and everything he needed to this particular place.

They had now been all over the Earth, had photographed in some of her most exotic and remote locales. From studio to city, Amazonian rainforest to Antarctic ice shelf, they had covered an extraordinary amount of ground.

Stone admitted to himself that for all the guilt he felt about how his photography was affecting the world, he was having the time of his life. The convergence of so much he had always sought was filling him with a joy previously unimagined. The whirlwind tour of the Earth had given him an appreciation of the planet granted to only a very few. It had certainly been made manifest in his photography. And what he now had with Charlie was something that yesterday seemed like a dream unattainable. It was by far the strangest, deepest, coolest, most complex yet maddeningly simple relationship he had ever had. The slightest pressure from any facet of their individual lives sent the whole dynamic careening off in a new direction. Yet miraculously, it had not derailed. It was something very special, even if he had yet to cross the boundary into—

"Charlie!" He waved. "Over here!"

"Where do you want your bag?"

"With us in the car. Wait up, I'll give you a hand."

The Pyramids at Luxor—The Campaign of The Century—Day 245

He stood on the balcony of his hotel room, still in awe at the sight before him, the ancient shapes that some say represented the Aspect of God, one side always and forever hidden. Joshua felt again the stillness, the slightest quaver of fearful awe, the humbling effect the enormity of their presence had on one's thoughts about the span of history, human life and one's place in the grand scheme. He mopped his brow, letting himself return to the present.

The days had passed in a relatively uneventful barrage of logistics and photo sessions. In fact, things had run surprisingly smoothly, thanks in a large part to Elora's highly competent production skills. He grudgingly acknowledged that she had done a very impressive job organizing this shoot. Unfortunately, it had left him very little time to spend with Charlie. Their last and biggest day of photography had already arrived and he had hardly seen her. He pulled the bill of his baseball cap lower to cut the glare, the sun loud on his skin. He checked his watch and breathed deeply. *Forty-five minutes 'til showtime.* His gaze to took in everything—the Pyramids, the crowds, the scaffolding in the distance, and felt for a moment the enormity of the weight he carried on his shoulders. Then the tight grip of arms encircled his waist and a face pressed into his back. He smiled, for it seemed the gods had answered his prayers.

He turned right into Charlie's waiting kiss, sweaty and sandy and oh how he wished this could go on forever. They finally broke and she looked at him, head tilted, teeth very white in her newly tanned face. "Miss me?"

He didn't even answer, just drank of her beauty like a man in a desert (which he supposed he was). He kissed her again, until she finally disengaged, gently, and reminded him they were almost ready. "You probably have a lot on your mind. I should go."

"Oh no, you don't." He pulled her to him. "I was just thinking—"

"Something you do a bit too much of, Mr. Stone," she said playfully, her hands on his chest as he cupped her bum.

"I know." He could feel how sweaty she was, how much he would like to—

"But, when you tell me what's on your mind, it's always—interesting."

Joshua laughed and tried to get that mind back on the job. Then said *to hell with it* and kissed her again. Finally he stopped and looked at the sky, hand on his hat bill as he checked the sun's position. They still had a bit of time. "I was thinking that sometimes you get tired of the whole 'whack, whack, whack' school of photography."

"What do you mean?" She stood in his shadow, noticing how he eclipsed the sun, how white her hands as they now rested in his.

"Charlie, have you ever seen the early guys' photographs? Wee Gee, Arbus, Cartier Bresson?"

"Yeah. Lots of times." She loved how his dark and honeyed eyes watched hers. "Even today there's stuff they shot that no one's touched."

"True." He pointed behind her, suddenly thirsty. "Pass me one of those ice teas, would you?"

"Sure thing."

She rummaged in the cooler and Joshua allowed himself to admire the clean line of her tanned legs. She wore a simple t-shirt, jean shorts, and a backwards bandana knotted above her forehead. Tufts of blond hair stuck up in all directions like frosting.

"By the way, you look very cute today."

"I know." She smiled and blew him a kiss. Though it was rather hard to see, she could somehow tell she'd made him blush. She finally found the cold ones down near the bottom and brought them back. She capped Joshua's bottle, then her own, and they mock toasted one another before getting down to the serious business of gulping. Joshua finished first and watched as Charlie drank her entire bottle, throat working, completely oblivious to the effect this had on him. He felt the southern regions stir and silently cursed the Campaign and its demands. Charlie finished, resting the still-cold bottle against her cheek, then turned her violet eyes to him. They were darker here, he noted, amethyst and serpentine.

"Go on."

"What?"

"With your thoughts, about the old masters."

Joshua's face went blank for an instant as he tried to recall what he had been talking about. Then he banished any non-old master thoughts (for now). "Charlie, the reason their work still stands the test is because they chose the moment. Or let it choose them. They didn't just stand around and grab everything in some motor-wind autofocus frenzy and sort it all out later." He took another sip of his drink, noticing with disgust that the tea was already warm.

"What do you mean?"

"I mean that what they did with their cameras was special. They saw with their souls, not with their wallets."

Charlie's face furrowed in concentration as she reknotted her kerchief. "And what you're doing with your camera isn't? Just because it's motor-driven? And you're getting paid?"

"I—I'm not sure."

"Joshua. This is really strange coming from you, especially this late in the game. What gives? Are you okay?"

"I'm wondering about the integrity of this whole thing, if I'm not doing something that's at best irresponsible, and at worst—"

"Evil?"

"Yes," he breathed, relieved she'd used the word he hadn't yet had the courage to.

Charlie finished with the kerchief. "Solipsum said something to me once, when we were shooting in Madagascar. 'Beauty must be served.' It's not the first time I've come across that phrase. I think he's right, Joshua. Our feelings and our consciences do the best they can to guide us, but sometimes I feel they're just there so we think we're in control when really there's some dark god behind the scenes who's pulling all our strings. Or maybe a bunch of them, and they're fighting each other with us as pawns. I don't know. Sometimes it makes me want to throw in the towel, but I don't."

Joshua was brought up short, forcibly reminded yet again that this beautiful blond girl was so much more than just a toy. And that if Charlie were a rose, her mind would be its scent.

"But it's working, isn't it? This whole 'liquid visual narrative' thing?"

She made a face. "Liquid visual narrative, my ass. Sometimes it all just sounds like so much Elora Campaign of The Century bullshit to me."

Joshua sighed. "I think you're right. But what's the answer? What should I do?"

Charlie's face lit up, as if all the knowledge in the Universe had suddenly made itself clear. "Simple. Shut–up and kiss me, you big lug."

He was just getting into it, the sweetness of her lips, when his walkie talkie crackled to life. "They're ready for you, Mr. Stone."

He stopped and held her face. "Time to go."

Charlie became serious. "We are taking the longest vacation after this. And nowhere exotic either. Just somewhere simple. And quiet."

"Deal."

He turned and began walking across the balcony. She let him reach the stairs before calling out, "By the way—nice bum."

He looked at her over his shoulder and smiled. "I know."

The Pyramids at Luxor

"You look like a raisin!"

"And you look like a piece of white asparagus stickin' out of a baboon's ass!"

A sunburned Russ couldn't believe the affrontery. *And from a dwarf named Hemo-goblin of all people! The fuck kind of name is that?*

"Why you little—I oughta throw you off the top of the Pyramid right now and watch you go splat!"

Hemogoblin gave him the finger, then grabbed a prop scimitar and began ginching over on fat white legs, the big sword held awkwardly in his stubby hands.

Solipsum looked over from the opulent couch he reclined on. He casually waved away a pomegranate offered by Quinby but took some wine from the other girl. The third continued fanning him.

"Russ. Don't irk the talent."

"Uh, yes, sir."

"Come here."

Russ quickly walked over and joined his Master under the shade of the awning. Solipsum looked cool and refreshed, his sculpted muscles oiled, hair pomaded, clad only in loincloth as he reclined on the Egyptian settee. He waved his hand in a gesture of dismissal and the three girls disappeared. "Russ. Phoena's gift to Joshua. Did he bring it?"

The assistant searched his memory. "Yes, sir. Yes, he did. But he hasn't worn them yet. They're still at the hotel."

"Get them. There is a chance he may have need of them."

"But, sir! If he finds out I've left the set, he'll kill me!"

Solipsum had been looking at the sky. His head rotated until the full power of his gaze was turned upon the hapless lackey. "Need I remind you who it is you serve?"

"N—no, sir."

"Good. Now hurry. Things are about to begin. If you run, I'm sure no one will notice your absence."

Russ turned to go.

"One last thing."

"Yes, sir?"

"Which one?"

"Uh—Quinby, sir."

"Not that one. I'm not quite finished with her."

"The Twins then, sir."

"Greedy boy." Solipsum smiled. "They will be in your room tonight. Now off with you."

Russ raced across the boiling Pyramid's surface as fast as his legs could carry him.

Hemo-goblin paused to light a smoke as he watched Russ run. *Looks like someone lit a fire under your ass, Turkey-boy.*

"Hey Dwarf, your not supposed to smoke up here."

Hemo looked up at Lance Boyko and grudgingly admitted the model looked perfect. A cleanly muscled skater-boy more beautiful than handsome with hair that looked permanently wind-tousled, he was dressed in that weird conglomeration of *Fa-shin, Inc.* merch that was supposed to make him look like all those Egyptian weirdos did, back when. "Next your gonna tell me they'll stunt my growth or something."

Boyko laughed. "Hey Dwarf, what's your take on how our shots are affecting everybody?"

"My take? The only take I'm worried about is my 'take-home.'"

"I'm with you, but still. My sister almost got caught in one of those riots."

"Yeah, well maybe you should tell her not to leave the house. I mean, what the fuck, it's just stuff, right?"

Lance shrugged. "I dunno. It's kind of confusing."

Hemo took a last drag and flicked the butt over the Pyramid's edge, taking a quick look to see if he'd hit Russ. He saw Lance's new girlfriend approaching and waved to her. "Hey, Alba."

"Hi, guys."

Alabasta Twigg slipped an arm around Lance's waist and Hemo cursed the fact he barely came up to her belly button. "Hot enough for you?" he asked.

She smiled. "It could be worse. We could be underground in New York."

Lance rolled his eyes. "Don't remind me."

"You know what's weird?"

"What?" asked Hemo, shielding his eyes as he looked up at her.

"I don't feel the urge to buy any of this stuff."

"Maybe because you're getting as much of it as you want for free. None of this shit fits me so I got my excuse."

"That would probably be true. If I actually wanted any of it."

"You mean you don't?" Lance brushed a strand of hair from her face.

Alba looked down at her sandals, then at each of them in turn. "No. I don't."

Hemo spread his arms and leaned back against the short stone balustrade. "Okay, I'll bite. Why not?"

She hugged herself and tilted her head to the sky, collecting her thoughts. Hemo loved it when she did that. "Something strange has happened to me since all this began. It's like I had some sort of fashion epiphany."

"Were you high?"

"Shut-up, Dwarf," Lance growled good-naturedly. Alba stuck her tongue out at him.

"Sorry," said Hemo. "What happened?"

"Well . . . I had a moment when I looked at myself in the mirror recently, trying to figure out why everyone was so gung-ho about my look."

"And?"

"I came to the conclusion that it didn't really matter what they thought. What really mattered was what I thought."

"I'm not following you."

"Well, what it really all came down to was *before* and *after*. That seems to be how I divide people these days. Into *before* and *after*. *Before* I started modeling, I really knew who my friends were. They were people who liked me for me, for who I was, as opposed to how I looked. *After* I started modeling, people treated me like some sort of thing, some weird perfect thing that they could say anything to, try anything on and basically fuck over as much as possible. In the beginning, I tried so hard to be that thing, even though I could never figure out exactly what it was. Then I had that day where I looked in the mirror and just said 'fuck it'. I don't care if I never figure out what that thing is, 'cause it doesn't matter. What other people think has nothing to do with my own happiness. And I suddenly figured out that all these people fighting over the clothing? The merch? For them it's the exact opposite. They think that by buying this stuff, they'll somehow find their happiness."

"Yeow!" Hemo stood. "That's pretty deep. Especially from coming someone who's supposed to be—"

"—meat for the camera?" provided Lance helpfully.

Alba and Hemo laughed.

"Go on." said the Dwarf.

"Well, it's like they've all been hypnotized or something. Into believing they actually need this shit, just to be themselves, you know?"

"Point," said Hemo thoughtfully.

Alba looked up at Lance and Hemo wished in that moment, more than anything else in the world, that a girl would look at him that way. A tall girl. He saw a frantically waving P.A. "Hey, guys? I think they're ready for us." He then held out his hands. "Come on, kids, it's back to the salt mines."

The three of them walked to the set holding hands, looking for all the world like a perfectly normal family.

Joshua stood on scaffolding forty feet in the air, the vantage from which he would take his final master shot. He looked down at the tremendous amount of movement and activity. It had taken approximately two weeks to set up for the past four days of intensive shooting. And it was not only Elora who had done an amazing job. He said a silent thank-you to her army of *Fa-Shin, Inc.* lackeys and palm-greasers as well. Tramping all over national monuments with scaffolding, generators and hordes of extras would not have been possible without a tremendous outlay of *baksheesh*.

He caught a glimpse of her running to put out some new fire and waved, even though he knew she could not see him. For some reason, it felt nice to see her put through her paces like this. She had wanted the most spectacular and unique photography he could provide, and these logistics were a small price. He smiled as a memory surfaced, the reflection of her face peeking out from beneath the covers on that pale and wintry day. How far they all had come.

He took in the sea of people that surrounded him and thanked God that the Pyramids were his last major location. "Rolling Stone", as his team had come to be called, was no longer able to quietly slip into a country with no more fuss than a normal magazine fashion shoot. The level of celebrity reached by practically everyone associated with The Campaign of The Century had seen to that. Information leaks now insured that no matter where they went, a crowd of eager spectators would appear, as if from nowhere. It looked like there were thousands of them here, all barely held back by the three hundred man security force hired by *Fa-Shin, Inc.*

He turned his attention to the squared-off top of the ruined Pyramid he would soon be shooting. It was still covered with rugs, furniture, urns and braziers, all meticulously researched to be as authentically Egyptian as possible. It had served as his main location for the past three days.

He saw Solipsum reclining under an awning, being catered to by Quinby and two other models like he was Cheops reborn. He shook his head in wonder. *I'm the one running this show and I don't get that kind of treatment. How does he do it?* As he watched, the entire cast began assembling, all dressed in *Fa-Shin, Inc.* merchandise that had been ripped, rolled, wound, wrapped, draped and deconstructed so that at first glance it resembled traditional Egyptian raiment. Wardrobe and Sindra's make-up personnel swarmed over them in preparation for the last shot.

He saw from the corner of his eye the huge thirty foot by thirty foot diffusion panel, the hot Egyptian sun softened by it. It was mounted on two massive pivoting grips that allowed the panel to turn and angle with very little human effort.

He thought about what he had already shot, the close-ups, pairings, detail shots and groupings. It was almost effortless, so easily had the cast slid into their assigned roles, as though guided by the hand of a distant yet powerful past, a past that in this country was like a living presence. A visitor here felt this very strongly but for Joshua it had become something he actually *saw*, for whenever he now looked through the viewfinder, the world changed. Or rather, his perspective did, for he now saw continuously what had earlier been glimpsed only as gaps and bursts of that other world. His camera had become like a strange new set of eyes. He bent his head to the viewfinder and watched as the overlay of modern-day Egypt disappeared and time shifted like the sands. He saw pageantry and drudgery, weddings, funerals, human sacrifice, Pharaohs and priestesses, beggars and grave robbers, queens, concubines, soldiers and slaves. All were so vivid and alive there was no doubt in his mind that what he saw was real.

For Gods *did* walk the earth back then. Beings of immense power, but petty too, ruled in their turn by drives as base and common as those of their supplicants. Large Gods and small, Gods of temple and tiny household shrine, of palace, river and tomb. Aman, Qetesh, Isis, Horus, and Osiris. The Gods of a nation.

And beyond this, he saw even more. It was as if the perceptual strata that separated the time stream became evermore transparent. At the last, they ceased to exist entirely, revealed as illusion imposed by Mind, deposed by Eye. He saw Energies and Entities, shaping and influencing, moving massively beneath the surface of events. Some good, some bad. Some very bad.

He lifted his face from the viewfinder and rubbed his eyes.

"Joshua?" Charlie's voice came to him from the walkie talkie's headset. "You are green for go. Repeat, green for go."

He paused, perfectly caught in the moment, balanced between the two worlds. "Okay! Let's do it!" he shouted into the headset's microphone.

His eye returned to the viewfinder. Past and present magically shimmered and intertwined and he knew these would be some of the best photographs he had ever taken. His finger pushed the button and it began. Poses presented and film wound as he barked orders into the headset, hearing his voice echo back from the hidden speakers on set. Things proceeded slowly, and slower than usual because he changed his own backs today. Then the pace increased and film started flying as the cast sped faster through their prearranged choreography. He felt the flow, the groove, and settled into it as image after image presented itself, the corners of his mouth rising in a smile he was completely unaware of.

On the ground, Elora grinned, happy as she'd ever been. It was almost as good as sex. Almost. She snapped some orders through her headset, tightening security near the scaffolding. Her gaze traveled upward to the lone man at its top.

What the hell? Where did that light come from?

She quickly rubbed her eyes, not sure of what she'd seen, then touched her headset's mike. "Joshua, what's going on up there?"

But for some reason, he couldn't hear her. *Sweet Jesus,* she thought, *am I the only one seeing this?* For the air around Joshua had begun to shimmer. As she watched, it grew brighter and brighter, until he was surrounded by a nimbus of golden light. She looked around her and realized with shock that *everyone* saw what she did.

Then the dusty throng was moving, slowly, like some great and lumbering beast of rock now come to life. They seemed drawn by a magnetic force, a siren call that occluded all shape of will. Elora behind the barricades felt their protean determination and knew it would not be denied.

Even the fucking security force is staring up there!

For they too felt the overpowering need to reach him, touch him. Suddenly the barriers came crashing down, screams filled the air, the crowd rolling forward like a breaker, pushing and shoving their way towards the scaffolding, shouting, shrieking, the unlucky quickly drowned in the surging tide of humanity.

Joshua continued shooting, oblivious to the seething mass below him, even as they began to climb the metalworks.

On the Pyramid's top, Solipsum, Phoena and Charlie all stared at the figure of Joshua, now bright as a pyre.

Charlie grabbed the walkie talkie. "Joshua! Look out!" she yelled. She saw he hadn't heard her. The headset hung about his neck, pushed back so he could shoot more freely. She looked down at the sea of heads, the fear creeping over her as even more clawed their way up towards Joshua.

A strange urge came over her then. She grabbed an extra camera, framed and shot by purest instinct the masses climbing the scaffolding, the shocked and gaping model tableaux in the foreground and the Pyramids behind. At the center of it all was Joshua, backlit by the sun, still shooting though he must have seen their reactions.

The roar of the crowd then became so loud he finally stopped. Men climbing the trellis, their faces ecstatic, had almost reached him. He looked around wildly then jammed the camera back to his face, shooting anything and everything, oblivious to the danger, unable to turn away, unable even to help himself. The scaffolding began to rock.

He heard a scream from the Pyramid's edge.

"Joshua!"

Looking down he saw Russ waving frantically.

"Catch!"

Joshua dropped his camera, the strap biting into his neck as Russ threw something at him with perfect speed and trajectory. His hand lifted and closed, catching the small and leathery hardness.

What the hell?

It was the case containing Phoena's glasses. He quickly put them on.

Solipsum on the Pyramid watched the spectacle and knew that things were moving faster than he had anticipated.

"Not yet, Joshua, not yet." For though he was surprised, he was not unprepared.

He moved behind a large urn and its screen of palms, unaware that Charlie was watching him. He stood and let his arms hang at his sides, fists slowly opening and closing. His breathing became deep and abdominal, brow furrowing with immense concentration as large beads of sweat blistered his forehead. His eyes slowly rolled to the whites.

Charlie almost cried out, fists covering her mouth. *Oh my God, what is he doing?* As she watched, he blew into his hand and captured a breath not of this world. The muscles in his arm coiled and he threw it skyward. Then his eyes rolled back down and he looked about, as though he had somehow sensed her presence. Charlie quickly ducked behind an urn, then peered about its base to find him gone. She heard the words "*To me!*" and stood just in time to see cast and crew surrounding Solipsum, their inertia shattered, everyone suddenly aware of the gusting winds that had sprung as if from nowhere.

Joshua on the scaffolding was jolted out of the viewfinder's world. The steel skeleton shook violently with wind and clinging body weight as the sandstorm grew.

The mass of people below roiled in confusion as the shrieking winds blew hot sand into their eyes and mouths. The climbers fell like tattered dolls, crushed in the turmoil as the mob-mind broke, survival all that mattered, men and women running for shelter, scattering before the terrible winds.

Joshua was trapped on the exposed metal. A gust almost lifted him and he cursed. He saw his cast and crew huddled in the centre of the set, then spied the buckling scrim, like a huge sail about to be ripped from its moorings. Windblown sand blasted everything and his vision became milkier as the sand scoured the lenses.

He frantically grabbed for his headset, one hand over nose and mouth, accidentally ripping the cable loose. "Fuck!" he spat, tossing it to the wind, then grabbed the radio from his belt. "Charlie! Watch me! When I hit the scrim, push the release!"

Then a thought

(save the camera)

exploded in his mind. He lifted it with two hands and instinctively knew that Charlie down on the Pyramid understood what he was about to do. He bent back as far as he could, then snapped forward, a trebuchet that hurled the camera to her. She could hardly see it through the wind and sand, then it slammed into her, a jolt of pain like a lance as she pulled the blocky metal into her belly. She rolled with the momentum, standing then, disoriented, to face the shrieking winds. One hand instinctively covered her eyes. She peered through finger slits and gasped as Joshua climbed onto the guard rail and—jumped.

Her head tilted back to see his body as it flew through the air, silhouetted against the sun.

He slammed into the scrim, hands gripping its frame, eyes lensed white in his dark and sandy face.

"Now!" he screamed.

Charlie jammed the button and watched as the huge scrim tilted slowly on its axis, straining as it fought the mighty storm. Then Joshua's weight came into play and it completed its rotation, safely lowering him to the Pyramid's top.

No sooner did his feet touch the stone then he yelled, "Blow the C02!"

Charlie blew the C02 claspers, releasing the scrim fabric from its frame. It fell on the cast and crew, where a forest of arms and hands shot up to pull it close before the winds could take it. The world became reduced to a beige, shrieking scream and the warmth and smell of their huddled bodies.

It was three hours before the storm died sufficiently to risk removing their covering. By then they were nearly buried. The extrication was slow but somehow joyous, the mundane task experienced with a clarity that only proximity to death could give.

They were nearly done when Joshua put his arm around Charlie and kissed her deeply, not caring who was watching. Neither did she. Solipsum began laughing, a deep and resonant laugh that came from the very depths of his being. A radiant Phoena, dressed as Nefertiti, joined them and they all put their arms around each other, laughing, cheering, sometimes crying, so very glad to be alive.

Stone watched his two models, noticing that for once, they were behaving like friends. He took off the glasses that had saved his eyes. They were opaque, so completely had they been scoured by the sands.

"Russ!" he called as he folded them away.

The assistant soon stood before him, sandy and disheveled, a huge grin plastered across his sunburned face.

"Thanks," said Joshua. "How did you know?"

"A little bird told him."

They both looked at Phoena/Nefertiti, who smiled as enigmatically as the character she had played that day.

Stone clapped his hands and all was silent. "I think, after this, it's time for a break. I'm giving you all ten days off."

The words had barely left his mouth before the cheering and whistling erupted.

Interlude Three—Vatican City

Cardinal Synn stood on a balcony of the Vatican Bank, surveying St. Peter's Square and the throngs of people. Some already carried Campaign of the Century bags, and that was very pleasing to his eye. He patted his ample girth and said a silent prayer of gratitude for the life he had been blessed with, a life of such rapacity and sensory gluttony as to rival some of history's greatest predators. All in the service of Holy Mother Church.

Cardinal Synn was acting head of the Vatican Bank, a position not without a considerable amount of power. It was a power he used as relentlessly in business as he did in the pursuit of ever more esoteric forms of self-gratification.

He had held this position for the past twenty years. The Bank was the largest of three that sat in what was effectively the world's smallest country, Vatican City, population 800.

It was an unusual bank, a bank which reported to no one, answered to no laws and was never audited. It had but one shareholder, the Pope, who took no interest whatsoever in the Bank's day to day "operations." This he left to that most trusted of his advisors, Cardinal Synn, who ran the bank ruthlessly. Lethally.

For the Bank was like a web, and he the spider at its center. Together, they had caught a great many flies—trusting, stupid, greedy flies. Drug laundering, outright theft from Holocaust victims and Mafiosi, Nazi gold, rampant currency speculation, scandal, cover-up and murder. All of these he had taken part in. But they were as nothing compared to the profits he foresaw from his co-venture with *Fa-Shin, Inc.* Or rather, his solo venture, as they would find out in one year's time, when a blind trust he had organized took over their entire company.

It had been very expensive, this funding of The Campaign of The Century, and perhaps he had placed more of the Bank's resources than was prudent in this one basket. But there was simply too much money to be made. As one of his contemporaries had so eloquently stated, "You cannot run a bank on Hail Mary's."

The Campaign was not even fully complete and the reports he had heard had surpassed even *his* expectations, which meant he had already won. Now he needed only to sit back and wait. Like a spider. As an added delicacy, it would be very nice indeed to see that sluttish Creative Director on her knees, mouth stuffed, her glottal begging the most pleasant of fugues as he signed the papers of transferal.

He turned from the balcony and smiled, then stepped into the room and girded his loins in preparation for his daily massage.

New York City, Stone Studios—The Campaign of The Century—Day 248

Charlie yawned and stretched, her feet twining with Joshua's. Her eyes wandered over his body and she said a silent thank-you for Sunday mornings, a small and lascivious smile steeling over her features. "God, Joshua, you are so much fun in bed."

"As are you, Platinum."

Charlie felt a little shiver. "So-ooo. You *did* see it."

"Yes."

"Why didn't you say anything?"

"Charlie, you have to understand, I've never been in this situation. To have feelings for someone so—close to me professionally. I guess I got a little—"

"Scared?"

He couldn't look at her and turned away, frowning a bit as he realized what he had almost thrown away.

Charlie propped herself up on her forearms. "Joshua, do you know how nuts you were driving me? I mean, I have *never* done anything that—forward—to *anybody*. I thought you didn't like me or—or, I didn't know what to think. And you mean if I hadn't made that first move, you never would have done *anything*?"

"I don't know, Charlie. Who can say?"

"But probably not."

"Probably not," he conceded.

Charlie flopped back on the bed and flung an arm across her brow. "Men!" she huffed.

Joshua moved closer to her and she lifted her head so he could position his arm-pillow. They watched the cloud-shapes chase each other for a long time, easily forgetting the dome's glass that separated them from the sky.

Joshua touched her face, fingers lightly taveling over the spray of freckles on the bridge of her nose. "I have to ask, with all we've been through, why can't we—"

She put a finger to his lips. "Shhhh, Joshua. Please, give it time. Just trust me on this. Everything will work itself out, okay?"

He sighed and lit a cigarette.

Charlie held out her hand. "Pass me one of those."

He looked at her curiously as he offered the pack. "I didn't know you smoked." The lighter flared briefly.

She exhaled and grinned. "Good sex makes me smoky."

"It's the one vice I can't seem to shake. Everything else has gone by the wayside."

Charlie slowly turned onto her belly, just as the sun broke past a cloud to bathe her in its clear, warm light.

"Joshua?"

"Yes?"

"Can I ask you something?"

"Sure."

"What's the story with you and Phoena?"

"Charlie, Charlie, Charlie . . ." He paused for a moment. "We go back a long way. I remember the year she came to New York, even then you knew she was going to be a star. God, the first test we shot was so mind blowing, *Vogue* ended up running it on their cover."

"That cover in your entrance hall was a test?"

Joshua took a deep pull and slowly pushed the smoke out. "Yes. Just her, I and Sindra. Those were the days. We were all so wild back then it's a wonder any of us are still alive."

"But she seems so together, both of you do. And when you guys are shooting, it's like you're all part of the same body. I've never seen anything like it."

"Neither have I."

"What else did you used to do?" She shifted, the muscles under her skin making her little dragon coil slightly, as if she, too, wanted to hear more.

"What else didn't we do. Coke, crack, DMT, ketamine, grass, hash, amyl nitrate, ecstasy, MDMA, Vodka 'Q's', you name it, we did it. It got so I could orchestrate the most fantastic high that lasted days, but my God, the come-down. It was almost more than I could stand. It would take as much as a week sometimes to get back to normal."

"Was Phoena involved in any of this?"

His eyes became flat and unreadable. "Yes, she was. Right in the thick of it. We probably both would have died if she hadn't found the way out."

"What happened?"

"She was stumbling home after our worst debauch ever. The shit that happened that night . . . She was muttering the standard crash-mantra, "Never again. Never again . . ." when she passed this Yoga studio. It was called Upward Dog. *Weird name*, she thought, *I wonder what's going on in there?* A week later, she took her first class. When she was sure, after six months, she told me. By that time, I was on the edge of death. Sure, on the outside, everything looked the same, but on the inside, I was a mess. Doing drugs everyday, just to stay on my feet, and damn, things were busy. It seemed that every time I turned around, Elora would book me for another job, each one bigger than the last. Phoena convinced me to do a week of detox, then try a class. It was one of the hardest things I've ever done. But that's what turned it around. After that class, she said to me 'Joshua? It's all here. Every place you ever wanted to go. This is the Gateway. But you have to do the work. Everyday. Otherwise, you'll slide. I know, because I would. I have. And we're both so similar it makes me sick sometimes.'"

"Wow, Joshua. I never knew. Were you and she ever—?"

"Lovers? Of course. For almost a year. But with all the shit we were getting into, we forgot what was special. Us. So we let ourselves slide, deeper into the Endless Party. It just got to a point one day where we'd seen too much of the darker side of each other's natures. Way too much. But we also decided that from then on, we would be friends. The best of friends. And if either of us ever got lonely, the other would always be there. But no strings. Ever."

Charlie carefully crushed her cigarette. "She's a very special person."

"Yes." Joshua's eyes had drifted upwards to the clouds massing beyond the dome's glass. "She is."

Charlie studied him for a moment, then waved a hand in front of his face. "Wooohooo! Earth to Stone! Earth to Stone! Come in please, Commander Stone!"

He grabbed her wrist and next he knew, she had straddled him and somehow pretzled his arm into a very painful joint lock.

"Hey! No fair! I give! I give!"

Charlie looked at him slyly. "You do, eh?"

"Yes! Yes! Anything!" he yelped.

"Well—okay."

She slowly slid off and Joshua's hand darted in to tweak her breast. She squealed but it was too late, his hands were already tickling her.

"No more! No more!" Charlie squirmed, feet kicking the sheets into a tangle.

Joshua finally eased off, gazing at her with emotions he had no name for. Then he laughed. "I still remember how you looked the night of the party."

"Not what you were expecting?"

"I didn't even recognize you in that outfit."

Charlie growled in surprisingly good Stone, "'And Phoena. Who is this stunning girl?'"

Joshua at least had the grace to look embarrassed. "Probably Sindra's make-up," he mumbled. "By the way, that was an incredible shot you took at the Pyramids. An award-winner for sure."

"You think so?"

"Hell, yes."

"Speaking of the Pyramids, what happened out there, Joshua? That storm . . ." She almost told him then what she had seen Solipsum do but something stopped her. "If it hadn't been for Phoena's gift . . . you couldn't see, could you? When you jumped?"

"No."

"Jesus. There were rumors, too. Of you being surrounded by some sort of . . . light."

"That's a load of eyewash, Charlie. You can't believe every superstitious—"

"Joshua, please don't lie to me. I saw it."

Her gaze was unflinching and he recognized with a start this must be what an adversary saw when she looked at him in combat. "This has something to do with the pictures, doesn't it? With this whole Campaign of The Century thing." Then she asked the question he had been hoping she wouldn't. "Am I the only one who knows there's something weird going on with these pictures? You said you'd tell me how you were creating these effects. Well?"

He hesitated for so long she wasn't sure if he would answer. Finally, he spoke. "They're not effects."

"What do you mean?"

"It's hard to explain."

"Try me."

"When the three of us work together, something happens. A . . . door opens. And I find myself seeing things that aren't really there . . . but that somehow make it into the final image."

"I don't understand."

Joshua looked up at the clouds again, as if they would magically arrange themselves into some sort of answer. "Charlie, most of the final images haven't been digitally manipulated. And I haven't done anything to the film either."

She gently touched his cheek, the directional light throwing half his face into deepest shadow.

"Joshua. You're scaring the hell out of me."

"What's scary, Charlie, is that I can't seem to stop."

She propped herself up on one elbow, a hand resting lightly on his chest, feeling his heart beat. "You're one of the strongest people I know. How can you not stop something?"

His eyes finally met hers. "Charlie, you know a lot about me but there's one thing I've never told you. The reason I quit photojournalism."

"I was at the peak of my profession when the war in Bosnia started. Winter of '96. By that time, I'd won practically every major journalistic prize there was, even the Pulitzer. I'd been shot twice, knifed once and almost run over by a tank. Been all over the world, to every hot spot imaginable. The Congo, Afghanistan, the Hindu Kush, even Laos.

But none of it seemed real.

The only thing that mattered was the moment. It was like the further I went, the closer I came to seeing—something. God, for want of a better word. It didn't matter how horrible the atrocity, there always seemed to be something looking back at me. Trying to tell me something.

Then came Bosnia. By that time I had some very good connections, on both sides. It seemed everyone knew me and understood that I never presented a biased view. My photography knew no politics. It only showed the human condition. In fact, if there was one word to describe how I saw, it was human. This allowed me the most incredible access to places simply denied other photographers.

I got the call late one night. A friend of mine, a major in the rebel army. He told me there was something very interesting, something I had to see, but that I must hurry. I dressed and geared up in twenty minutes and ran to meet him at the helipad. We immediately took off. No lights, no flight plan, and a vector that took us deep into enemy territory. We flew for what seemed like hours, skimming the treetops and hugging the cliff faces. It was one of the hairiest rides of my life.

We finally landed in a valley and started hiking towards a grove of trees. The moon was full that night and with the snow acting as a reflector, it was eerily bright. We arrived at the grove and the major called a halt. He lit a cigarette and squinted at me over the flame. "What you are about to see has only been rumored about in the Western press. We have very little time. And you cannot use the flash. Now go and take the pictures. The world must know what is really happening in this war."

So in I went. No lights, rock steady hands and high speed film. What I saw there haunts my sleep to this very day. I stepped into the grove, and at first, I couldn't understand what I was seeing. Then my mind finally grasped what my eyes already knew, what I had somehow already found myself shooting.

They were bodies. Thousands and thousands of bodies. Men, women, children.

But mostly children."

"The 'Missing Years'," Charlie murmured.

"Yes. The 'Missing Years'. I had found them, though I didn't know it at the time."

I walked among them, shooting away at anything that caught my eye, instantly composing, framing, finding. Then the strangest thing happened. I seemed to—step outside myself. I reached the point I had been striving for all those years. Amidst that horror and waste, I found myself seeing—God.

And her name was Beauty.

Beauty in a child's snow dusted eyes, as they found Infinity in the winter sky. Beauty in the grace of a mother's arms, holding a child who would never cry. Beauty in the jut and splay of a forest of limbs, delicately edge-lit by the cold full moon. Beauty in a pool of blood so black it looked like a hole in our Reality.

I shot it all.

Even after I'd run out of film, I kept shooting. I still don't know why. Something compelled me, something so powerful, I was helpless before it. A puppet. Even when the major shouted at me to come back, I couldn't stop shooting. They finally dragged me out of there and stuffed me back in the chopper. If it hadn't been for the major, they would have shot me and left me to join those on the other side of the lens.

I watched the sun rise as we flew back and knew that my life had changed forever.

Upon our return to the base, I left immediately. Didn't even process the film. No one could believe it, but no one stopped me either. Somehow the story had already gotten out and no one wanted to get in the way of a crazy man. After all, don't we all secretly fear that madness is contagious?

I came back to the States and did the one thing I shouldn't have. I developed the film. Seeing what I'd shot somehow closed the circle and I finally touched what I'd been searching for all those years. From that moment on, I knew I'd never take another war photograph. I also knew that I would never forget those images, those people.

I took a year off, just to decide what to do, to come to terms with what I had seen that day, both in the valley and in myself. I came to the realization that I loved Beauty in all her forms, but that she was like a flame. And that if I came too close, I would be consumed. Then I caught a lucky break. Elora gave me a small fashion job. I still don't know why. But that shoot opened up a whole new universe for me. That's how I came to be a fashion shooter."

Charlie had thought she was getting to know Joshua but after this . . . the realization dawned on her that she and Phoena were probably the only two people who had ever heard this.

"Joshua, that's an incredible story."

He looked into her eyes, searching for something, eyes so arresting and fathomless he thought sometimes he would tumble into them and become lost forever in their fractal depths.

"Charlie? What I met in the valley that day? I'm meeting it again here. And God help me, I can't turn away."

Tears began to run down his face, even as Charlie felt herself slammed with a sadness of such immensity, it was like a fist to her heart. She almost screamed to the Universe, "But we've hardly had any time!"

Because she knew in that instant she had lost him.

Interlude Four—Paris

Fabien Rousse sat at a café on a boulevard in Montparnasse, contemplating life. More specifically, the situation in which he now found himself, with his new girlfriend. You see, they had just had another fight, a big one. All because of those stupid photos that everyone in Paris was so crazy about. Everyone except him.

He stared down at his latte and sighed.

There will be no sex tonight. Such is the price of having a girlfriend as beautiful and as willful as this one. It is always one or the other. Either I am right (no sex) or wrong (sex). Very rarely have I found the middle ground with this one.

He lit a *Gaulois*, pausing to inspect the matchbook's cover. Phoena gazed back at him.

Pretty girl. Even prettier than Juliette. And that is saying something.

He exhaled and looked up, scanning the sea of faces walking along the boulevard. He saw his girlfriend clutching a mass of bags and waved. "Alors! Juliette! Over here!" *Women. Always shopping.*

Then he froze. It was as if a light had burst in his head. He looked again and saw the flood of people with their various bags, all with Campaign of The Century images on them, then back at the matchbook cover, to Phoena's eyes. Then again to the marching bags, their bobbing faces floating like the torn-up pieces of a photo someone had tossed on the sea. And just like that, he had it.

He laughed quietly to himself, shaking his head as he did so. Because Fabien had figured out the secret of The Campaign. Why it worked. He was not really looking at millions of images. He was looking at only *one* image. And how that image revealed of itself was determined as much by what it showed as by what he allowed himself to see. And the definition of 'image' became broader and broader the more the Campaign permeated him, so he could go deeper and deeper into that one image, infinitely, because it had no maximum magnification. Just like Reality.

He saw that he *had* been right in his evaluation of the images (Pretentious Shit).

And that Juliette had *also* been right in *her* evaluation of the images (High Art of The Kind That Can Change The World).

Now, if he could only convince her that once, just this once, maybe they were *both* right . . .

Juliette came to greet him, holding aloft her several shopping bags. She had a smile on her face that could light the world. "Fabien! Mon amour! Regarde!"

Well, Fabien thought, *maybe there will be sex tonight.*

New York City, Central Park West—The Campaign of The Century—Day 249

Charlie had finally decided that enough was enough. There was simply too much weirdness going on with Joshua, Phoena, the Campaign and damn near everything else in her life and it all pointed to Solipsum. Especially after hearing Joshua's story. The time had come to visit his apartment.

"Daughter? Be careful."

Their eyes met in the rearview and Charlie wished she could tell the Driver what she was up to. "Don't worry, I'll be all right. I know what I'm doing."

"I hope so. Still, if you need help, call. I will be here right away."

She'd left the cab and walked into the building, thinking about why exactly she hadn't confided in Phoena. It wasn't like she didn't trust the other girl. She just wished she knew more about what had happened between her and Solipsum.

It had been easy enough getting in. It was just like her friend Quinby had said: show up at the front desk looking really sexy and speak the words "Beauty must be served." She was wearing a short summer dress she'd borrowed from Phoena that clung to her like her own skin. Her underwear consisted of a micro thong that would barely cover a gum drop, a short black wig and green contacts. She hoped it would be disguise enough. The doorman's eyes had fastened to her breasts like limpets but he'd still made her repeat the words twice, this time as he looked her in the eyes. Security, it seemed, wasn't quite as lax as she'd been led to believe. He finally allowed her to go up to "Mr. Solipsum's suite," so that she might "make herself at home." All this with an oily fecundity that made her want to scrub.

She stood now in the empty hallway looking down at the plastic card in her hand and wondered *what the hell am I doing?* She glanced up and down the hall, sure that at any moment Solipsum would return. *Come on, Cherry Cora, you know he's shooting so let's get this over with.* She quickly slid the card into the thin vertical slot, watching as the door hinged inward of itself.

She stood there for a moment, not sure whether to flee or go forward. It was the white that drew her in, the overwhelming impression of white. She stepped across the threshold, low heel click on white marble floor. A sense of movement caused her to spin, just in time to see the door closing behind her soundlessly. Solidly. She felt the first faint touch of fear.

Don't be scared, Cherry Cora. Where there's a way in, there's always a way out.

She relaxed herself with that thought, slowly blanking her mind and opening her sensorium, the dead bird's foot key now clutched tightly in her fist.

The first thing she noticed was the quiet. Not an ordinary quiet, but a stillness—a complete and utter absence of any sound, ambient or otherwise, like the jungle when it was waiting for something to happen. She felt the air on her bare skin, how uncomfortably cool it was, almost enough to raise gooseflesh. And the entire apartment smelled of nothing, as though she stood in a complete and utter lack of presence. The only part of her unaffected by the cool was her shoulder, her dragon shoulder.

She shook off the growing feeling of unease and walked down the carpeted steps into the sunken living room. The air stirred, bringing to her the smell of something sweet and rotted. Then it was gone. She shivered involuntarily, feeling like a character in a Z-grade horror movie.

God, I wish this place wasn't so white. Somehow that makes it even more creepy.

She quickly scanned a living room that looked more like a set from a photo shoot for an architectural magazine than anything habitable. Pristine. White. Sterile. She got an impression the whole thing could be cleaned with a hose, and this, not its visual aesthetic, was its primary design mandate. Beyond some magazines scattered on a coffee table, the room looked like it had last been used a month ago? An hour ago? Impossible to tell.

She turned and went back up the stairs, into the kitchen. It was no different, so creepily clean she was afraid to touch anything, like someone could perform

(surgery)

experiments in here. She opened the refrigerator's stainless steel door to see it fully stocked with every sort of gourmet delicacy imaginable. Many were things she'd seen but had never tried. There seemed to be an inordinate amount of red meat, but not the kind that came from the supermarket. This looked more like wild meat. Game. *Maybe that's what smelled.* Somehow she didn't think so. She closed the door and hurried down the hallway, looking for the keyhole home to the thing she held so tightly. Her black wig was getting a little itchy, a vague awareness that she'd already spent too much time in this place beginning to gnaw at her.

I don't get it. What does this open? He doesn't seem to lock anything up. Then a small thought tugged at her. *Maybe it's because none of this stuff is of any value to him.* She remembered the mysterious sandstorm and realized that though she didn't yet know how, these two elements were somehow intimately linked.

She took a quick peak in the bathroom. *Nothing here,* she thought, and turned to go. Then something caught her eye, a spot of color under the clear glass basin. She dropped to hands and knees, peering at what looked like a pool of

Blood! Holy spit, that's blood!

She crept closer, extending a finger, almost touching the tensile surface when something shimmered. She scrambled back with a cry, chest tightening, hyperventilating, then closed her eyes and calmed her breathing consciously. *Relax, Cherry Cora. No one can hear you. This place is like a vault.* She stared again at the pool, fear and curiosity rippling over her features, edging closer to watch as it shimmered again.

Omigod, it's Phoena!

The image slowly faded, the last of its sorcery consumed. Charlie rubbed her eyes, spooked.

She quickly stood and edged around the pool. Time was running out. Her heels sunk into the carpet as she hurried down the corridor, doors on either side. Then she saw the last one ahead of her, the one with the scarlet handle. She reached it, hand with key extended, and stopped abruptly. *Where's the keyhole?* She slammed her palm against the white wood in frustration and was startled when it swung inward. A moment's hesitation and she pushed the door wider, about to step through when she saw it.

The picture.

She found herself frozen, unable to move, pinned by the man in the image before her. He looked like Christ, bearded and crucified, the thorns of his crown long and cruel. The blood ran freely down his face in rich red streams, the only color in what was otherwise a black and white photograph. It was one of the most extraordinary black and white photographs Charlie had ever seen. She drew back and gasped, recognition slamming into her like a brick-bat to the head, the key falling to the carpet from her nerveless fingers.

For the man staring back at her was Solipsum.

She closed her eyes, then opened them again, the photo so vivid, so lifelike he seemed to be standing in the room with her. A memory surfaced and she swallowed. *B—but that's impossible!* Because she had suddenly remembered where she'd seen this image before.

A breeze stirred the curtains through the open window, breaking the spell. She bent to retrieve the key and happened, still crouched, to looked at the photograph obliquely. A tiny divot, some sort of debossing, disturbed its otherwise smooth surface.

She approached the photograph and saw a small hole, but the wrong shape. *Try it, Charlie, what have you got to lose?* She had brought the key to within an inch of the black circle when the birdlike flanges uncurled and rearranged themselves, twining around one another like blind worms. She felt the movement through the key's thin shaft, almost dropping it in revulsion as they found the hole and disappeared into it. There was a small oiled "snick" and the door opened. Charlie stared, feeling the cold hand of fear delicately trailing its long and icy nails down her spine. And knew this was not her place.

Oh God, Charlie, do you really want to see what's in here? A tiny voice arose inside her, the warrior voice she sometimes thought of as her dragon's. . .

Without fear there can be no courage

She stepped forward and a sound broke the stillness, like something thrown into hot oil. It became louder and before her horrified eyes, the door's frame began to spack and rackle with malevolent veinings of energy. They raced about the frame, red and black and yellow, branching, questing, a fork spearing out at her, quick as a snakehead. She threw her arms up, the lethal bolt impacting her shoulder, right where the dragon sat. Her body thrummed, as if something were fighting to enter, to penetrate her flesh. Then the feeling disappeared. She lowered her arms, just in time to see a fresh bolt seek her out. No time to think, only move, turning her shoulder, feeling the raw force as it slammed into her, drawn as if to a lightning rod. More bolts sought her as she lurched forward, chin tucked, shoulder high, wave after wave of dark and vicious energy exploding into her, trying to kill her, the magic determined not to let her pass. Her feet began slipping as they fought for ground, the doorway not a plane now but a corridor, the lethal bolts a furious twisting storm, all crashing into her dragon, her shield, only to die in black and fiery blossoms. A surge of pure adrenalin pushed her forward with all she had left, finally bursting through the doorway.

She almost collapsed, hands to her knees as she breathed in huge and ragged lungfuls of air. Her shoulder felt hot, almost burning, but curiously painless. Her eyes were drawn to the tattoo, and for the briefest instant she thought she saw it—move. Her lids snapped shut, black energies still strobing behind them, and when she opened her eyes again, she saw only ink.

Then the stench hit her, fetid and raw like some dirty animal's lair. A cough tickled her throat and her eyes watered. She knuckled them and walked deeper into Solipsum's inner chamber. The Room seemed vast, impossibly vast, with ceilings and a spaciousness that the exterior architecture could not possibly have contained. The Room did not lack in personality. Everywhere she looked there was a strangeness. Furniture that appeared more grown than carved, sculptures brooding and massive, paintings of historic events but from some alternate universe, horrific and sensual. There were other things too: diagrams, books, things she had no name for, and were those

(medieval medical instruments)

tools? Those surfaces not covered by cryptic diagrams, paintings and tapestries were black. It was a very special black though, that seemed more simple absence than any sort of paint. It hurt her eyes if she looked at it too long. Her gaze traveled down to see she had wandered onto an ancient tapestry, its colors rich, adorned with pictures of people

(fucking)

dancing? Then her eyes were drawn deeper, because sexual abandon was the least of what she saw. Things began to move, bodies thrusting, sweat gleaming on a curve of buttock, the entire black deviancy slowly coming to life. A man's head turned toward her, invitation in his eyes, a promise on his lips. A tiny sound escaped her and with a huge effort she wrenched her gaze from the sight before her. Eyes straight ahead, she hurried off the thing, feeling the pebbled movements of what lived in it through her shoes. The little voice inside her became urgent. *Hurry, Cherry Cora! You don't have much time!*

Sweat ran freely down her temples now and her eyes were grainy from the contacts she hadn't worn in years. Then she saw the enormous painting on the wall. It appeared to be a blueprint, a huge diagram of something that looked like Joshua's studio, but rendered in a way she would never have imagined. As if someone had dissected its very soul. She stepped closer, the detail in the drawing remarkable, lines representing ley and energy branching off, and a word, "Ascen—" Something punched through her concentration like a frozen needle sliding into her flesh, telling her it was now and immediately time to *leave*. She spun about, racing from the room as though it were collapsing in upon itself, turning to slam the door and palm the key as she caught her breath.

She heard something, sounds coming towards her from down the hall, someone walking, faster and faster, and the panic set in. She saw the open window and realized she had no choice. Before she knew it her shoes were off and tossed through the frame, then one leg out as she straddled the sill. She took the last second to pop the key into her mouth *hurry Charlie!* then slid her body through the window opening. *Which way, which way?* Then she saw it, a long and vertical concrete abutment, an architectural affectation shafting up to her right. She swung out, leg and arm still gripping sill as her left hand groped for purchase. The wind was blowing, buffeting, stronger and colder than she would have believed. Her hand continued reaching, *reaching*, wind blowing, dress riding high, too high *fuck the modesty and find the handholds!* Half inch grooves lined the building's sides and suddenly it all came back in a rush, the training, the training, it's all of the mind and the mind controls the body. That and whatever you do, *don't look down.* She inched over, leaving the safety of the sill, fingers and toes gripping concrete grooves, prehensile. Then her arm swung around and she had it, concrete abutment body-wide *thank God! thank God!* as she hugged it. She gripped and clung, thighs and forearms, fingers and toes finding the grooves, her life now hanging by how much flesh she could wedge into the tiny runnels. *Breathe, breathe, breathe, Cherry Cora,* already the strain had kicked in, wind and cold and *my arms hurt! legs scraped, fingernail popped, bleeding toes, it hurts, it hurts! fuck the mind noise, grip or die!* Then she steadied her breathing, feeling the Now, texture of concrete, grit, dirt, the very air.

She turned her head to see the open window, the vague shape of someone reflected there. She watched, eyes blinking, squeezing away wind-tears, as the shape became Solipsum. *Oh please, oh please, oh please don't look.* Luckily, astonishingly, her prayers were answered. She breathed a tiny sigh of relief, muscles screaming, body clinging, *trapped, still trapped*, the next thought forming, pushing at him, *leave, leave, leave! so I can get back in!*

His hand reached out and pulled the window shut.

She slipped.

Utah, Meg's Desert Cactus Travel Lodge—The Campaign of The Century—Day 249

Russ guzzled his fifth beer, belched softly and figured that'd be it. Wouldn't do to be too hungover for the Mesa Shoot set-up. He sat back in a chair on the porch of what was probably the rattiest fleabag motor-

inn he'd ever stayed in. *But what the fuck, it's clean and they got cold beer. What more could a man ask for?* A picture of
(*Charlie*)
someone popped into his mind and he angrily crushed it.

The sun burned its way into the horizon and Russ settled back, savoring the quality of the desert light. It brought back a fond cascade of prurient memory, the Twins and Egypt and the wonderful way they—*fuck, could those two fuck. They whipsawed each other like it was the last day on—*

His cell phone rang. Not the special one, the normal one.

"Yeah?"

"Russell."

"Who's this?" He belched.

"Bokken."

Oh fuck. Russ sat down abruptly, chair legs slamming into the old wood of the porch. "*Sensei.*"

"I have some information for you. If you are not too busy drinking."

"Yes, *Sensei.* I—I mean no, *Sensei.* I'm not too busy. I'm listening."

"That drawing you gave me? The one of the tattoo?"

"Yes, *Sensei?*"

"I have discovered its origin. And you were right. When I first saw what you had given me, I thought you were playing some sort of joke."

"No, *Sensei,* I would never do that."

"I did not doubt it. But the . . . gravity of what you gave me . . . I telephoned an old friend in Japan, *Sensei* Miagi. It took him some time but he finally found the answer. I was very surprised. I did not think to ever have such a thing cross my path."

There was a silence that Russ patiently waited through. If there was one thing he had learned in all his years of training, it was never to rush *Sensei* Bokken.

"That tattoo?"

"Yes, *Sensei?*"

"It adorns a woman. A very special woman. Russell, as I told you when you reached black belt, there are those in the world of martial arts who exist on the surface, there for all to see. Then there are—others. Who exist beneath the skin of the world. Whose skill level passes so far beyond what you or I or anyone I know is capable of. This tattoo belongs to such a one."

"*Sensei—*"

"Let me finish. This *irezumi* is unique in all the world. Anyone who attempts to reproduce it simply dies. Anyone. For you to have seen this thing—in America? It simply cannot be. It belonged to a woman who was special to the *Yakuza*. A legend. An assassin of extraordinary skill. She is rumored to have dispatched men and women the world over. People of the highest standing. People so well guarded that they were impossible to kill. Yet still they are dead.

"About a year ago, word began coming out of Japan. From the streets. That this woman was no more. That someone known as the Winter Queen had decided she be removed from the Game. Nine assassins were each given the assignment. And a tenth as well. Someone very special. They converged on the woman's home and found something they did not expect. A bloodbath ensued. The details are unclear. But at the end, the tenth succeeded where the others had failed. For one such as her to be dispatched—I do not want to think of whoever it was that did this. Where did you find this tattoo?"

"*Sensei*, it—it is on the arm of a girl I met. An assistant in the place I now work."

"Hmmmm. So the rumor is true. *Sensei* Miagi told me that this woman had a student. Only one. A girl. A *gaijin*. With black hair."

"*Sensei*, the girl I saw the tattoo on has blond hair."

"A simple thing to alter. What else do you know of her?"

"Her skill level is extraordinary. Sh—she's better than me, *Sensei*. But she doesn't know it. There is only one other thing about her. She has eyes that are—"

"Violet, are they not?"

Russ almost dropped the phone. "H—how did you know?"

He heard a deep sigh on the other end. "Russell, whatever you are involved with, go no further. Even as a student, this girl would know far more than you. In fact, I suspect she knows even more than I. More than I would want to know. Of dark things. Black things. Things that cross the boundary between this World—and the Next."

"But *Sensei*—"

"Russell. Listen to me. Leave this thing alone. Promise me."

"I—"

"Do you promise?"

"Yes, *Sensei*."

"Good. I must go now."

"*Sensei*, please, wait!"

"What is it?"

"What was her name? The assassin?"

"Haiku. Her name was Haiku. Good bye, my student."

Russ found himself listening to nothing but dead air. He sighed and sat back, suddenly sober and craving a cigarette, unaware that he had dropped the phone. His mind was in a turmoil but one thing stood clear. He had to make a call. A special call. With the other phone. The red one.

New York City, Stone Studios—The Campaign of The Century—Day 249

"Jesus, Charlie, how did you get back in?" Phoena looked over at her friend, seeing again the small white bandages on her fingers and toes, so stark against her tanned skin.

"I—kicked in the window."

A chill came over Phoena despite the warmth of the late afternoon sun. She realized in that instant how close her friend had come to death, and the sudden thought of her world without Charlie was more than she could bear. Then she raised her sunglasses, Charlie's words fully registering. "You kicked in the window? With your bare feet?"

"Yeah. I had one chance. If the glass was too strong, well, that would have been it."

"But—but that's impossible."

Charlie sighed and turned on her side, wincing a bit as her scraped legs brushed against one another. She snuggled deeper into the towel. "No, Phoena. Not for me. Not with the stuff I've learned."

"The stuff you've—?" Phoena stood abruptly. "We need more cocktails." With that she disappeared inside.

Charlie took the time to relax, or at least try to. She looked at Bruun, who was sleeping on the towel beside her. He seemed to be smiling. As she watched, he stretched out a hind leg and pawed the air a few times before relaxing again with a small cat-sound. She smiled and scratched his head, then gently rubbed his raggedy ear between her bandaged thumb and forefinger. He began purring and she wondered what it would be like to live his life, if only for a day. She gazed out at the pool, seeing the tiny riffles of water, highlights like pins scattered across their tops. She felt very still today, but somehow completely alive, aware of the minute detail in everything that surrounded her, almost as if she were experiencing the taking of one continuous photograph.

Phoena returned with a pitcher of the frothy green and very alcoholic drink she'd concocted earlier in Joshua's blender. She set it down on the table between them with the exaggerated care of the slightly drunk.

Charlie watched as she refilled both their glasses. "That's a really nice swimsuit, Phoena. Goes with the rad body."

"Thanks. Believe it or not, it's from 1964. Rudy Gernreich." Phoena's fingers idly traced the black straps that crisscrossed the taupe wool bikini. "Joshua bought it for me, back when."

"When you were lovers?"

Phoena shielded her eyes. "He told you that?"

"Yeah. He told me pretty much everything, but severely edited."

"That's okay, Charlie. There's not much about me that I wouldn't want you to know. Not now." Phoena lay down on the lounger and turned on her side. "So. Out with it. Where did you learn all this karate stuff? Rumor has it you even beat the crap out of Russ."

"I didn't. In fact, he could have killed me, but—God, Phoena, do you really want to hear this story?"

"Uh, YES."

Charlie moved closer to the edge of her lounger and lowered her sunglasses. Bruun took the hint and jumped off the towel. "Okay, here goes. But have patience, Phoena, I've never told anyone this."

"I grew up in Tokyo. My Mom taught English and my Dad was a small time advertising photographer. He was really good but he never learned how to play the game. That and the fact that he was a *gaijin* insured he would never rise much above the level of salaryman. But I never really figured any of this out 'til later. I was fifteen when they died. We were coming home from a night on the town. Mom had just gotten a raise, and we'd decided to celebrate.

My Dad wanted to take the main road but I wouldn't hear of it. "Where's your sense of adventure?" I cried as I pulled them along down this short cut I'd spotted. The alley looked like a much cooler route than the stuffy old road we always took. Little did I realize that that simple girlish decision would end up changing my whole life.

As we walked through the narrow alley, I looked up and saw an old lady in a window. She looked down at us and seemed about to

(shout a warning, to)

say something but then she

(saw one of them was a gaijin and)

seemed to think better of it. I heard a child cry and then the window slammed down as she ducked back inside.

Mom and Dad laughed and Dad called her a silly old woman. They were both a bit drunk but we were all so happy. That's probably why we didn't notice we were being followed. There were seven of them and they must have been high on something.

It started when this cocky kid a few years older than me suddenly appeared out of the darkness and blocked our path. He was dressed in black, his face so white it seemed to float.

"*Gaijin* filth!" he yelled, "Why don't you leave our country and take your corruption with you!"

"Yes!" another one blustered as he joined them. He had really bad acne and seemed as scared as me.

"B—but leave your wife and daughter behind," the third boy stammered, fat and sweaty as he stepped out of the night. Four more boys then slunk from the shadows like dogs. They all wore black and that was when I realized they were part of some gang.

"Good suggestion," said the first, obviously their leader. He was all bravado as he tried to bolster the others. I somehow knew that none of them had ever done this before.

Then they surrounded us, knives and martial arts weapons suddenly in their hands.

I spread my arms and stepped in front of my parents. "Mom! Dad! Get behind me!" I tried not to sound as scared as I was. They all burst out laughing and I knew we were in big trouble.

"So. The little cub has teeth." the leader sneered. Then he came forward. He hesitated for a second as he seemed to notice

(how young she is! She cannot be more than fifteen! But so beautiful! And her eyes! Ayeeeah! Violet like the neon of the Ginza! I must have her. I will show her)

something. Then he yelled to the others in Japanese. It was some sort of street slang that I didn't understand. They started moving and seemed to be everywhere at once. I went into a defensive stance, like I'd been taught, and then the leader suddenly attacked. His hands were like lightning! I barely managed to defend myself even though I knew he was just playing with me. *This is way different than the dojo,* I thought. Then I heard the scream.

"Dan!"

I looked to see Mom kneeling beside my poor Dad. The front of his shirt had this horrible red stain that spread quicker than I would have believed. His eyes stared up at the night sky and I realized with a shock he was dead. One of the gang members stood nearby, holding a dripping *tanto* at his side.

"I'll kill you, you fuckers!" I shrieked, then lunged toward the leader. He easily evaded my first attack, then blocked my kick.

"Now, now, little Kitten, didn't your *Sensei* teach you never to fight in anger?"

He brushed past my guard with total contempt and slapped me. My ears rang and I tasted blood in my mouth. Someone grabbed me from behind, and before I could remember what to do, my arms were pinned. The lesson came back and I tried to scrape his shin, only to get punched in the solar plexus for my trouble. It was the hardest I'd ever been hit and God! I thought I was gonna die. The pain was incredible! My body went limp and I started to cry. *Fuck, Charlie, your dad is dead and this is the best you can do? Fight them!* But my body wouldn't listen. I could only stare, helpless, as events unfolded around me, like some nightmarish *No* play. I saw my mom grab the fallen knife that had killed my dad, lunging for the gang leader. He deflected her, and as he did, I managed to kick him. It was weak, but enough to make him sloppy. His block went too far, the knife going straight into one of the gang creeps that was facing me. The fat and sweaty one. He went down so quietly, sighing a bit, like a balloon with the air let out. Then the leader went nuts.

"Old whore!" he yelled, his voice breaking as he delivered a blinding *shuto* strike to my mom's throat. I heard this horrible sound as the cartilage cracked and watched as she collapsed in a heap, dead.

"MOM!" I screamed.

"Shut up, half caste bitch!" The leader was breathing hard now. "Hold her!" A simple robbery had turned into a double murder and I guess he figured, *what's one more body?*

Then I saw him staring at my breasts and knew that wasn't all he had planned.

He reached out and grabbed the front of my dress. "Now, it is time to see if you are a real blond." He ripped it down. I felt the cool night wind on my body and tried to cover myself. The arms holding me gripped tighter. I glared at the leader through my tears and vowed he was not going to have me.

Suddenly I heard this—voice. It was powerful and imperious and seemed to come from everywhere at once.

"Even she is more than a match for your shriveled apparatus."

He turned to look back down the alley, his hand still gripping my dress. "Who dares?"

In response, a *sai* came whizzing through the night air, spearing the throat of one of the gang. He sort of gurgled, then fell. No one moved. We were all completely immobilized. Then someone quietly whispered . . .

"Haiku."

One of the others turned to him and I heard his voice go up a notch. "But—but she does not exist! She is only a legend!" It was the kid with the acne.

The leader shoved him. "Idiot!" he hissed, "Tanaka is dead. Is this the work of a ghost?"

"We are all dead," Acne moaned.

All of us turned to the mouth of the alley where Haiku stood, edge lit by the streetlights. My first thought was *she's so tiny. Almost as small as me.*

Then the leader pointed and yelled, "Get her!"

What I saw next will stay with me 'til the day I die. Haiku's command of several martial arts was surpassed only by her fluidity. Her grace made it seem like the gang members were frozen as she killed them, one by one. She left some time between each, just enough so his friends could see him die. Then she killed the next. And the whole time, she seemed a bit disgusted, like she had to take the trash out and had forgotten to wear her gloves. Finally, only their leader remained.

"I will savor killing you," he snarled and lunged for her. She brushed aside his attack like she would a fly, then drove a *sai* into his stomach with so much force the tip came out his back.

Her smile was like ice as she brought her face close to his. "Now, now, didn't your *Sensei* teach you never to fight in anger?"

Then he fell to the ground, his sagging weight pulling her weapon free with a small sound.

I looked at her, my voice breaking. "Who—who are you?"

"My name is Haiku. Come, we must go. The police will be here soon."

"But my mom and dad—"

"They are dead. Nothing we can do will change that. Come!"

So began what was to be for me a life unlike anything I could ever have imagined. You see, Haiku was an assassin for the *Yakuza*, one of their best. And she decided to take me under her wing. She began teaching me everything she could. And I soaked it up like a sponge. I had entered a secret world—even my hair was dyed black and she made me wear contacts so no one would get curious about who I was. I—"

Charlie stopped and looked at the other girl. "There's more. Actually a lot more."

"But?"

Charlie gave her a small smile. "Let's take a little break. The rest gets pretty—intense." She reached for her drink and drained it.

"Hey, you're burning up," said Phoena. "Want some lotion?"

"Okay."

"Turn over, lobster girl."

Charlie obediently flipped onto her front. Slowly.

"Can I sit on you? Will you be okay?"

Charlie lifted her head. "I'll be fine." She took a quick gulp of her magically refilled cocktail and lay back down. Phoena gently straddled the other girl and spread some fragrant aloe-coconut lotion on her hands, carefully applying it to her friend's skin.

"Phoena?"

"Yeah?"

"When you said there's not much about you I don't know, that wasn't quite true."

"Oh?" Phoena undid Charlie's bikini top and started applying lotion to her back. "Relax, Charlie, you are way too tense." She felt the muscles beneath her hands loosen, then heard her friend's muffled voice.

"You never told me where you came from. How you got to be a supermodel."

Phoena put a daub of lotion on Charlie's dragon and just let it sit there, like a little hat. She giggled a bit, then rubbed it in. "You know, we're kind of alike in more ways than one. 'Cause I've never told anyone my story either."

"Not even Joshua?"

"Not even Joshua." Phoena sat back and put her hands on her thighs. "I like you, Charlie. You're funky and cool and cute as can be. There's something about you that reminds me of me, way back when. And some day, you're going to make a great photographer. Besides, you are now officially my best friend."

The young assistant propped herself up on her elbows and brought the back of a hand up to touch her forehead. She rolled her eyes in mock swoon. "Oh, Phoena, stop. I'm getting misty."

The model playfully swatted her bottom.

"Owww!"

"Whatever, Clinging Ninja Queen with Buns of Steel." Phoena clambered off her friend carefully and lay back on her own lounger. She took a long sip of her drink then held the cool glass to her cheek, just enjoying the sensation. Charlie watched with a tiny smile, somehow very happy. She noticed the light on Phoena's face, her eyes like precious tourmalines, the pendant she had taken to wearing a deep and numinous scarlet.

"Did you ever wonder what my real name is? Well I'll tell you. But—" Phoena held up a finger. "You realize, of course, you are sworn to secrecy. 'Cause *no one* knows this."

Charlie rolled onto her back and solemnly held one hand in the air while the other covered her heart.

"It's Raspudka Suklofsky."

"Ra-*spud*-ka?"

"Not 'Ra-spud-ka'. 'Rahsh-pood-ka.'"

"Did—did they used to call you 'Spud' in high school?" asked Charlie as she tried to hold back the laughter.

"Does the word 'pummel' mean anything to you? How about the word 'crab claw'?" Phoena then reached over and gently squeezed an injured Charlie-toe.

"Hyuh! Hyuh!" Charlie yelped.

"Now that I have your attention, do you want to hear this story?"

"Yes, oh yes! Please, Phoena!"

"If I hear one more insult . . ." Phoena's pincered digits lingered in dangerous proximity to a fresh Charlie-toe.

"I'll be good! I'll be good!"

The fingers squeezed together, just missing the bandage as Charlie squealed.

"That'll be it for you. Got that?"

Charlie nodded vigorously, trying not to giggle.

"Okay then. Where was I?" Phoena looked for her drink, finally found it right where she had left it, took a huge gulp, then wiped the green froth from her lips. She sat back and sighed.

"Can you imagine growing up with a name like that? The teasing I took? Until my body—But I'm getting ahead of the story. Let me start at the beginning."

"Ever been to South Carolina? No? Well, let me tell you, it's one of the most beautiful places on God's green earth. And tucked away in a little fold of all that beauty is Precipice. That's where I grew up.

Dad died before I was born so it was up to my Mom to raise me and my two older brothers. We lived in the deep woods in this cabin that had been in my Mom's family for generations. It was big and old and always run down. We never had any money to do more than patch work fixin' on it. But when you're a kid, you don't really notice stuff like that. Hell, I never even knew we were poor 'til I started going to school."

Charlie quietly refilled Phoena's glass, noticing the accent that had crept into her friend's voice, and how very far away she was from where she lay right now.

"Growin' up with two older brothers, I learned a lot about the woods. Hell, I was such a tomboy, people thought my parents had three sons instead of just Cody n' Bryce. They took me huntin' and fishin' and taught me just about everythin' there was to know about trackin' and woodcraft. Even how to throw a knife.

All that runnin' around the woods also kept me away from the house. 'Cause Mom had gotten herself a boyfriend. Kenny. He was a lazy fuck, but good lookin' in a weasely kind of way. Kenny worked down at the mill. That's when he was workin' and not drinkin'. One day he put the two together and ended up losing three fingers to a rip saw. That was the end of Kenny's days at the mill. He started spendin' more and more time at our place, getting' drunk and wallowin' in self-pity like a baby in a dirty diaper.

I tried to get Mom to clear the jerk out but she wouldn't hear of it. See, Dad died at the mill and Mom wasn't about to lose another man to that fuckin' place. So she put up with his shit. This went on for another four years, 'til the night everything went to hell.

It was the summer I turned sixteen. It was the best and worst year of my life. I basically turned from ugly possum to belle of the ball in eight months. All my curves came in and the baby fat disappeared, practically overnight. It seemed like I got taller too, but it was maybe just the new geography made me look that way.

When I came back to school in the fall of that year, boys were trippin' all over themselves in the halls whenever I walked by. Suddenly I wasn't "Suck-a-lot-sky" anymore. And I still didn't really get it. It was all so totally bewilderin', to be confronted by that *wantin'* thing in people, all because of how you looked. But it was fun too. Didn't take me long to learn how powerful a thing beauty can be, good an' bad. See, it wasn't just the boys in school that were takin' notice. It seemed ole Greasy Kenny wasn't so drunk he didn' notice the changes I was goin' through too. It started out with him just happenin' to come into my room when I was changin' or the bathroom just as I was comin' out of the shower.

I told my brothers about it but they just laughed. Told me I was crazier than a shine-blind coon. "He's just a harmless old drunk," they said. Well, it turned out he wasn't so harmless after all. But I'm getting' ahead of myself. Like I said before, it was the best year of my life.

It probably would have been the peak of my existence, if Rothman hadn't come to town."

Charlie blinked. "You mean—"

"Yup. Rothman Cartilage. The agent's agent. Also known as 'Bite Radius' cause that's how you measure the chunk he takes out of you. But this was still early days for him. He was big, but he hadn't gone supernova yet. He'd just been booted out of *Elitist* for 'financial improprieties' and was drivin' through South Carolina on his way to God knows where. Back home to Hell, probably. I met him when I was working after school at Katie's . . ."

Phoena's mind took her back to that long ago summer, when she was a young girl waiting tables.

"I remember it like it was yesterday. There was no one in the place except one non-descript man sitting in a booth by the window. He was still looking at the menu when I came up to him. "Are you ready to order, sir?"

"The steak, I think. Raw. I mean rare. And coffee. Black."

"Would you like a baked potato or the fries with that?"

"Neither. Just the steak." He put the menu down then and finally looked at me. "Oh my. Aren't you the most stunning thing I've seen in an age."

He smiled and that was when I first saw his shark-like grin.

"Uhhh, thanks, I'll go place your order." *Jesus, that was creepy,* I thought. I spun his order and picked it up in no time, him being the only customer. Then I walked over and plopped it down. "Here you go, Mister."

I watched, fascinated, as his mouth chewed the—I was going to say meat. But that's not really what went through my head at the time. The word that popped into my mind was "flesh". He chewed the flesh that I had set before him. For some reason that distinction seems important. Really important.

"Mmmm. Very succulent."

I'd seen enough and turned to leave. That's when he grabbed my dress and I saw the weird prosthetic he had in place of a hand, extendin' beyond the cuff of his jacket.

"Not so fast, blossom. How would you like to make five million dollars in the next two years?" He yanked me a little harder. "Look at me when I'm talking to you, girl."

It almost ended right there. But I did look at him, fire in my eyes. "Fuck you, Mister. Who do you think you are?" I pulled away, not even noticin' how his pincered fingers took a piece of my dress.

"Wait. Hear me out. My name is Rothman Cartilage. I scout models for *Elitist*. Or at least I did, until I figured out how much better off I'd be on my own. I found Linda, Dane, Telura and Harlow Bleak."

I whipped around. "Sure you did!" I said in my most sarcastic voice, Then I turned to go.

"Wait. Pick one."

"What?"

"You heard me. Pick one," he enunciated. I could see his teeth.

"Okay. Harlow."

"Know her voice?"

"Yeah. From that new *Dwhor* ad she's in."

He pulled out a state of the art cell phone and punched in fifteen numbers. It was like no phone I'd ever seen, and his fingers flew over its keypad like some master pianist's.

"Babe? It's me. How are things on the Côte? . . . cool . . . don't burn. What's up? Not much. Just touching base. Hey, do me a favor? Say hi to a friend of mine."

Then he handed the phone to me with another shark-like smile.

"Uhhh . . . Hello?"

And a voice I instantly recognized as Harlow's said, "Whose this?"

"Ras—Raspudka. My name is Raspudka."

And Harlow laughed that musical laugh that I would come to know so well. "That'll change." Then she shifted gears. "Did you pick me?"

"What?"

"Did he tell you to pick one? Just answer yes or no."

"Yes."

Harlow laughed again. "Well listen up, chicken on a bun. He'll deliver. Do whatever he says and you'll go straight to the top. But never trust him. Cause he'll fuck you in the end, right in the hole where your heart used to be. And you have to want it bad. Real bad. Otherwise walk. Now. Got that?"

"Yes."

"Good. So . . . decide. . ." There was a *click* as she hung up.

And I decided. Right then and there. "Okay Mister. Start talking."

Well, we sat there for a long time. A couple of hours passed like minutes and after it was over, I knew that my life had changed forever. He gave me a card and told me what hotel he was staying at. We were going to talk some more tomorrow and then go from there. As it turned out, things ended up moving faster. A lot faster.

I was walkin' back to the cabin where we lived and boy did I have stars in my eyes! I couldn't believe I'd just talked to one of the biggest models in the world. Then I saw the lights spilling from the window and my mood turned sour. If the lights were still on, it meant *he* was still up. Waiting. Watching.

Sure enough, when I got to the porch, there he was. Lounging in the doorway, drunk, holding a bottle with that three-fingered club hand I couldn't stand to look at. The other hand was playing pocket pool. He reeked so bad of booze it was like his skin was farting liquor.

I briefly thought of mom and my brothers, visiting her sister. Maybe it would have all turned out different if they stayed home. I never forgave them for what happened.

Kenny belched, then wiped his mouth with the back of the club hand. "Where the fuck have you been?"

"I had to work late."

"Work late? It's eleven-o-fucking-clock late. Why didn't you call, you little bitch, I was worried sick!" he said, suddenly the model parent.

I stood there with my hands on my hips and let him have it. "Worried about what, you creepy ped, you might miss your bedtime ogle?"

Then I squeezed my boobs at him. Probably not the smartest thing I ever did. It really made him mad. His pissy little eyes got even redder and beadier. Then he bellowed "That's enough!" and fucking backhanded me.

I couldn't believe it! I put my hand to my cheek and tasted the blood in my mouth. Boy could he hit! One of my front teeth felt loose. I opened my mouth to touch it and next I knew it had fallen into my hand. I started crying, my poor tooth clenched in my fist. "That's the last time you ever hit me, you bastard! I'm outta here!"

He lurched away from the doorway and staggered towards me. "Where do you think you're going?"

And like an idiot, I stayed there and answered him. "I met someone whose going to make me a star. I'm leaving tonight."

He almost fell down, he started laughing so hard. "Oh, that's rich! Har, har, har, har!" Then he got even angrier. "You're not going anywhere, except to bed. Now!"

And this weird light came into his eyes. Like he knew there was no one around and he could finally do what he'd been fantasizing about for God only knew how long. He dropped the bottle, grabbed me and spun me around, then started groping me. I almost choked on the stink of him, booze and sweat and week-old piss. I started screaming and he covered my mouth with that—hand, like some fat white turtle. Uggghhh! I lost it and bit down as hard as I could. Blood squirted into my mouth and I felt it rip as he wrenched it out and damn, you should have heard him scream!

I ran inside, looking for something, anything to hurt him with. The kitchen was right by the door and a big old pot was boiling on the stove, but way too big for me to lift. My eyes were darting around desperately. Then I saw the kitchen knives and grabbed one, crying so hard I could barely see.

I gripped the knife in two hands and turned, screaming, "Come and get it, you fuckin' bastard!" He just smiled and grabbed this old axe handle by the door. Started slappin' it into the bloody turtle hand. Thwack. Thwack. Thwack. He didn't even seem to feel it. Just standin' there. I didn't know what to do. So I drew my arm back and threw the knife, just like I'd been taught. And it missed by a fuckin' mile.

He laughed and I thought, *Good work, Spud, you stupid cow! You just disarmed yourself.*

Then he started walkin' towards me, like he had all the time in the world, smilin' as he said "You are goin' to get it, you little bitch. You are *so* going to get it!"

The worst part was I could see the bulge in his pants, like a piece of pig iron. I just froze and watched him as he came, my mouth numb where my tooth used to be. He stopped in front of me, smirking. I could feel the hot stove at my back and knew I had nowhere to go. Then he swung the axe handle. I didn't even have time to think, just move, diving to my left. Everything happened so fast after that! I heard a crash, then a huge whumph! and felt this sudden heat. When I turned to look, he was burning. Burning and screaming. I just had time to glimpse the broken shelf support he'd hit instead of me. There must have been something up there that wanted the fire.

Then he was lurching towards me, this flaming boogey man and, Charlie, the fucking smell was sick. Like roasting pork. God, it was horrible. And his face—melting—as he screamed "*I'll kill you, you fuckin' bitch!*"

I scrambled backwards on all fours, looking for the door. Already there was smoke and fire everywhere. I couldn't believe how fast the place had caught. Kenny was stumbling around, screaming and screaming, bumping into stuff, setting it on fire. I could just see the door, prayin' and prayin' he wouldn't find me. He came real close once and even over the roar of the flames, I could hear it, his fat—sizzlin'.

I finally crawled through the door and got outside onto the porch. I staggered to my feet and made it to the grass before I tripped and fell. I just lay there, breathing and coughing and rubbing my eyes. One of them felt puffy and was hard to see through. I was a mess of hurt. Then I sat up and looked back at the house, going up like a match. All I could hear was the fire. At one point I thought I heard him scream but I never saw him again.

Then I took off. Breathin' hard, mouth bleedin', my sides hurtin' from runnin' so fast. I don't even remember how I got to Rothman's hotel.

I must have been a sight, standing there with my clothes all ripped, covered in soot, the blood 'n snot runnin' outta my nose and one eye black as a lump of coal.

He took one look and said, "I take it your parents didn't agree?"

I turned my head and spit some blood onto the gravel. Then I looked back at him through my one eye. "It's worse than that."

He scanned the parking lot to see if anyone had noticed us. "Fuck. Get in." He grabbed my arm, gave a yank and slammed the door. Then he pulled out the first aid kit and started cleaning me up.

"Hmmm, not so bad. Some cuts and scrapes, that tooth will need replacing but nothing broken. You should be okay in a couple of weeks. Now sit still . . ."

I told him what had happened as he cleaned me up. He was almost done and was swabbing antiseptic into the last cut. When the pain flared up where he'd touched, I just gritted my teeth.

"Ohhh, tough, eh? By the way, you have an exquisite body."

I couldn't believe what he'd just said. "Mr. Cartilage, after what I've been through, I can't deal with no more—"

"Don't worry, Raspudka. My sexuality does not intrude upon my work. Appearances to the contrary, there is probably no one on the planet you would be safer with."

And I believed him. As it turned out, that was just about the only thing he didn't lie about. We left that night and I've never been back since.

As we drove away, he turned his face to me in the fading light and said, "That name. It has to go."

"But it's my name!"

He looked at me like I was the greenest girl in the Universe. "Names are power. And after hearing that rather remarkable story, I think it's best we christen you—Phoena. Now say it."

"Phoena."

And it felt so right, I could see it in his eyes. Then he laughed and laughed that sharky laugh as we drove down the last lone stretch of highway.

The next five years were some of the best and worst times of my entire life.

Someday I'll tell you about them in detail but for now, let's just say it was one fuck of a ride. He introduced me to everything I'd ever dreamed the industry was about. And that was only the beginning. He took six months to put my book together. Only the best shooters, but not just established guys, new photographers too. Photographers he had his eye on. Comers. He knew that letting them shoot me now would work to his advantage down the pike. Smart man. *Very* smart man.

At the end of the first year, I was off to Europe. Milan, then Paris for more editorial and finally, Germany for the money. He never let me forget that. "Money is the life blood of the industry," he'd say, "No blood, no life. No life, and you'll end up back in Buttfuck, South Carolina, waiting tables and blowing truckers in the Johnny on the Spot out back."

I don't know what it was. Timing? My looks? Him? He explained it once by saying, "Phoena, in every age, there arises a confluence of forces that together elevate an individual far beyond the norm, into the stratosphere. You are such an individual."

I got good at the money part. Making blood flow. That's when the partying started, or rather got out of control. Because we'd barely left South Carolina when he introduced me to drugs. Nothing heavy, just a joint or two. Then once we were in New York, and I had to deal with the brutal schedule of making myself over and shooting, shooting, constantly shooting, well—that's when the coke started. Just some bumps to pick me up at first, but I really started to dive by Year Two. And still my career kept going up and up. There didn't seem to be any end in sight.

And I finally got to meet Harlow. We ended up becoming best friends and going through some wild times together . . ."

Charlie looked at her friend and said quietly, "Then she died in that horrible car wreck."

Phoena sat up slowly and put her face in her hands for a moment, then raised her chin and swallowed. "I was there."

"What?" Charlie swung her legs to the ground and almost stepped on Bruun. "But everyone knows she got too high and drove off the edge of that cliff."

"No." Phoena shook her head. "She wasn't alone. The driver lost control and smashed us into the rocks. When I came to, Rothman was there and the next thing I knew, he took care of everything." She started to cry.

Charlie could not believe what she had just heard. "God, Phoena." She quickly gathered the weeping girl into her arms.

Phoena sniffled. "I've never told anyone that."

They looked into each other's eyes, deeper and deeper, their gazes unwavering, for a moment that seemed to stretch to infinity. And something passed between the two. Something that took them both by complete surprise. Charlie leaned a bit closer, never breaking contact with Phoena's green, green eyes. She marveled for an instant at how heightened her senses were, how it seemed she could taste every molecule of Phoena's scent, mingled with lotion-smell and the slightest trace of alcohol. Then, as if by magic, the distance between them was no more. Their lips touched and they kissed, very lightly, very tenderly. Charlie's hand slowly closed over Phoena's breast, feeling the powerful beating of her heart, the warmth of her skin. Then she felt Phoena's hand on her own, pressing it closer. Charlie had no idea how much time passed before they separated to gaze once again into each other's eyes.

Then Charlie asked the question they had both been dreading. "Who was driving?"

Suddenly, Solipsum was there between them.

"Me."

Book 9

"All that we see or seem is but a dream within a dream." —Edgar Allen Poe

New York City, Stone Studios - The Campaign of The Century—Day 249

Charlie wondered how much he had seen, the alcohol roiling in her guts. "Uh, w—we were just talking about you, Mr. Solipsum."

"Shut up, cunt." He looked at Phoena. "Tell her. The whole truth."

"But—"

His gaze became a piercing luminosity that would not be denied. "Tell her."

"Milan. That's where I met Harlow for the first time. We were in a club, dancin' and partyin'. You know, the usual crowd, models, play-boys, hangers on, when in she walked. She was one of the most beautiful women I'd ever seen. Everything stopped. Except the whispers.

We were introduced and as soon as I heard her voice, my mind flashed back to that long ago phone call. She remembered it too. We both laughed and she said, "Now you're called Phoena." Suddenly it seemed as though we'd known each other forever. Then she introduced me to the exquisite man she was with.

That was when I first met Solipsum.

In an instant, the magic circle closed and from that point on, we were inseparable. The three of us became the talk of the town. We went every-where together, did everything together.

Everything.

Strange, isn't it, how you think you've tasted all there is of pleasure? And to one day discover you've visited only the smallest part of an infi-nite garden."

She sighed and lay back on the lounger, the setting sun edging her, deep in the remembering of it.

"Continue, Phoena." Charlie was struck by how beautiful his voice sounded in that moment. "Though you almost seem to be enjoying this a bit too much."

"As much as you did that first night, Trey?" She turned her head and looked at him in a way he had never experienced. "As much as we both did?"

Her words silenced him. Charlie looked at them both, their profiles kissed by the dying sun, each face so intent upon the other. She remembered how they had looked in the Station, the almost unbearable tension/attraction that had emanated from them. And she realized with surprise they were equals.

Phoena finally spoke. "The one thing we didn't do was shoot together. It was weird. Really weird. We'd be optioned all the time but something would always come up. It was like Fate had determined we would never appear on film together. At least not then.

"It was only three months but they were the most intense three months of my life. And then we went for the drive in the mountains. And something happened. Something so strange . . ."

She hesitated, the past a crushing weight of tortured metal.

"Tell her." Solipsum had found his voice again. "*Everything.*"

"It was such a gorgeous day, blue sky and the cool mountain air. We'd even brought a picnic basket and some wine. Trey was driving and Harlow was beside him. We were just laughing and having fun, not a care in the world. Then Harlow invited me to come sit on her lap. I started clambering over the seats and looked at Trey and he—did something."

Phoena stopped, her eyes finding Solipsum's for a split second, to see again what they had seen that day.

Charlie glared at the male model, her friend's hand so cool in her own as she took it. "What? What did he do?"

Phoena shivered and exhaled slowly. "He showed me his *true face.* I almost lost my mind. I—I can't even describe what he—really looks like. You still don't understand what he is yet, do you?"

Solipsum prodded her with his shoe. "Finish it."

She looked down woodenly and obeyed. "After that, everything was suddenly instinctive, every nerve in my body, screaming at me to get away. I scrambled and my foot must have hit his gas foot, 'cause suddenly the car zoomed forward. I was thrown into him and his hands lost control of the wheel. By the time he shoved me aside and grabbed it again, the truck was nearly on us. I was sure we were all dead. There was only one way for him to veer. Into the rocks.

"Harlow died instantly. I ran over to her and thought for a second that she was okay, she looked so peaceful. Then I saw the angle of her head and went into shock. I couldn't believe *I* was still alive. And Solipsum. He was pretty fucked up. Was. Until he—repaired himself. Then he pulled out his cell and called Rothman. I don't know where he was that he got there so quick but before I knew it, they were—fixing things. Together."

"Fixing things?"

Phoena sighed, her shoulders rounded, her voice small with shame as she looked at Charlie. "They were salting the site with booze and pills. So it would look like an accident. Then they threw her body over the cliff. The two of them. And I just watched until they led me away."

Solipsum looked up from inspecting his nails, a completely inappropriate smile on his face. "Wow, Phoena. What a heartbreaking story."

"Shut up, you—*monster*!"

Bruun hissed from beneath the lounger. Solipsum looked at the cat and laughed with genuine delight, as though he knew some strange and delicious secret. Then his eyes found Phoena's. "Me? A monster?" he asked conversationally. "Have you looked in the mirror lately? Who is the real monster? Hmmm?"

Phoena's expression wavered, then collapsed, a horrible animal sound torn from the depths of her being. She fled the poolside. Charlie was about to follow when Solipsum's eyes pinned her like slitted headlights. "Not so fast, little monkey."

She noticed that something had appeared in his hand. It took her a second to realize what he held, then the shock took her breath. "Wh— where did you get those?" she gasped, unable to tear her eyes from the sight of her black wig and the severed head of her special doll.

"Now, now, you visited my home. Isn't it fair that I visit yours?" He tossed the wig and doll aside as though they were dead animals. "If you ever enter my home again uninvited, the next piece of sushi you eat will be your own. As I feed it to you." He made a lapping gesture through forked fingers, his tongue muscular and sinuous.

Charlie almost screamed, her heart pounding wildly, shaking with terror.

"Go to Hell." she managed weakly.

"From there." His eyes burned. "Like it better here."

And then she ran, Solipsum's laughter echoing in her ears.

Interlude Five—Cyberspace

Mola existed in Cyberspace only as an idea, a node of order in a seemingly endless sea of chaos and crashing waves of data. Yet for all that, she was alive in a way no human mind could conceive of. In a way that let her know what the final result of The Campaign of The Century might be, and the true nature of Solipsum's plan. She could not help but feel admiration for him. The sheer audacity was on a scale that impressed even her. She wondered what it would be like, when his plan cracked Cyberspace open like a cheap locket. How much things would change. Or would they just expand to accommodate? As she dipped and sailed amidst the wall-like tsunamis of ons and offs, ones and zeroes, Mola smiled. Because it was not dread that filled her.

It was anticipation.

New York City, Stone Studios—The Campaign of The Century—Day 250

Joshua Stone sat in the special room with the unmarked door. It was the room in which he did the work he could only do alone. The room not meant for others to see. He was deep in thought, surrounded by images he had created for *Fa-Shin, Inc.* The Campaign of The Century was nearly complete. All that remained were pick-up shots and the final, master studio shoot of Phoena and Solipsum.

The entire room was filled with images from the Campaign. They surrounded him in silent tribute to his sheer talent, will and professionalism. And he didn't care. All that mattered, all that had ever mattered, was the photograph. This was how he had lived his life, and that was why he was the perfect man for this job.

Sometimes he felt he should let the world in on his greatest secret: he really had no idea what he was doing. Never did. Never would. All he really knew was how to go to the well, and which well to go to. As to what would come up? It was anybody's guess.

He stood and wandered around, looking at the photographs taped and pinned to every available surface. Photographs of New York, Los Angeles, the giant spruce trees of British Columbia, South Beach, Montana, Texas, Spain, the American Northwest, Arizona, an abandoned factory in Germany, India, Africa, Monte Pichou, Easter Island, Brazil, a Tokyo Subway, the swamps of New Orleans, the Golden Gate Bridge, China, Egypt, Greece, Paris, London, Antarctica amongst the penguins and Cyberspace. The images were all amazing, but as they progressed, he finally began to acknowledge how dark they had become. And that hiding behind the façade of art was no longer an excuse for irresponsibly pushing any button in people just to thin their wallets.

Joshua opened a drawer and pulled out his Egypt glasses, absently running a thumb pad over the sand-blasted lenses as he looked at an image from the Pyramids. It was but one of the many, many images where the world as he had seen it through the viewfinder was what the world now saw in the finished ads. How strange and frightening this was. It was also the most powerful and seductive thing he had ever experienced, a force he now found himself helpless before. In the beginning, it had been something so magical, he had convinced himself it could happen only once, not even sure that he hadn't imagined it. But his vision kept shifting every time he looked and soon it was no longer the exception. He felt himself now at the center of a great wheel, where time was at best a muddy concept. The closer he came to the hub, the greater the overview he gained, the greater the layering and non-linearity of creation. He felt that he was on the cusp of figuring it all out, if he could only keep his eye to the viewfinder long enough.

He wandered over to the enormous light table that ran the length of the entire west wall. The sea of transparencies almost seemed to mock him, so powerful was each individual image. Yet when seen all together, they diluted one another's impact, like a buffet of the richest foods rolled up and tablecloth-burst against a wall. The visual noise they generated, the way each screamed for attention, finally became too much and he turned away.

The wind was gentle tonight as he stepped onto the small balcony. He leaned against the railing and lit a cigarette, gazing out at the carpet of tiny lights so far below.

His mind was in turmoil and he remembered what Elora had said. "It's your photographic soul, Joshua." And he laughed aloud because he finally understood the meaning of those words.

But though he plunged down some dark creative whirlpool, his heart held him high above the churning maelstrom, buoyed by his love. *So this is what it's like. How could I have lived for so long without touching this? Charlie, God, I wish I could ask you what to do. But I'm scared. Not of what you'll say, but that I'll ask to shoot you, to somehow drag you into this from the camera side.*

And that you'll say "Yes."

He arced the butt over the railing, watching the orange pinprick diminish into nothing.

New York City, Coney Island—The Campaign of The Century—Day 252

Charlie furtively glanced around to make sure no one was watching, then tossed another fish to the seal she had named Maybelle. She rarely came here but when she did, it was always with treats. The animals just made her feel so very blue. It was almost like they were trying to communicate something to everyone they met, to beam some lesson from their doleful eyes as they slouched in dirty homes that no one seemed to look after, their coats now lackluster, surrounded by their grubby toys.

Why, why, why is it necessary for them to be here?

For some reason, this made her think of Phoena and Solipsum and what had transpired at Joshua's pool. The model had disappeared and it had taken Charlie two days before she was finally able to reach her, only to be told her friend needed some time alone. *God, what did I do? But she liked it too, I know she did.*

Charlie sighed and reached into the *McWrong-alds* bag that she was using to camouflage her treats. She pulled out another fish, tossed it and noticed too late that a couple of children had seen her. *Oh fuck* was her last thought before the two came rushing over.

"Hey!" one whined, "yer not supposed to feed the animals."

He couldn't have been more than twelve but already sported a pierced ear, a *Day-Glo Abortions* t-shirt and a cigarette tucked behind one ear. His shirt was so loud Charlie's eyes felt violated. She somehow knew they should both have been in school. "I wasn't feeding them."

"Bullfuck!" his friend screeched, then burped with even more volume.

Day-Glo smacked him upside the head. "Ya stupid mutant! This ain't the neighborhood Lola to be impressed by yer gas."

Burpy ducked his head and peered down at his toes but couldn't keep the smile off his face. A hefty kid in a striped shirt, he had the most incredible lighter-thumbed foof of red hair, and more freckles than pennies in a wishing pool. Charlie laughed despite herself. "Tell you what, if you guys promise to stay quiet, I'll let you each have a fish when we get to the penguins. What do you say?"

The boys eyed one another, some secret signal passing between them. The two then began shrieking and laughing with such enthusiasm Charlie let them carry the bag. She walked to the Penguin Pool, a boy on each side, both of them running to keep up.

"So what are your names?"

"I'm Nathaniel," the skinny boy piped, "better known as Nate."

"And I'm Oswald, but people call me Oz."

"When they're not calling you Whale-O!"

"Shut-up, blood fart, they do not!"

The two started tussling.

"Boys! Boys! We don't want to attract attention," Charlie admonished as she separated them. "We won't be able to feed the other animals." Both of them immediately stopped struggling, then looked at her contritely before shuffling along with the nonchalance of drug dealers.

They reached the Penguin Pool and as if on cue, ten of the birds left their roosts and flocked to the rocks nearest the small glass wall.

"They *know* you," Oz breathed as Nate looked at her with new respect.

Charlie reached into the greasy goodie bag and pulled out some sardines, careful of her bandages. She crouched low and doled them out, looking each boy sternly in the eye. "Do *not* wipe your hands on your pants. You'll stink to high heaven for the rest of the day."

"Don't worry, we won't, we won't."

The boys snatched the fish and before Charlie could stop them, flung all their sardines over the rail at once. The penguins jumped into the pool en masse, squawking and splashing in a feeding frenzy. Even Charlie could not help but laugh as the commotion showered several tourists and soaked their baby.

"Jesus, let's get out of here." She quickly grabbed them both by the hand and all three scooted to the next enclosure just as several zookeepers converged on the Pool.

Charlie turned to Nate and crouched so their eyes were level. A cigarette had magically appeared in her hand. "Got a light?"

"Hey! Where did you—" Nate's hand darted to the empty place above his ear and his eyes went huge as he looked at the zoo-girl. "Damn, you're fast."

Charlie just smiled, then her eyes went far away as Nate pulled out some matches. She remembered the last time she had smoked. And the story she'd heard from the man she—loved? She looked at the two urchins and decided she needed some advice. "Can I ask you boys something?"

"Sure! Anything!"

"If you knew someone, someone you really liked, and they told you their heart—no, let's be honest—their soul—everything they were—was given away to—"

"Another girl?" asked Nate.

"Another guy?" Oz was more astute.

And Charlie shook her head at what Fortune had thrown in her path.

"I'd dump him," from Oz.

Nate affected a fierce scowl. "Me too."

"But what if it wasn't some*one* he gave his soul to, but—some*thing*?"

Nate's little face clenched in disgust. "That's even worse."

"Why?" The blond girl looked at him so openly, Nate wondered if you could be twelve years old and fall in love.

"Because he's a junkie," Oz said quietly.

Charlie sat back, the breath leaving her, stunned by the utter truth of what Oz had just said. In an instant, she knew she could no longer be with Joshua. Not as lovers, if that's—

"Yer not going out with one, are you? Yer way too pretty." Oz looked like he was about to cry.

"No," Charlie murmured, "not any more." Then she mentally shook herself. "Come on. Let's go wash our hands and get some ice cream."

"Yay!" the boys screamed.

Nate looked up at her. "My hands are already clean."

"Oh yeah? When did you clean them?"

"Right now!" He grabbed Oswald's hair and wiped his hands in it. Oz erupted in shrieks of fishy outrage, his chubby arms wrapping around Nate's body grabbing fistfuls of shirt as he feverishly swabbed his own hands. Charlie could only shake her head helplessly and try to put some distance between her and the stinky boy-storm.

Sometime later, they were all sitting on the steps near the exit, happily bloated on too much ice cream.

"Well, you guys, I have to go. But I want to thank you for your advice. I really mean that."

"Aw, no! We were just getting to know you." Both boys looked so crestfallen Charlie had no idea what to do. Then a sudden inspiration hit her. "See that tree over there?" They all turned to look in the direction of the huge old oak she was pointing to. "If you ever see a *McWrong-alds* bag stuffed into that hole, take it out and look inside. There'll be some way to contact me. Check it on the first of every month, okay?"

The boys' eyes lit up.

"Just like spies." Nate whispered loudly.

Charlie brought her head close to theirs and said, "Good luck, fellas. I'm sure we haven't seen the last of each other."

"Hey. We don't even know your name."

"It's Charlie. My name is Charlie." She was about to stand when Oz grabbed her hand.

"Hey, Nate said—oof." Oz doubled over, the air whooshing out of him, Nate's elbow buried in his side.

"Shut up! Don't tell her what I said. That was before we got to know her."

Charlie turned to the redheaded boy. "What did he say, Oz?"

"H—he said it would be so cool to touch your boob."

Charlie glared at Nate. "Is that true?"

"Yeah," he muttered, eyes downcast as he shuffled his feet. His little face then turned redder than Charlie had ever seen anyone turn. Except perhaps herself. And that's what did it. She lifted his chin and looked him in the eyes. "Okay."

"What? You mean . . . ?"

"Yes."

His small hand tentatively reached out and gently squeezed Charlie's breast like it was the nose of some huge plush toy. The hand quickly darted back and he looked at her with his big blue eyes. "Th—that was so cool." he stammered, grinning.

Charlie tousled his hair and mentally chided herself for corrupting a minor. But, she figured, if she were a boy, wouldn't she just die if a girl said "yes" to that request?

She finally stood and looked at them one last time. "'Bye Nate, 'bye Oz."

"'Bye Charlie."

She walked away, one road closed and another now suddenly open.

Utah, National Monument Desert—The Campaign of The Century—Day 253

Hank Steadman gazed out across the Arizona desert and felt a sense of peace and serenity that few people would ever experience, especially those not blessed with living here. There was a silence that seemed to make a moment stretch forever. It was a feeling he greatly enjoyed. He had to admit to himself, however, that it was quite an amazing experience, to see his home from this particular vantage point.

He stood atop a mesa where he and some other cast members had just finished shooting for the day. The primitive rock formation was massive, with a tent that housed their gear and grub set up at it's furthest extremity. It had taken two helicopter trips to get everything up here, but from the smile on that boy Joshua's face, it seemed it was worth it. Hank looked over at the welcome warmth of the big bonfire and figured he'd have a smoke before he got himself some chow.

Be nice to hunker down by that fire too. It's colder than a banker's heart up here.

As he rolled some tobacco, he noticed a figure striding towards him, silhouetted by the flames. Judging by its size, it could only be Joshua Stone.

Been around a long time, and I thought I'd seen it all. But I ain't never seen a man dance with the Devil the way this boy does. And he's leadin'! Don't that beat all. You just best be careful, Joshua. Cause when you play with fire, sooner or later—

He lit his smoke.

—yer gonna get burned.

Stone lifted a hand as he reached him.

"Hank."

"Huh."

"You got an extra one of those?"

"Roll 'em myself, boy. I can do one for you. Less'un you prefer to roll yer own."

Stone shook his head and waved a hand. "Go ahead, I'd appreciate it."

"Hold mine then, son."

Steadman began to roll a perfect cigarette with the effortless grace of years. Joshua watched him work, looking at his craggy face in the firelight. It was a face so lined and seamed it reminded him of a rock formation, alien and blasted as the surface of the moon.

Steadman squinted up, his eyes almost invisible in the fleshy creases of his face. "You know what yer getting' yerself into?"

"Not sure I follow you, old timer. You mean these pictures?"

"Them. Him. Her. The whole ball of wax."

"Honestly? No. Not anymore." Stone sighed and let his eyes drift to the fire.

The older man grunted with resignation. "What I figured. Here ya go."

He handed over the cigarette and they smoked in silence for a few moments.

Stone tilted his head back and seemed to notice the stars for the first time, the moon a tiny crescent of fingernail. "It's a beautiful night, isn't it?"

"Ayuh."

"I know this may sound kind of strange, but if you were me, what would you do?"

Hank Steadman smiled, as though he'd been waiting for this question all along. "Why, hell boy, that's easy. I'd drop the whole thing faster'n you kin spit. Now. While you still got the chance. And git as far away from that Solipsum character as you can."

"I—can't."

The old man stood, dropped his smoke and ground it out under the heel of his well-worn cowboy boot.

"Then keep this in mind, son. People, and experiences, they kin be a lot like drugs. And if you crave it, then you're a slave to it. And you strike me as someone stronger than that. Much stronger."

"Thanks, Hank."

The old man took his hat off and inspected it before looking back at the photographer. "Git some sleep, boy. We got a long day ahead of us tomorrow."

He put his hat back on and began walking towards the bonfire.

Interlude Six—Toronto

Melanie Temple was dressed in her best and on her way to what she knew would be the raddest rave of her life. She saw her reflection passing in a window and knew she was cute. Chubby, but cute. She smiled and shrugged and figured, what the hell, life could be worse. At least these baggies looked good. She continued walking the streets of downtown Toronto, hurrying a bit because she didn't want to miss a thing. A necklace of gelatinous ecstasy pills in the shape of gummi bears bumped against her neck, *Fa-Shin, Inc.*'s logo lightly emblazoned on their little bellies. She brought the necklace to her mouth and chewed off two of them.

Hope these are as good as Dolly says they'll be.

Melanie couldn't help but notice those cool *Fa-Shin, Inc.* ads that were all over the place. Somehow she didn't find them as invasive as a lot of the other stuff she usually saw. They didn't talk down to her, didn't make her feel not good enough. They were everywhere, sometimes on the most startling surfaces. She saw a bus shelter with Solipsum on it. Someone had added a markered word balloon that said

I'm cold.

She stared at it, the combination of words and image affecting her as neither would have individually.

She kept walking and saw more bus shelters with Campaign images similarly altered.

This itches.

C'mon, it's for a good cause.

Then one of them stopped her. It was a particularly striking image of Phoena's face, her eyes like luminous emeralds, her expression one that seemed to break past all of Melanie's defenses, to leave her hopelessly vulnerable to whatever Phoena wanted to tell her. On this one were markered the words

I will never love you.

She stood and absorbed and was, for an instant, overcome by the certainty that this simple phrase distilled the entire essence and lie of advertising.

Because it did.

Then the drug's trickle branched and Melanie began to twinkle, twinkle, little star. Slowly, the people she passed took on the faces of Phoena and Solipsum. It was such a subtle process that she wasn't even aware of it.

She finally arrived at the warehouse that was host to *DESTINY 438— ADULATION*. She presented her ticket to a Solipsum, was frisked by a Phoena and made her way inside where she was soon greeted by her friends, who all wore Phoena and Solipsum. Melanie didn't notice a thing.

Dolly/Phoena greeted her, unaware their faces were the same. Her eyes were as large as a baby seal's and she grinned like someone in a comic book. "So, how are they?"

Melanie hugged herself. "Swank! Totally swank!"

They were joined by Dolly's boyfriend Skid, who they saw as Solipsum. Skid thought he was seeing double but figured two Phoenas had to be better than one. Everyone who had taken the drug was affected in the same way. Ignorantly immersed. And if you were to look down on the crowd from the ceiling, and see anyone thus affected represented as a pulsing dot of color, a strange thing would happen. The pulsing dots would coalesce into something familiar. Something you once glimpsed in a blond girl's hair . . .

New York City, Macy's—The Campaign of The Century—Day 254

Rothman Cartilage was doing something he rarely did, because he frankly detested this activity. He was shopping. For a gift.

"That will be $18,073.56, please."

The pert and friendly salesgirl who was obviously meant for better things gave him a winning smile. She was already calculating her commission as two words

(wage slave)

appeared and disappeared in Rothman's mind.

"Here."

His prosthetic hand rested on the counter, an *American Impress Black Card* pincered between its two organically functional plastic "fingers."

"Oh." The girl's hand wavered, wanting/not wanting to touch it, as though Rothman had placed a sexual truncheon on the glass in front of her.

"What's the matter? Never seen one of these before?"

"Sorry sir," she said nervously, "you just caught me off guard."

"Never let your guard down, my dear. There are things out there that— bite." The Agent smiled, then looked up and saw a massive image of Phoena, his creation, and Solipsum, his nemesis, looming over the counter. *My, my, my. You're just everywhere, aren't you? I'm beginning to wonder who really got the better deal. You? Me? Or Solipsum.* His eyes lingered for a moment on the unusual piece of jewelry that adorned Phoena's neck.

"Sign here, sir." The salesgirl hesitated a moment, then plunged ahead. "Uh, may I ask you something?"

Rothman was becoming bored. "What is it?"

"Where did you—"

"Lose the arm?"

"Yes."

"A boating accident. I met a more—accomplished predator."

The girl was puzzled. "I don't understand."

"You weren't meant to. Now, could you wrap that please? My manual dexterity isn't what it once was."

"Right away, sir."

His cell phone rang. Once.

"Yes? Oh, it's you. Of course I've seen them. How could I not? They're everywhere. It's the most astonishing Campaign I've ever seen. When? Tonight? Impossible. You've got what? The deed? To the Club? I'll be there. Give me one hour." He clicked off.

The sales girl handed him his package. "Thank you, sir. Have a good day."

He raised an eyebrow. "You don't really mean that, do you?"

"No. I don't." She smiled boldly.

He considered her for a moment, then decided. "Good. Honesty is always an excellent beginning."

"What do you mean?" she asked, completely unaware that her life had just swerved across some invisible meridian and now traveled in the suicide lane.

"Have you ever thought about becoming a model?"

New York City, Stone Studios—The Campaign of The Century—Day 255

Charlie had been walking down the hall from the pool when she heard the sounds. She entered the main studio and found her friend huddled on the couch, sobbing. "Phoena! What are you doing here?"

She ran over and knelt beside her. "Are you all right?"

Phoena nodded mutely, still turned away.

It was the first time she'd seen the other woman since that day Solipsum had found them. She'd talked to her on the phone but Phoena had seemed distracted, saying that she couldn't see anyone for a few days. There had been something in her voice that had made Charlie listen. And now to find her here.

She felt something brush her thigh and looked down to see Bruun gazing up at her. He seemed agitated, and as she stroked his head, she was briefly overcome by the strongest conviction that the small mammal knew exactly what was going on.

She reached out a tentative hand she let rest on Phoena's nape. "Why are you crying? What's wrong?"

Phoena turned her wet face towards the young assistant, her voice ragged. "I don't know if I can go on with this anymore."

"What do you mean?"

"It's Solipsum. I—I'm scared, Charlie. Scared of what he might do."

"Is that story really true or—"

"Am I crazy? Go ahead. You can ask that."

"This may sound strange but—I believe you. I don't think you're crazy. Because something really weird happened to me at the party."

"What do you mean?"

"I think he tried to force his way into my mind. But he couldn't."

Phoena wiped at the tears, her eyes narrowing. "What else?"

"I—I didn't want to tell you everything that happened when I broke into his place. He has a secret room, that's bigger on the inside than it is on the outside. There was a picture of Joshua's studio, a painting with all these strange lines coming off it. But Phoena, it was the *door* that threw me, the door to that room. It's a giant photo. Of him. He's done up like Jesus, bloody thorns and all. He even had a beard. I've seen that picture before and I'm pretty sure I know where. There's other stuff too. Like the sandstorm . . ." She sat back on her heels, her face stiff and anguished. "Phoena, I'm so sorry. But I didn't want you to think *I* was crazy. I didn't want to lose you as my friend and because I—I found myself liking you in a way that was—more than friends." Her voice trailed off, the last words directed at her knees. Then she looked up, the tears welling in her eyes. "You don't understand. I've lost so many people . . ."

"Charlie." Phoena sat up. "You aren't going to lose me."

She pulled the other girl close and kissed her forehead. Then some strange impulse overcame her and she kissed Charlie's eyes, tasting the salty tears, the young girl's lashes soft as belly fur. Charlie's lips parted as though she were about to speak. She found herself meeting Phoena's gaze, her hands slowly coming up to rest on the model's face, now knowing she was not alone in what she felt.

"Oh Phoena, I—I really want to kiss you right now. Like I've never wanted to kiss anyone in my whole life. But we can't have any secrets. This is way too special." Charlie sat down beside her. "There's one other thing you have to know. You haven't seen everything Joshua's shot so far, have you?"

Phoena shook her head. "Just the stuff that's been published, nothing else. It's part of our contract. No one sees anything until it's out there. It might distort his vision or something."

"I think that's only part of the reason. There's a lot more going on here than you know about. Something really strange is happening when he shoots you guys."

"What are you talking about?"

Charlie gave the model's shoulders a squeeze and got up. "Come on. I have to show you."

They walked through the main dome, down corridors and up staircases into areas of the Studio that for Phoena became increasingly unfamiliar. She had thought she'd known Stone Studios and was startled to discover that Joshua's home, much like his mind, showed of itself only what it wanted.

They had just finished climbing a set of stairs she was sure she'd never seen when they turned a corner and began walking down a white corridor. It twisted sharply away from the dome's natural curve and finally ended at a large, unmarked door. Phoena watched as Charlie hesitated, then punched in a code, her face a strange mixture of awe and fear, like a penitent entering the ruin of a dear and sacred shrine. Phoena felt something cold stir in the pit of her stomach, warning her not to go in. She looked down the corridor to see Bruun sitting there, just watching them, and somehow knew he would go no further. Her heart sped, her feet almost stepping back when Charlie took her hand and pulled her across the threshold. Together they entered Joshua's Image Room. The room where he worked alone. The room not meant for others to see.

Charlie threw a light switch and images seemed to burst upon Phoena. She found herself overcome by a reaction so visceral, it was like a punch that kept sinking into her. A thought

(so this is what Infinity does when you ask it to pose for you)

entered her mind, then was obliterated by what she saw on Joshua's walls. Hundreds and hundreds of images from the shoots that had already taken place, all of them stunning. Yet she knew instinctively that looking at them together like this was something that was never intended. It was like seeing an ocular distillate that ran the gamut of the visible spectrum, then veered off into territories unknown. It was nearly enough to cause spontaneous blindness. And there was something else, a pattern she could just discern . . .

Charlie stood in front of her, hugging herself as though it were cold, dark skin and white bikini, fingers truncated by her small white bandages. "It's almost too much to look at, isn't it?"

Phoena had trouble finding words, her eyes involuntarily drawn back, again and again, fighting her will as they sought to suckle the images.

"I—I don't know what to say." Her voice began drifting. "They're magnificent . . . compelling . . ."

She felt the presence of some vast and unfathomable—thing, a black and wet malevolence lurking just behind the sea of frozen faces, riveted eyes and zippered mouths, the flesh as clothing superimposed on solarizations of limb and bone, the mutant extrusions of priapic parody, the cockswells and cudgels and cuntings of want, the whole shell shocked trampoline of eye chaff presented obliquely so she barely registered how thinly it sliced her brain into predetermined pressings of want.

Then came the loinprod buyprod eatprod fuckprod, stippling her mind, her body slowly heating, secreting in uncontrolled empathy with buttons pushed wantonly, randomly, slickly, the effortless mastery of complete and utter madness imposing itself like cement.

Her mind, shrieking, reared as it tried to make sense, to slot and bracket and somehow order the photographic slivers of slash and flow as they faster and faster realigned themselves. Because God help her, no matter how she saw them, they all fit. She tried to back away, her mind now a tiny fingernail paring, clinging to some cliff of photographic sanity as it tried to find shelter, any shelter, any semblance of normalcy, to take it in her arms, to somehow underpin the whole rotted eye-fuck that tottered on the abyss of insanity.

And Solipsum was everywhere, but in a way she had never seen, never been privy to. He was strewn and draped, leaning and basking, there, not there, cuttings of his eyemelt boring into her brain, an encroachment of shambling gibbering lunacy she finally tore herself away from, lids slamming down so that her eyes could breathe again.

"Jesus . . ." She gasped. "I—I knew he had a dark side but never anything like this. And these effects. I've never seen anything like them . . ."

"They're not effects."

"What do you mean?"

"I'll tell you in a minute. Keep looking. What do you feel?"

Phoena turned back to the images, eyes this time slitted to the thinness of paper cuts. She saw again that vague yet pervasive pattern, like some sort of symbol. "It's hard to describe. I feel like something's shifting inside me—opening—like a door—I want to walk into them—into whatever it is I see just behind them—calling to me."

Charlie cupped her chin, thoughtful. "It's like staring into a black hole. I feel my will being drained. It's a major effort just to tear myself away."

Phoena now had the trick of it. She closed her eyes and opened them again on her friend. "What the hell is going on?"

"I don't know. But somehow it involves you and Solipsum, and whatever is happening when Joshua shoots the two of you. It's like he's creating some sort of visual symphony, though what this is going to do as people see more and more of it is anyone's guess. I'll tell you one thing though, selling clothes will be the least of its effects." She grabbed the other girl's hand. "Come on, there's one last thing."

"What?"

"I want to show you where I saw that picture. The one of him on his door."

She pulled Phoena—a Phoena who was so very relieved that they were not staying *in there*—down the hall to the room that held the Wishing Wall.

They entered and pulled up chairs to sit and look at the Wall itself, Joshua's inspirational image vortex, the hundreds of photos, drawings, paintings, sketches and diagrams culled from a thousand sources.

Phoena leaned back and stared at the sprawling collage, which seemed to her like some tiny mutant offspring of what she had just seen. "What *is* this?"

Charlie turned in her chair and slumped back, suddenly tired. "Joshua's Wishing Wall. He says it's like staring into the Muse's pool. If you look at it long enough, something creative's bound to emerge.

Like Narcissus looking at his reflection, thought Phoena.

"This is where I'm sure I saw that Jesus picture." Charlie leaned forward and pointed. "And there it is."

They stood and approached the wall.

Phoena instantly recognized the features of the young bearded Christmodel, crowned and crucified, his face dark with blood. She angled her head. "But he's upside down."

"No, that's how he looked in the magazine."

"What magazine?"

"This is part of an editorial, a really famous editorial that appeared in *The Flesh.* I knew where it came from when I saw the shot on his door. But it can't be him."

"Why not?"

Charlie unpinned the magazine page and rotated it. Phoena stood closer, an arm naturally slipping around Charlie's waist as they peered at it together. The assistant's fingernail tapped the lower corner. "Can you see this? It's too blurry for me to make out."

Phoena slowly read the words "Cruci-Fixation. Photography by Bailey David. 1966." She drew a sharp breath. "Jesus, Charlie. That means he has to be like, sixty years old or something. What the hell is going on?"

An idea came to her and she carefully folded the picture, putting it in an envelope she found on a work table. "Come on." She grabbed Charlie's hand and they began walking back down the corridor, to the gauzy brightness of the main dome she could just make out in the distance. "There's only one person who can help us get to the bottom of this."

"Should I call us a cab?"

"No. A travel agent."

Charlie's eyes widened. "Where are we going?"

"London."

Book 10

"Growth for the sake of growth is the ideology of the cancer cell." —Edward Abbey

"Our culture has made us all slaves to an idea, an idea that takes precedence over everything, over our own lives and the lives of others. And slavery to an idea is far more dangerous than slavery to a human, because we do not even know that we are slaves. We pass through our days with the freedom of a dog who never reaches the end of its leash, certain that what we see is all of reality, all there ever was, all there ever will be, all that is possible. Having enslaved ourselves to this idea, we then enslave others, passing on the knowledge of how to be a slave from father to son, father to daughter, mother to son, mother to daughter, sibling to sibling, teacher to student, owner to labourer, boss to employee, slave to slave.

It's not easy to remove this leash we're not wearing, to break this leash that doesn't exist. How can I be a slave when I live in the land of the free? I choose my jobs, I choose where I live, I choose how I spend my time. I am not enslaved to industrial mass production. I am not enslaved to the perception of others as objects to be exploited. I am not enslaved to anything. I am a free man, and nothing you can say will convince me otherwise." —Derrick Jensen

30,000 feet, somewhere above the North Atlantic, New York to London. 1st Class.

Phoena sat on her wide and very comfortable seat and still felt claustrophobic. She always did on aircraft. She looked down at the complimentary magazine the stewardess had dropped on her tray and Solipsum's eyes met hers as though he were really there. Her hand covered it and pushed it away.

Fuck, even at 30,000 feet I can't get away from that—thing.

Charlie sensed her agitation. "Are you okay?"

"Yeah, I'm fine. It's just—" She turned to her girlfriend, hand lightly brushing away a strand of hair. "Whenever I stand back and try to see this objectively, everything seems so totally over-the-top crazy, like I'm in a comic book or something."

"Phoena, it may be crazy but it's happening. And everyone's being affected. Take a look." Charlie pointed to the headline of the New York Times she had been reading.

50 MORE KILLED IN LOS ANGELES!
Shoppers Riot as Department Stores Run Out Of Merchandise

"But just what *is* happening? I mean, this is like no other job I've ever shot. The images are crazy, fantastic, dark, light—"

"—and everything in between. I know what you mean," finished Charlie. She put the paper away.

"People are dying. And I think somehow we're to blame, because we helped create these photos."

"But, Phoena, they're killing each other over the *stuff*, the *Fa-Shin, Inc. stuff.*"

"No, Charlie. People are dying because they *want* that stuff. The specifics of what they want is interchangeable. *That's* how *Fa-Shin, Inc.* is making so much money. The key is *us*, because we *induce* that want. Through the pictures."

"So what can we do? Stop?"

"No. It's too late for that. They'll just run the photos they already have and then we'd be out of the loop. We have to figure out what's really going on, then we'll know what to do. And speaking of the photos, let's start with them. You said Joshua wasn't using any effects. So how is he doing it?"

"I don't know."

Phoena drew back. "You don't?"

"No," Charlie shook her head emphatically. "I have no idea how he's producing the stuff we saw in that room. Yeah, there's digital guys working around the clock and Joshua's got every lab in town booked 24/7 but he's still producing work that should be taking way longer to finish."

"There must be *some* explanation."

The other girl looked down at her hands for a moment, as if deciding something. Then her eyes met Phoena's. "This may sound crazy but—"

"What?"

"He's doing it 'in camera.'"

"I don't understand."

"Phoena, when I print his contact sheets, hell, even when I get the film back, it's already there. All the stuff you saw in that room? *It's already there.*"

"That's impossible."

"That's why I didn't think you were crazy. Because I knew about this. The first time it happened, I sort of blocked it out. I figured Joshua was using some secret cutting-edge technology he wasn't telling me about. But when I asked him, he couldn't really answer me. He said that what came out was how he was seeing things as he shot them."

Phoena gaped. "That's crazy!"

"Is it? Look at everything that's happened to us so far. This Campaign that's making people kill each other, the sandstorm that came out of nowhere. And I think we both agree that Solipsum's not really—human."

"Charlie—"

"Wait. Let me finish. Maybe what Joshua is doing is just bending up time or something. Accessing some weird field of—visual possibility. Like a savant."

Phoena gave her a quizzical look. "That's just way too—quantum for me, Charlie. I think it's not so much what Joshua is doing that we have to worry about. Strange as it may be, it's just a manifestation of something bigger. Of what's really going on. And *that's* what I want to know." She slumped back in her seat, crossed her arms and sighed deeply. "Solipsum's at the center of all this. I can feel it. And that picture is the key. It's funny, after all I've been through with him, I still can't turn away. Here I am on some wild goose chase because—oh God, it's like he's the most powerful magnet in the world."

"Well, you can sure see it in the pictures. They chose well. I don't think there are two other people on the planet who could have pulled this off. Never in a million years." Charlie looked out the airplane's window for an instant, then back at her friend, eyes bright with the reflected ambience of the sky. "Phoena, what happened between the two of you? You seem to hate him so much I can feel it, but when you're in his arms, you . . . love it, don't you?"

A look of disgust came over the model's face. "Yeah. I do. It all comes back to the first night I met him. The night the three of us first slept together. Something happened that I can't remember. It's like trying to look at an object past a really bright light. I know there's something there but I can't for the life of me make out what it is. It's like my soul and my body both know but they haven't let my mind in on the secret."

"Phoena this may sound funny but I think he feels the same way about you. He seems to have this total contempt but I saw his face when you said, 'As much as we both did that night?' He looked almost . . . human. Like there was something he wanted and for all his power he couldn't have it. Unless you gave it to him."

"But what's his plan, Charlie? And don't kid yourself, it's his plan, not Elora's. One look at the two of them and you know right away whose driving that train."

"All aboard!" Charlie bawled, "The Elora Express is now leaving the station. Whoo! Whoo!" She began to make grinding motions with her hips as she pulled on an imaginary whistle.

Phoena elbowed her as she tried to hold back a giggle. "Piglet."

Both girls began laughing, honking and shrieking like children, much to the consternation of the other passengers in first class. Phoena finally wiped a laugh-tear from her eye. "Seriously. Do you have any theories?"

"No. Not yet. But I think a lot of things are gonna come clear once we get to London—"

"—and figure out why he's the spitting image of a model from a fashion magazine that's sixty years old." Phoena sat back, unaware that the flat perspective of the magazine in front of her had changed. The eye portion of Solipsum's face on the magazine's cover had begun to bulge, as though something were

pushing

its way into this portion of reality. It looked around and saw from its fisheye perspective a very distorted view of them both.

Phoena sat up. "Charlie! Do you get the feeling we're being watched?"

Charlie's eyes darted about, then she saw the magazine. "What the hell is that?"

"Oh my God," Phoena whimpered.

She saw the staring eye, and all thought fled. Her hand grabbed a swizzle stick and savagely thrust it into the magazine, penetrating its surface as it went through the cover and into

Solipsum's apartment

piercing

his left eye.

"BITCH!" he screamed, his head whipping back in a stream of blood.

On the aircraft, the girls huddled together, both shaken to their core, staring at the quivering stick.

New York City, Stone Studios—The Campaign of The Century—Day 257

Joshua was standing in his Image Room once more, surrounded by photography from the last shoot. It was very—*provocative? No. Tell the truth, Joshua. At least to yourself. Charlie already said it. These pictures are evil.*

He felt utterly drained, almost old. He remembered the dream again, the one he'd had the previous night. A dream of his Muse. But this time it had been different, this time he had seen her on Earth looking even more radiant and somehow—real. And this time he could only watch, powerless to help, as she lay on a golden altar, in a beautiful bower, trees and vine leaves gently blowing in the summer breeze.

While the Gods of Commerce viciously raped her.

Fat and bloated things they were, with pendulous bellies and wrinkled hairy skins, their pricks like rolled up wads of bills, shoving them in, shoving them in, as her face turned to him and the tears of the World streamed down her cheeks.

Then he had heard their voices, inviting him to join them.

He had woken up screaming, sheets soaked, heart pounding, to find Charlie gone. He was frantically reaching for her when he remembered she had left for England with Phoena. He'd gotten up from the bed and walked around, his heart finally slowing as he came to the realization that after this, he would not take another picture for at least five years, maybe ever. And never again for money, for it was not only his Muse he'd felt being raped, it was his own creative soul. It was not something he wished to experience ever again. And if his photography was the price, so be it.

His eyes took in the images that surrounded him, images that embodied both the Dark and the Light, Hell and Heaven for want of better words. He wished more than anything he had ever wished for that he could stop. Just simply stop. But he knew he could not, for the thing inside that had propelled him to heights of creativity known by so very few wouldn't let him. It demanded that everything be sacrificed to it. Everything and everyone. He then came to the final realization that he would have that night.

This included Charlie.

Interlude Seven—Miami

Tina Flare ducked behind a clothing rack as another display case was smashed. She was fucking freaking out, because she had never felt anything this intense in her life. She moved aside some *Fa-Shin, Inc.* merchandise and peered out at the rioting crowd.

Who woulda thought! A fashion cult, right here in South Beach. And for what? A towel. A fucking towel. With Solipsum's face on it.

She looked up at the backlit displays, not even noticing the broken glass that fell from her hair, to see Solipsum and Phoena smiling down on the boiling mass of people like dark and silent gods.

Fuck, they almost seem to be enjoying it.

Bits of clothing and other less identifiable detritus flew through the air as the screams and breaking glass punctuated what was now a general roar. Someone rushed by, clutching a scrap of towel, face bloody, laughing insanely. She ducked behind some dresses as the figure stopped and peered about.

I have to get out of here.

She saw her friend Norman wandering towards her in a daze, blood running from a cut on his brow. His clothing was ripped and his eyes had the same glazed quality Tina had seen in damn near everyone today. He stumbled along the crowd's fringe, oblivious. "Oh God, what's happened to you?"

She rushed out into the aisle, clamping down on the fear and grabbed her friend just before he wandered into the thick of the riot. She absently noticed the towel scraps everywhere as she pulled Norman along, a Norman who was feebly trying to pick up those very same scraps.

What the fuck is going on?

"Norman! Snap out of it!" She stopped and grabbed his head with both hands. "Snap out of it!" Norman didn't even see her. Then his face broke into a huge smile and she felt a wave of relief wash over her. Until he shoved her aside. She turned around in time to see him running towards the store's front doors.

The *Fa-Shin, Inc.* trucks had arrived.

London, England—The Campaign of The Century—Day 257

Neither of them had gotten any sleep and as soon as the plane landed, Phoena and Charlie took a taxi from Heathrow to the hotel. After checking in, they went up to the single room they would share by some unspoken agreement and started to unpack. Both had brought very little clothing, as they would only spend two days here before returning for the Campaign's final shoot.

Phoena snapped the closures on her suitcase and stowed it under the bed, then grabbed a towel and turned to Charlie. "Can you order up some room service? I'm going to take a quick shower before we go see Bentley."

"Sure, what do you want?"

Phoena's thoughts were drawn back to what they had seen on the plane. "Nothing with eyes."

"Eeewwwwww!" Charlie winced. "That was totally uncalled for." They looked at one another and grinned, the mood now somehow lighter. "Just for that," Charlie said, "I'm getting you a shrimp sandwich, with all their little heads still attached."

She crept around the bed and brought her fingers up on each side of her face, waving them like tiny antennae as she made peculiar shrimp noises. Phoena screamed in mock terror as Charlie chased her about the room, knocking over a lamp before tripping and falling onto the bed. She was immediately whacked by a cushion Phoena had grabbed from the sofa. A massive pillow fight ensued, punctuated by squeals and shrieks as neither girl showed mercy. Only the sound of a fist pounding on the wall finally caused the girls to stop pummeling each other. They stood face to face, tense and gasping, then simultaneously threw their pillows away before collapsing in a heap of muffled laughter. Phoena finally went to the bathroom for a now much-needed shower.

Charlie finished unpacking and was idly leafing through some tour guides when the inspiration hit her. She was still talking on the phone when her friend emerged from the bathroom in a cloud of steam.

". . . and FedEx it. I need it here pronto," she said in hushed tones. ". . . I can't tell you," she giggled, ". . . it's a surprise. Thanks, Humber, you're the best." She hung up and turned to see Phoena drying her hair. "Food'll be here in ten," she said brightly.

Phoena was mildly curious as to what *that* was all about because Charlie was a terrible at hiding things. But before she had even finished toweling her hair, the food did arrive and she forgot.

After some surprisingly succulent sandwiches, they took a taxi to *PRY*. The magazine was located in a very impressive suite of offices at Canary Wharf. The elevator shot them up to the 85th floor and they walked into a reception area opulent and glacial. A desk that looked like an overturned ashtray hid the receptionist.

"Hi, we're here to see Bentley," said Phoena.

There were some furtive movements and the distinctive smell of nail polish came and went. Then a plummy voice intoned, "I'm sorry, Mr. Sween doesn't see anyone without—"

Charlie had found something on the floor. "Is this yours?" She held the thick pornographic Japanese comic book between two fingers.

"Give me that!" The receptionist snatched it back and finally looked at the other woman. "Oh! My God! You're Phoena!"

"So I've been told. Can you please buzz Mr. Sween? He's expecting us."

"Uh—uh—right away."

The girls were quickly ushered into Bentley's office.

"Hi, Bentley."

He glanced up from the papers he had been skimming. "Phoena! And Charlie!" He stood and grinned, then quickly strode around the desk to embrace them both. He was dressed in old twill pants and a raggedy cardigan and Phoena could smell the pipe smoke on him when he hugged her. She looked past his shoulder at the magnificent view of the Channel and wished with all her heart that this was just a social call.

"God, it's good to see you two!"

He saw Charlie's bandaged fingers, so at odds with her summer dress. "What happened?"

"A darkroom accident. I'll be okay."

The next few moments passed in a burble of fond memories as they recounted adventures they'd had and almost had on that special night. Charlie had just finished laughing at Phoena's delicious Arragon story when Bentley decided to confirm something. "Rumor has it that was the night Elora offered Joshua a billion dollars to shoot the Campaign."

Charlie shrugged, her eyes innocent. "Maybe. I never heard it, though."

He believed her. For about a tenth of a second. Then he turned to Phoena, sensing in her posture an urgency she had disguised well thus far. "So, to what do I owe this delightful surprise? What brings you to England?"

Phoena reached into her bag and pulled out the complete issue of *The Flesh* that Charlie had found. "This. Do you know anything about it?"

Bentley's eyes widened in recognition as he reached for the magazine. "Blimey! Yes. Yes, I do." He sat down. "This was their last issue. Also their biggest seller. It's still a legend in the industry. That story stirred up so much shite—but that was a long time ago. Sixty years now, at least."

"Who's the model?"

Bentley removed a pair of reading glasses from his breast pocket and put them on. "If memory serves, his name was Malcolm. A real up-and-comer. Could have been the next big thing. Would have been if—"

"What? What happened?"

"He died. And no one knows how."

"What do you mean?"

Bentley sighed and removed the spectacles, pinching the bridge of his nose. "Well, it's all a bit vague, really. Sort of a legend in the Industry, don't you know. It seems that directly after that shoot, the photographer, Bailey David, had some sort of party. Him, Malcolm, some other people. Even a Royal, if I'm not mistaken. While they were all in their cups, some other 'guests' arrived. At least, that's what the Yard was able to piece together from what was left. They all died, you see, and rather messily I'm afraid."

"And the story still ran?" asked Phoena.

Bentley smiled at her naïveté. "Of course! Nothing moves a rag like scandal. You should know that."

Charlie looked up from the magazine. "What do you mean, 'messily'?"

"It was like someone had stuffed them all into a blender, put it in the middle of the floor, set the dial to—what's that French word? *Frappé?* Then turned it on without the lid."

"Eeeewwwwww! Gross!" Charlie exclaimed, completely repulsed and secretly fascinated.

"Who would know more about this?" asked Phoena.

"Why?"

"I can't tell you. Not right now."

"Does this have anything to do with this unbelievable Campaign Joshua's shooting?"

Charlie looked at the writer slyly. "It might."

"Charlie!"

Bentley glanced at the young assistant, then at Phoena. "Okay. Now you've got my nose up. Out with it. What does some sixty year-old scandal have to do with The Campaign of The Century?"

Phoena sat on the edge of his desk, her hand unconsciously pushing the magazine away. "Tell you what, Bentley. I'll give you something. A taste. But you have to promise to sit on this until I give you the okay."

"You Yanks. What's the matter, don't you trust me?"

She stood and folded her arms, face set, her eyes impenetrable. "My way or you'll never know. Decide."

"All right, all right, you've got a deal. But only if I get an exclusive."

Phoena pretended to think about this. "Done."

They shook hands.

"Now, give."

Phoena pointed to the last picture in the spread, the one of Malcolm crucified, and spun the magazine so Bentley could see it reversed. "Remind you of anyone?"

He put his glasses back on and adjusted them. "Vaguely . . ."

"Look closely. Past the beard and blood."

Bentley recoiled. "My God! Solipsum! But how—?"

"That's what we're here to find out."

"This is incredible. Now that I see it, the resemblance is astonishing. They could almost be the same person. What's going on?"

"Honestly?" Phoena shrugged. "We don't know. That's why we need your help. With all your contacts, you're the only person who can get to the bottom of this."

Bentley brought his hand up and absently rubbed his mouth. "There's a little feeling I get whenever I'm on to something hot," he said pensively. "A burning sensation at the base of my spine."

"And you're feeling that now?"

"Yes. Like someone's stuck a glowing ember under my skin. It hasn't been this strong in years. Maybe never. I think you're onto something, Phoena. Something big." He stood. "Where are you staying?"

"The Strand."

"Of course. Give me the rest of today, probably some of tomorrow as well. This is fifty years old, it's going to take some digging."

Phoena's expression became serious. "Don't take too long. Something tells me we have very little time."

They began walking to the door.

"What'll we do while we wait?" asked Charlie.

Phoena smiled. "Why, see London, of course."

"Yippeeeee!" Charlie raced down the hall.

Bentley laughed as he put his arm around the model's shoulders, letting Charlie get ahead of them before speaking in a low voice. "There's just one other thing, luv. That feeling I get? It also means that something bad is about to happen. Something very bad. For God's sake, Phoena, be careful."

She kissed him on the cheek. "Don't worry, Bentley. I have Charlie to protect me." Then she put her arm around his waist as they walked past the receptionist to the elevator, just in time to see Charlie in fierce concentration, practicing some sort of push kick, toes just brushing the elevator button.

Interlude Eight—Los Angeles

Tag Orbit had always been good at climbing, but he had never figured he would be able to combine it with his other favorite pastime—painting. That was until he discovered the aerosol. Now he was having the time of his life. For the past four years he had quietly been terrorizing Los Angeles. Or rather, the billboards of Los Angeles. He marveled at how easy it was if you just followed one simple rule. Don't ever tell anyone what you're doing, 'cause sure enough, the wrong people would figure out who you were and shut you down.

This Campaign of The Century thing had been absolutely amazing. It had allowed him to express himself in ways he had never dreamed possible. By painting a strategic bullet hole in a forehead here, (leaking, of course), a skull overlay there, horns here, and wings there, he was able to alter The Campaign of The Century in very profound ways. He had, in fact, taken it over—at least in L.A. At times he even considered himself Stone's co-creator, such was the power of his "enhancements." What they'd done was bring to the forefront what had always lain beneath. The story still got seen, but now it was absorbed through the lens of his graffiti. It had caused people to think, to feel, more deeply. Only a few of them, but it was a beginning. And although he did not realize it, he was the first embodiment of the Power of One. Like a pebble in a pond, or a butterfly's wing in South America, he affected the future with a five dollar spray bomb in ways as far reaching as they were unpredictable.

Tonight he was going after his biggest prize, the massive new vertical billboard on Sunset Strip. He was dressed in black and knew he must be quick. It would be bullet holes this time. Big ones. Right in the middle of their foreheads, dripping carmine red for as far down as it would run.

He began his rappelling descent of the massive billboard that featured Solipsum and Phoena's faces, cheek to cheek. He stopped at forehead level and pulled out two cans of spray paint, one red, the other black, duct-taped together. He quickly sprayed the bullet holes, then saturated each with so much red they began, as planned, to run. The night breeze ran fingers through his thick brown hair and he had never felt more alive. He started to laugh, spontaneously, hysterically. Then he gripped the rope, planted his feet and sprung off Solipsum's face to make his way down.

And everything changed.

He became aware of something tracking his progress. Watching him. His head whipped around frantically, muscles rigid, barely registering that the nylon rope was now cutting into his palms. *Where are they? Where the fuck are they?* Then the eye in front of him slowly blinked.

Solipsum's eye.

In the photograph.

His heart started pounding, mind shrieking that this couldn't, couldn't, *couldn't!* be happening even as Solipsum's face turned to him out of the billboard.

Massively.

Tag felt himself shrivel under the gaze of something he still refused to believe was real, the seep of his own hot terror piss barely registering as Solipsum's hand emerged from the billboard and casually flicked its fingers.

"Be gone."

Tag's last thought as he arced through the night was that it must have been magic paint or something, because when that face had turned, so too had his paint, becoming blood as it ran and ran, all the way down past cheek to chin.

Then he smashed into the middle of the Boulevard, where traffic swerved to avoid his shattered body.

Unsuccessfully.

London, England—The Campaign of The Century—Day 258

Bentley had only been able to turn up one lead. Phoena and Charlie found her at a nursing home in Hampstead. She was a very old lady who happened to have been Bailey's receptionist at one time. She only contributed one word to their search.

"No—"

But she pointed them to another person. And like following a trail of verbal breadcrumbs, Phoena and Charlie soon found themselves taking some sort of whirlwind tour of London, from famous landmarks to clubs and restaurants to dingy back alleys. Phoena was forced to do something she rarely did, because it gave her no pleasure—not any more. She used the full force of her beauty and celebrity to extract as much information possible in the short time they had left. This meant she had to wear the disguise she had taken to wearing since the Campaign images had started appearing. She now used her celebrity only when they'd found who it was they sought, deftly as a surgeon's scalpel, a little here, a little there, with a blade so fine you couldn't even tell it had drawn blood. Or information, as the case had been.

"I don't think I've ever heard —" a copper said,

"Of the bugger—" sneered a punk,

"But—" a housewife reflected,

"I might know—" a cab driver remembered,

"Someone—" a young schoolgirl knew,

"Who can help you find—" the model pointed them,

To an older model who did not have pleasant memories of "That old pederast."

"Long gone—" another model said wistfully, absently picking at the scabs on her arms.

Her booker didn't add much. "And good riddance—"

"To bad rubbish, I says," another booker piped up.

"And who are you—" a drug dealer inquired,

"To be askin—" a mover demanded,

"Oh! Well! Why didn't you say so? I've never met a real live super-model before." the old lady exclaimed. She then began prodding Phoena with her umbrella to see if she was real. Charlie didn't even bother holding back the laughter.

Another drug dealer remembered something. "Wait a minute—" as he scratched his head,

Turned out a club doorman knew, "There's a rumor—"

A record store clerk reflected, "Something about—"

The ice cream vendor almost remembered it, "Some sort of—"

It was a bartender who finally pointed them in the right direction. "Derelict Hilton—"

A drunk slurred, "Can you imagine such a thing?"

Another drunk looked over at them. "Where?"

Phoena and Charlie finally arrived at an industrial wasteland, colloquially known as the "Derelict Hilton." A cardboard sign hung forlornly from the chain link and announced this to any prospective lodgers. The girls looked at it briefly, then threaded their way through a slit in the mesh. They stood for a moment, taking in their surroundings, the jagged hulk of an abandoned factory squatting in the distance before them. Charlie pointed and Phoena saw the movement of people far ahead. They began walking over the broken concrete and rubble, weeds and bits of industrial flotsam poking up from the gravel like shell-shocked refugees. They finally reached a small knot of vagrants and Phoena asked the closest a question regarding a certain Bailey David.

He looked her up and down before snarling, "Well, that little piece of information—"

Another bum shouldered forward. "Is going to cost you."

They found themselves surrounded by a feculence of homeless who appeared to have materialized from nowhere—The Legions of Filth. The girls instinctively spun to guard each other's backs, heads turning, eyes darting, the stench almost beyond belief. The ring of broken men tightened, eyes bright with remembered lusts, eager to sample what had fallen to them, here in their place of power.

Los Angeles—The Campaign of The Century—Day 258

Peeva Slatern sat in a chair and calmly waited for the little red light on camera one to start blinking, as she had so many times before. Peeva was host of the enormously popular television show *Decadence Weekly*. In a world saturated by media coverage, Peeva's show had managed to claw its way to a niche at the very top that none of her competitors had been able to crack. Some of this success was due to Peeva herself, some to the look and pace of *Decadence Weekly*. But the real reason the show was such a mammoth hit was because it was broadcast live and orchestrated so things—happened. Unscripted things. "Moments," as Peeva had come to call them.

Her cameraman waved to her and mouthed a countdown. Five . . . four . . . three . . . two . . . one . . . and they were off.

The intro music began and Peeva looked at the full house, secretly very pleased. This would be one of the most popular shows ever. The degree of interest in this whole Campaign of the Century thing was unlike anything she'd ever seen. People were absolutely *feverish* to know more.

She glanced at a monitor, to see what the camera saw. The *Decadence* studio still looked like the most modern of TV interview set-ups, complete with wraparound LCD projection screen on which an innocuous cityscape was currently visible.

The music died, replaced by wild cheering and clapping as the blinking lights instructed the herd. She smiled as she waved them to quiet, her teeth like mints on a string.

"Tonight on *Decadence Weekly*, people are talking about what many are calling the advertising coup of the century."

Images from cities all over the world flashed on the screen behind her. And everywhere The Campaign of The Century dominated. Images of giant billboards, bus shelters, shopping bags, t-shirts, matchbook covers, riffling magazine pages, and shoppers, shoppers, hoards of shoppers, buying everything in sight.

"The consumer spending frenzy that has been sparked by this Campaign is unequaled in the annals of modern history. A massive payday for some, but does *Fa-Shin, Inc.*'s brilliant strategy have a darker side? With us tonight is the mastermind behind the entire Campaign. Ladies and Gentlemen, please welcome Creative Director for *Fa-Shin, Inc.*, Elora Gorj."

Elora came striding into the TV studio in a low cut designer dress the color of fresh money, body toned and eyes burnished. She crackled with energy, on a high no drug could touch (though she had made several attempts tonight). The studio audience went crazy, their applause and whistling like a carpet of sound for *Fa-Shin, Inc.'s* Creative Director as she made her way across the stage. She air kissed Peeva and sat down in a chair opposite her.

"Elora," the hostess gushed, "You look stunning tonight."

"Thanks, Peeva, I do, don't I?"

"Uh—right." *Jesus, don't trip over your own modesty or anything.* "So, how does it feel to be the architect of the greatest advertising campaign in history?"

Elora leaned forward to better display her cantilevered breasts. She licked her lips.

"I'll let you in on a little secret. It feels *great.'*

Peeva noticed some white particulate matter around Elora's left nostril. It was not a sight she was unfamiliar with. A brief thought

(ask her for some)

surfaced before another

(she's higher than a fucking kite!)

replaced it.

"You have no idea how amazing it is to have everything you've worked so long and hard for finally come to fruition."

"But tell me, Elora. Many are saying that this whole campaign is nothing more than a thinly disguised art-wank that runs interference for the biggest cash grab in history."

Elora held up her hands, kliegs flashing off her silvered nails. "Whoa, Peeva. Nobody's forcing anybody to buy anything. It's a highly competitive world out there. We've had the balls to do what no one before has ever attempted and now we're able to reap the rewards. Fortune favors the bold." She sat back, satisfied.

"Indeed. And what rewards. Your third quarter earnings are about to come out and industry experts are predicting a 1000% jump in profits. And this from a company that's already one of the biggest in the world."

Elora smiled. "We may be one of the biggest but we're also one of the best."

"But what about the persistent rumors of deplorable Third World sweatshops where workers are paid pennies a day?"

"What about them?" Elora became indignant. "No one has ever proven anything. And no one ever will."

"Because *Fa-Shin, Inc.* covers its tracks so well?" Peeva smiled sweetly.

"Because those rumors are patently false."

Peeva sensed the coming of a "Moment" and laid a card to speed its birth. "Just like the rumors you've been planking the Campaign's top male model, Solipsum?"

"Jealous, Peeva? Oh, I'm sorry, I forgot. Your tastes run more to Phoena, don't they?"

Trumped! Peeva backed off. For now. "Uh, why don't we go on to something a little less—prickly?"

"Why don't we," *douche nozzle!* Elora crossed her legs and sat back, miffed.

Peeva dusted herself off. "Let's take a closer look at some of the images from The Campaign of The Century."

Another montage came up on the massive LCD backdrop, this time at a slower frame rate. Both Peeva and Elora turned to look at what had started to materialize, quickly becoming lost in the sea of images unfolding before them. As the photographs flowed and dissolved into one another, they were treated to what it was like to experience Joshua's images from the point of view of the consumer. And it became very evident that he had more than fulfilled Elora's wildest expectations, that he had indeed created a totally organic liquid visual narrative.

The audience was rapt. They leaned forward in their seats, as if to more fully immerse themselves in what they were seeing. The editing of the montage was magnificent. Someone had even set the flow to music, music that Elora could have sworn she had heard before. Music that somehow fit perfectly with what she was seeing. She looked back for a moment at the studio audience, then at the screen again, and found herself caught in the limbo of inducement and result, cause and effect, astonished by the sheer power of what she had had a hand in creating. Then it came to her. The music. Where she had last heard it. And the circle came to a close inside her head with an almost audible snap. She realized in that instant that though she had believed otherwise, believed it with all her heart, she had never been more than a puppet, dangling from strings controlled by the hands of a master manipulator. Thoughts flashed in her mind like exploding glass, each refracting and reflecting a tumbling other, building to a blinding nova of realization that almost caused her to scream out loud. Sweat began to bead her forehead, vision going white at the edges. Even Peeva noticed something was wrong and turned to ask if she was all right. The expression on her face was the only genuine thing she had shown all night. Then the music, the music she last heard at the Seventh Level, began to fade. The studio lights came back on and things returned to a semblance of normalcy. She shook herself slightly, turned back in her chair and looked out at the audience. Her vision adjusted to the new level of brightness and it became obvious that people had been deeply affected by what they had just witnessed. She heard sounds, laughter, crying. Then the screaming started. Peeva was motioning frantically to someone off stage to cut to a commercial, for the first time in the history of the show. As Elora's eyes finally returned to normal, she understood why.

It appeared that eighteen people in the front row had voluntarily blinded themselves.

And Elora finally asked herself what was *really* going on.

Book 11

"The sleep of reason breeds monsters." —Goya

London, England—The Campaign of The Century—Day 259

"Here now! Who the fuck do ya think ya are, comin' here all hoity-toity like yer some sort of supermodel?"

Phoena looked at the man in front of her, intimidated as much by his physicality as by his stench. Even with shallow breaths she felt like a toilet brush was scouring her nasal passages. She began breathing through her mouth, studying him. He was younger than she'd first thought, fat like sewage in a sausage casing, clothes at a fashion crossroads where Bike Courier, Rave, and Dickens were beating the fuck out of each other. The bitterness came off him in waves, lining and creasing, his mouth pushed together like a small word.

"I'm looking for the world-renowned photographer Bailey David."

The bum absently scratched a flea bite. "No one here by that name. Now feck-eff, whydon'cha? Before there's trouble."

Phoena dropped her voice. "Too bad he's not around. I'm from Cranston and Porridge. It seems a certain Bailey David was left a rather substantial sum. By his late brother Malcolm." With that she turned to go, and could tell by the creeping fust that he was following her.

"His brover Malcolm? Well, why din'cha say so, ya strumpet."

Phoena spun about and quickly stepped back, some animal instinct keeping her distant. He smirked at her reaction, then cut to the meat. "Substantial. How much would that be?"

"That's for Bailey, not for you."

"Fuck it. We'll just take wot you got then have our way with you."

Charlie brought her fist before the man's face and opened it. He quickly shuffled back when he saw what lay there. A soft murmuring arose from the other men as they, too, retreated. Phoena looked at the strange key-like object, then at the other girl. Charlie's eyes never left the crowd before her. The man they had been talking to then turned.

"Come wif me," he said, trudging away.

The homeless parted and they followed him down a wide alley, two enormous factory shells looming on either side, skirting puddlings of old machinery and broken glass as though traversing a minefield.

Phoena glanced at her friend. "What just happened?"

"Something made me pull this out." Charlie showed her the key.

"Is that what I think it is?"

"Yeah."

"Why did it work on them?"

"I think it opens other things besides that Room. People's minds, other doors of . . . possibility." Charlie stopped and held the key out. "Here, Phoena. I want you to take it."

She was about to refuse, then something made her change her mind.

"All right," she said as her hand closed over it. "For now."

They hurried to catch up to their guide who stood before a lorry dock, its steel roll door jammed open with two cinderblocks. "Here we are then." He levered himself up and crawled under it with a grunt.

The two girls looked at one another, then Charlie jumped up and disappeared under the metal rolldown. A few seconds passed before Phoena saw her hand emerge and make a come-hither gesture. She squeezed it, squirmed under—and entered another world. It was very dark and quiet, except for the odd drip and the patter of tiny feet. She found Charlie's hand and they followed the bum towards the room's only light source, an oil drum fire burning in the distance.

As they came closer, details slowly emerged from the gloom. There was old sofa on which sat a huge heap of rags, the oil drum, boxes, junk, wires and bottles. Lots of bottles.

"I've brought you some people."

The rags shifted and spoke. "I thought I fookin' told ya never to bring anyone—"

"They used that word. 'Malcolm.'"

The heap sucked in a breath and levered itself up to a sitting position. Feet plopped to the ground, bottles clinked, layers of clothing shifted and Phoena finally made out the shape of a man. He wore a filthy and tattered overcoat, bulging pockets pendulous with the weight of succor. Underneath was a vest that had at one time obviously been red but was now so stained and threadbare it reminded her of a scab. His black pants were shiny and she could see dirty long johns through the holes in them. She took in his ancient face, a splotchy purple from years of drink, wattled cheeks covered in a gray cilia of greasy whisker. The only anomaly was a large pair of wraparound designer sunglasses, *Pucci* by the look of them.

"He's blind," Charlie whispered.

The bum tilted his head, as if he wasn't quite sure he'd actually just heard a girl's voice in this shithole. His face turned to the fat youth, his voice a gin-soaked barnacle. "All right, fook oof then, Crebsy, I'll take it from 'ere."

Phoena gave Crebsy some money, trying not to touch his hand. He snatched the bill, blew her a kiss as he silently cursed her, then shuffled off. The creature on the couch made no sound until Crebsy was well out of earshot. He began rubbing his hands together and Phoena sensed how afraid he was.

"You tell 'im!" the air hissing out of him fiercely, "all these years and I stuck by me word. I never told a soul. About any of it!"

Phoena paused, digesting this new morsel. "Well, maybe it's time to start."

"Wot?"

"Tell me, Bailey. What makes you so afraid? And who's Malcolm?"

"You mean 'e din't send you?"

"No, he didn't."

Bailey wiped his nose with a sleeve. "Then why are you 'ere?"

"To stop Him."

The old man wheezed, then began to laugh, a laugh that quickly degenerated into a wracking cough. He hacked up something red and black that he spat towards the oil drum.

Phoena shuddered, then regained herself. "There must be a way. But I need to know what he is. Where he came from."

"Never! There's nofing you can say or do—"

"I'll tell him where to find you. I work with him practically every day. I'll tell him that you spilled your guts. It will be interesting to see how long he makes you last."

"But—but—I'm jus' a defenseless ol' man!" Bailey cowered like a beaten cur, and Phoena felt a sudden stab of pity. She quickly stifled it.

"So what," she snapped.

He sighed and sagged into the ratty sofa, its springs *shreeping*.

"C'mere. At least let me see 'oo I'm speakin' to."

Phoena dutifully went over and sat near him. He exuded some sort of perma-stench,

(oldsocks-cancer-cockcheese-vomit-piss-rubbing-alcohol-and-impacted-shit)

that immediately caused olfactory shut down. She swallowed, then took his hands and guided them to her face. They were surprisingly gentle as they traced its contours, eyes first, then downward as fingers touched her cheeks, his thumbs her nose and lips. And somehow before she knew it, he was groping her breasts, hands kneading, thumb-pads rolling—she slapped his mitts away as he cackled with glee.

"Been awhile since I felt tats that firm. And they're real, too, aren't they?"

"All right, Bailey, you've had your fun." She pulled her coat more tightly about herself then glared at him, forgetting for a moment he was blind. "But I'm not in the mood to fuck around anymore. Too much weird shit is going on and too many people are dying. Now, out with it!" Her voice reverberated and they all turned their heads to follow the carom of its echo.

"All right, all right. Don't yell at me anymore. Please. I'll tell you. Everything. But on one condition. Yer a model, aren't chew? And at the top of yer Game. I kin tell. The years go by but there's some fings yew don't ferget."

"Get to the point."

"I want a kiss."

"What? After what you just pulled? Never in a million years!"

"Just one little kiss," he pleaded. "Fer an ol' man 'oo used to be someone. Please?"

Phoena saw his poor designer sunglasses and knew he held the key to everything. She rolled her eyes and looked to her friend, who shrugged sympathetically and mouthed, *What are you gonna do?* Charlie then grabbed her own breasts silently, eyes squeezed shut as she sniffed the air like a mole. Phoena gave her a particularly dark look before turning back to the old man on the couch.

"Deal."

Bailey settled back amidst more *shreeping* as the girls dragged over a couple of abandoned kitchen chairs. Charlie found some broken plywood skids and fed them into the oil drum. The flames fell upon the dry wood, the consumptive illumination strangely beautiful as it flickered over the flesh of the old man and the two young women. Bailey turned his face to the heat, rooting for a bottle he finally took a long snoutful from. The burn went straight from throat to gut before a heat to match the fire's spread through him. Then he judged himself ready.

"Aye, you should have seen it. London in the swinging Sixties, booze, drugs and birds galore. And no fookin' AIDS7. You can't imagine it, girl, it was a fookin' Wonderland."

Phoena sat back in her chair. *Oh yes I can*, she thought.

"An' I was at the top o' the heap. Shootin', fookin', partyin', it's a fookin' wonder I'm still alive. But even wif all that, it wasn't enough. I got bored. Sensory overload or somefin'. Anyhoo, I was havin' one of me parties, famous for'em I was. I'd invited a small but select group to this one, includin' one of the royals, Phillip, way removed, if ya know what I mean. 'e suggested we 'ave a bit 'o fun wif some black magic shite 'e was dabblin' in at the time. Well, me, I was game for anyfin' in those days. I said 'Sure mate, bring whatever ya need.' Turned out it was the last party I ever frew. 'Ere were five other people 'ere that nite. I'm sure by now yu know 'oo they were."

Phoena remembered what Bentley had told them before they started their search. "The Edensbridge Massacre. Britain's equivalent to the Manson murders. But you were supposed to have died there. How come you're still alive?"

"Because 'e made sure of it. But we're getting ahead of the story here. We were partyin' pretty heavily and one fing kind of led to another and next I knew, we were 'avin' ourselves a bit of an orgy."

"What a surprise," said Phoena without surprise.

"I still 'ad the set up from a very weird shot I'd done for the *FLESH*."

"Cruci-Fixation." Charlie's voice was soft. "The last shoot you ever did."

Bailey's head turned towards her like a canker on a stick. "Aye, that's the one. And Malcolm, that beautiful young boy who was in that shot, well 'e was one of me invitees that night. So we strapped 'im to the cross again, upside down just like before, only this time 'e was naked. And then the royal drew this Pentagram around 'im and started lightin' all these black candles 'e'd brought. It was weird, let me tell you. You could feel the power buildin' in the room . . .

But we were all so fookin' high. I'd never felt that charged in all me life. Things were goin' great until Mr. Head-up-'is-Arse Royal pulls out this knife, and the next thing ya know, 'e's makin' all these weird little cuts on the boy's body. By that time, even poor sweet Malcolm, fooked up as 'e was, knew somethin' was a wee bit off kilter. So 'e says 'e's had enough and 'e wants to come down. I went over to accommodate the lad and found meeself wif a knife wavin' in me eyes.

'I'm not *finished* yet!' the little Royal screamed. Like some wee tot caught tannin' bugs wif' a magnifin' gless. An' he was wankin' too! Then 'e yelled at me. 'Fetch something to catch the blood, Bailey. Do it *now!*'

Don't know why I listened to 'im, it was like I was underwater . . . Fookin' drugs! Brought a tray out from the darkroom, didn't even look in it. Maybe if I 'ad, it all would've ended right there. I came back and shoved it under Malcolm and that's when crazy Phillip slit 'is throat!

Fook, the blood that poured out of that poor boy. All 'e could make was this gurglin' noise, an' 'is eyes—pleadin' for mercy the whole time. It was fookin' 'orrible. We all stood there starin' and there was nothin' we could do.

Then I started to notice, I guess we all did, that as much blood as was comin' out of him, not a single drop left the tray. It was like a 'ole that didn't seem to have any capacity to get—full—you know?"

Bailey shifted on the sofa and took another drink, a long one, shuddering as the memories pressed in, the alcohol his only buffer. "After that, things got really weird. You see, whatever was using that tray as a window started to—suck—so's all the blood was drained out of the poor boy.

Then the sounds started.

Horrible noises, all crunchy and squishy-like as Malcolm's bones an' innards were liquefied into some sort of gruel. It poured out of 'is throat and into that damned tray. When the last of it 'ad gone, the husk that was 'is skin slipped the ropes an' fell off the cross. *Kersplash!*

Then a deathly silence filled the room. Even that fucker Phillip quieted down, what wif all the weird shite e'd bin chantin' while all this was goin' on. I got up and looked in the tray an' finally saw what was there. What 'ad been doing all the suckin'.

It was a print of Malcolm, from the shoot.

It 'ad been floatin' in some developer and I'd forgotten about it when me guests arrived. There it was, just breakin' the surface, that god awful mixture of blood, developer and Malcolm—stretched tight as a drum, like it was waitin' for some kind ov signal.

Then Lizzie screamed—and the Print started to spin. Slowly at first, then faster and faster, blood flyin' in all directions. An' like smoke risin' from a cigarette, somefin' began to materialize in the air, a couple of feet above it."

He leaned towards them and tilted the bottle to his lips, throat working as the oily light painted his face like something from the Pit. He lowered it and coughed once, his voice now rough. "I don't know what I expected, some sort of demon maybe.

But not—*that*.

It was the most stunnin' creature I'd ever seen, like the distillate of human beauty. I almost couldn' look at it, but I couldn' tear me eyes away either. None of us could. We were all struck dumb, just standin' there, starin', blood and God knows what else drippin' off of us.

Then it opened its eyes.

Wot looked at us from behind those eyes was so utterly—alien—it defied belief. Because you see, wot we were really lookin' at was Malcolm. But a Malcolm so far beyond 'imself, it was like 'e'd fulfilled every ideal of human potential. Become a god.

An' 'e was—bigger somehow. In every way, if you know what I mean. Like 'is skin could barely contain whatever energy was givin' life to the boy's shell. Then it opened its mouth and laughed. And all 'ell broke loose. Literally.

Wot 'appened after that . . . well . . . believe me, missy, yer better off not knowin'. Can't say 'ow long it went on. Seemed like days. Probably less than an 'our.

Last I saw was Phillip die.

Last I 'eard was the sound of that fing . . ."

He lowered his sunglasses.

. . . eatin' me eyes."

Phoena stared at his ruined sockets in horror. Black and empty as open mouths, they swallowed the firelight with a hunger that would never be satisfied. "Jesus, Bailey! That's—" The words remained lodged in her throat.

"Wot?" He slowly put his glasses back on. "You don't believe me?"

"No. I believe you. It explains far too much. And I thought I was losing my mind. But between then and now, that's a sixty years. Why did he take so long to start killing again?"

"Not 'e. It. Don't confuse what 'e looks like wif what 'e is. That's a big mistake. And as to why It took so long? I fink It began by learnin' to be human. To curb Its appetites. So as to draw the least amount of attention to Itself. I think It 'ad to learn to—savor. Or else It would've perished a long time ago."

"Is there any way to kill It?" asked Charlie.

"I don't fink It can be killed. Least not like us. But there *is* a way to send It back to where It came from. But it's one 'ell of a long shot."

"How?" Phoena demanded.

Bailey's mouth stretched wide and it took her a moment to realize he was grinning. "Not so fast, girlee. I think it's time for that little item of barter we discussed earlier. It was a shag, wann'it?"

"A kiss. Our deal was for a kiss. That's it."

"Well, what are ye waitin' for?"

Phoena saw his face moving in, lips like two pieces of turgid liver, flecks of spittle on his chin and gray whiskers, and all she could do was close her eyes.

London, England—The Campaign of The Century—Day 259

"Seeing" was not really the right word, thought Solipsum as he gated through limbo. When he moved from place to place, through the images of himself that acted as Gateways, his sensorium experienced a vastly more—open—perspective of Reality. Time, dimension and distance were all malleable, illusory. It really all depended on one's level of awareness.

The rainy stain glass runnings of color began to solidify, shimmering and clarifying as a tiny pinpoint in their center expanded, interlocking, unfolding, telescoping, until he stepped through the *GQ* cover and into—

Bentley Sween's apartment.

He noted as he became three dimensional that as always, he had arrived in the same clothing as the image through which he had Gated. His hand shot to his eye, feeling the patch there, reminded again of his carelessness. He swore silently, cursing Phoena.

The room in which he stood was large and low-ceilinged, with bookcases and clusters of heirloom furniture huddled on rugs that had seen better days. Table lamps and wall sconces provided a torch-like illumination, insular and splotchy, the ambient light almost nonexistent, objects falling quickly into blackest shadow. A Bentley who fit perfectly with the room stood before him.

Solipsum gazed at the writer with complete confidence, and utter contempt. "Where are they?"

Bentley took a sip of his brandy before answering. "I think you're rather too late, old man. They've probably found him by now."

"You are not at a dinner table, scribbler. You will tell me where you've sent them. *Now.*"

Bentley took another sip, then tilted his head and looked at Solipsum lazily. "What happened to your eye? Oh, let me guess, poking around where you don't belong? I suppose that's the price one pays for being a bit of a Peeping Tom, wot?"

Solipsum advanced, eye aglow like some great cat's, his teeth grinding. "Your torment will be—"

"Oh, do shut up, Blinkey. Before you embarrass yourself further, I suggest you look down."

Solipsum did. And realized to his shock and embarrassment that he had allowed himself to become very neatly trapped, by blithely Gating through a magazine that lay within a Circle of Binding. And not even Solipsum could defy the Laws that enslaved him to whomsoever had bound him thusly.

He lunged towards Bentley, the movement inhumanly fast, his whole head distorting to such a hideous degree it would cause immediate insanity were it looked upon directly.

Bentley averted his gaze but did not move, confident the circle would hold. There was a great burst of light and the smell of charred flesh, slightly rotted, filled the air. Solipsum rebounded, tendrils of smoke drifting from him, the flesh of his hands and face a bright red that was already fading.

Bentley's eyes hardened. "Try that again and I'm going to make a phone call. To someone who would be very grateful indeed to have a Master Demon of the Seventh Level as his personal slave."

"So. You know what I am."

"Yes. Took a bit of legwork, and guesswork." Bentley allowed himself a small smile. "Surprising, though, how everything fell into place once I permitted myself to believe you weren't—human."

"You have done well, Bentley. Now, let me go and I will give you anything you desire."

The writer was enjoying himself. This wasn't turning out to be as hard as he had been led to believe. "Anything?"

Solipsum's gaze became liquid, his voice warm with promise. "Including Phoena's love."

Bentley suddenly realized the stakes were much higher than he'd thought. "Y—you can do that?"

"Yes."

He paused, and let himself imagine a life with Phoena. She was everything he had ever dreamt of in a woman. Beauty, intelligence, grace . . . he slammed the lid of that Pandora's box before it opened far too wide. "Sorry old chum. It wouldn't be cricket."

"But—"

"Shut up. Last I looked, I was the one in charge here. Now, as you are bound by the Circle, so are you bound by my will. Answer me. What is your plan? How does it involve The Campaign of The Century? And what will happen to Phoena and Charlie?"

"May I smoke?"

"By all means."

He tossed a pack to Solipsum, who caught it easily with one hand. "Do you have a light?"

Bentley snorted. "Please, you're a demon. Surely a little fire is the least of your abilities."

Solipsum smirked as a small flame issued from the tip of his thumb.

Bentley watched the display, feeling himself somehow mocked. "Enough delay. Answer."

Solipsum exhaled and looked up. "Truthfully? I can't. Or rather, I can, but with your limited sensory apparatus, you wouldn't understand a fraction of what I am about to do."

Bentley put his glass down and made his second mistake. "Then I command you to expand my sensorium. But only temporarily. And only enough to accommodate your—communication."

"Very well."

The writer felt a slight tingling in his head that disappeared faster than a cheap high.

"That's it?"

"Yes."

"I don't feel any—wait a minute . . ."

The tingling had returned.

Solipsum calmly smoked, his eyes never leaving the other man's. "In three days, it all comes to a head. Everything I have worked for, all this time."

Bentley's eyes widened. "Yes. I see it . . ."

The tingling branched through his prefrontal lobes, externalizing as a halo of light.

"Do you see how it all fits together?"

"My God! It's so horribly ambitious. But the payoff . . ."

Solipsum smiled. "Beautiful, isn't it?"

"I never imagined . . ."

"No. You didn't."

"But this means . . ."

"You're finally getting it, aren't you . . ."

The entire room now blazed, Bentley its center, radiant.

" . . . so it will . . ."

"Yes. Follow it to the end . . ."

"Oh . . . my . . . God . . ."

Solipsum smoked, calmly watching as Bentley's brain exploded through the top of his skull. Bone and blood geysered up, ribbons of multihued *kundalini* energy intermingling with viscera and spinal cord.

Solipsum took a long last pull from his cigarette, then smiled a smile that did not quite reach his eyes.

"Exactly."

Interlude Nine—Tokyo

Nori was in the subway station, patiently waiting for the Tokyo mag-lev bullet train. She was surrounded by hundreds of commuters, all on their way home. She looked over and saw a businessman furtively buying schoolgirl panties from a vending machine. His angle prevented her from seeing whether it was the "new" or "used" lever that he had pulled. Not that it mattered.

The train pulled in, and she and the rest of the quietly seething mass were herded aboard by the white-gloved attendants. The doors hissed shut and Nori looked up to see she was surrounded.

By herself.

Ads from The Campaign of The Century featuring her and Solipsum used all available ad space in the car. Elora had decided that deeper penetration into the Japanese market required Nori replace Phoena in certain ads.

Then she felt the furtive touch of the first hand on her leg. Being groped in a Tokyo subway was nothing new. She swatted the hand away as she would a fly. But then another hand, bolder than the last, squeezed her breast. She turned to react and felt the knuckled push of three erect phalluses on her thighs and gluteal crevice. As the train hurtled into the tunnel, she heard the whispers begin.

Nori . . . Nori . . . Nori . . .

She tried to scream but a hand had already covered her mouth. Her last sight before the crush of bodies pulled her to the floor was of her own face, staring back, as if from a mirror.

London, England—The Campaign of The Century—Day 259

A half bottle of very expensive wine, delicious and clear, sat beside two glasses on the small table by the bed—a bed Phoena and Charlie were lounging in, naked and languid with the tawny memories of what had come before. Smoke curled lazily from the tip of Charlie's cigarette, edge lit by the afternoon sunlight as it streamed through the room's huge windows, drapes softly billowing in the late summer breeze.

Phoena looked at her beautiful friend and just enjoyed her for a moment. How the rays of sunlight painted her now as they played off the planes and angles of her face, the exquisite musculature of her body, how it shimmered in the molten gold of her hair and limned the fine down at the nape of her neck. In that moment she felt herself transported, to a place beyond time, an infinite Now where they were the only two people in the whole wide world, each drawn to the other like a lodestone, helplessly compelled by something

(love)

she could not yet admit, not even to herself, that evolved and grew and gleaming, changed and oh, how she wanted to take and give and drink all of this exquisite girl in one long and never ending draught.

Her toes reached and stretched, then curled against Charlie's back. "Mmmmmm, how I love the way you smell . . ." she murmured.

Charlie looked at her lover, casually reaching down to play with Phoena's baby toe, trying to distract herself as she felt the blood rising in her face.

" . . . like some wild orchid that no one's found yet. Primal, delicate—earthy . . ."

Charlie kept blushing more deeply with each word until she couldn't stand it any more. "Orchid? God, Phoena, I always thought I smelled like a—a soggy hamster when I—exerted myself."

Phoena laughed and hugged her close, burying her face in Charlie's soft and golden mop. She marveled again at the feel of her lover's body, how light she was, yet taut and firm, like pliant steel. And felt her own body responding, flowering, the heat slowly building once again. *God, what is she doing to me?* She almost reached for Charlie, then slowed herself consciously. *Savor, Phoena, savor . . .*

Charlie idly traced a finger along her lover's thigh. She still could not believe what she had just experienced. It was like walking through the window of an actual photograph, into a reality she had never imagined could exist. *So this is what it's like on the other side.* She burrowed deeper, nuzzling Phoena's throat, gently kissing the hollow, then looked up at this woman whom she had once thought would remain forever some unattainable photographic icon. "Can I ask you something? It's kind of—personal."

Phoena nodded.

"Did you ever—" Charlie hesitated, then tried again. "I mean, you know . . ."

And Phoena grinned a wicked grin, leaning in until their noses touched. "—get kicked out of Girl Scouts for eating a brownie?"

"Phoena! God!" Charlie fell away, blushing and laughing and thought that if any more blood rushed to her head she'd turn into some sort of Missus Tomato-head, permanently. "I'm going to get a t-shirt. It's getting a bit chilly."

Phoena was sipping her wine when Charlie crawled back over the covers and sat on the bed's edge. She lit a cigarette, then leaned back, mouth an 'O' as she blew a ring towards the ceiling. Phoena watched, eyes straying to her lover's breasts, following their contours even as Charlie turned to give her the full effect of the words printed on her shirt front: I PHUCKED PHOENA.

"Ahhhhh! Charlie! Where did you get that?" Phoena grabbed a pillow and began pummeling the other girl.

Charlie tried to get an elbow up, laughing so hard she missed the block. "Oh, Phoena. An assistant was wearing it at Joshua's party and I just had to get him to send it. I thought if we—you know . . ."

Phoena stopped, pillow raised. "Does that mean I have to get a matching shirt that says 'I CHEWED CHARLIE'?"

Charlie yelped and dove on her and they laughed and wrestled like otters at play. Phoena finally settled back against the headboard. "Okay! Okay! Whew! Let's take a break for a minute, and if you're lucky, maybe I'll answer your question. Maybe."

Charlie gave her the big eyes. "Please?" Her hand snuck over and grabbed Phoena's breast.

"Charlie!" Phoena swatted the hand away and pulled her lover down beside her.

"Are you going to be good?"

Charlie nodded.

"Okay. Harlow was the first girl I was ever with. And believe it or not, the only one. 'Til you. "Charlie smiled a small and special smile because words could not describe how that had made her feel." There was just something magical and sexual about her that made it so it didn't matter that we were both the same. Girls, I mean. She came from such a different place, not at all the frivolous creature she let everyone think she was. I remember once we were sitting across from each other, naked. We'd just finished eating some fruit and were both sticky with juice. I started getting very turned on and touched her face, but she stopped me. 'Try this,' she said, and took my hands. Then she held my wrists as I held hers and looked deep into my eyes. 'Feel my heart,' she said, 'as I feel yours.' So we sat there, just looking at each other and feeling each other's heartbeats. I lost all track of time. Then the most remarkable thing happened. Our hearts started to beat in unison. I could feel it. Physically. The room seemed to—disappear—as I *literally* felt myself drowning in her eyes. Then we made love. Or at least I think that's what we did. It was so beyond anything I'd ever experienced . . ." She shrugged helplessly.

Charlie gazed at her, more than a little wonder in her eyes. "Could we . . . ?"

"Yes. I think we could." Phoena continued the slow, unconscious caress of her lover's hip. "I think we could but—"

"Not yet." Charlie finished, and laid her head on Phoena's breasts, listening to the beat of her heart. Phoena gently stroked the other girl's hair as they relaxed into the silence, just comfortable in each other's presence.

Phoena finally nudged her. "Charlie?"

"Yeah?"

"All talk of mystical who-knows-what aside, you must know that was one of the best times I've ever had. With anyone."

"M—me too."

"But I have to ask—"

"What about Joshua?"

"Yes."

Charlie was silent for several moments. "I think I've lost him," she finally said. "To whatever is happening to him when he takes those pictures."

"His Muse."

"Is that what it is? I—I don't think so. When you look at his work, all his work, before he started shooting the Campaign, that's his Muse. This other stuff is different."

"What do you mean?"

"It's like some sort of photographic drug he's on, giving him a power he never even knew existed. And he can't walk away from it. Like that time he was in Bosnia and found those children."

" 'The Missing Years.' "

"Yeah."

Charlie took her lover's hands and squeezed them tightly. "Phoena? I think he's gone too far. Down a road I just can't follow. Not anymore. He's chasing something that he'll either catch or die trying to. I met some kids at Sea World and they set me straight. He's behaving like some sort of—fuck it—I'll say it—junkie. And those pictures. They're evil, Phoena. Just evil. I thought I had what it took to be a great photographer but if I have to—to be like that, to sell my soul—I just can't. I thought I loved him but I just can't." And then the tears came.

Phoena gathered the blond girl in her arms. "Shhhhh, Charlie. It's going to be all right."

"God, it's just gotten so strange! What Bailey told you, do you believe him?"

Phoena sighed. "Yes. There's no way he could make up a story like that. It reeks of truth. And his eyes . . ." She shuddered at the memory.

"What about Joshua? What can we do?"

"Save him. Or at least try."

Charlie wiped a tear away and bit her lip, an unconscious gesture both fearful and sensual. "How?"

"Let's go over what we know. Solipsum is a demon from Hell, masquerading as a male model. He has powers and an agenda we don't know about—yet. What else?"

Charlie's expression became thoughtful. "He can use pictures of himself as windows to see through. Can he also use them as doorways to travel through?"

"That's scary. Really scary. Let's put that one hold for a minute. What else?"

Charlie paused. "Well, what is he doing here? I mean. You know him, right? I mean, really *know* him. What's your take?"

Phoena put her hands behind her head and looked up at the ceiling. "I remember him being like a starving man at a banquet. He stopped just short of gluttony but I never saw anyone who enjoyed—sensation—so much. Any sensation, even pain. Sexually, he was insatiable, and very inventive. That combination, plus his sheer physicality was almost too much for Harlow and me. And that's saying something. Maybe that's all he's doing here, just enjoying himself. He reminds me of something I saw on a shoot once. I had a strobe pointed at me and the little light inside burned out. You know the one?"

"The modeling bulb. The one that shows you what the flash will do."

"Yeah. Just before it blew, it flared so bright it was almost blinding. I remember thinking, 'What a great light. But it can't last.'"

"Do you think it's the same with him? He's burning so hot, and with such a great light, that he's frying the filament? His body?"

Phoena sat up, seizing on Charlie's last words. "That's it! It must be! Remember when you showed me Joshua's images? He looked like he was rotting in some of those shots."

"Picture of Dorian Grey."

"Exactly."

"Okay. So let's say he is looking for a new body. Couldn't he just grab anyone?"

Phoena shook her head. "I don't think it works that way. It's like running a million watts through a hundred watt bulb. It would just blow."

"And I guess for him, most people are hundred watt bulbs."

"So who is the million watt bulb? And how do you find him?"

"Or her."

"Or her? I mean, sure. Why not? It could be a woman, couldn't it?"

Charlie's eyes darkened. "I think it's you, Phoena."

"What?"

"And he found you by sleeping with you."

"That's the craziest—"

"Think about it. He's a demon, true, but he's also here, on Earth, in the physical realm. There's lots of weird stuff he can do, but there are rules. Just like he probably can't teleport himself from place to place randomly. He'd need a picture to gate through. I think he can maybe guess if a new body can hold him. But then he has to go inside, physically. To be sure. At least a part of him. Like—"

"—testing the waters."

"Yeah. And then he knows."

"But why am I still me? Judging from Joshua's pix, he's almost burned out Malcolm's body. Why has he waited so long? Why didn't he kidnap me long ago and take possession of his new home?"

"Because there are rules. Some of them we know, and some of them we don't."

"So you think The Campaign of The Century is just a big ruse to—"

"Get into a picture with you."

"To somehow recreate the circumstances of his birth?"

Charlie gripped the other girl. "That's it! He has to perform some rite. While the two of you are together in a tray of blood and developer. In a photo."

"I think we're close. I mean, I can understand orchestrating The Campaign of The Century, because I guess the rules say I have to be with him of my own free will. But why wait 'til the end? He could have taken me over after the first shot."

Charlie shoulders slumped a bit. "I know. That's where it all kind of falls apart."

"If I'm still me, it means there's something he still needs. Maybe he's looking to get it with the last shot, 'Ascension'."

"Oh My God! That's what I saw in his room. That's the word!"

A strange calm settled over Phoena. As if she had already known this last shoot was where they would make their stand.

Charlie got up and paced the room. "How do you fight a demon? Holy water? Crosses?"

"By using what Bailey David gave us. He said we had one chance, and that we'd 'know the when and where of it'."

Charlie sat down again. "It's not enough. As Joshua says, you always gotta have a back-up plan."

"Any ideas?" Phoena reached for her glass of wine, its rim clicking her teeth. "Fuck," she muttered and sat up, one of her front teeth at an odd angle.

"What's the matter?"

"Nothing." Phoena had quickly brought a hand up to cover her mouth.

"Come on, let me see."

Phoena now had both hands up. "No way," she said, her voice muffled.

Charlie quickly straddled her, easing Phoena's hands away. "Let's see, let's see—oh my God." She stared for a moment, a slow smile spreading across her face. Then she gently lifted the porcelain tooth out.

"There. Are you happy?" Phoena gave her the hockey grin.

Charlie said nothing and carefully put the tooth on the bedside table. Then she brought her mouth down on Phoena's, kissing, kissing, her tongue gentle and insistent as it explored the gap in her lover's smile.

New York City, the Financial District—The Campaign of The Century—Day 257

Elora Gorj was being greed-fucked by Solipsum in her office and she'd never had it so good. She looked at the shadows their moving bodies cast on the wall and just had time to think how like some exotic flower they appeared. Then sensation demanded she return her attention to what she was experiencing.

All thoughts of confronting him had been put on hold, even to asking why one of his eyes was filled with blood. Because this was without a doubt the peak sexual experience of her life. The sensations she felt were pushing the electrical capabilities of her body's synapses to their limits. And beyond.

She heard his voice behind her.

"My, my, my. What a greedy little thing you are, Elora."

"Ohhh . . ."

"Would you like more?"

"Yes, oh God, yes!"

"Then here . . ."

Solipsum began to take things to a whole other plane of experience. A plane visited by only a very few in the course of human history. It began with the Eighth Level of Tantric sex, the level where primal energies were exchanged. A level that normally took ten years of careful practice and total mind-body discipline to achieve. Then he took her beyond.

As for Elora, she had long since exceeded her ability to describe what she was feeling. But not her capacity for experience. She had now reached the place where irreversible physical damage occurred. And she didn't care. Because she was experiencing—simultaneity.

"My—my—God, what—what—are you—doing? I can feel you fuck-ing me . . ."

"As I'm being fucked by you? Incredible, isn't it?"

"Yes!"

"But wait, Elora, there's more. Much more."

"What—is that . . ."

"Why it's me. *All* of me."

"But how can you be in two places . . ."

She caught a glimpse of Solipsum's tail, glistening and monstrous as it disappeared behind her.

She lowered her head as wave after wave of pain and pleasure washed over her, so intense they paled everything that had come before. She be-came dimly aware of an internal tearing, a liquid flooding . . .

"Oh—oh—I've never felt that before—no more, please—it hurts . . ."

"Too late, Elora, too late . . ."

Solipsum built the momentum far past what she, or for that matter, any human, was capable of. At the end, their bodies moved with the quantum speed of electrons.

Book 12

"You come to love not by finding the perfect person, but by seeing an imperfect person perfectly."
—Sam Keen

". . . Nothing shall be deliberately or unthinkingly allowed to detract from the central movement of our culture, toward monolithic control, toward production—which, after all, is nothing but the turning of the living . . . into the dead. Production is the manifestation in the physical world of the psychic process of objectification. It is the turning of the subject (a cow, for example) into the object (. . . a hamburger, a leather coat . . .). To do so necessarily kills the subject, first in the objectifier's experience, and then in the physical world.

Production, however, is not the end point. Production, deified as it has become, is not the god who stands behind the god. The god who stands behind the god is annihilation. Where does our production lead us? Psychic death. Emotional death. Physical death. And, as should be increasingly clear to anyone paying any attention whatsoever, it is leading us ever more quickly toward the death of every living being."
—Derrick Jensen

New York City, The Campaign of The Century—Day 260

Dear Quinby,

Great news! It's almost over. There's something I'm going to pull with this last sanction, something that will slip through the financial cracks when it all comes down and no one will ever notice. It's dangerous but it's too good a chance to pass up, too good a chance for us Quin, for us to finally say goodbye to the whole rotten stinking mess and just check out. We'll take off to that little island we went to last year, the one I'm about to buy. Yes, Quin—buy. Just like I promised you all those years ago in Monte Carlo. 'Cause you know I'm a girl of my word. God we were so young, then, weren't we? What days those were!

But this one's going to be hard, Quin. Really hard. He's the toughest bastard I've come against so far, a fat spider sitting at the center of his web, who thinks he can't be touched. But I have a surprise on my side.

Remember how you told me once you didn't think I ever got scared? "How could you?" you said. "World class spy, villains, gadgets, license to kill? It's the most fantastic game in the world!" Then you kissed me and pulled back and looked into my eyes, into my soul, as you said, "God, Jane, don't you know you'll live forever?" I'll never forget that, Quinby. Never. But I'm gonna let you in on a little secret, lover. I DO get scared. So scared sometimes I can't even move. And then I think of you and what we have together and somehow find my heart again.

God how I miss you! Your sunny face, your crazy laugh, the smell of you, the taste of you, that yummy, yummy body. I could just squeeze you so hard . . .

It's almost over. Then we'll be together. Wait for my word, then meet me where we had ice cream last time I was in town.

And bring your suitcase, girl of my dreams.

Love, Jane.

Quinby stood huddled in the rain beneath a neon sign, the turquoises and pinks highlighting her wet face. She crushed the letter she had already read so many times and swallowed. *Godammit, why am I so weak? She loves me! More than anyone I've ever been with, boy or girl. Yet I'm betraying her, with someone who treats me like a toy. Oh God, what am I doing?* She looked down the street to see Solipsum walking towards her and quickly stuffed the little ball of papper into the pocket of her white raincoat. She waited patiently as he approached, so many thoughts racing through her mind, so many memories of what they had shared, still lost in them when he found her.

"Quinby," he said quietly. "Do you know what stands before you?"

"I—think I do." She looked up from the reflections in the wet street and as she found his ice blue eyes, everything suddenly became very clear. "It's yours, isn't it? This whole Campaign of the Century thing."

Solipsum smiled, his teeth very white in the neon's glare. "After tonight, the world will be a very different place. Very. Its dark beauty will finally be brought to the fore, humanity as you know it a thing of the past. Would you join me in such a place?"

Quinby lit a cigarette, took a slow and thoughtful pull. "What would I have to give up?"

"Everything."

She considered what he had said, considered all that had passed between them, and all that could yet come to pass. "What would I gain?" she finally asked.

"Everything."

She dropped the cigarette, the sensation of smoke no longer satisfying, her hand in her pocket, touching the letter. "Trey? I think I'm going to pass. 'Cause this time? The story might have a different ending. And this time? I'm cheering for the home team."

Solipsum's eyes widened, the rainwater dripping from the points of his hair. Quinby thought he'd never looked more beautiful.

Then he did something that surprised them both. He leaned in and kissed her with all his dark essence.

"I release you," he said softly, and walked off into the rain.

New York City, Stone Studios—The Campaign of The Century—Day 260

Joshua gazed out the dome at the gathering clouds, as if they held some clue as to how he should proceed. The sky was almost black now, only dollops of gray cream remaining that looked as though they too would soon be swallowed.

Going to be one hell of a storm.

He looked at Phoena and Charlie and was hard pressed in that moment to decide whom he loved more, whom he would save if he could choose only one. He shivered at that thought, wondering where it had come from. He brought himself back to the present, how all the bonds he shared with them had been strained to their limits by what they had just dropped into his lap.

It was the last day of The Campaign of The Century. And it had almost not been the last day, because his main model and first assistant had disappeared. Both had now returned at the eleventh hour. They all sat on the circular couch, the mood as fragile and tense as a prison reunion. He noticed how nervous they were, and how this must reflect on what they had just told him, what they somehow expected him to *believe*. It was simply too much to swallow. A man usually in control of his emotions, he tried to keep his voice level. Then the intensity that was almost his trademark betrayed him.

"You are both fucking nuts! And late. I didn't think you guys were going to make it. If you hadn't called from the airport—you were both supposed to be here yesterday. Now you show up with the—craziest story I have ever heard. Even if he is some kind of demon, what the fuck is he doing masquerading as a male model? What's his purpose? It doesn't make any sense."

"Joshua. You've got to believe us," Charlie pleaded. "Everything Bailey told us ties in with what's been happening. I mean, look at your images. They've become—windows on Hell."

Stone's face tightened. "Charlie, you are way out of line. These images are some of the best work I've ever done."

Phoena's voice cut through him like a saber. "Wake up, Joshua. Just because a thing is beautiful doesn't mean it isn't evil. You of all people should know that."

Images from the Campaign loomed in his mind and he finally saw them for what they were, the immensity of what he had done rising up in him like a continent vomited from the Earth. And he knew she was right. So terribly, terribly right.

"I . . ."

Charlie lifted her hands. "Please, Joshua. Just hear us out."

New York City—The Campaign of The Century—Day 260

Solipsum hurried to the studio, Quinby's face finally fading from his mind as he thought of what lay ahead of him. He could barely contain his joy.

At last. The final day. And not a moment too soon. I doubt that I could have maintained this form for more than a few hours. All goes according to plan.

The wind picked up, whipping the rain into his body. He tilted his head to look up at Stone's studio, the icy needles striking his flesh, merging into rivulets that ran down his face unheeded. He saw the domes backlit by lightning that slashed the night, scissors stabbed and ripped through black velvet. He ducked his head and began to cross the street.

Three intersections away, The Driver switched on his wipers and started his engine as the skies opened and the rains descended in force. The cab rolled forward, fat droplets spattering the windshield's dirty glass, beating a watery tatangelo.

It was time.

The Driver stared out at the city's streets for what would probably be the last time, and knew he had waited too long. As a Guardian, he should have seen this coming long before now. He just hadn't understood what was happening when the photographs started appearing everywhere. He smiled grudgingly at the demon's audacity. To hide something so obvious in something so obvious. And now, it was probably too late.

He stared at the mandela dangling from the rearview mirror and began to chant. "I will kill him, I will kill him, I will kill him, I will kill him . . .", each utterance pushing the car faster, speedometer edging higher 'til the needle pegged at ninety. Suddenly, Solipsum loomed in the glass before him. The Driver pushed the gas pedal to the—through the floor. His last sight before the cab slammed into Solipsum was the demon's startled face.

Then he exploded through the windshield as the car accordioned against the creature's immobile body.

Time slowed, his mind perceiving his flow through it as though through a clear treacle, fully aware of every detail as his body crashed into the asphalt in a shower of shattered glass. The cab's speed was undiminished, it had just changed vehicles, becoming instead his body's meaty momentum. He slid and skidded and rolled before slamming into a lamp post. Hard. Through it all, his eyes never closed. Now the pain came like a freight train, his body a pig bag stabbed by a million scalpels. The effort to hold back the scream almost broke him.

His legs extended before him, splayed and useless. He tried to move his left arm and was stopped dead by a searing pain. He looked down to see the thin splinter of bone jutting through the ripped fabric of his leather jacket, gleaming wetly in the streetlight. Yet though he was dying, he was very strong. He slumped back and focused his mind, shutting down those body areas of no further use. His good hand crawled towards his jacket pocket, even as he saw movement across the street. The Glock he pulled out weighed more than life. He cocked the trigger, hand like a rock, the gun pointed at Solipsum who advanced like a jungle predator, eyes burning in the rain.

"Die," he muttered as he squeezed the trigger, and miracle of miracles, his aim was true, he *knew* this, hand slipping, heart rejoicing as the perfect brain shot sped towards its target.

Until the demon plucked the bullet from the air.

The Driver's hand fell to his side, gun clattering on the concrete and he couldn't understand why. His brain was still telling it to fire, fire, *fire*! He felt the distant crackle of breaking fingers as Solipsum knelt on his right hand. His eyes began to tear, not from pain, but from the immensity of his failure.

Solipsum looked down at the Driver, then at the bullet in his hand before tossing it aside. He felt so very alive, supremely aware of everything around him, the hissing rain and distant sirens, the whole world compressed to their interlocking eyes. "What did you hope to gain, old friend?"

" . . . Charlie . . ." the Driver mumbled through shattered teeth.

Solipsum leaned closer, seeing something for an instant in the Driver's face, in the tortured mosaic of shredded flesh and embedded glass. Then he blinked the rain from his eyes.

"They are all dead," Solipsum whispered, "they just don't know it yet. But I'll be sure to give Charlie your regards. Just before I fuck her brains out. Literally."

With that, he leaned over the Driver and unhinged his lower jaw. Three rows of teeth extruded, splitting gums in a razored rictus. This time the Driver did scream.

Until Solipsum bit off half his head.

Stone Studios—The Campaign of The Century—Day 260

Joshua could not believe what he had just heard. "So that's his plan? To take your body? Jesus, Phoena, this is incredible. I mean, a demon from Hell, instigating The Campaign of The Century, just to get a new body? It's a little much." He sat back and folded his arms across his chest, his jaw thrust forward, mouth a thin line.

"Don't you find it the least bit ironic that this final shoot is so similar to 'Cruci-Fixation'?" Charlie asked.

"For a body, I can buy that. But to orchestrate The Campaign of The Century? Why so many shoots? Why not just one, do the switch and get on with playing?"

"Because there's more." Phoena stood and walked to the dome's edge. She gazed out at the city, at the coiling black fury of the sky. She could feel the answer, slippery yet close and plosive as a school of fish whenever her grasp closed around it. "There's something we're missing and Charlie and I haven't been able to figure out what it is yet. But whatever he's got planned, it's big and audacious, just like he is." She came back to sit on the edge of the coffee table and face him. "Look how much trouble he's gone through. How much work he's put into this. He's convinced the biggest fashion corporation in the world to instigate an ad campaign so totally unlike anything that's come before, it's a miracle he got it past their front door, let alone onto the front pages. He managed to somehow get Rothman to release me from my contract, something I didn't even think was possible." She took his hands without even being aware she had done so. "It all comes together tonight. Joshua, I know this creature, I've *been* with him. Even though we don't know for sure what he's got planned, I do know one thing. We have to stop him."

Stone sat forward, his eyes drawn to the pendant Phoena wore about her neck, to its muted red reflection. He looked away in frustration, finally admitting she was right. "Okay. How?"

"With this."

She pulled a vintage *Bronica* out of her hand bag.

Stone looked at it curiously. "I don't get it."

"It's Bailey's camera. The one he used on 'Cruci-Fixation'."

She passed the camera to Stone, who turned it in his hands, well aware that he held a piece of photographic history, wishing he had more time with this exquisite relic. Something caught his eye, a discoloration on the lens mount. He peered at it closely. "What's this? Rust?"

"Malcolm's blood."

"Jesus. What did Bailey say?"

"There's a roll of film in it. With one frame left. One chance. If you capture him at just the right moment, his soul, if you can call it that, will be frozen on this piece of film and he will be forced to return to Hell. Forever."

"And if I miss the shot?"

The green in Phoena's eyes deepened. "We're finished."

"Great." He carefully set the camera down. "What's the back-up plan?"

Charlie looked at them both. "Here's what we've come up with—"

"Joshua?" the intercom interrupted. "Solipsum is here."

Stone's face went slack with the realization that they had just run out of time. "Damn. I can't have him wait, he'll get suspicious." He thumbed a button. "Okay, Trish, send him up. And Trish? After he gets in the elevator, I want you to go home, got that?"

"But, Joshua, I thought we were going to celebrate."

"Listen to me. I want you to go home."

"But—"

"We'll have a special celebration tomorrow. Tonight's going to go very late. Okay?"

"Okay," she answered, sounding unsure.

"And Trish? Once he's up, bring the elevator down and lock it."

"But how will you get down?"

"I have the key."

"But that only works when—"

"Trish! No more questions. Just do as I ask. Please."

"Okay, Joshua." The intercom went silent.

Stone felt a sudden foreboding, as if that were the last time he would ever hear Trish's voice. He offered a silent prayer to whatever gods watched over him that they look after her too, especially tonight. Then he looked at each of the girls. "Okay, we have five minutes. You're right, Phoena. This last shoot has to take place. It's the only way we can find out what he really wants. We don't have a choice. Bailey David said we had to capture him at the right moment, which means, I think, his moment of greatest vulnerability. If he needs your body, he has to leave the one he's in now. So he'll be weakest when he's between his body and yours." His voice became thoughtful. "And like you said, if his plan is to do the switch tonight, he's going to need to somehow recreate the moment of his birth, right down to the tray of blood and developer. And the all important print." He picked up the *Bronica* and stood.

"So, here's the plan. After we're done, I'm going to give him that opportunity. We'll process and contact, same as always. Everyone will stick around, just to make sure I've got the shot. But this time, I'm going to get very excited about one particular image. And because it's the last shoot, I'll insist on a celebratory print. I'll get Russ to pull it. From there, the ball will be in his court."

"Isn't that dangerous?" asked Charlie.

"Yes. It is."

"But we have no choice." said Phoena, giving voice to what was on all their minds.

"We do have one major thing in our favor." Stone held up the old camera. "The element of surprise."

"How do we use the *Bronica*?" asked Charlie.

"You'll take it and set it up on a tripod behind me. We'll camouflage it with some lights so he doesn't see."

Phoena watched Joshua's hands as they touched Bailey's camera and felt very cold for an instant. "What then?"

"Attach the radio synch to it so that we can trigger it remotely. Charlie and I will each have one receiver. That way, if either of us becomes—incapacitated—the other can push the button."

You're handling this like a photo shoot, thought Phoena. *You have no idea what we're up against.* But all she said was "This is going to be tricky."

"Yes. But it will work. Trust me."

She nodded. "Then let's do it."

New York City—The Campaign of The Century—Day 260

Charlie had just finished positioning the *Bronica* when the elevator doors opened and Solipsum entered the studio. His hair and skin glistened with rainwater and she swore she had never seen him look more photogenic.

Stone shook the model's hand. "Have you seen Elora?" he asked.

Solipsum looked surprised. "No one called you?"

"No. Why? What's happened?"

"I'm afraid she's had an accident. Reaching for something."

"Is she—?"

"Oh, she'll be fine. They just gave her some sedatives that have knocked her out, poor girl." He doffed his coat and looked at them all. "Shall we proceed?"

Thus the evening began.

The Campaign of The Century ended as it had started, simply, with the original crew of Joshua, Solipsum, Phoena, Charlie, Russ and Sindra the only ones present. A symmetry not unnoticed by Charlie.

Her eyes met Phoena's and she felt her heart swell. Then, before she could help it, they drifted to Joshua, who smiled at her as he smiled at no one else. The guilt she felt was strong, the relief stronger still. She couldn't decide in that moment what frightened her more: what the night would bring, or the day, when she told Joshua she had left him for Phoena.

She watched as Solipsum draped his coat over a chair before walking to the make-up room with Phoena and Sindra. She almost dropped the transmitter when he winked at her in passing, as if he could somehow see her secret heart.

She turned back to the set to do a final check. The cove tonight was set to black but the floor had something special on it. No projection for this, the final shoot. Joshua wanted texture and realism, thus the panels had been overlaid by plaster, lightly roughened. It had been painted black, but for the pentagram in scarlet, so crudely rendered as to be almost splashed, surrounded by black candles. The main light was a massive 10K spot, clamped to the catwalk and pointing straight down, its thick lens almost a meter across.

Charlie looked up at it and could barely make out the lumpy shape of her back-up plan, lurking in the shadows. She walked over to the girder nearest the set and checked the 10K's switch, then absently tested the tension on the cleated rope that should not have been there. The one she hoped Solipsum wouldn't notice. She finally looked to the dome and the lightning blasted blackness beyond, to offer her own silent prayer.

In the make-up room, Sindra applied the last touches of body-glisten to Solipsum's naked torso. *No pudding on this boy*, he mused as he daubed away. *It is like painting a piece of marble.* But for some reason, he did not feel the delicious sexual tension that sometimes came, and was one of the things he enjoyed most about his work. For he knew that creativity and self-indulgence were but two sides of the same coin.

Solipsum looked into the mirror at the woman who was the key to all he had planned. She sat in a director's chair, completely oblivious to her surroundings, probably in some pre-shoot meditative model state. But Solipsum was not fooled and knew by her expression she was reliving something sexual.

What could it be? he wondered sarcastically. "Phoena."

"Yes?" She looked at him in the mirror, startled and slightly irritated by the interruption.

"I would just like to say that it has truly been a remarkable experience working with you."

Phoena was a bit surprised. But then she had suspected the night would go like this, every word and action loaded. "Likewise, Trey. But I also have to say that I'm glad that after tonight, I'll never see you again."

The demon smiled. "Never say never, Phoena."

She ignored this and looked instead to Sindra, who nodded that he was done. She shrugged into her robe and rose to leave. "I'll see you on set, Trey."

Solipsum turned his body slightly, watching her reflection recede. Then a movement caught his eye, Bruun creeping into the room. *"Ah, just who I was waiting for."*

The cat sat at a safe distance, his silver fur unusually bright, regarding the demon warily as its voice spoke in his head.

Look at you. In that pathetically weak form. It would be the easiest thing in the world for me to get rid of you now.

You would not dare. My death might—

Not just your death, you stupid creature. Also your disappearance.

Bruun looked to the door, tensed to bolt when he found himself frozen, limbs gripped in an arthritic pain decades accelerated. His head and forepaws twitched spasmodically.

The only reason I am letting you live is so you may bear witness to the outcome of tonight's events. To see who lives and who dies. And who becomes my thrall. Then will I take you back to Hell.

And if I don't?

I will peel the last of your lives from you.

My life means nothing, if in forfeiting it I can thwart you.

Brave words, little mammal. Solipsum lunged and Bruun's heart nearly stopped.

Sindra threw up his hands in exasperation. "What are you doing? Stay still. We are not finished yet."

Solipsum relaxed and made a dismissive gesture. Bruun felt the pain depart instantly, his relief so powerful he collapsed on his side, panting.

Remember. I do not even want to see you until the morrow or your life will be forfeit. And for nothing. Because if I have to delay my plans by killing you and hiding your carcass, I will do things to them all that you cannot begin to imagine. Now run and hide.

Bruun bolted.

Stone Studios—Main Studio

Phoena entered the main studio to see Joshua and Charlie deep in conversation, standing on the pentagram. The shaft of light from the 10K high above cascaded over their heads and shoulders, illuminating yet isolating their figures. Joshua was like a thing unearthed, a statue carved from the heart of a meteor by some long dead civilization. Charlie looked almost insubstantial beside him, as if she stood on the cusp of another world.

She joined them, seeing now the tension in Joshua's face, the lines bracketing his mouth deep as seams in a wall of coal. She could feel the love he had for Charlie, and for herself.

"Just in time," Stone said quietly, holding up a transmitter. "Charlie's rigged the *Bronica* and we're each going to have one of these. Here's how they work. The red light means it's on." He turned the small plastic box to display the glowing red LED. "The green light means the safety is disengaged and this center button will fire the camera. You shouldn't need to know any of this, but in case something happens, now you do. Just be very careful when this light comes on. Push that center button and it's all over. We only have one shot."

His glance flicked to the gleam at Phoena's throat. "Your pendant."

"Yes?"

"I want you to wear it."

"Aren't we supposed to be naked?"

"Yes. But somehow it fits."

Phoena nodded in agreement, a small tight smile on her lips.

Joshua then spread his hands in a gesture she had come to know so well. "Okay, girls, it's showtime."

For this, the last shoot of The Campaign of The Century, despite all that had gone before, and all that was yet to come, the team ran like a well-oiled machine. Phoena and Solipsum stood naked on the set, like a dark and primal Adam/Eve whose love would blaze a path across an alternate human history. The sexual tension between the two became palpable and thick as Joshua fired away, effortlessly moving together, sometimes dominant, sometimes submissive, changing roles as they used to clothes. Their bodies appeared sculpted in the dramatic light that concealed and revealed, revealed and concealed, Phoena's shard aglimmer, Angel and Devil, Heaven and Hell, so in synch they moved as one.

Joshua was almost silent because they required so little direction. His eye, mind, spirit, Solipsum, Phoena and all they were/could/would ever be were joined in a unity that went beyond time. And he felt for an instant that if he wanted to, what he saw through the viewfinder would finally become reality.

It was as though he had never been so fully transported. That line, that line, that simple line, the curve of flesh as it crested and ebbed, now him, now her, now him again, the light and dark in constant cut, flowing and defining, receding and advancing, now shy, now bold, now brazen and rapacious as it twinned between the blade-gap in their bodies, joining, lifting, gifting and presenting to his hungry eye the crescents of flesh, the sultry stare, the lips on arc of throat so white, the razor teeth that delicately bit, both now lost in the moment/each other, flesh and identity melting away as they rocked and gripped and teased and sucked the very essence from the ether, to go so far beyond anything he had ever shot he felt as though his bones had turned to blood.

Two hours passed like minutes and then suddenly, it was all over. He raised his head, as though surfacing from a deep pool, and said the three words he wasn't sure he would ever say again.

"That's a wrap."

Thus The Campaign of The Century ended.

Everyone looked at one another and for one brief instant, they forgot who they were and simply basked in a profound sense of accomplishment. It was as though each recognized that what they had been through these past months represented the peak of their careers, perhaps even their lives. Though similar heights may yet be scaled in the years to come, The Campaign of The Century would forever stand alone, never to be surpassed.

The laughter came then, and not a few felt their eyes well with tears, such was the enormity of what they had collectively experienced, the sense of accomplishment and completeness that settled over them. Joshua opened a very expensive bottle of champagne and soon each of them held a glass. They all looked at him and he paused, finding the eyes of each of these people whom he had come to love. Then he held his glass high.

"Beauty *has* been served."

Six glasses tinged, the note pure and sweet, then everyone drank to a job well done.

Joshua took his time, savoring the champagne from a bottle he had secretly thought he would never open. Then he called for his second assistant. "Russ, if you would be so kind as to process the film. Run it normal. No, on second thought, push it half a stop."

"Right away, Boss."

Joshua put his arms around Charlie and Phoena and everyone made their way to the lounge. Charlie immediately saw the oysters and rushed towards them with delight. She wondered when he'd had the time to organize these, but then allowed herself to finally relax into the moment, to let him have his magic. She sucked one into her mouth, savoring the firm and slurpy flesh that definitely—

"Reminds you of something?" whispered Phoena with the sauciest of glints in her eye.

Charlie coughed as the heat rose in her face.

Sindra came over to rescue her as Joshua brought Phoena another glass of champagne. Then the stories came, most not yet tall with the telling, memories of places and people, light and love and pictures, pictures, pictures. Enough to last a lifetime, or so it seemed tonight.

Charlie had rarely seen Joshua so at ease. The negative in his features had somehow totally given way to the sunny and positive. He was a man with an enormous weight lifted from his shoulders. Seeing him this way, she felt that everything would work itself out, even their own relationship.

Russ finally returned with the contact sheets and everyone looked at Stone expectantly.

"Okay, folks, I know no one is supposed to see anything until it's published, but since this is the last shoot, I think this time I'll make an exception. So, let's take a peek."

Solipsum, Phoena, Charlie, Russ and Sindra all crowded around to inspect the contacts. They were in that moment united in the joy of creation and each understood, on the most elemental of levels, that the whole truly did surpass the sum of the parts.

No one commented on the fact that Solipsum and Phoena had wings in every single frame of film.

Stone was on the ninth sheet when his face lit up. "Wow! There it is!" He had found an image that was so stunning, it was immediately obvious it would become the capstone of the entire campaign.

Joshua, Phoena and Charlie now all understood why the demon had waited so long. A picture of this caliber could never have been created without all that had come before. It was arguably the finest image he had ever photographed.

Solipsum smiled with deepest satisfaction. For him, everything was now nearly complete. He had finally come to the end of a long and dangerous journey, and nothing more stood in his way.

Joshua handed the sheet to Russ. "Hit me a 16 x 20 fiber of this, pronto."

"Right away, Mr. Stone."

The assistant hurried off once more to pull a print from a shot he couldn't *believe* Joshua had gotten as everyone crowded around to look at the rest of the contacts.

Stone Studios—Lo-Tek Darkroom

Russ closed the darkroom door and turned on the small stereo. The strains of Sade's final album slowly filled the room as he began preparations for the 16 x 20 print. He pulled out the three big trays and filled them with chemicals: developer, stop bath and fix. The taps were then turned on and the temperature carefully checked before he ran water into the fourth. The soothing splashing lulled him and his eyes drifted to Charlie's "Platinum?" Polaroid tacked to the ledge above the sink. The Polaroid that had quietly become infamous throughout the entire city. Just seeing it took him back to that day, the day of the casting, when first she had walked into all of their lives. He remembered how she had stood there, so brave in all her nearly naked glory. He thought he'd understood beauty with his years of assisting, seeing the parade of supermodels and camera chicken jading him into the conviction that beauty could somehow be reduced to breasts, face, legs and ass.

It was still hard for him to admit how wrong he had been, because Charlie that day had awoken in him such an overwhelming tide of lust, love, jealousy, rage and simple fucking wanting. The memory of it still burned in his brain like a white hot spike that had never cooled. His fingers reached out and lightly touched her picture. And he wished that it were all somehow different, that he hadn't mouthed off to her at the party and he had just been . . . a better person.

Then he remembered how she had insulted him, and he smashed his fist on the sink's edge. *Shut it down, Russ. You made the right decision. Fuck her. She had her chance. Now it's too late.* He turned on the enlarger.

The neg went into the carrier, the main lights went off and the safe lights on. He leaned in and did a grain focus check, the orange light bathing his face in the colors and contrasts of an accident scene.

"Okay, Russ, let's see how good you are. See if you can nail that exposure on the first try."

He dialed in the numbers, punched the timer, and the enlarger's light came on. Phoena and Solipsum's winged forms hit the paper in negative, and he watched as if he could somehow see the mystery of the paper's halides reacting to the light.

Then for a split second, he did.

"What the fuck?" He jumped back and rubbed his eyes, opening them again just as the light snapped off, the exposure complete. He stood in the orange glow and stared at the paper. It sat there, inert. His hand reached out, gingerly touching it, feeling its cool pearl surface. Then berating himself for a fool, he lifted the easel blades and dropped the sheet into the developer.

He watched a minute go by on the timer as he gently agitated the tray. Ever so slowly, Phoena and Solipsum's negative images became positive, and Russ felt himself moved by the sheer power of what he saw. "Where did those wings come from?" he whispered. "And that thing around her neck. It's red! But this is a black and white!"

He lifted the print out to check it, and as he watched, Solipsum's face detached

from the paper's surface, rising and expanding until it floated before him. He felt the hairs on the nape of his neck rise as the head turned to him, solarized and dripping, eyes like twin eclipses.

"Russ. Bring the Print, *as it is*, with the tray into the main studio." The thing's voice was hollow and thick with effort.

"But it hasn't finished developing yet."

"I know, halfwit, that is the point."

"But as soon as light hits it, it'll be—"

"Bring it out," snarled the head, "NOW!"

Russ almost jumped out of his skin, dropping the print, which slid back into the tray of developer. He was still watching Solipsum's head discorporate and did not notice the falling print knock Charlie's Polaroid into the tray as well. It slipped beneath the print where it lay, hidden.

He grabbed the tray and flicked the main light switch with his foot, then began lugging it down the hall to the main studio. As he walked, he stared at the 16x20 through the sloshing developer, unable to believe his eyes. *Fuck! This print should be black. No stop, no fix, what gives?* The shard around Phoena's neck was as red as a drop of blood. Then he mentally patted himself on the back.

Because he had nailed that exposure on his first try.

Stone Studios—Main Studio

Russ arrived in the studio and looked up through the dome to see the electrical storm raging outside had grown worse.

Stone saw him and set his glass down. "Russ, what are you up to? Just the print, man, not the whole frigging tray."

"It's not for you. It's for Him." He finally let Stone see the long buried contempt surface in his eyes. Then he turned his back and placed the tray in the exact centre of the Pentagram, checking its position carefully before relighting the black candles.

Stone walked to the set. "For Him? What are you talking about?"

Solipsum set his glass down and wandered over to join them. "Why, the end of the Campaign, Joshua. The real end. Nothing more. Nothing less."

Stone turned to the model. "Cut the shit," he snapped. "What the fuck is really going on, Solipsum? What are you? I'm pretty sure you can't be human."

"No. I'm not. Would you believe I am a demon made flesh?"

Stone heard the other's words, slowly feeling their clear and weighted truth. "Yes. I think I would." He paused. "But you're not what I thought you would be."

"And what did you think I would be? This?" Solipsum projected for an instant as a cartoon devil and they both laughed. Joshua hadn't expected the demon to have a sense of humor.

"No, no, not that. Maybe a rep, or an agent," he said and they laughed again.

"Let me ask you this, Joshua Stone. What do you think is happening through our photography?"

"I honestly don't know."

"Then I will tell you. You are far more powerful than you realize. In fact, your inner eye is so powerful that it has commenced prying open the Doors of Perception. It is allowing you to see what truly is."

"But why am I the only one who sees this, why only through the view-finder?"

"Because your conscious mind is still not ready to relinquish control. It won't let you see because it does not *want* you to see."

"I don't understand."

"Let me ask you this. You think you have seen it all, don't you? I find it so ironic that even with such limited visual capacity, you are one of the great seers of this plane. It would be humorous were it not so piti-ful. To think you actually believe you can see when your limited visual apparatus is incapable of taking in more than the tiniest fraction of the spectrum of light. I tell you now you have not seen a billionth part of a billionth part of the wonder that is Creation. It is like hearing only one note of a symphony and complaining of the quality of the music. I offer you this, Joshua Stone. Say the words and I will lift the scales from your eyes, that you may behold all of which I speak."

"No!" Charlie screamed, "Fight him!"

Joshua turned to her with infinite regret. "It's already too late. It was too late after I took the first picture."

Solipsum just smiled.

Stone turned back to the demon. "Yes. Do it."

"Take up your camera and come with me, Joshua Stone. I would give you my final gift."

Then he followed the demon to his destiny's end. Because for Joshua Stone, it had always been about pushing the envelope, redefining bound-aries and truly going where no man had gone before. He could no more resist the demon's offer than Icarus could the sun.

They stepped onto the set where the demon disrobed. Light began streaming from Solipsum's form, as though his outline was a hole punched in this Reality, letting the first rays of Creation shine through. Joshua began to see. Worlds and spectrums of luminescence previously unknown, let alone imagined, filled his vision. Macro and micro, quan-tum and cosmic, all visible simultaneously from a fractal vantage that stood outside any notion of space or time. The most beatific smile overcame his features, the sternness softening as his finger futilely clicked the shutter on a camera that could never record what he saw. He began mumbling, ". . . beautiful . . . so beautiful . . ."

He was dying. A part of him knew that. But another part also knew that this time, the Clouds were real. And that this time, he would finally get some film he could look at when he came back down to Earth. He saw his model, the Muse that had inspired him for his entire life, soar higher and higher. He poured on the speed, trying to catch up. Just a little further—he was almost there—the light unlike anything he had ever experienced, a light no film on earth had the billion f-stop latitude necessary for its capture. He caught the briefest glimpse of her face and saw in her eyes that thing he had sought for so very long. Then she smiled, beckoning him onward. And as he soared higher and higher, he finally went to a place beyond even Solipsum's reach.

He fell to his knees and slowly, his hands lowered the camera for the final time. Charlie gasped as his face was revealed. Where his eyes used to be, his beautiful brown eyes, only empty sockets remained. Tendrils of smoke drifted from them as two thin streams of blood ran down his cheeks like tears.

Solipsum turned to the two girls, the glow around him fading.

"Die, you fucker!" Charlie screamed as she pulled out the receiver, jamming its button with her thumb.

Solipsum just laughed. She looked at her hand, then back to him, pushing the button repeatedly, futilely. She quickly glanced at the camera and saw the green light flash with each thumb push. "What the hell?"

"Trying for that *Kodak* moment?" Solipsum asked her calmly. "Probably best if you take the lens cap off first."

"But I did!" she cried.

"And I put it back on." Russ stepped into the light and smiled at her.

"You piece of shit," spat Phoena. "I can't believe you're helping him."

"Fuck you, supermodel. He's gonna help me get what's mine."

"What's yours? Wake up, Russ. He's a demon, for fuck's sakes. The only thing he's going to give you is—"

"Charlie." said Solipsum.

Phoena's eyes went wide. "What?"

"That's what he asked for. That's what I promised him. And I always make good on my promises."

The model's heart began to pound as though she were buried alive. "Not this time," she said and stepped forward.

A hand touched her shoulder, stopping her gently but firmly. "This one's mine," said Charlie.

Russ walked to meet her, in no particular hurry. He shook his limbs, loosening up, then waved her forward. "Okay, Charlie Brown. Let's do it."

She hesitated for an instant, struck by something in his voice, something that almost sounded like regret, then cursed her lack of focus and sunk into a stance.

They began circling each other, the Dance had started—until Solipsum froze them with a gesture. His agenda would not permit—he paused to reconsider, intrigued. "You know, I really do want to see this. Proceed."

Then the battle was joined. Each already had the other's measure and they proceeded to attack, feint, defend, looking for openings, any openings, strikes darting swift as arrows, hands, feet, knees, elbows, all precise, ruthless, no quarter asked and none given.

Charlie remembered in a flash how insistent her teacher had been about basics and rigorous technique. "They are like a, b, c's," she was told. Only when you had learned the alphabet, then could come words, sentences, prose, poetry, and finally—grace.

She ducked a roundhouse/hook kick reversal that she actually saw coming. *Have I found his rhythm or did he telegraph that?* Some instinct told her to move diagonally and fake low. And there it was, the opening, side kick pistoning even as she saw it. She heard Russ's muffled grunt as the edge of her heel impacted, dancing away before his foot could take her knee.

Sindra made a sound like a squeezed toy. "Get back!" Charlie yelled without turning her head. She kept moving around Russ, circling, forcing him to turn, then kicked high, driving up his guard. Her leg came back, barely touched the ground, then lashed out in a front push kick, the ball of her foot a battering ram smashing into the exact area she had hit earlier. She heard the crack and knew the battle had turned. Russ was now in serious trouble. He rolled backward, the pain in his side like a blade, barely dodging Charlie's descending axe kick, coming to his feet for a brief respite. Then he surprised her, switching styles and launching a furious kung fu attack that flowed through tiger, dragon, crane before a snake strike, blindingly fast, nearly smashed her temple. His hands became a blur, weaving a complex tracery, an ancient pattern designed as much to hypnotize as to confuse, to somehow cause *tsuke*: the Lapse. She snapped out a double roundhouse, low, then high, *fuck! too slow!* her foot suddenly trapped in mantis arms, his knife hand already moving to her knee cap. Without thinking, she spun in his grip, the crescent kick catching him full in the head.

He staggered backward, hands clutching his face, side wide open for her hammer fist. He screamed as Charlie's blow drove bone into lung.

She circled patiently, taking the time to breathe, breathe, breathe. She knew that even now, Russ had what it took to kill her, that there was no animal more dangerous than one that has been cornered. She glided in and quicksilvered a palm heel to his broken ribs. He overreacted to the feint, the pain blinding him, his guard too low and she got inside past the point he could drive her back. The strikes and blocks then came so fast, Phoena couldn't even discern where one movement ended and another began. Charlie flowed like water, rolling off each block into another strike, using the hapless Russ's own energy to magnify her blows. He finally missed a block and she landed a vertical fist to his ribcage, feeling it give. He staggered back, leaning against a girder, a hand clutching his bloody side.

"I could have won." He took a deep breath and she could hear the air whistling in the wound. " 'Cause I knew the magic word."

"Russ—"

"The word that would'a made you lapse . . ." His mouth filled with blood and he spat out a great wad of it, smearing some on his face as he dragged a forearm across it.

"Russ! We can get you to a hosp—"

"Haiku."

Charlie's hands dropped as she stared at him in shock. "Where did you—?"

"It doesn't matter." He staggered, a hand gripping the dome-girder, pulling him upright. "I didn't use it. That should say something, shouldn't it? Maybe there is hope for me." He smiled the smile she had last seen when they were underground.

She felt her chest tighten. *Why didn't I say 'yes' to him? It was only a date. Things could have been so different. He doesn't need to die, Charlie. You don't need to add another name to that list. Talk to—*

"Finish it," he rasped.

"No. We are getting you—"

"Finish it! At least let me die a warrior."

He attacked, a clumsy fumbling kick she easily sidestepped, into the circle of his guard, there to deliver the *shuto* strike to his exposed throat. She put everything she had into it, trying by main force to somehow end it quickly. She felt the cartilage crack and saw his eyes bulge. A horrible memory briefly surfaced

(mom!)

that she crushed almost instantly, stepping back as he clawed at his shattered windpipe and slowly collapsed to the floor.

She looked down at his body, sickened. She had killed before and had hoped never to experience that feeling again. There was no romance in what she had done, no glory. Only finality. She suddenly gained an enormous insight into Haiku, understanding now how much that person had had to change to be with her.

She brought an arm up to brace herself against the girder, feeling the rough edges of the rope she had tied there earlier. The adrenaline/endorphin surge passed, leaving her utterly drained.

Phoena rushed to her side, asking over and over if she was all right. Charlie could barely focus.

"That was very good," said Solipsum, impressed. "How would you like to replace Russ as my Familiar?"

"Bite me, vermin."

"If you insist."

The demon walked towards her and Charlie could only watch as the whole lower half of his face transformed. With a sound like ripping sack cloth, long razored teeth, some triangular, some serrated, filled his mouth. His head distended, slime oozing ropey and clear. She almost pulled too soon. *Wait . . . wait . . . he's nearly there . . .* then he passed into the Pentagram's center. She yanked hard on the rope and heard a *pang!* as the safety bolt sprang free. The demon looked up, just as the 10K spot and eighty sandbags came hurtling down on him from the catwalk high above. There was a loud metallic *cruunch!* Then nothing.

Sindra rushed to the set. "Is he dead? Is he dead?"

"Get away!" Charlie screamed, "Don't touch—!"

A fist punched through the wreckage and grabbed the horrified Sindra's shirt. He struggled and mewled, feet sliding as he was pulled closer and Charlie had to look away. Everything inside her was screaming run, run, *run!* and she threw her weight forward to break the fear, stumbling into Sindra then wrenching him back with all she had left. His shirt ripped and they fell to the floor.

"Sindra! Sindra!"

A sound made her look to the heap of wreckage, to see Solipsum's other arm emerge. She watched as it bent, the muscles dense and quivering as he tried to lever himself out.

"Help me, Charlie, we have to move him," said Phoena urgently.

She grabbed Sindra's arm and together they dragged him to the dome's rim. The rain fell in sheets now, a solid undulating curtain, the lightning blasting their faces.

"Wh—where am I?" His eyes blinked open, hands feebly clutching at the tatters of shirt cloth.

"Listen to me," said Phoena, her voice low. "You have to get help. The police."

"What?"

"Can you stand? He's coming."

"I—I will try."

They helped him to his feet. Phoena took his shoulders, forcing him to look at her. "Take the stairs. The elevator's no good."

"My phone . . ."

She shook her head. "The storm's probably killed it. Get to the stairs. Try it there. But either way, get out of here. Find help. We'll try to delay him."

Sindra looked at them both, then past their shoulders. His eyes widened. "My God!"

"Hurry!" Charlie screamed. The thunder crashed so loudly she thought the dome would shatter. Sindra tore his eyes from what he was seeing, spun and fled. The two girls looked at one another. Each could see the terror in the other's eyes, but there was something else too, some strength born of Sindra's rescue. Phoena touched Charlie's face, about to speak when they heard the crash. They watched in sickly fascination as the twisted form of Solipsum rose from the rubble of sandbags and lighting wreckage, extricating himself with insectile delicacy.

"Fuck," said Charlie, "This is going to be way harder than we thought."

The demon brushed bits of glass from himself, his head lolling like some ponderous sunflower on the stalk of his broken neck. "Not bad. Not bad at all." His mouth as he spoke was almost vertical. "If I were human, I would be dead." He then grabbed his head with both hands, the vertebrae crunching as he wrenched it hard to the upright.

"There. Much better. I'm impressed. The camera was a particularly intriguing touch. If Russ hadn't seen that, you would have had me."

He began hobbling forward, his walk improving, body affecting continuous repairs until he stood before them, human again, bits of him still twitching.

"Now, where was I? Oh yes. The camera. I knew you two were on to something when I tracked you down on that London flight. But I had no idea you would actually be able to find that old pederast, let alone learn of my origin. Well done."

He lifted a hand and a bolt of hellfire shot from his extended fingers, destroying the *Bronica*. "So much for that. Now, I think we've had enough distraction. Come, Phoena. Come and meet your destiny."

"Wait." She held up her hands. "One thing. Why me? Did you really go through all this just to get a new body?"

Solipsum looked at her, genuinely surprised. "New body? You think—" He doubled over and began laughing.

The two girls looked at each other, completely baffled. This was the last reaction either had expected.

"You think I went through all this just to get a body? No. I want— need—far more." There was a small sound as he straightened a finger. "You still don't understand, do you? Then let me explain. It's all about Power, Phoena. Ultimate Power. Over this world, and after that, who knows?"

"How?"

"Through the Ritual we are about to enact. A Ritual whose potency has been exponentially multiplied a thousand times by Joshua and the remarkable images he has created over the past nine months. You see, the Ritual normally acts as light through a Lens. But when there is more than One, it can act as light through a Prism. It allows me to facet my consciousness into as many shards as there are images I have participated in."

Confusion crept over Phoena's features. "You mean—that wherever you appear, in all the ads we've shot, you would be able to somehow— see through them?"

"No. *Be* through them. Literally. Millions and millions of them. Each image come to life as a separate demon, yet united in One Mind. My Mind. Then Hell will reign on Earth. And I will rule over it. All." His mouth widened. "Amazing, isn't it?"

"But—but where is the Prism?" asked Phoena uncertainly.

"The Studio," said Charlie, the answer now so obvious as she remembered what she had seen in the Room that day. "The Studio is the Prism."

Solipsum turned to her, all his teeth now visible. "Yes."

"Run Phoena!" She lunged for the girder and the 10k's switch, hoping the light would still take juice. She threw it, shielding her eyes just as a huge flash exploded.

Solipsum howled as shards of glass and metal peppered his back, distracting him as Phoena raced across the studio.

The demon's eyes blazed. "You little bitch!"

He limped towards Charlie, his right leg mangled, pieces of the 10K's glass still burning into his flesh. His hands rose and bolts of hellfire shot from his fingertips, barely missing her as she dodged and rolled.

"Stay still!" he yelled, crackling energy slashing the studio as he tried to kill her, Charlie zigzagging, never stable, the concentrated energy exploding all around her, white hot coals of it, closer and closer. She had almost made it past the final wall to safety when a slash of green shot by and seared her arm.

She cried out and tripped, scrambling to recover, reaching out blindly to grab a metal outcrop, swinging her body just as another bolt burst through the wall, spraying molten slag. Then she too was running down the hall.

Solipsum staggered after her, cursing as he left a trail of blood, glass and pieces of himself.

"Charlie! In here!"

Charlie slammed the Wishing Wall's doors and turned to Phoena, panting. "Well, that partially nailed the bastard, but it isn't going to stop him. He is one tough mother. It won't be long before he finds us. Any ideas?"

"None," said Phoena, trying hard to hide her desperation. Then she saw the other girl's arm, the skin cracked and bleeding. "Oh my God, are you all right?"

Charlie said nothing, her face a mask of pain. They both jumped as the Wishing Wall door cracked and a ferocious pounding began outside.

Charlie reached for a chair. "Quick! Grab something!" she shouted as she jammed it under the door handles.

They feverishly threw furniture against the door as the pounding became more frenzied, splinters raining from the tortured wood. A hand exploded through the door and Phoena screamed. It groped the air violently and grabbed her hair, pulling until Charlie picked up a floor lamp and bludgeoned the thing savagely. Bone cracked and the hand withdrew. The girls heard a frustrated keening sound. Then it stopped.

Charlie's eyes met those of her lover. "What happened?"

"I don't know."

She looked around, wrinkling her nose. "What's that smell? It smells like—"

(rotted luxury)

They turned, just in time to see Solipsum step through an image of himself pinned to the mosaic. He lurched towards them.

"Phooooeeeennnaaaaa . . ."

Charlie ran and launched a flying side kick, but Solipsum was not Russell and his speed was inhuman. He grabbed her leg, tossing her aside like a child's doll. She hit the wall hard and landed in a heap, the demon already upon her crumpled form.

Oh my God! Did he kill her? Phoena then saw the rise and fall of Charlie's chest and felt the relief wash over her. Until Solipsum unhinged his lower jaw.

"Stop! I beg you!"

The demon lifted his head, all pretense of a human façade discarded, hideous to a degree beyond anything Phoena had ever seen.

"Why?" His voice seemed to rend the very air.

"Because I love her."

He spat out a tooth. "Pathetic." He turned back to finish what he was about to do.

"Wait!" She stepped closer. "I'll come with you. Of my own free will." An insight flared in her mind. "You don't have enough power to complete the Ritual and bend me to your will, do you? You can only do one, unless I cooperate." She saw him hesitate and pressed on. "You're so close. Why take a chance? For one life? Come on, Trey—decide."

Solipsum's face compressed to normalcy.

"Done."

Charlie was drifting, surrounded by black. It was not unpleasant, just—black. She felt like she could go on like this forever, were it not for the tiny wet rasping sensation she felt on her face. Errant drops of thought slowly cohered. "Ohhhh, where am I? What's that on my face? Stop that!"

She opened her eyes, the room sideways, Joshua's cat staring at her. "Bruun! What are you doing here?"

She attempted to rise, then collapsed again as the nausea took her. Her fingers gingerly probed her face, hoping she wasn't hurt as badly as she felt. She realized the lights were flickering and the hairs on her arm began to rise. A sudden vision blossomed in her mind, a fingernail drawn across a wrist, Solipsum's wrist, blood welling, then slowly dripping into a tray where it disappeared in puffs of smoke.

She sat up. "It's starting."

The pain hammered her as she tried to stand, the wall helping. Then she began limping down the hall, away from the main studio.

Phoena stared at Solipsum, the last vestiges of her will completely drained. She could only gaze helplessly into his eyes as the lower halves of their bodies commingled in a smoky stream that descended into the tray. The beautiful dome had cracked in several places and rain poured down. Intermittent lightning flashes illuminated everything in harsh contrasts. She could just make out amidst the massive chunks of dome glass and shattered furniture the bodies of Joshua and Russ. Solipsum's voice was everywhere as he chanted and intoned in a language not of this Earth. The words left his lips, then came alive as faint electrified glyphs that hung suspended in the air.

Charlie found herself in Lo-Tek, desperately sweeping chemicals off the shelves, searching. "Where is it? Come on, come on, where is it?"

Bottles shattered, boxes of powder exploded, tongs, canisters and reels flew in all directions. Finally, her hand closed around the small bottle, not even checking its label as she grabbed it, the glimpse of yellow through the milky plastic enough. Then she raced from the darkroom, praying it was not too late.

In the main studio, Solipsum had nearly completed the Ritual of Transference when Charlie burst into the room. She just had time to register the strange effect created by the merging of Solipsum and Phoena's bodies, the shard about her neck now glowing. She heard his voice, so fractured and vibratory it was all she could do not to clap her hands over her ears. The final sound had almost left his throat, a rumbling *ohm*-like proclamation.

"*Solipsum!*" she screamed, and ran towards them.

The demon's head turned sharply, eyes yellow and wide. His voice broke off and the energy in the room palpably diminished. Raising a hand, he fired a flurry of bolts but the Ritual was demanding too much of him and none could find its mark. He began droning again, lightning flashes limning Charlie's body as she streaked towards them. Water poured down through a crack above her, cascading over her as she ran through it, splashing into her eyes. She opened them and jumped, a bolt nearly taking her leg, then slipped in a puddle and lost her balance. She went with it, rolled with it, the next bolt exploding into the floor beside her. Then a huge ball of hellfire, green and crackling, filled her vision. Instinct took over and she released all muscle tension, dropping to the floor and sliding on her side, stopping just inches from the tray. Her hand ripped off the bottle's cap and dumped the contents in.

The stop bath touched the Print and Solipsum shrieked, suddenly affected by a monstrous pulling, like the gravitational field of a black hole. His screams rose higher and higher as he elongated to capillary thinness. Then he was sucked into the tray. His eyes found Phoena's as he disappeared, the look of loss and frustration they contained impossible to describe.

Phoena's body, like a film running in reverse, slowly became whole as she felt his presence leave her. She looked at Charlie, lightning flashing her face, the storm now boiling, as if it had become the manifestation of Solipsum's impotent rage. Her heart felt squeezed by the hot hand of an angel, life and love and fierce compassion filling her as her eyes took in the soaking form of the girl before her. The girl who had just saved her life. She was bleeding from a dozen cuts, her clothes torn and dirty, and her poor arm! She looked like she could barely stand. And it suddenly seemed like the most important thing in the world was to just hold her.

"I love you," she said walking forward, testing her body.

And Charlie's eyes went wide.

"*Wh—what's happening to me?*"

Phoena watched, stunned, as Charlie's body began to fade.

She ran the last few steps and reached out, hands tearing through the ghostly wisps of her lover's form as though through rotted fabric.

"CHARLIE!"

But it was too late. She turned to look into the tray and there she saw the floating Print. Charlie had replaced her as the figure in Solipsum's arms, and in the tray's upper corner, she saw a Polaroid afloat, the word *Platinum?* still visible. But the figure had been punched out, and only a white silhouette remained.

Book 13

"There is no excellent beauty that hath not some strangeness in the proportion." —Francis Bacon

"Be the change you wish to see in the world." —Ghandi

New York City, Stone Studios

Phoena stood trembling, physically and psychically dazed, the devastation on a level she had difficulty comprehending. The deaths were still not real to her. She stared about, at the furniture blasted to pieces, walls scorched and blackened, machinery and parts of girders melted to slag. Everywhere were scattered chunks of the dome's glass that glistened in the rain. Everything that Joshua had worked so hard for, all those years, gone, along with the man himself. It was far too much to take on right now.

She fell to her knees in front of the tray and stared at the Print, at Charlie nude in Solipsum's arms, at the look on her face and the arch in her back, the strange wings that rose behind her and the round ripe curve of her buttocks gripped by the demon's hand. She saw the claw that extruded from his index finger, dimpling her lover's flesh and the tiny bead of blood that had started the slow meander down her pale, pale thigh. The only thing missing was the scarlet pendant which Phoena could still feel about her own throat. Something surged inside her then, a rising tide of lust and jealousy so powerful she almost cried out. Because she wanted

(them both together)

things to be as they were before. Then it hit her. Charlie was gone forever. Her Charlie.

"We beat you, you fucker!" she screamed to the cracked and bleeding studio, to the violent storm beyond. "We beat you. . ." she whimpered, collapsing, hugging her knees as the tears finally came, tiny rippling rings spreading over the surface of the Print as they fell soundlessly into the tray.

"You must go to Hell."

"What—who?" She looked up, startled.

Bruun sat before her, eyes bright, his fur soaked by the rain. Lightning made burning cracks in the sky behind him. She felt/heard it again.

"Hurry. The Gate is closing."
She gazed at the cat in wonder. "I can hear you in my mind."
His head tilted sardonically. *"It is like a miracle. Get up. He has Charlie. Hell is vast and the longer we wait, the harder they will be to find."*
Phoena stood, then formed the thought instead of speaking the words. *"How do we stop him?"*
A picture bloomed in her mind. Her eyes traveled past the small mammal to the still-kneeling form of Joshua Stone. She sloshed through puddles, past the smoldering ruin of the sofa and crouched before him, a tumult of memories threatening to overwhelm her. Then it was as if she heard his voice, faint yet distinct. *Later, Phoena. There will be time to mourn me later.*
She looked at his remarkable face as the rain misted them both, the emotion transporting her. Her eyes were drawn down to the camera that still hung about his neck. His favourite camera, the one he had photographed most of The Campaign of The Century with. She realized in an instant that whatever magic existed in Joshua's camera was at least as powerful as Bailey's. Probably more so. She gently lifted it by the strap, then kissed his wet forehead. "Rest now, Joshua. You've earned it."
She turned the camera over, cradling the lens between the soaked legs of her jeans. "Please, have film left in here. Just one frame. Please." But the only thing staring back from the frame counter's tiny window was a zero.
"Damn! Empty!" And almost gave up, then felt something by her leg. She looked down to see that Bruun had dragged the Polaroid back over.
"Use this."
A quick check of the tabs by its exit slot revealed there was one left. She switched backs and looped the camera over her head, then ran to the tray where he waited. Her eyes went to the cat. *"How?"*
"Give me your hand."
She crouched low, fingers extended, not quite sure—then he bit her. She yanked her hand back and glared at the animal. "Dammit, that *hurt!*"
Bruun gazed at her calmly. *"Let some blood drip into the tray."*
Phoena clamped down on her anger and did as she was told. She watched, incredulous, as the Print became smaller, rotating, then spinning, round and round as it descended into some sort of Vortex. Its milky edges beckoned like an illuminated tunnel, her mind dimly registering she had seen this shape before.
"Step in."

She surprised herself by doing just that. She looked at Bruun one last time, then stepped into the tray and vanished. The cat jumped in just as the Gate's edges curled in upon themselves and collapsed into its center.

The studio was finally still. Rain still poured through the cracked dome but none were left who felt it. It descended, oblivious, washing the dead, as lightning flickered like sodium through eyelashes.

Hell

Blackness.
Rich.
Thick.
Like floating in ink.

And she was floating. Or at least she thought she was. *Where am I?* Charlie's eyes slowly opened. Everything was blurry until—

"Jesus! What the hell?"

—her eyes racked focus and made clear the thing that was almost touching her face. It peered at her, curious, tilting its fly-like head, and she saw her naked body pinned to a wall by viscous bands of blood, reflected hundreds of times in the facets of its compound eyes. Then she felt its pincered digits as it scampered down her body to land on the floor with a plop. It waddled away on wrinkled legs, its bloated baby's body still mottled blue from some long forgotten immersion. It began addressing what looked to Charlie like a massive sculpture of bone-ish glass, all blistery knots and taut organic protrusions.

"Master. She is awake."

Nothing happened. Charlie began to take in her surroundings. The room was large yet somehow intimate, with ceilings high, then arching higher, to peak and cradle and finally bring back the strange and shifting glow that blanketed everything. The floor and walls were of scarlet glass, bloods and blacks in slow intermingle. They too were possessed of some shifting translucency that seemed permanent, until her eyes returned to find it subtly altered. Stone sculptures of naked children acted as smoldering braziers, hollowed skulls the fire's bed, a yellowy mothlight shafting and fluttering through the holes in their distended bellies.

The furniture and décor were so cutting edge it almost made her eyes bleed. The style they embodied, their sheer *thing-i-ness*, was what was just around the corner, what would always be just around the corner. Walls, furniture, paintings, lighting, all seemed conceived by some master industrial designer, equal parts visionary and lunatic, given tools of ritual and the infinitely malleable stuff of souls. It was all so darkly fantastic, so stylistically perfect, she felt every induced craving she might ever have, every yearning for that perfect thing—satisfied.

Then she saw that all of it breathed. And even the furniture had pores.

It was so jarring a Reality her mind was momentarily overwhelmed and stopped. She found herself observing as the Witness, a place she had only ever reached in deepest meditation. And most exhaustive combat.

Details continued to present themselves. She noticed a floating coffee table on which were scattered issues of *VOGUE—HELL* and *VANITY DARK*. The cover of one featured a stunning beauty shot of a model whom Charlie recognized. She was the same girl Phoena had pointed out to her earlier during their fateful day in Times Square. Fawn, the heroin girl.

A movement caught her eye. The fly-headed infant stepped back to give room to the thing she had thought was a wall or a piece of furniture. It slowly turned, and she recognized Solipsum.

He stood revealed in all his glory, the very distillate of toxic Beauty. His form was both male and female, but combined in a way that had no bearing on human aesthetic or reality. It was like looking at an aspect of Beauty personified, one that was constantly changing, shifting, redefining, eating of and vomiting itself, faster and faster and faster and faster as it chased and was consumed by its own corruption. And she recognized that what she was seeing was the embodiment of Style.

Charlie squeezed her eyes shut. "Stop. It hurts."

"Is this better?" His voice was surprisingly mellifluous.

She let her eyes open to see his shape shifting had halted and he embodied the form she was most familiar with. Then she saw the tail she had not seen before, barbed and black like a manta ray's. He stood resplendent in an elaborate trench coat, high collared and gleaming-black. Upon his head he wore a circlet of gold with tiny horns of blood red glass. His chest was bare and she could see the gill-like abdominal muscles that ended in a V at the waist of his black leathern pants. A ribbed codpiece completed the ensemble.

"Thank you. Where are we?"

"Home. Hell. The Seventh Level. Whatever you want to call it."

"You're kidding."

"Does this look like I'm kidding?"

He raised his arms and the walls disappeared. For a single instant, Charlie caught a glimpse of what Hell looked like, fully revealed.

It was so vast that any concept of space and distance was rendered utterly meaningless. She instantly knew that though she perceived this place as physically real, it was actually a place of the mind. And beyond. Perception here occurred instantaneously and the first thing that hit her like a captive bolt shot to her brain was that Hell was conscious. The very ground, the rocks, monuments, organ buildings, glyphs, streets, fundament and architecture and things she had no name for, all malignantly aware. Inhabiting this host were demons and souls, billions and billions and untold billions of them. Demons major. Demons minor. Souls as bricks. Souls as mortar. She sensed its tremendous age, the layering of demon and human soul, like some cancerous loam that fed and fertilized the whole anew, ad infinitum. It was a place whose overarching quality was its complete apathy to human suffering. It was so vast even Solipsum was dwarfed. And she understood instantly how he would dream to carve out his own realm in a place less crowded, less endlessly kinetic, less filled with bladders, arteries, organs, creatures that moved and sucked and ripped and fucked-and-did-it-all-again-and-againandagainandagainandagainand

her mind almost shattered.

She threw her head to the side, eyes slamming shut, trying to unsee the things she had just seen.

"My God. I— I . . ." She closed her mouth, aware of how near she had come to becoming some gabbling, shrieking shade had not Solipsum restored the walls. A tiny thought

(*who will save me*)

surfaced before she crushed it. ". . . I had no idea."

She consciously slowed her breathing, then lifted her chin to look at him. "How did I get here?"

"That's what I'm trying to figure out. "The demon seemed lost in thought for a moment.

Charlie took the opportunity to test the jellied bands that held her. Their touch was intimate yet firm and she understood they too were alive. She braced her back against the wall, slowly pushing her hips forward, arms and legs leveraging. The bands tightened just as slowly, insistently, painfully, to relax when she did. *No help there.* Then she noticed that her efforts had only caused her pain where she strained against her bonds. The other pains, the other body-memories, had mysteriously disappeared. The only odd sensation she felt was a pulsing warmth in her left shoulder, centered on her dragon. Then a black and heavy shroud of fear began to smother her, stronger than she'd ever felt it, and on its heels despair, massive and crushing and in her mind she cried out for Haiku. And something happened. She felt her own mind

shift

and she became for an instant both herself and her teacher, in two places at once, perspective two yet one and the words rose strong and clear and true in both

(delay him)

and she found herself relaxing as the Haiku/Charlie duality faded to a point just beneath her consciousness. *Delay him. How do I*—a thought flashed. "The Polaroid!"

Solipsum's expression became flat. "Yes. But it should only have been able to affect the transference of my consciousness to your body. That is all. For the spell to bring you here—there is far more going on with you than meets the eye."

He walked up to the wall and peered at her curiously, as though she were some carnival homunculus floating in a bottle. "Tell me Charlie, what makes you so special?" He brought his face very close to hers, brazier-light dancing in his pupils, the gamy essence of his scent enveloping her.

"Nothing!" she recoiled, cheek flattening against the wall.

Solipsum raised a hand and extended his index finger, enjoying how she watched, transfixed, as a claw extruded. With slow deliberation, he lightly touched her throat. A bead of blood welled, fattening into a droplet that he quiveringly lifted and brought beneath his nose. He closed his eyes and slowly inhaled its fragrance. His mouth finally opened and his tongue, forked and long, licked the droplet from the claw.

He almost choked.

"By the Pit! This cannot be!"

Charlie felt the thin line at her throat burning, the anger rising. Her chin dropped and her hooded eyes looked directly into his with fierce defiance. "So. Now you know my secret."

Phoena was awakened by the screeching of gulls, as if from a dream. Her eyes opened and the first thing she noticed was the vault of the sky? *is that what it is?* roiling above her. Clouds of blood and black, like infusions of watercolor in some torpid liquid, randomly copulated their way across an expanse so vast it seemed she saw the whole of this world's sky at once.

She sat up, the heat hitting her like a mouth-clamped garden glove, moist and loamy, alien and somehow very alive. She rubbed her eyes, not really sure if what she was seeing was what she was seeing. All about rose mountains, craggy and ancient, gnashing black teeth that bit the sky. In the distance, she could just make out the odd shadowy flappings of some indistinct forms, like bits of skin nailed to barn board.

She noticed something lying beside her.

"The Print," she breathed.

She saw again her lover's helpless face and Solipsum's knowing leer, still unsure whether she wanted to burn this thing or step into it. Her hands rolled it into a tube as she looked away. After securing it with a hair elastic, she stood and stretched, noticing for the first time she was not wearing the same jeans and t-shirt she had worn when she'd left. Her upper torso was now clothed in a leather vest the color of old blood, ribbed and tied with thongs and clasps. She ran her hands over it, marveling at its softness. They encountered the camera and she held it out for a moment, trying to tell if it, too, was somehow altered. It looked unchanged, the Polaroid tab still visible by its exit slot. Her hands then traveled lower to feel the same soft leather snugly encasing her legs, intimate as a second skin, and on her feet were large treaded boots that came to just below her knees. Her hair too felt different, longer and wilder and *auburn!* she noticed as she picked up a strand. She felt the weight of metal ornaments and *are those bells?* She shook her head and heard a tiny musical tinkling that brought a smile to her face. Her hand went to her throat, already knowing that her shard would still be there, its coolness somehow comforting. Then she felt a lump in her pocket and she knew that something else had also made it through.

She walked a bit, just getting used to it, the boots already very comfortable. *Where are we? This looks like some sort of mesa. Some sort of* . . . the gull-noise intruded once more. Only it didn't quite sound like birds.

What is *that?*

She wandered to the mesa's edge and dropped to her belly, creeping forward so she could peer down. And gasped. Hundreds of feet below was a crashing sea of fire and blood, filled with millions upon millions of souls, as far as she could see. The gull-noise was the sound of their screams as they burned and drowned simultaneously. She could only stare and stare, rendered speechless by the sheer magnitude of what was unfolding before her.

"Their torment is endless. And they have it easiest."

"What—who?"

She turned her face to see Bruun and was startled by his appearance. In Hell he manifested as a simple stuffed animal made of cloth, like a child's toy that had been washed many times. Even his raggedy ear translated and she found herself staring for a moment at the loose threads that hung about its shell. She sat up as he came closer and saw he was as small as any five year-old child. "Where are we?"

"Where do you think?"

"Hell?"

Bruun did not answer. Instead, he pointed with mitten paw behind himself. She scrambled to her feet to behold an enormous archway, massive and ancient beyond all reckoning. It appeared carved from some charred and porous emotion, stone that was like nothing she had ever seen. Chiseled deep into it, in letters older than time, stood the words

ALL HOPE ABANDON YE WHO ENTER HERE

These were the Gates of Hell.

They walked towards them and Phoena gradually became aware of the light. It was like the light in a painting, subtle as it revealed, sometimes flat, sometimes glimmering, the light a liquid that fell like metal mist.

They came nearer the Gates and Phoena felt their dark and hulking weight, as much in her mind as through her eyes. Detail emerged. That was when she first saw the carvings. They covered every available surface, scenes of torture and rapacity of such exquisite and malignant detail they seemed almost alive. They were stunning, erotic beyond anything she had ever seen, the moment of their capture balanced on the blade of orgasm. She stopped to stare at a frieze of three men and a woman joined in a union *charnelle* that would make de Sade blush. She drew nearer, repulsion and fascination moiling inside her. "My God. Whoever carved these must be some sort of genius. I've never seen anything like them."

Bruun's button eyes blinked at her curiously. "What do you mean?"

"These carvings." She ran her hand appreciatively over a sculpted buttock.

"They aren't carvings."

Her hand snapped back.

"They are souls."

Phoena gaped at him.

"And whatever they endure and participate in moves at the speed of blood congealing."

She turned back to stare at the figures, so many of them, as if she now could somehow see them move and could not help but think what it would be like to be locked in an act that progressed so slowly, pain stretching into new pain, the torment of pleasure forever unfulfilled . . .

The earth shook beneath their feet. Indistinct and edged, it emerged from the gloaming like something from a pool, the oily, hellish light sticking to it, licking it, lacquering the monstrous three-headed form that lumbered towards them, scaled and muscular and prehistoric in its presence. It arrived, planting taloned feet the size of swine, a reeking mass of fur and feathers and God knew what else. Questing heads lunged about, all different yet vaguely human, attached to tentacle necks that writhed and undulated, snake-like.

One head was wolfen, but stripped of all flesh and fur, a lupine mask of muscle and teeth and tendon and bone, like some discarded hunter's trophy left on a stump to rot. Phoena immediately thought it the ugliest, but not by much. Another was hugely beaked, with slitted eyes sewn to each side of its elongated skull. The last looked like some sort of jaguar crossed with a grub.

"What the fuck is that?" she whispered.

"The Gatekeeper."

The Wolf Head spoke. "Halt! Who goes there?"

Bruun looked up at the creature fearlessly, his little voice clear and strong. "It is I, Bruun, and Phoena, a mortal."

The Gatekeeper laughed and Phoena almost covered her ears, the sound a knuckling of bones and breaking things, shriek-coated in triplicate with blackboard nail drag.

"Long has it been since you have graced these portals, €ϖφℨℨεϖðόὀφΞɾϕδ. What brings you here? And why should I grant you Passage?"

"I come because a Demon Lord of the Seventh Level seeks to upset the Balance."

One of the Gatekeeper's heads S'ed forward to stare at the cat boldly. "And why should that concern me?"

"It shouldn't. Far be it for me to disturb one such as yourself with the mundane doings of the physical plane."

All three heads thrust towards him, snake-necks whipping back and forth in frenzy. "Be careful, €ϖφℨℨεϖðὀφΞɾϕδ," the Gatekeeper boomed. "I do not tolerate disrespect and will *not* be trifled with. I was ten times ten thousand universes old when you were but a gleam in the Creator's Eye."

It farted derisively.

"My apologies, oh, Gatekeeper." Bruun bowed his head. "I meant no offense."

"Continue." This from the Parrot Head, mollified.

"I ask that you grant us passage to cancel the debt of blood you owe. And to transport us directly to Solipsum's realm."

"Solipsum! Your former Master. A powerful enemy you have made. You ask for much, €ῶφꝢꝊεꞷꝊꝊφΞꞃφδ. Perhaps too much. Passage I will grant, and to both of you. I am in a generous mood. But transport? This requires an additional price."

Phoena finally decided to speak. "And what might that be, oh Gate-keeper?"

A head, the lupine one, leaned in and sniffed her none too delicately, then reared back, eyeball rolling. "At last! The mortal speaks! I did not think the music of your voice would grace my ears, unless it came as screams from the Pit."

"The price, Gatekeeper. What is the price?"

Bruun was horrified. His mitten-paws tried to tug her back. "Phoena," he whispered urgently, "you know not what you—"

"Enough." She yanked her arm away. "It's time I pulled my weight."

The Gatekeeper had watched the exchange with interest, heads darting and whispering among themselves. It finally spoke. "Very well. That thing you carry beneath your arm."

"That you cannot have."

"The thing you wear about your neck."

"Nor that."

"Your last chance. Deny me this and the price becomes your lives."

The heads writhed slyly. Phoena said nothing, waiting.

"Your left eye."

"Take it and be done."

A wing lifted and a clawed hand darted forward to draw out the prize, popping it into the wolf head's mouth. Phoena screamed as the wound was instantly cauterized, clutching her hands to her face as the other two heads snapped and fought, shrieking in outrage at their denial of the morsel. "Very tasty. Mortal flesh is such a delicacy and—"

"She has paid, Gatekeeper" Bruun spat. "Let us be off."

But the Gatekeeper had not yet finished eating. Finally, with a smack of its wolf-head lips, the creature belched and they were ready. It knelt and they climbed aboard its back. The Gatekeeper then spread wings far wider than Phoena would have imagined, and before she knew it, they were off. The wind pushed back her auburn hair, bells tinkling faintly, the breeze strange and cool on her naked socket as they climbed swiftly into the red and black sky. She looked down once to see the Gates diminishing below, then stared, slack-jawed at the astonishing panorama unfolding before her eye. She absorbed it all, her mind expanding painfully to accommodate shifts of scope and scale that were simply outside human understanding. Buildings and statuary cobbled with eyes, monstrous gargoyle edifices prickling with bone-spur, organ-like causeways and mummified hearts the size of skyscrapers, all crowded and fought, reaching it seemed less to touch something than to escape their present circumstance.

The Gate Keeper dipped beneath an archway that stretched for leagues, she and Bruun ducking as condensates of something fleshy dripped onto the creature's feathered hide. They came upon a gristly spire partially covered in bone scaffolding, creatures swarming over its surface, hard at work eating it or building it, she could not tell. Banking round this, they passed a court yard gathering of creatures human and otherwise, a party it appeared, and she caught the reek of flesh, seared and basted, the scent so strong both mouth and eye involuntarily watered. She watched, fascinated, as the creatures greedily devoured the flesh that had been set before them, grunting and slorphing. An enormous black edifice lifted itself from the ground to hang in the air ahead of them. They flew and flew and seemed to come no closer and she finally understood they were yet miles distant, the thing that huge. It resettled itself as she watched, indifferent as plague as it squatted and crushed the teeming mass of people? souls? below it. She felt Hell's pulse then, its slow and malignant majesty, proud evil following its own stately progress, pomp and ceremony timeless and ingrained. She finally gave up trying to codify and define, to somehow make it all fit into what she thought she thought reality should be, and simply let her feelings of terror, revulsion, hatred and even pain slowly fall away until only awe remained, touching her to the depths of her soul.

"Master! Intruders!"
Relish's bloated baby-limbs flailed with agitation, fly-head twitching as though the sanctity of the room would be breached at any moment.

With a gesture, Solipsum materialized a scarlet oval on the wall before them. It blistered slowly, reflecting brazier-light and ceiling coruscation before its surface broke and rolled, resolving into a rippling mercurochrome.

Charlie saw them then, two tiny figures on the back of some strange flying creature. As she watched, they become larger and larger, until she recognized Phoena. Her heart lifted and she felt a tiny surge of hope. *She came! I can't believe she came!* And she understood Haiku's earlier words.

"Phoena and that cursed animal," the demon snarled, his eyes cold as he glared at Charlie. "It appears they've come to rescue you. Let us prepare a welcome. Relish! Awaken the Woman of the Walls. She is to bring back only their hearts. The rest she may do with as she pleases." He turned back to the scrying pool.

"Solipsum! Wait!" Charlie strained futilely at the already tightening bonds.

He glanced at her over his shoulder, waiting.

"I'll tell you where I came from, how I came to be. Why I'm still of use to you."

"It doesn't matter." His voice became bored, as though he had hoped to hear something more enticing. "You will tell me anything I wish to know. And when the novelty of your torment has worn off, I might still have use for you. As a towel." He returned to the Pool. "Relish—"

"You can still do it, you know."

"Do what?" His tail swished impatiently.

"Open the Gate."

"How?"

She pointed with her chin. "Look, Solipsum, look at what she brought with her."

Then he spied it, held tightly in Phoena's hand. "The Print!"

"Or the Gate, depending on your point of view. And if my—condition was enough to get me here, isn't it enough to open the Gate again?"

Relish nodded vigorously. "She is right, Master."

"Shut up!" he snapped and his tail lashed out to sweep the creature off its feet.

He began walking towards her. "You are right, Charlie. Blood never lies. I will let them approach. But while we wait," he pulled up a chair, "I will hear your story."

Interlude Ten—Rome

Dolce Vitalia stood with her hands on her hips surveying the mess before her and swore vehemently. "Fungula!"

She was a good looking woman in her thirties, passionate and curvy and tough as girder rivets. She had to be, to survive for as long as she had in the totally male-dominated garbage collectors union of Rome. She wore filthy overalls, huge gloves and a bandanna. A cigarillo dangled from the corner of her mouth. Vito thought she could not have looked any sexier. "Va Fungula! Fungula! Fungula!"

She tossed the cigarillo aside just as he joined her. "What's up?"

Dolce pointed at the reeking mess that had already attracted flies and a couple of stray dogs. Several garbage bags had burst and the ground was half covered in coffee grounds, orange peels, rotted meat, spaghetti and a seasoning of well-used kitty litter. A magazine sat in the center of it all, Phoena's face looking back at them. The image they saw had become iconographic, it was so pervasive. Dolce suppressed a shudder because she had seen that face before. When it was not so famous, as it loomed larger in a tiny sports car's windshield—*but no. It couldn't be.*

Dolce shut down the memory with another torrent of Italian abuse. Even Vito, who had taught her most of what she knew, was shocked.

He put his hands on her shoulders. "Bella, Bella," he soothed, "Take it easy. Leave it. We can't take anymore anyway. The truck is full."

She looked at him, surprised. "What? We usually do six more neighborhoods." His eyes were brown and his Roman nose descended almost uninterrupted from the plane of his forehead. She restrained an urge to touch the stubble on his jaw.

Vito shrugged and let his hands drop. "It's this Thing, this Advertising. People are buying shit like crazy."

"And the more they buy, the more they throw out."

"And that's why we work like dogs. With no raise. But Bella," his eyes became serious. "We are not the only truck. The whole fleet has this problem. Rome is overflowing with garbage."

Dolce kicked one of the plastic sacks. "Then there is nothing we can do. Fuck it. Let's get out of here."

They left the pile of garbage in the middle of the street. The two dogs who were waiting at a safe distance approached and circled the bounty, snapping and growling at each other. Then suddenly, both pounced on the magazine. Their heads whipsawed furiously as their jaws locked, claws scrabbling, each trying to wrench the prize from the other. Dolce turned back to see Phoena's face, just as it was ripped in two, each dog tumbling backwards with its spoil. She gasped and shuddered, quickly crossing herself. Because it *was* the same face. The face of a girl she had left for dead. Then she was running back to the truck, gulping air, the image of that beautiful face being torn asunder playing over and over in her mind.

Hell

Phoena stared about herself mutely as she and Bruun continued on their journey aboard the flying creature. They now passed over areas less populated, but the strangeness of the land did not diminish. Instead it seemed to encroach upon them even more, mountainous ruins looming to either side, black and gray and twisted things that brooded like old kings, the ancient remnants of Hell's earlier tenants. Irregular openings in their rotted faces emitted a weak and ruddy light that glistened greasily from the skin of the distended bladders that hung in the air around them. She hadn't been sure these things were alive, until some sort of bird-bat had come too close to one and gotten itself eaten. The pain in her left socket seemed oddly distant, as if the sensory overload she was experiencing had short-circuited a portion of her brain. She noted through her remaining eye the other winged animals(?) that had once or twice ventured near. They quickly disappeared, however, upon recognizing the Gatekeeper. It was strangely quiet, only the rushing wind, the tiny tinkling of her bells and the muscular flapping of the Gatekeeper's wings breaking the stillness.

Her hand went up to adjust the patch she had managed to fashion from pieces of leather and a jacket-thong. She glanced at Bruun and was reminded of something the Gate Keeper had said. "What did he mean? 'Your former Master'?"

Bruun regarded her, his face simple and innocent as the wind played with the threads of his ear. "I was once Solipsum's Familiar."

"Like Russ?"

"Russell? That one was at such a larval stage in his servitude I am surprised Solipsum even used that word. No. The role of Familiar is much greater, as are the promised rewards. But in exchange, you must do all that is asked of you."

"I don't understand."

"I . . . brought him souls, Phoena. For his pleasure and torment. Many, many souls."

"What happened?"

Bruun's head dipped as he looked down, lost for a moment, the memories crowded and painful. She reached out and gently touched his shoulder, marveling for an instant at how tactile his cloth skin felt. "It's okay. Whatever you did, it's in the past."

His eyes were like wet black stones. "Everything has a price, Phoena. Everything."

"How did you come to Earth? To be a cat?"

"I'd found a strange anomaly in his home, a hole in Hell, a passage that led not down, but up. To Heaven, I think. At least that's what it looked like. I slowly started sending souls through it, sensing in their escape the possibility of my own redemption. This went on for some time until I became greedy. Careless. So of course I was caught. I thought I'd managed to escape with my life, through the very conduit I'd sent so many. But when I stepped across the threshold, everything went black and I knew somehow that Death had found me. When I became conscious, I was in your Realm and not in the Place Above at all. It seemed I had not yet paid my debt. I also found I had been granted that most special of gifts—"

"The physicality of a cat."

"Yes."

"So you became some sort of . . . Guardian? On Earth?"

"Yes. Before I was forced to leave Hell, I was privy to his plans, including the one that has brought us here. When I found myself in cat-body, on the earthly plane, I knew what I had to do. To stop him. To somehow make a difference. But even cats, I found, can experience their own Hell in your world."

"But you don't look like a cat here. Why?"

Bruun gazed at her for a moment, about to speak when something caught his eye. He pointed. "We are almost there."

They rounded a huge crag and Phoena almost cried out. Dominating the sky before them was an architecture so monstrous and vast it defied belief. Hulking yet delicate, it emerged from the piss-light like something from under a child's bed, a fully realized nightmare that changed and grew, even as she looked at it. It was shrouded in a yellow mist that clung and caressed like disease, a clean and complex geometry of curving spline and up-ended dome, basilica and battlement pulvinating into groupings of growth that radiated and interlocked, a viral Escher-logic of malignant perfection wild with fronds that grew from its corpus for hundreds of feet in either direction. Their surface seemed to ripple and sway until they flew closer and she saw their thorny spines bristled with the remnants of a vast and vanquished demon hoard, still impaled and writhing.

One of the Gatekeeper's heads turned to look at them while the other two continued craning forward. It was, of course, the ugliest one, which seemed to have taken a liking to her. "There it is. You will have only one chance. His defenses are too strong for me to risk a second pass. As it is, I cannot even land. You must jump." He veered closer until they were only ten feet above a cancerous outcropping that pulsed evilly.

"What?"

Bruun stood. He offered her his paw. "Prepare, Phoena."

She hesitated, clearly unhappy with their situation. "An eye doesn't buy much these days, does it?"

Bruun ignored her. "There! Jump!"

Phoena followed him and landed with a *whhumpff*. She quickly stood and looked back at the Gatekeeper, who hadn't even slowed. "Wait!" she called, "When will you come back?"

The ugly head turned to peer at her. "Come back? The deal we negotiated was for one way Passage only. Your return is your affair. Good luck!" He flapped away on his leathery wings.

"Great," said Phoena dusting herself off. "Where are we?"

Bruun looked back over his shoulder as his foot touched the first of many steps. "His home." He gestured impatiently. "Come, this way. We must hurry."

Phoena scampered after him, bells tinkling. "Is Charlie safe?"

He stopped and blinked. "Yes. For now. She is very powerful, far more powerful than the demon knows. He thinks he has slunk back to Hell with a plaything. It won't take him long to realize his ambitions can still be made real."

Phoena gripped a stone-shape to balance herself. "You mean he can use Charlie to recreate the Gateway?"

"Yes."

"How? I thought it was me he needed. And besides, we have the Print." She held it up to emphasize her point.

"*That* is our only bargaining chip. As for his need of you, that was on Earth. Things are different here. Very different." She looked at his face and was once again reminded of the startling change he had undergone since their arrival in Hell. "What made Charlie special on Earth makes her extraordinary here. In the history of this Place, there has never been another like her."

"What do you mean?"

His little dough-nipped legs took several steps as he turned to face her." You still do not realize what she is, do you? She has never told you her whole story. I will tell you what I know. It is very important. But we must hurry. Come, this way."

They crossed a tiled landing and walked towards a huge and ornate doorway. Behind it, the steps branched and looped, joining and inter-twining with the thorny fronds that blossomed to either side. She looked at those distant steps and somehow knew that she would not fall, even if she were upside down relative to where she now stood, that gravity would be bestowed by whatever her feet were in contact with. Spatial geometry played no role here, location resided independently of itself. It was the landscape of the mind.

Bruun stood before the door and began speaking in a strange voice a language she had never heard. His small forelimbs made traceries in the air that stirred it into currents she could faintly see. He stopped abruptly, arms hanging at his side, panting. "It is not working."

"What's not?"

"My words of opening have been rescinded."

He turned to her and she was shocked to see the defeat in his eyes.

"I am sorry, Phoena. I do not know what next we should do."

"Is there some other way in? Some secret way you know of?"

He shook his head and spread his arms. "These defenses are new." He pointed to a cluster of speared demon corpses. "And very effective. We can try—"

"Wait. I have an idea."

She stepped closer to the door and studied it. Looming fifty feet and stretching out to either side, it looked less like a door, more a barrier carved from petrified bone and banded with thick straps of gut. Metal studs were spaced at intervals, each embossed with a different glyph. Phoena stepped back and let her eyes defocus, searching for the pattern within the pattern. Then she saw it, far to her right, a rectangular shape she could barely discern.

"Come on," she said and took his hand.

Soon they stood before the faint outline Phoena recognized, the door within the door. At its center were three holes spaced around a penta-gram.

Bruun's shoulders slumped. "We have nothing to open this with."

Phoena gave him a small and evil smile as she reached into her pocket. "Oh yes we do."

"You may begin at the night you met the assassin."

"You already know? Of course. You were lurking by the pool before you scared the hell out of us."

Solipsum smiled at the memory, then gestured. "Speak."

Charlie's eyes closed for a minute, as her mind took her back to that long ago time. That special time. She knew that if Phoena was to have a chance, she would have to share with the demon that most intimate part of her life, that which he had tasted in her blood.

"I—I started training with her. She told me once that I'd barely made it under the wire. Because in martial arts, when you learn as a child, it doesn't just become a part of you, it *is* you. Which I guess is true for anything. She was relentless in her teaching, as though she were determined that I would some day be as good as her. As if.

I had been with her for five years on the night everything changed.

We were in her underground dojo, at the tail end of her most brutal training session ever. It was fully equipped, but not like a conventional school. Because it reflected *her* training, by people whose knowledge had mostly passed from this Earth. She had taken what they showed her and went even further, combining it with very esoteric stuff she'd picked up in India, where she studied *Yoga* and *Tantra*. And darker things.

I was her only student.

That night we were both in our black gi's, sparring lightly, working on movement and anticipation, no contact, no weapons, just our bodies. And as we worked, something arose within me that I'd never experienced. A sort of groundless—awareness. It was as if some dormant sense had come fully and completely awake, like it had been waiting patiently for my body to just let go and utilize it.

Haiku picked up on it instantly.

The next thing I knew, she was driving me back with full powered kicks and strikes and combinations that came so much faster than anything I'd ever seen her do before. The sweat started pouring off us both but neither of us was breathing hard. It was all technique and spirit and balance and flow and—*awareness.* Somehow I was able to block and counter everything she threw. Then she upped the ante, moving faster and faster, using techniques I'd never seen, let alone been taught. And somehow I just *knew.*

Then I saw it, for the first time ever: an opening. I took it, spinning and side kicking her in the stomach at full power. She flew back and grunted as the air whooshed out of her. I was devastated. The awareness left me instantly and I was slammed back into being Charlie. I ran over but she was already on her feet. Instead of being mad, she was happy.

Her eyes shone as she took my hands in both of hers. "Very good, Charlie. Very good. You have become so skillful. You finally—*feel*. I am impressed. You have learned to channel your anger. Your parents would be proud."

Tears came to my eyes as she hugged me. Then she stepped back.

"That will be all for today. Let us spend some time away from this place. Tell me, Charlie," she said with a mischievous smile, "is your karaoke as good as your martial arts?"

Next I knew, we were in a small bar in the nightclub district. It was dark and mysterious and just a little bit smoky. We were very drunk. I'd had a bit of *sake* before but nothing like we drank that night. The little porcelain cups seemed always to be brimming. Before I knew it, she'd coaxed me on to the stage. There were only a few people in the place but it didn't matter. I sang my heart out. It was an old Kinks song . . .

"Well that's the way that I want it to stay,
And I always want it to be that way for my Lola,
L-O-L-A Lola."

I staggered back to the table, grinning like a fool. "Your turn." I sing-songed.

Haiku got up and a bunch of sake bottles fell over, clattering against one another. She ignored them as she staggered off to the stage, trying to maintain a straight line. After finally getting up there, she waved an arm drunkenly in the direction of the dj. " 'Ray that one again," she yelled.

She tried to sing my Kinks song, but just failed at it miserably. It seemed her pronunciation went all to hell when she got drunk. And she was very drunk. The letter 'L' was especially hard for her. She finally gave up and managed to weave her way back to the table. She hugged me and we both collapsed in fits of laughter. *Lola* was still playing in the background.

"I've never seen you drunk before," I said. "You seemed to be having trouble with the L's."

"Yes. Espe-sherry cherry co-ra."

"Like this. Co-la. Co-la. Try it."

"Co-ra."

"No." I cupped her face. "Watch my lips. Like this. Co-la."

Back and forth we went. Co-la. Co-ra. Co-la. Co-ra. Our faces moving closer and closer. Then we both stopped speaking, inches apart, just staring into each other's eyes. Then something arose, something neither of us expected, never in a million years. Faintly in the background I could hear the lyrics to that song.

"Then I looked at her and she at me,
Well that's the way that I want it to stay,
And I always want it to be that way for my Lola."

Then we kissed.

Next I knew we were home again in Haiku's incredibly spacious and beautiful loft. It was a mark of her extraordinarily high standing in the Tokyo underworld that she was allowed a place this big. We stepped into the living room, shaking rainwater from our hair, laughing nervously, both of us still drunk. But I don't think either of us was quite as drunk as we pretended. The air was too charged with the thing that had arisen between us. I think we were both so deeply aware that we had to go forward, into uncharted water, or forever go our separate ways. Haiku leaned over the stereo and put on an old Riuychi Sakamato CD. Then she turned to me, everything a little sparkly from the rain.

"Charlie, may I ask you something?"

"Sure."

"You are very beautiful, Charlie-san. Why is it that you do not have a boyfriend?"

The last question I expected. I got very embarrassed as I tried to answer her. "After that night with my parents, I just didn't think I could— I've never met anyone I wanted to—but I'm still—God, this is hard to talk about . . ."

We'd both wandered over to the couch and sat facing each other.

She took my hands and said, "Charlie, there are paths of pleasure other than those you can walk with men. Would you like to learn?"

"Yes," I breathed.

God, she showed me things I never dreamed were possible. But that's something . . ."

And Charlie decided that the rest of her story was hers and hers alone, even as it came unbidden, even as she felt again the strange duality rise within her, experiencing now with two minds, two souls, hers and Haiku's, their body-memory one, the surging tides of lust and life and love undying.

(. . . I was trembling like a leaf. Even her slightest touch seemed to cause the most electric tingling sensations on my skin. And she knew it, her hands running over my body, stopping just short of the places I wanted her to touch. I strained forward, but they would flit away like butterflies, only to return, lightly, lightly, over and over, and her lips just brushing mine as I stood there, helpless. Then she began caressing my breasts, in small circles that got tighter and tighter, cupping their undersides before slowly closing in on my nipples, which were harder than I'd ever felt them. God, I was so sensitive! My body was like a wire and she the current. Then she gentled me, guiding me through what I was feeling, making me breathe. To draw it out.

She was so delicate yet clear in her intent, her hands and mouth so—certain. Then finally she undressed me. It was almost unbearable—each button, each snap, the slow agony with which she unwrapped me, like I was the most exquisite of gifts. She would sometimes stop and kiss me unexpectedly, my nose, my earlobes, the freckles on my pulsing throat, whenever the mood took her—those lethal hands still working, working, but weightless now, light as drifting cherry blossoms. I was down to my bra and panties when I stopped her. "Now it's my turn," I breathed raggedly.

She was wearing this beautiful turquoise sheath of the rarest silk. When I unzipped the back, she shrugged and it fell to the floor. I gasped as several things struck me at once. How beautiful her naked body looked. How dark she was between her legs. And how many scars she had. But the most striking thing—my God, the memory is still so strong—winding its way down from her left shoulder, all around her body to end at her ankle was the most magnificent tattoo I'd ever seen. It was a dragon, a special dragon. Shimmering and green and mythic and so detailed it seemed to be some special kind of alive. Like it was her ferocious guardian. I was stunned. It was almost too much to take in. Because I had never seen her naked. Nor she, me. And then . . .)

(. . . it was my turn. I slowly took Charlie's face and kissed her delectable mouth again, then pulled away to look at her once more. I saw her little freckles and beautiful eyes, her mouth so full and lush, the lips now darker with all our kissing. The pressure was building in my own body, the fiery ki so intense it was like a small sun, burning in my core, everything heightened by the obvious fact she had never done anything like this before. Her skin was like warm silk that rose to my touch, blushing. I unclasped her bra, her beautiful breasts filling my hands, her nipples the

palest pink. I slowly lowered my mouth, first to the one, then the other, using my tongue and teasing their tips. I could feel her hands, wanting to, starting to caress me. Each time, they would be interrupted by another wave of sensation.

Then I finally touched her.

There.

Just there.

Between her legs.

She moaned softly, and I felt how wet the material of her panties had become. I brought my fingers to my lips and tasted her, all the while looking into her eyes. Oh how she tasted! Like the honey of a wild orchid. She smiled shyly and I saw in the green and mauve of those faceted depths that she was enjoying this as much as I. Then I knelt and slowly lowered her panties, to finally gaze upon her. She was like a jewel, nestled in a blond ruff the softness of a lion cub's fur. I gently ran my hands over her, cupping her bottom, her beautiful bottom, like two halves of a perfect melon. Then I could wait no longer. I buried my face in her pelt, feeling her heat and wetness as I breathed deeply of that delicious scent. I began caressing her nether lips, slowly, so slowly. Then I brought my mouth down and . . .)

(. . . she tasted me! I felt like an electric shock had left her body and entered mine. I couldn't help myself as my hands, it seemed, with a will of their own, grabbed her hair and pushed her face into me. She started doing things with her mouth that made me gasp, I couldn't help it! I felt her hands holding my bum, pulling me into her as she licked and nipped and stroked and sucked, sometimes gently, sometimes firmly. I was drenched—moaning and crying, my whole body shaking. It seemed to go on forever, this wave, building and building, sweeping me up with a power and a force I couldn't resist. I felt a scream building up inside me and didn't know what to do. So I pulled her up and just started kissing her and kissing her, tasting myself and her face was so wet I pulled back and thought *is that me?* Then I saw the tears. She looked at me and her tears just came and came. I suddenly realized how incredibly lonely she must have been. Master assassin, all those years, with no one she could ever turn to, to trust, let alone—*love?* That was when my heart broke, right in two. I hugged her so hard her ribs creaked. Then we fell to the floor and just devoured each other. She was . . .)

(. . . so eager. She learned very quickly. We were both at such a peak of physical conditioning the art of love became unto a sacrament. It seemed I cried forever.

From Joy.

The Clouds and Rain came for her almost faster than they did for me, the muscles of her lithe body taut and quivering, and her eyes! those violet, violent eyes! Like a galaxy exploding, and I, drowning in them, a sea of sensation, crying out as shudder after shudder wracked her/ my/our body, both of us using the Awareness now, joined in something I never believed existed, let alone that I could touch, as we were both carried up and up and UP until it seemed we found the face of God. It was something . . .)

. . . I am not going to tell you about, Solipsum. It's—private."

"Continue," the demon graciously conceded, still savoring the intoxicating flood of images that finally slowed and dissipated. For it seemed that here in Hell things truly were different, and Charlie's mind was no longer closed to him.

"What followed next were the best three years of my life. Not only did my martial arts' training take on a new dimension, I learned from Haiku the arts of flower arranging and calligraphy as well. All of this began to have an amazing impact on my photography. For the longest time, taking pictures was something I only dabbled in, but now my photographs seemed to resonate with the lushness and complexity that was my life. Even Haiku was impressed and thought I could make a great photographer . . .

(. . . I kept my professional life completely separate from the life I now had with Charlie. She was aware of what I did, but never involved in any way. And though I sometimes disappeared for weeks on end, the duration of these trips grew shorter, even as the time between them became longer. For I had found in Charlie that which I had never thought to find, that which I had coldly mocked and closed myself off from my entire life.

Love.

She taught me to be a child again. She taught me to enjoy the "goofy pleasures," as she called them. I didn't even feel ridiculous when she surprised me once with a birthday party, just her and our cat, Miko. I tried to protest, saying that it wasn't my birthday, that she didn't even know when my birthday was. She looked at me with those eyes and said it didn't mat-

*ter, that when you loved someone, every day was like a birthday. She had
put up decorations, and we all wore hats, even Miko. There was a special
chocolate cake with one candle on it, that she solemnly made me blow
out. Then she did a little dance, holding Miko's paws as they turned in a
circle. The cat looked so confused, all I could do was laugh. Then she and
I danced and danced and it became something so magical, the very air
around us shimmering. Then we kissed, for what seemed like hours, tasting
the chocolate on each other's lips before we made love.*

*   It all ended . . .)*

. . . one night during training, we were taking a water break and it just
kind of dawned on me. How lucky and grateful and almost overwhelmed
I felt for the gift I had been given in Haiku. Friend, master, lover. I had no
idea these three dynamics could coexist so harmoniously in one person,
let alone in a relationship. And the fact that she was a girl just added to
the dynamic.

I guess that in the end, I was living in a fantasy world. After all, she
was an assassin, and one day that was bound to catch up with us. It finally did.

The attack came suddenly, right in the training hall. Which meant we
were as ready as we would ever be. It was arrogant on the part of whoever sent them, but the message had to be clear. Even at her peak, Haiku
and her cub were no match for the woman known only as the Winter
Queen.

They were wrong.

We almost won.

My God, you should have seen her. She was awesome. I realized that
though I thought I knew a lot by this point, it wasn't the tiniest fraction
of what she knew, never mind what she could do. Nine of them fell. Masters all, the very best. But the tenth—he was special. Huge and masked,
with weapons and skills I'd never seen. But she had. She seemed to know
him because they spoke together, in a dialect I didn't understand. It was
the only time I ever heard fear in her voice. They fought for so long,
neither tiring, neither giving ground. Then he slipped and she laughed,
her sword floating by his guard to slowly slide into his side. He countered with such a furious backstroke it would have cut her right in half
if she'd been there. Then she was moving backwards, pressed hard and
I saw she was about to stumble over one of the other's bodies. I shouted
a warning and that was—a mistake. The mistake of an amateur. It never

should have distracted her, but it did. Because she cared for me. That's what killed her in the end. She turned her head just a fraction of an inch but it was all he needed. His sword came across in an underslash and just—ripped her wide open. I screamed and ran to her, still not sure what had happened.

The tenth assassin looked at me and laughed. But I could see the wound she had given him was taking its toll. Worse than he knew. He tried to cut me down as I knelt there, and the pain stopped him cold. Then we both heard the sirens in the distance. I wiped the sweat from my eyes and when I opened them, he was gone. I had never seen his face.

I looked down at Haiku, cradling her, crying, trying to stop the blood that poured from the huge wound in her abdomen. Her pain must have been unbelievable. She finally focused her eyes and grabbed my sleeves, still so very strong.

"Ch—Charlie. Listen. The police will be here soon. You—you must leave. Look in the small table in our room. Under it is a secret compartment. Open it and you will find all you need. I am so sorry Charlie, but—but our time is over."

"Let me call. . ."

"No, Charlie. It is too late. The wound is too deep. Please go. Quickly."

"No! I won't let you die! I love you!"

"And I love you, Charlie. But you must do as I say. Go. *Now!*"

She looked at me with a fierceness I had never seen. As if all her love, her very essence, was distilled into that moment, into something she could send to me by the very power of her gaze. Then she died.

I couldn't even cry out, I was so deep in shock. A white hot rage came over me, and I swore I would destroy whoever had taken her life. If I died in the process, then at least I would meet her in the afterlife. Or so I hoped. I was a wreck, covered in her blood. Then the sound of the sirens, closer now, finally pierced my haze of grief. I kissed her one last time and gently lowered her to the floor. Then I ran to our room. It was the hardest thing I ever had to do. But she had trained me far too well to disobey. More importantly, it was her dying wish.

I looked in the compartment and found the money and a passport, as if she had known this day would come. Under them was a surprise, a letter of acceptance from the New York School of Photography. It was to be her last gift to me. The tears came again and threatened to overcome me. Half of me wanted to stay and find the tenth assassin, but I had seen them fight and knew I was no match for the man who had killed her. My death here would serve no purpose. So I left and went to America. To photo school."

"God, how I loved her. I'll never get her out of my mind. If you can tell me one thing before you take my life, Solipsum, I would like to know who killed her. I swore revenge and even if I never leave this place, perhaps I will meet her assassin here."

"That one is under the protection of Another. And he yet walks the Earth."

"I demand you tell me—"

"You demand? You *demand?* Have you forgotten whom you address?" He slapped her twice, very fast, very hard.

Then he heard a tiny roar but before he could react, Charlie's dragon bit him.

He bellowed, more in surprise than pain, the little creature's teeth sinking deep into his hand, its eyes afire, still half skin-drawing, not yet fully emerged. Solipsum's other hand shot out and gripped its head. He began pulling.

"Nooo! Don't hurt her—"

Charlie's mouth opened wide in a scream, but only a high thin note emerged. A bolt of white fire shot up her shoulder, igniting like a phosphor in her brain as Solipsum ripped the little dragon from her flesh. He threw it aside, its body flying through the air to land in a heap, bloodied and twitching. Relish scrambled over and watched it raise its head to emit another tiny roar, a roar that was cut off when he shoved it into his mouth, teeth crunching noisily.

Charlie shrieked, "I'll kill you," her bonds almost strangling her.

Solipsum snapped his fingers and she froze. "You will do exactly nothing, except what you are told. Now shut up."

He turned to his servant. "Relish. Watch her. I must think."

Then he stalked away.

One foot in front of the other. One foot in front of the other. And don't look down. Phoena had been repeating these words over and over, the mantra helping to numb her mind to what she was beginning to see as a hopeless quest. She and Bruun now descended a set of seemingly endless steps. With no hand railings. They were cracked and ancient, slippery with some sort of hellish lichen that made for treacherous footing at the best of times. Having only one eye wasn't helping matters. The steps followed a wall that was itself even older. Mottled with grayish discolorations, it sloughed off pieces of itself like diseased skin that sometimes looked at her.

She pushed a piece of hair from her face and heard again the high and rising cry, oddly feminine, that seemed to come from all directions at once.

What is that? God, there are so many weird sounds in this place.

Her skin felt clammy in the damp and humid air, the strange tribal leathers she wore touching her with an undeniable but not uncomfortable intimacy. She forced her mind back to the present, to their relentless pace, the tireless Bruun leading them God only knew where. Suddenly she could not go any farther, she had to rest, if only for a moment. She watched his retreating back, noticing again his ragged ear. "How do you know where we're going?" she asked loudly.

He looked back at her. "You must be quiet, Phoena. You will attract the attention of whatever lurks here."

"Okay. Enough of this cryptic nonsense. If I don't get some more answers, I'm not moving another inch."

Bruun halted his descent and turned to her with his button-like eyes. "What do you wish to know?"

"Why do you look like a stuffed toy?"

His eyes darted briefly to the shard about her neck. "Because Hell is a place of archetypes. We appear as our true essence."

"And your true essence is . . . ?" She looked at him again and saw in the simple features of the stuffed creature the innocence and unconditional love that shines from all animals.

"I—understand. But what about me? Why do I still look like me?"

"Because you are under my protection. It hasn't been necessary for you to touch this part of your soul. You still journey through Hell as a human."

"Oh."

"May we continue?"

"One last question," her curiosity getting the better of her. "What did you look like, when you were his Familiar? What did your true essence used to be?"

Something swam then in the depths of his eyes that scared her more than anything she had thus far seen. His snout opened and she saw for the first time his sharp and tiny milk teeth.

"Do you really want to know?"

Before she could answer, a horrible cry split the air and they both turned to the parting mist before them, to be confronted by the most fantastic creature Phoena had ever seen. A Harpy-like bird woman with taloned feet and pearlescent scales floated towards them on enormous rotted gossamer wings. They were buffeted by a wall of fetid air, pressed back against the moist and slimy walls. The creature hovered and Phoena stared at the deep diagonal slash across her chest, a hideous wound still oozing and unhealed, bequeathed by some warrior angel in that long ago Battle. But the creature's face was what Phoena found most striking. Human and heartstoppingly beautiful, all her features flawless in their structure and symmetry, skin of alabaster, eyes a milky marble, her lips the perfect recurve of an Amazon's bow. The whole of her was suffused with an ineffable sadness that Phoena could feel, tugging at her soul.

The Woman of the Walls.

Then the illusion was shattered as the thing's mouth opened in another earsplitting shriek, jaws lined with needle teeth as she swooped to attack.

Phoena and Bruun tried to bolt down the stairs, but the flying creature easily blocked their descent. *Damn, that thing is fast!* Phoena thought. She looked past the monster, almost immediately overcome by profound vertigo, the steps descending forever as they dwindled in the mist below them. There was nowhere to hide.

Then, before her eyes, Bruun—changed. He dropped to all fours as his whole body expanded, muscle and tendon growing, stretching, bulging, cloth becoming fur, his stubby tail now long and lithe. He looked to her like some great and prehistoric predator cat, the slabs of muscle dense and packed, the only white his sabred teeth. She felt the sudden push of wind as the Woman halted her attack, shrieking in outrage, only to be answered by Bruun's deep-throated roar.

The cat reared and swiped at her with a massive paw, claws long and sharp as daggers. The Woman tried to flee but Bruun was too fast, slime and organs exploding as he partially disemboweled her. The creature shrieked in agony, body recoiling and convulsing, her tail a whiplash hawser that swept Phoena off her feet. She tumbled down the steps and instinctively opened her hands to break her fall, only to watch the Print she had so carefully guarded go spilling off the edge and into space.

Still sprawled, she looked up to see Bruun and the Woman locked in a ferocious battle when the thing suddenly spied the falling Print. With cry of triumph, she tried to break free but Bruun hung on, claws sinking deeper as his powerful hind legs tractioned grooves in the treacherous stone. Suddenly, the Woman's head disattached and she extruded a dragonfly body from her own neck. Spreading newly wet wings, she blurred them dry and dove for the Print. Bruun was left gripping her empty husk, shredding it with a roar of frustration. He dwindled, reverting to his stuffed form. Pearly linden leaves of the Woman's skin lay scattered about as he rose to his feet. He looked at Phoena, who was completely stunned by what had just passed.

"What are we going to do now?" she cried.

Bruun gently took her hands in his paws. "Come. We must go on. I know a shortcut. But it is dangerous. Very dangerous. And if we become lost, our return will be measured in geological time."

Interlude Eleven—Las Vegas

Chip Chance was dealing Blackjack from a seven deck shoe at the *MGM Grand*. He looked about him from the depths of the Money Pit and thought *What a bunch of fucking losers. Look at them. Used-up chain-smoking bloated old freezer eagles pissing away their kids' college money. Is there anything more pathetic?* Then a little voice inside him said "Yeah. You." And he realized he was as old and as washed up as they were. In a town that reported 1% of its revenue, where sixty billion annually was sucked out of the economy into a pyramided vortex that outflowed God-only-knew where, he was but a cog in a vast and complex machine. That despite all his dreams and goals, that was all he had ever been, and would ever be. He looked up and saw across the lobby one of the images from that ad campaign by *Fa-Shin, Inc.* that had caused such a stir lately. The one the Gaming Commission wanted shut down because it seemed the suckers were staring at it when they should have been gambling.

In that moment, something inside him snapped.

His hands, always by far the most graceful and eloquent part of him, began to move, to "talk," with a will of their own. Before the players knew it, the buttery slide of the cards had altered, a twenty-one had appeared where it never should have. An old lady with hair like blueberry candy floss shrieked with glee. But the dealer seemed to have forgotten about the eye in the sky.

"Aw Chip! What the hell are you doing?" Salvatore Bavarsi, casino manager, sat back and shook his head, saddened more than he would have believed as he watched his friend from childhood do the one thing he should never have done in this town. His hand went to the phone, security's number half punched when the ad on the back of the magazine he'd been reading stopped him. It looked to be a smaller version of those other weird fashion ads that had sprung up all over town. He found himself staring at it, lost in it, as time opened for him like a lover's arms, welcoming him back to the easy, crazy days of his youth. Days he'd shared with Chip.

His own liquid visual narrative ended and then began again as he set the receiver down and opened up the special computer program. The one he wasn't supposed to have access to. The one that controlled the odds of every slot in the casino.

Hell

Solipsum surfed the Sea of Hell. Twisting and turning, he ascended and declined the waves and spouts of crimson sea, balanced on some curved and sleek impossibility. It was a sea that was shockingly and intelligently alive. He always did this when he needed to think. As he did now.

His mind seemed separated in two. Half concentrated on reading the chaotic temperament of the waters which were trying to kill him. The other half concentrated on the question at hand, the opening of the Gate. Dare he attempt such a thing? Very difficult on Earth, an Opening here was much easier, but only if the proper elements were at hand. And they were. Such a plan was also fraught with great peril, because the chaos that governed much of Hell would greatly influence such an Opening in ways that were as unforeseen as they were unexpected. For even in Hell, there were Rules. Opening a Gate here could rend the very fabric of Reality. And that concept was too much even for Solipsum's mind to hold right now.

He continued surfing, putting the question on hold. As he rode through the churning Zen-like calm of a Red Tunnel, a hand suddenly emerged from one of his gill-like abs. A tiny face followed it. "Help mm-meeeeeee . . ." it puled.

The face was half dissolved, acid-eaten and barely recognizable. Then it became evident that what at first appeared to be a hand was instead a claw. A prosthetic claw.

Solipsum glanced down in mild surprise. He then pushed the creature back inside himself. "Rothman. You obviously need more digesting." The gill resealed.

He looked up again and was confronted by a towering wall of crimson water. Gliding effortlessly to avoid its forward face, he angled in beneath the frothy cusp to ascend the now accessible side. He shook the blood-water from his eyes, body at one with the thing he rode. Solipsum cautioned himself yet again to be careful. He risked all by surfing this Sea—it was one of the few things that could kill him. For only a thing immortal could kill a thing Immortal. As he rode the crest of the thousand foot wave, with all of Hell spread out before him, he laughed a laugh of such shimmering insanity even the sentient Wave drew back.

He realized how much he had missed what he now did, how it was the very risk of Death that sometimes made life so intoxicating. *This* was his nature.

And he finally knew what he had to do.

Charlie opened her eyes and wondered for a split second how much time had passed since the demon had left, and whether Phoena was still alive. Her limbs were starting to ache as the bonds tightened mercilessly to support her sagging weight. Then a wall grew a doorway and Solipsum strode into the room. He was wet with something that looked faintly red, like diluted blood. It raced and lifted with questing psuedopods even as it evaporated. As he walked towards her, she could not help but notice how refreshed he looked. His eyes glittered like chips of fired obsidian.

"Charlie. A virgin. Who would have thought." His laughter, loud and harsh, rang from the walls.

"Master!" Relish scurried in brandishing something. "The Gateway!"

He presented Solipsum with the rolled up Print, covered in viscous white slime.

"At last!"

The demon took it and made a flicking motion with his wrist.

Charlie watched as it telescoped towards her, the emulsion unfurling from its paper base like a membrane. Her eyes squeezed shut and she recoiled as it covered her, molding to her body and face like a second skin she could feel her own skin drinking in. She coughed and sputtered, the bonds tightening as her lungs filled with fluid. Then the feeling passed and she opened her eyes. Her own face stared back at her from the tops of her breasts, from the mirror her skin had become. She lifted her head to look at Solipsum, to see him smiling in a way she found extremely disconcerting. Then her eyes traveled down to below his waist where something—unspeakable—stirred. The fear surged like acid, eating at her guts, but she could not look away. "Wh—what happens now?"

"We open the Gate. With your vestal blood."

"This is going to hurt, isn't it?" Her voice was very small.

"You have no idea."

It's almost like Earth she thought as they trudged along the cliff's edge. *But meaner, all jaggedy and black, like everything wants to cut you.* She looked off towards the horizon, light shafting down through the scud of low black clouds, their edges underlit by a malevolent glow that simmered in the distance. The chasm yawned to her right, a mile or more down.

Some short cut. But I am not giving up. Fuck you, Trey Solipsum, demon from Hell or whatever you are. You are not going to beat me. Not this time.

The camera was a comforting weight about her neck and she knew that though they'd lost the Print, with this they still had hope.

Bruun stopped in front of her so suddenly she almost stumbled into him. "A Minion," he whispered. "Let us hope there is only one."

"What—?"

Then she saw it, blocking their path. It was small, only three feet high, rear legs hinged backwards like some giant insect's. It stepped closer and peered at them curiously, body lean and ropy, all muscle and sinew, covered by a black reflective skin like glossy oil. But the creature's most remarkable attribute was its face, with features so simple and expressive they reminded Phoena of a drawing. It seemed to have decided something. As they watched, it extruded a part of its body until it held a spear, wickedly sharp and chitinous in large three-fingered hands.

Then it was running towards them, powerful legs eating the distance. Bruun stepped in front of her, flowing into his fighting form. He lunged forward, massive jaws snapping shut but the creature was too quick. It stabbed the spear into the ground and vaulted through the air with it. A quick somersault, a screech, then it laid the cat's back open with the spear's razored tip. Bruun shrieked in agony and Phoena could only watch in horror as the wound instantly festered, the hellish poison that coated the Minion's blade eating into his body. The cat fell to the ground, the pain so intense he lapsed back to his stuffed form. She heard a sound like Christmas ornaments shattering and turned to see the Minion, it's drawn face all teeth and grin, something dangling from around its neck as it laughed at them.

"Get it!" Phoena screamed, "it grabbed the camera!" She pulled Bruun to his feet and he staggered a bit, then waved her forward, trying to block the pain. She ran after the creature as it scrambled towards a black, serrated ridge, almost over the top when she lunged, catching the camera's trailing strap. She yanked hard, bringing the thing up short, its body almost horizontal as its neck snapped. Bruun behind her made a sound and she quickly pulled him to the ground. Together they watched the little Minion's body tumble down the slope, straight into a nest of other Minions. Bigger Minions.

Phoena could not believe her eyes. *There must be hundreds of them.*

The baby Minion's body came to rest at the forefront of the mass. Two adults pushed their way through and bent to touch it. A momentary silence, then a terrible wailing pierced the air. The mother saw a movement, her head jerking up to see girl and cat, peering over the ridge's crest. She began jumping and pointing and suddenly the entire horde was boiling up the ridge in attack.

Phoena and Bruun turned but it was too late, the cliff edge loomed and there was nowhere to go.

"Get behind me," Bruun roared as he tried to change.

Phoena did but quickly saw his pain was too great, parts of him changing, then snapping back to Bruun-toy. And though he was still very quick and strong, they were no match for these things. It was only a matter of seconds before they were driven towards the cliff's edge. Phoena looked over her shoulder to see a thread of yellow, some great and fiery river, far, far below. One of her feet slipped. She screamed as she tried to balance, arms windmilling, the sickening sensation of nothing but air as she fell over the cliff's edge. A flailing hand brushed Bruun's body, grabbing and sliding but finding no purchase on his cloth skin. He too slipped backwards, her weight too much. *That's it! We're finished!* flared through her mind when her fall was stopped, arm almost wrenched from its socket. She looked up to see Bruun gripping the cliff edge with one paw. *Oh fuck of fuck oh fuck!* her mind shrieked as she balanced in space, only her death grip on his hind leg between her and certain doom. She felt the camera strap slide and instinctively turned a booted foot up, catching it just in time. *For all the good it will do.* She looked up to see the Minions pointing and shrieking as they hurled insults and spears.

And she knew that this time, they were well and truly fucked.

Charlie was beyond pain. She had no idea her body could experience this depth of sensation. And she knew she could never be as she once was. The spiraling, swirling matrix, the Gateway she and Solipsum had co-created, yawned wider and wider until it engulfed her entire field of view. She had no choice but to enter. Her perception shattered as she felt her consciousness facet into billions and billions of individual visions, visions of faces, people, crowds, all races, all colors, all staring back at her. She realized she was simultaneously experiencing the point of view of all of Joshua's images, as she looked out at all those viewers looking in. At once.

She became aware that what she had merged with was that thing, that pattern, that—Suchness made flesh.

She finally understood the seduction of pure Evil. And as with any seduction, she had to come to it of her own free will. Solipsum could not force her.

And God help her—she wanted to.

For in the final analysis, it was all about Power, what you were really like when there was no one left to tell you to stop.

She felt a Force, dark and massive and ancient as Death, a cool wet hardened pulsing thing of such immensity it was like a planet—pushing through her—waiting to join with her.

She tried to resist, but it was utterly futile. Her mind began to shred as she felt herself letting go. A tiny part of her that was the Charlie she knew screamed and screamed and screamed. . .

"Call for her and she will come."

"What are you talking about?" Her arm and shoulder were a burning agony and she knew she couldn't hold on much longer.

"The Sword. Call for her and she will come."

"I can't . . ."

She looked up at Bruun and the Minions and the sheer face of the looming cliff. Spears cut through the air around them, missing by mere inches. *They're just toying with us. It will all be over soon. I'm sorry, Charlie. I tried my best.* She felt her grip loosen as the calm of impending death settled over her like the warm embrace of an old lover.

Bruun's eyes found hers for the final time and his voice, though low, seemed to fill her very soul. "Focus, Phoena. Let go your mind."

"I—I—"

"The Sword, Phoena! Manifest her or we die!"

To her complete surprise, her mind let go and the world went white. The drum sound came crashing down upon her, throbbing, pounding, as it bore the voice, the chant, the words she suddenly understood. Her mouth opened wide as a scream burst forth, rocketing up from the core of her being, the shard around her neck burning hotter and hotter, first red then white as it seared through her flesh. Her throat split wide as the scream became longer, a piercing ululating shriek as the metal finally subsumed into her body. She felt a molten fusion consume her, raging unchecked through body and blood, the pain now of molecular intensity. Every bone, every muscle, every cell supernova-ed in an ecstasy of light and became something—more. Flesh ripped, ribs cracked, her femurs splintered and reformed, expanding as her body stretched, lengthened, grew. Her mind cleaved and it all came flooding back as she finally re-membered who and what she was. She felt the shining essence of her will take the wild and fiery thing inside her and shape it, molding its en-ergy, channeling the whole of it down to her right hand where it emerged from her body.

As a beautiful, burning Sword.

Energy still crackled about her, the air laden with the reek of brim-stone. Then the coiling streaking bands of light subsided, to reveal a be-ing transformed into something so beautiful and deadly even the Minions were rendered mute. She looked up to see an expression on Bruun's face she had never seen. Fear. And pain? Then she realized she was crushing his small cloth foot. The one she still clung to. Needlessly.

She vaulted back onto the cliff face, tumbling through the air to land like a leaf on legs that felt longer, more powerful and *pointed?* Phoena looked down to see they had changed into delicate gazelle-like hind limbs, fur-covered and cloven-hooved. Her leathern vestments had ex-panded too, and hugged her newly muscular torso as closely as they did her previous form. She shook her hair, bells louder now and deeper, Sword held aloft as she *roared*. There was a deathly silence in its wake. The Minions gazed now upon a being transformed, light years beyond the frail thing they had earlier seen as sport. She had become some-thing both Dark and Light, equal parts of Heaven and Hell, a pagan foot planted firmly in each Place. She had become again that which she had always been.

The Angel Raphaela. Of the Fallen.

And it instantly became clear to her why she had been the only vessel that could withstand Solipsum's presence.

Her mouth opened wide and she laughed a laugh of utter madness as she advanced on the horde, Sword scything through their tight and screaming ranks. The creatures of Hell fell back in terror and confusion, then pushed by those behind, renewed their onslaught with even greater ferocity.

Bruun crawled back onto the cliff top and saw through Phoena's new limbs the vicious battle that ensued. A battle she was winning. He marveled for an instant at what she had become. He saw the Minion corpses heaped around her, the ground black with ichor. Screams of the living and dying filled the air, the battle's din incredible. Suddenly he convulsed as the pain crashed through his mind's last defenses, the poison finally coursing through his body unchecked. Then he felt something, a different sensation, a coruscating ripple through his very soul—the rend in the fabric of Reality. Pushing himself upright with the last of his strength, he stood on his stubby feet. "Phoena! The Gate is opened!"

She turned and a Minion slipped her guard, a spear growing as it ran towards the cat. Bruun snarled, claws extruded, already swiping at its head when the poison reached his heart and—squeezed. Pain like a thousand suns flared and blinded him, slowing his paws. The Minion easily ducked, planting its feet, its entire weight behind the savage spear thrust that pierced the cat's exposed belly. Blood and stuffing gushed out as the creature twisted the blade, Bruun's eyes bulging with disbelief.

"NOOOOOOO!" Phoena screamed as her eye met his, already rushing back, too late, too late.

The Minion was still frantically reabsorbing its weapon when Phoena's blade sliced down like an axe and cut the thing in half. Bruun collapsed to his knees, the blood soaking into his cloth skin, the Minions screaming in triumph. As one they rushed Phoena and she was almost buried in their writhing, glistening bodies.

Then she let go the last vestiges of her humanity.

The blade became a blur as limbs and heads and pieces flew, her speed and strength terrifying as she killed the filthy creatures with a complete and utter lack of mercy. Everything was subsumed in a scarlet rage she so fully reveled in, roaring, laughing, screaming, swinging, gore splashing the fur of her legs, skin and leather dripping with it now, the Sword a scarlet arc as she gave in to her birthright. The power flowing through her limbs was unlike anything she had ever felt, like nothing she ever dreamed could exist. Hack, slice, pivot, backslash, flow. Soon her feet no longer touched the ground, the blood and corpses too thick. The Minions' screams, the clash of battle, her own curses, all of them blended into one continuous sound that became louder and louder, whose rhythm she felt in her very soul. Her arms hacked faster, chest heaving until with a sudden sweep of her Sword, the last three Minions died and she was left alone, ankle deep in gore.

It was over.

She sheathed the Sword at her back and quickly turned towards her small companion. He lay as she had left him, cloth now crimson, surrounded by heaps of the butchered dead. Blood trickled from the corner of his snout, the mortal wound in his belly already black with corruption. She dropped to her knees and touched his cheek. The black buttons of his eyes opened, shiny with pain and she felt the hot tears well in her own right eye. She cradled his head and brought him close.

"You are almost there." His voice was very faint. "Past those rocks . . . the final doorway."

"But—"

"Go. Please."

She began sobbing. "You can't die! Not after all we've been through!"

" . . . save Charlie . . . and everyone else . . . if you can . . ."

Then his little body went limp and his soul left him.

Phoena's face tilted back to the vault of the sky as she loosed a cry of such rage and anguish as to almost tear her heart out. For all the good it did. She bowed her head, spent, then said a silent farewell to this strange animal who had come to mean so much to her. She was about to stand but instead reached out to touch his face one last time.

"Goodbye, Bruun. I—I hope they have lots of treats for you in Heaven." She kissed his forehead, then wiped the last of the Minion blood from her face and stood, feeling her anger now like a living thing. Her eye blazed in the transformed planes of her face and a horrible smile of anticipation touched her lips.

Wait until he sees me now.

She found the camera by the cliff's edge, and using the straps of her corset, bound it tightly to her body. Then she set off for the final killing field.

Interlude Twelve—Berlin

Christian Briggs, frontman for the band *Bardo* looked out at the crowd and felt for a second that strange sense of unreality wash over him again. Blonde, lean muscled, more striking than good-looking, his voice was an instrument of the gods. It wasn't the first time he'd felt this rush, and he hoped it wouldn't be the last. Even after all these years, he still couldn't quite believe how big they'd gotten, playing now to crowds so huge they needed a space that could land a school of zeppelins.

He peeked past the curtain at the stadium, and had to admit 'the word as stone' Nazi architecture thing worked like a motherfucker. Only this time, those draping swastika flags had been replaced by Campaign of the Century banners. Each was at least five stories tall and there must have been fifty of them ringing the stadium. *Fa-Shin, Inc.* had pulled out all the stops as their exclusive sponsor this tour. (Christian smiled when he remembered what that had cost.) The effect of the banners was very potent. Solipsum here, Phoena there, other people/models/creatures/who knew what, all of it more art than advertising. And Art, he had discovered, was very much like Power. Neutral. Same as music. All of them just vehicles for the message.

He stepped onto the stage still soaked with sweat from their last song, wading through little drifts of flowers and panties, the crowd going nuts, screaming and waving and he knew if he asked they'd do anything for him. Just as he'd probably do anything for them.

The chair was waiting, his favourite guitar already leaning against it. A quick mike check, then he was noodling away, the band giving him space, not really sure what he was up to, not really caring 'cause he'd show them soon enough.

It came out a little choppy at first, probably because he'd started with one song and it took awhile to realize he was actually playing two. When he did, he let the first one, the planned one, go, wanting to see where this other song would lead him. It started coming easier then, the melody taking shape, riffing off some strange shit he'd heard at a club he'd been to, last trip to the Rotten Apple. Some club with a scarlet door. His fingers found the notes and as they did, a hush fell over everyone, so huge and expectant he swore he could hear a girl in the front row drop an egg. Then he picked it up a little, Brady on the base the first to get it, laying down the line and adding a bit—but the right bit—which is all Malchuck on the drums needed. Freaky Frank in his wizard coat kicked in with the keyboards and there it was, the whole thing rolling out the door, screams coming from the crowd like they recognized the song.

He looked out as he played, at that sea of faces and arms and waving glow sticks, at the ads that hung and dominated and looked down on them all and suddenly a great big bubble of *fuck this!* burst inside him. The melody rocked faster and he kicked aside the chair, the band getting wilder as he sliced through the chords, and then he was singing, making up the lyrics, singing against it all, the dead-end jobs, the grinding debt, the fucked up state of everything, the beggaring of our natures and how powerless we feel and it all made perfect sense. The crowd was on its feet, singing it back to him, swaying, surging, touching, lighter spark shimmering, someone torching a Solipsum banner as onlookers cheered. Then another one went up, and another one. It got hotter and brighter and at some point he realized he wasn't singing in English anymore, or German or any other language for that matter. Neither was the crowd. But they both somehow understood each other.

Sweat was pouring off him, hands wringing, cajoling, teasing it from the guitar, his voice like the birth of a storm, and he'd never felt like this before, never held a crowd in his hand like a woman's face and it all came together in a final peak, ecstatic, orgiastic, the crowd one voice and him one voice, *believe*, they sang, *believe* he sang back, higher and higher it took him/them, the energy incredible now, bursting from them both, the crowd one thing, one entity reaching for him, closer and closer their energies came, his, the crowd's, his, the crowd's until neither could wait any longer and he reached out to that girl in the front row, reached out to her hand, the crowd's hand, all those people, and through her, they *touched*

and became One.

Hell

Phoena burst into Solipsum's inner sanctum to be confronted by a sight she would take to the grave—and beyond. A giant swirling Vortex that defied all laws of time and space loomed before her: shards, outward looking windows, the simultaneous perspective of all of Joshua's work. And God! How it pulled at her, like being in Joshua's special room. But this was different, as different as reality was from photography.

She noticed a figure at its center, naked, beautiful and—*silver? Is that Charlie? Why is all that blood at her feet? And that look on her face, the same as on the Print. Oh God, Charlie, what has he done to you?*

She saw Solipsum then, standing on the other side of the Vortex. He looked magnificent, the very embodiment of virile vehemence. He spoke and she heard a sound, a sound that cracked the very air, cascading through her, resonating, vibrating, a sound she had never heard but instantly recognized. The sound of her Own True Name. Her blood began to sing as the power and recognition flooded through her, all of it crashing back, the memory of that night she had blocked for so long.

The night they had made love in their archetypal forms.

Solipsum smiled as he saw the realization dawning in her features, a genuine smile, as one bestowed upon an equal. "I never dreamed you would get this far, let alone that you would actually remember."

"What have you done to Charlie?"

"Isn't it obvious?"

Phoena's eyes strayed to the pool of blood at her lover's feet and she knew how he had opened the Gateway. A volcanic blast of rage almost consumed her.

"I'm going to kill you."

Solipsum laughed. "Over that?" He made a dismissive gesture. "That is but meat, while we, on the other hand, are Gods. That night we joined—have you forgotten how magnificent that was?"

"No. I haven't forgotten." She looked at Charlie and something happened. It was like a window thrown open on the dusty and unused spaces of her soul, the light washing over everything—cleansing, illuminating, purifying.

Her eye found Solipsum's and her smile became terrible. "I've remembered it all. How I became as I am now when we made love, how much I enjoyed what happened that night. To the very depths of my being." She slowly unsheathed her Sword and pointed it at him. "But that doesn't change what you are, you bastard! You're a thing, Solipsum, a mockery that sucks the life from everything it touches because it can't come to grips with the depths of its own loneliness. No matter how many pictures you're in, how many people you fuck, how much you kill and hate, you'll *never* know what it is to be loved, though you secretly yearn for it with all your black, black soul!"

Solipsum recoiled, eyes bulging, his face suddenly slack. Phoena finally felt that horrible weight of lust lift as she regained control of her body, no longer ashamed of what she'd done or how it had made her feel, *no longer confusing a physical sensation with who she really was.*

Her vision went red as she held her Sword aloft, the energy crackling up and down its gleaming length. She stood at the ready as Solipsum strode towards her, his black leather trench coat discarded, lifting and snapping in his wake. A long and brilliant blade of Hell materialized in his right hand, glowing like some air-burned glyph.

Phoena snarled, hooves set on the hard stone floor as she dropped to a crouch with her blade held high. Solipsum circled, Sword moving in lazy arcs, its tip flicking out like a serpent's tongue, testing her guard. She sensed in his movements a subtle shift, an almost unconscious attention to her blind periphery as he toyed with her, teased her, she almost hypnotized before his mouth opened wide in a terrifying scream as the downswing came at her.

She met the attack head on, the two blades crashing in a shower of sparks, steel ringing like notes from the One True Song.

Then it was a game of slash and parry, twist and thrust, the two Swords meeting again and again, their edges almost fused, their contact so continuous. The demon used a two-handed grip that was slightly slower but so much more powerful. She felt each bone-jarring impact in her shoulders and arms, marveling that her blade had not yet shattered. And he smiled all the while, that secret and compelling smile he had used to such effect in all their many pictures.

Then he came too close, trying to jam and overpower her, to force the battle to a speedy end. She saw his mistake and let him move in, timing his commitment, suddenly pivoting, deflecting the thrust and reversing her blade to lock his guard, trapping him. She braced her legs and put her back into it, forcing his Sword down lower and lower, until the hilt of his blade touched her thigh. He smiled.

Why is he—

She felt a massive spear of pain as the blade concealed in the hilt of his Sword plunged deep into the meat of her leg. She howled in anguish and instinctively kicked up, almost hitting his face, hoof clanging off steel. He wrenched his Sword free with a curse, hilt blade retracting.

Fuck, fuck, fuck, I did not see that coming!

Her leg was afire, blood pouring from the hole in her thigh, the leg almost buckling under her. His tail lashed out, coiling around her good leg like a whip. He yanked hard, and gravity took her. She fell backward but instead of fighting the motion, she rode it, kicking high, Sword arm managing a perfect upstroke before she crashed to the floor. She heard the sound of steel on stone and wondered how that could be.

Until she saw his severed hand, still clutching his Sword, and knew she had struck true.

She quickly scrambled to her feet, triumph gleaming in her eyes, ready to administer the *coup de grace*. He grimaced at her, clutching the stump of his right hand, but the blood was already slowing to a trickle. As she watched, the hand on the floor flew backward, reattaching itself to his wrist in a writhing fury of knitting vein and artery. Solipsum swung his Sword experimentally, laughing heartily at her dismay.

Then grew to twice his former size.

And sprouted three more arms, all holding Swords.

She instinctively covered her wound with her free hand, trying to staunch the flow of blood. *Fuck, Phoena, don't just watch the show. Something happened, he fixed himself, he's giving you the clues, think, think, think or fucking die . . .*

Then she felt the energy emanating from her core, a cool and blue and soothing balm, healing, healing, pain dissipating and *oh god he's figured out what I'm doing, here he comes . . .* and then there was no more time for thought as four blades came at her, two a side.

Parry, deflect, bells ringing, her arms working faster than she had ever used them, not even able to thrust or slash, parrying, parrying, only parrying as she was forced backwards by his relentless advance. She felt a heat behind her and kicked back, cloven hoof shattering a child-brazier. Burning embers sparked through the air, a tiny meteor fury, some smoldering in her hair until she shook her head violently.

She thought for an instant about Charlie. Then remembered the nothingness she had seen in her eyes when she first came into the room. *He's done something to her and she can't help you, Phoena. You're on your own.* Two blades almost made her pay for the lapse and she lashed out wildly, a lucky swing grazing his face. His head jerked back, crown flying as he staggered, disconcerted and she took a moment to breathe, breathe, breathe.

"Didn't like that, did you?" she taunted, panting now. "Even though you can fix yourself, that model thing runs pretty deep. Your face, your face, your pretty face."

In answer, he whirled the four blades so quickly their arcs became solid, like the spinning wheels of a chariot. She thought ruefully that what she fought now was a far cry from the Minions she had battled earlier. Fighting the master was not like fighting his servants, and giving vent to fury far different than going past it.

She felt the deep throb in her leg, the flow of blood now slowed to a trickle. But the wound and the ceaseless battle had taken their toll and she knew she would soon be finished. *There must be a way to beat him. There must.*

There isn't, Phoena.

Her eyes widened and she suddenly knew that he had probably been able to see her thoughts since the moment she'd arrived. As she watched, he grew again, more arms sprouted, and then he was attacking for what she knew was the final time. Her arm came up, legs braced and body leaning to ward off his downswings *clang! clang! clang!* Her muscles screamed, her whole body a symphony of pain as she turned the edges of three blades, then kicked him in the groin—to no avail, his codpiece more than decoration.

Blades attacked from all sides now, a moving steel cage, the demon's ten arms like battling a threshing machine. Her body bled from a dozen wounds, Sword hand slick with her own blood. Perhaps were that Sword and her abilities not so new to her, she would have been able to relinquish the conscious control necessary to defeat him.

Such was not the case.

She pressed on and gave the last of what she had. The battle's pitch built to a feverish intensity, then all ten Swords united as one and crashed against Phoena's lone blade. It shattered and she stood holding what was left of its magnificence.

One of the pieces slid over to where Charlie stood on the cusp of the Vortex. It bumped against her feet. It was enough to finally distract the silver girl from the hypnotic spectacle she had almost become lost in. She looked down at it, curious.

The demon was now nearly twenty feet tall and before Phoena could even think to run, his Swords disappeared and he snatched her up with two hands, finally noticing the little camera around her neck.

"What's this?"

Two more miniature arms grew from the ones that held Phoena, talons slicing straps until he gripped the camera. Then both arms and camera expanded in size so the demon could better see what he held. "Joshua's toy? Ha, ha, ha, ha, ha! Very good, Phoena, very good!"

The formerly small camera was now much larger than Phoena, and Solipsum moved it below the struggling girl, the better to see her face when he crushed her.

"We could have gone so far together. But it's too late now."

She finally ceased her movements and looked up at the towering demon's face, his razored teeth glittering, eyes burning with triumph. She saw the giant swirling Vortex of shards behind him, some with images, some with reflections of her, the camera and his extended hands. She remembered the Station and an inspiration nova-ed in her mind. Her leg began to rise, just as she heard his voice.

"Goodbye, Phoena."

He squeezed and she screamed as two of her ribs snapped.

Charlie had lost a great deal of blood and was very weak. She could sense how things would be if Solipsum won. How she would not die but rather merge into what was to become. This was something he had not told her, perhaps because he had not known.

Her eyes defocused and she saw Clarity for an instant in the chaos of the Vortex. She remembered that day in Joshua's studio, when she'd encountered something larger than she was.

Something she'd had to go around.

Not through.

And she finally knew what she had to do.

"Demon!" her voice a crystal, clear and ringing. "Turn and face me!"

She picked up the shard of Phoena's Sword and prepared to drive it into her own throat.

Solipsum's head jerked around and Phoena saw the fear grow in his eyes. She looked at Charlie, at the shard edge poised beneath her chin, and thought *so this is how it ends.* Her eyes found those of the silver girl's and she heard the words, shining and beautiful.

"I'm sorry, Phoena. I love you."

Phoena's eye squeezed shut and she felt the tears come. The immense pressure had stopped, the demon distracted. Still the waves of pain smashed into her, again and again, and all she wanted to do was sleep. To just forget it all and sleep. A memory flashed in the darkest depths of her consciousness, like sunlight glinting from a mirror in the Station, the Station, seeing herself, her leg raised . . . She opened her eye and saw again the Vortex swirling behind Solipsum, some images, some reflecting, reflecting, reflecting . . . and there it was, the answer, lifting her leg, his name torn from her throat . . .

"SOLIPSUM!"

His head turned back, hands already squeezing, her ribs grinding, the pain like the spears of Christ as she gritted her teeth and hissed,

"Smile, fucker!"

then stamped down with all her strength on the camera's giant shutter. A huge flash erupted, blinding, illuminating, Phoena suddenly consumed in every wavelength of light, gamma, ultraviolet, infra red and light she had no name for, dancing and overlapping, plunging her into an implosion of vastness that short-circuited her entire sensorium.

In Charlie's mind, something had happened. The relentless push she had felt before was gone and she found herself surrounded by—space. So much space. Worlds of possibility spun and collided, crashed and blended, and she understood that the same instant she had always recognized whenever she looked through the camera was the same instant in which the Universe existed.

The Now.

And everything that ever was
everything that would ever be,
all the Charlies she ever was,
and all the Charlies she would ever be
joined together in a sea of she,
manifesting simultaneously.

In that instant, Charlie touched the hand of God, and realized that it was her own. That this was true for everyone and everything.

And she became filled with an overwhelming sense of awe at the astonishing simplicity of it all.

Interlude Thirteen—New York City

Swinington Marzoopiel knew that he would die in the next three months and there was nothing he could do about it. Oh sure, he'd tried every major drug cocktail, radiation nanotherapy, even holistics. Everything money could buy. And it was not enough. Because he had AIDS7, a virus that mutated so quickly his meager defenses were as tissue to a bullet.

He stood now at the threshold of *Barmey's*, one of his churches. One of the places where he had worshipped with a devotion that would shame even the most pious. The fact that his worship had taken the form of shopping in no way diminished its purity.

Yet all he felt now was a crushing sense of betrayal. For he had discovered that he prayed to a god that could not hear him, because it never had. A god whose bloated interests he had served and served well his whole adult life. Mammon. Or as he had come to know her—*Style*. He had perpetuated her agenda and been her high priest by constantly, ceaselessly selling that which was new. Making sure that it appeared on TV, in magazines, on billboards and bus shelters. Never questioning the merit of a thing, its newness passport enough to go to the front of everyone's attention. To numb and dumb a people so sense-bludgeoned they could only crave the poison that was killing them. This poison he administered: the *useless new*.

He stepped into the store, knowing this might be his last time in the *Church of The Buy it NOW!* As he merged with the throngs of shoppers, he once again marveled at the Campaign Joshua, Phoena and Solipsum had co-created. *My God, the response. Who would have thought that in this day and age people could be so moved to do something.* A small memory surfaced, something to do with lab animals and cocaine. How they would forgo even food in favor of the drug. How they would eventually starve to death, still shoving their little bodies against the coke dispensing lever even though it dispensed no more. He pushed the thought aside, striding deeper into the store.

As he walked past displays and backlit Campaign of The Century ads, he was surprised that what used to excite him no longer did. Gone the were the allure of clothes and ties, the siren call of designer *dreck*. Perhaps the proximity of death had given him a distance he had never had. A distance that allowed him to see for the first time what a terrible waste of potential humanity had become. Tears formed in his eyes and he thought,

As I stand here dying, what has given me the most joy in my life?

Images flashed—his childhood, brother, parents, teachers, a trip to the Appalachians that had changed his life. His first gay experience. Being run out of his small town, with nothing but the clothes on his back and the tears on his face. Acceptance by a House in New York when he thought he would die of starvation. And in all these thoughts, through all these images, did a single instance of "shopping" arise?

No.

He stopped, momentarily stunned by this revelation. He looked down at his hands and realized that he had inadvertently wandered over to the fragrance counter. He was holding a bottle of *CHOKE*, the new fragrance by *Fa-Shin, Inc.* He looked up and his eyes met those of a young white male clerk, obviously gay, obviously a massive fashion victim. All around him people shopped with the frenzy of crack addicts on paycheck Friday. The young man smiled and his eyes went wide with sudden recognition. "You're Him! Swinington Marzoopiel! The Stylist of the Stars!"

Swinington just smiled. The clerk looked down at Swinington's hands and gushed, "It's the latest. It smells sooooo good!."

"No. It doesn't."

The boy looked confused, his eyes then riveted by what they saw in the other man's.

"It smells like what it is." said Swinington. "Rotted Luxury."

He jumped up on the counter, then took the bottle, turned and hurtled it at a massive back lit display. The image that had become the corner-stone of The Campaign of The Century, Phoena and Solipsum kissing, shattered into a million pieces. There were a few screams and sparks from the arcing wires. Then nothing.

Silence.

Swinington jumped up onto the counter and yelled "All of you! Listen to me! Look at that sign! *Look* at it! Before I smashed it, it held you in its thrall. It was Mother, Father, Brother, Sister, Lover, Friend. And they all whispered the same thing. Buy . . . buy . . . buy . . . But look behind it. Look at what's really doing the talking. What is forcing you to do something you don't want to do. What is really *there*!"

From the crowd, a tiny voice, a child's voice, said, "Nothing."

"That's right. NOTHING! The emperor has NO CLOTHES! It's a fucking PICTURE! And IT WILL NEVER LOVE YOU! Don't listen to NOTHING anymore. Don't listen to NOTHING masquerading as SOMETHING that gives a fuck about you. You don't need anything to be yourself. You never did. AND YOU NEVER WILL! What's really there? NOTHING!"

The Power of Change resides in the Power of One.

Then another voice was heard. "Nothing!" And another. "Nothing! Nothing!" More voices joined in. "Nothing! Nothing! Nothing! *No Thing!*" There was a loud crash as another back lit display was destroyed. More people took up the chant. *"No Thing! No Thing! NO THING!* . . ."

Swinington jumped off the counter, his boot heels crushing broken shards of Phoena and Solipsum's faces. He looked up, back at the hole where the display used to be. And saw, in one startling instant, a girl,

naked and beautiful and silver staring back at him, tall as its frame. He reached for her and reality
   shifted.
   She smiled and shook her head. Then, as if something had just occurred to her, she made a gesture with her hand. Instantly his whole body was electrified, as if every cell had realized its true potential and expanded into something—else. The pain left as quickly as it came, and he collapsed to his knees, whimpering with relief. His head came up to see the mysterious girl had almost disappeared. Then she turned back to look at him. One last time.
   "Charlie?"
   Charlie raised a finger to her lips. "Shhhhhhh."
   Then reality reasserted itself and became three dimensional once again. Sounds intruded and he realized that he'd better pick himself up and get out of there, before he was arrested. He stood and squared his shoulders, the sunlight edging him like a lover. Broken bits of glass fell away as he strode towards the exit and the dawn of a new day.
   For the tide had turned, the Campaign of The Century had tipped.
   The *other* way.

Hell

   When next she opened her eyes, Phoena found herself lying on the floor, battered, bloody and still behooved.
   So it wasn't a dream . . .
   She slowly rose to her feet, lowering her head as she placed a hand over her side, focusing on directing that blue and cool energy she had felt earlier. Immediately the pain in her side subsided, slowly decreasing to a level she could tolerate. She lifted her face and almost screamed, so real was Solipsum in the photograph before her. She stepped closer and looked at him frozen, his expression a mixture of fear and determination, muscles rigid, veins like bridge cables as he tensed to squeeze—forever.
   She paused for a moment to tie her hair back, then wandered around to the back of the image, curious. It was blank and smooth, except for the printing along its bottom edge: *Polaroid Color*. And a number.
   1000.
   She shook her head in wonder, bells lightly tinkling, wishing that Joshua were here to see this.
   She turned to the Vortex, whose relentless pull had finally ceased. Millions of shards, like tiny jewels of perspective, hung in space—waiting. A stunned and naked Charlie stood surrounded by them, still hold-

ing the broken blade of Phoena's Sword to her throat. Her silver skin reflected the shimmering maelstrom, and Phoena found herself overcome
by emotions she had no name for.

She slowly made her way to Charlie, Sword hilt sheathed. Her lover
looked at her, hands steady as a rock as they gripped the blade, eyes
gleaming with the light of distant stars. "Phoena? You look—different."

Phoena just smiled.

"I'm not all—back yet. I can still stop it. The buying . . . the madness . . ."

"Charlie?" Phoena spread her arms, palms open. "I think it has to
happen of their own free will."

The silver girl sighed and lowered the blade. "You're right."

Phoena glimpsed a Vortex shard and gasped as she recognized Swinington in its tiny plane. Then it winked out. As she watched, others slowly
began to extinguish themselves. "What's going on? What does it mean?"

"It means they aren't staring anymore. It means they're deciding for
themselves whether or not to look at images designed to manipulate
them. I—I think they're finally growing up."

She touched Phoena's cheek. "What happened to your eye?"

"Plane fare."

"What?"

"I'll tell you later."

Charlie's gaze dropped to the floor for a moment, then returned to this
woman who had come to mean so much to her. Who had journeyed to
Hell for her. *But I'm tainted. Will she still want me after . . .*

"You know what he had to do to me. To open the Gate."

"Sshhhh. Never mind. It's all over now."

"He took my dragon, a—and God, Phoena! He killed Joshua and
Russ and so many people. . . . . . ."

Phoena didn't know what to say. Charlie's face was a silvered mask
of anguish, and as she watched, mercury tears streamed slowly down her
cheeks, cutting through Phoena's own reflection. Then it all became too
much and the mirrored girl burst into tears, collapsing into Phoena's arms.
It seemed that all her grief, and the world's too, came flooding out in a
wave of emotion so powerful Phoena found her barriers breaking down,
even her wounds forgotten, so at the last, she could only cry with her.

Long moments passed before Charlie finally raised her head and looked
into Phoena's remaining eye. Then she deliberately pulled her lover's face
close. "You came for me, Phoena. You came to Hell for me."

"For us."

Charlie felt the joy blossom in her, stroking her lover's hair, feeling how matted and bloody it was, feeling in that texture how hard Phoena had fought for them. For her.

"I love you, Phoena. And I always will."

"I love you too."

Phoena pulled back so they could kiss, deeply and passionately, tasting of and drinking of each other, and time, for each, stood still, their souls transported for that small eternity to a place beyond everything.

They slowly separated and Phoena tilted her head to offer a small smile. "Now let's get the fuck out of here. Before we get all mushy on each other."

Charlie laughed and Phoena marveled at how much she sounded like her old self. In that instant, though Phoena knew her friend had changed, she somehow knew that what made Charlie the remarkable girl she was, remained.

"How do we . . . ?"

"That's the easy part. Watch this."

Phoena repaired her Sword with the slightest effort of her will, then sliced a Gate in Solipsum's reality. "I'm learning . . ."

As they stepped through, Charlie finally understood the meaning of the Symbol.

Epilogue

*Fa-shin Inc.'s Campaign changed the world. In the beginning, it was even in the way we thought it would. No company in the history of the planet had ever seen such profits in such a short amount of time. But as we learned to our dismay, and ultimately our destruction, consumer wealth is a resource like any other. When it is depleted past a certain point, without thought as to gradual replenishment, without thought **that people are human beings and not simply living wallets,** then you are left with nothing.*

*Because a large piece of the debt incurred by the general public was loaded onto our Buy It Now! cards. No one thought about **what would happen if everyone suddenly decided they weren't going to pay.** We didn't believe such a thing was possible. We were simply too arrogant and complacent in our surety that the herd would never behave in unison. **But they did.** A hard lesson. One that proved the death of Fa-Shin, Inc.*

Here my critics will doubtless accuse me of some nebulous and totally inappropriate spirituality. But I will say what must be said. What is in the final analysis, the truth.

Joshua Stone's images had an agenda of their own. Beyond Fa-Shin, Inc.'s. Beyond even Solipsum's.

People finally woke up to the rampant consumerism that had almost destroyed their lives. They slowed down in their buying, suddenly harshly and intelligently selective. They became aware of how they had been manipulated into buying things they didn't need and didn't really want, all to fill the void in their lives. They began to ask simple questions. And if the answers weren't forthcoming to their satisfaction, they simply—stopped.

The effects of the Campaign didn't end with its demise. They continue to this day. Because the spine is broken. Consumerism just doesn't know it is dead.

Yet.

—from Poverty Whip—An Inside Look at The Campaign of The Century—Maurice Vellum

Center Island, Toronto, Canada

"No one really believes you, you know."

Phoena looked at Magma, immaculate in her shiny white raincoat so at odds with the dull and waxy pallor of her face. She could see the mixture of perverse curiosity and pity in the other woman's pale gray eyes. *At least you still have two of them.*

"Let it go, Magma."

"I won't, Phoena. I simply won't. They still haven't found his body yet. And that whole story about him going insane and killing Joshua Stone and that other boy—it simply makes no sense. Trey would never—"

"Wouldn't he, Magma? I think you and I both know he was capable of worse. Much worse." Phoena produced a dry smile. "Don't tell me after all the years you spent with him you didn't know what he really was."

The booker's mouth trembled. "What do you mean?"

"It doesn't matter. What does is that you're finally free of him."

Phoena saw doubt, confusion and finally acceptance swimming through Magma's eyes in the time it took to draw a breath.

"You're right. I am free of him," she said quietly.

"And you own the top agency in the world."

"Unless Rothman Cartilage stakes his claim."

"I somehow doubt that will happen. But who knows? He may still turn up. I mean, Elora did, didn't she?"

"Yes," said Magma with an expression if distaste. "Half dead in that insane asylum in Luxembourg."

Phoena was suddenly very tired. "I have to go now. It's been a pleasure." Without waiting for an answer, she began making her way through the throng.

She came closer to the huge portrait of Joshua, its lower quarter obscured by heaps of wreathes and flowers, their colours saturated, fragrance now muted by the light rain. She had scattered his ashes earlier in the day and thought for a moment how strange that had felt, to hold him in her hand.

The turnout still surprised her. She hadn't expected it and she certainly hadn't planned for it. That meant a lot of these people would probably be stuck here, now that the service had ended. Already the campfires were springing up and the sun had not even set.

It seemed every person Joshua had ever known had decided to come. Oh sure, there was the expected collection of family, friends and former lovers, models, make-up artists and magazine mavens. But there were also a great many people Phoena had never seen, and at first she couldn't understand why they had come. The only thing they had in common was an expression of peace, as though some monumental weight had been lifted from their shoulders. It took her awhile to figure out that it was the Campaign that had brought them here, the Campaign that had required this final touchstone. Because Joshua's work had somehow catalyzed them all into a spontaneous action that had broken the back of a thing the world had thought untouchable. So they had come to see him off, to laugh and cry and curse their own gullibility, to share and hug and hold and tell, all of it under a younger Joshua crouching in a helicopter's bay with a slightly bemused gaze, as though he couldn't quite believe what they had all created.

Phoena felt the tears come again, slightly surprised that she still had so much sorrow left inside. She let the memories take her, as they so often did these days, memories that now straddled two worlds, one so fantastic she still had trouble believing it existed. The acrid stench of minion blood suddenly filled her nose and she exhaled sharply. The revenant vanished. But not the feel of killing in her good right hand.

"Hi, Phoena. Are you okay?"

She slowly unclenched her fist. "I'm . . . not really sure. It all still feels slightly surreal. Like he'll somehow magically reappear with this puzzled look on his face and ask us what all the fuss is about." Her eyes found Quinby's. "What are your plans after this?"

"Jane and I are taking an extended vacation. Somewhere nice and hot. And quiet. What about you?"

"I think Charlie and I are going to take the advice of a certain stylist we both know."

"Is it true? That Joshua willed it all to you and her?"

"You mean the studio? Or should I say what's left of it."

"Yeah. Rumor has it the real estate alone is worth a fortune."

"It's not something I'm really thinking about now, Quin." She paused, then asked softly, "Are you sad he's gone?"

"Who, Joshua?"

"No. Solipsum."

"Sometimes. But most of the time I'm glad. It lets me pretend I'm stronger than I am. Who knows where things would have gone if he was still here. I think you know what I'm talking about, don't you?"

"Yes. I do." They were silent for a moment, birdsong clear and beautiful in the air around them. Phoena turned to the other girl. "Quinby, you don't know anything about what happened to Joshua's camera, do you?"

"His camera? What are you talking about?"

"It seems to have disappeared. Charlie thought it would be a good idea to have it here at the funeral but now I can't find it. I think someone may have stolen it."

"Maybe one of his fans. Was it important?"

"Only in a sentimental way. It's all that's really left of him. Besides the pictures, I mean. I like to think there's a little piece of his magic in it."

"I don't think you need a camera to feel Joshua's magic, Phoena."

"What do you mean?"

Quinby made a graceful gesture that took in the sea of people and campfires before them. "That's magic. And it's probably all the magic you'll ever need." Her eyes were laughing as they found the other girl's.

And Phoena smiled for the first time in what felt like forever.

One Year later—Somewhere in Oregon

It had been a lot different than she'd expected, slow paced and easy and so dreamy-comfortable she still couldn't quite believe it. But, she supposed, it had to end some time. In fact, she was a little surprised things had lasted as long as they had. The old pick-up began protesting so she shifted gears and it crested the hill, grumpy but compliant. The wind ruffled her hair, gravel crunching as she coasted down into the valley, the smell of green summer filling the cab. Her eyes found the small cottage, lit by the rays of the dying sun and she marvelled for an instant at how relaxed she had let herself become in this place.

She turned into the driveway and Betty Blue rolled to a stop, engine still rattling even after she'd pulled the key. Her hand touched the box of prints on the seat beside her, nudes of Phoena she had shot in the wilds near their home. Her career had now blossomed into something so unexpected—fine art of all things—it still brought a smile to her face. Notoriety, it seemed, did have its uses. It had certainly made her some money, money they didn't really need. Phoena had shown her a bank book once with a balance she'd mistaken for the account number. They still hadn't figured out what to do with Joshua's final gift.

She lifted her head and gazed out at the land, the land, the beautiful land, trees burnished by the molten sunlight, glimmers from the water on their little trout pond, already lost in the fractal complexity of it all, the Clarity that the Symbol had bestowed bloomed everywhere now, overlaying and underpinning all that she saw, a poetry, a visual tapestry so complex yet simple that sometimes she felt she would burn in the ecstasy of it. But already it was fading, like a photo left too long in the sun.

And she knew this level of perception would soon be gone completely. Which was maybe for the best, considering.

She slumped back in the seat, throat tight and painful, tears welling as she reached into the pocket of her flannel shirt. The writing swam before her and she crushed the paper, fist slamming into the old truck's cracked vinyl seat, making the box of prints jump. *You have to tell her, Charlie. Before it's too late.* She wasn't even aware that her hand had crept beneath her shirt again, lightly rubbing the soft smooth skin of her belly, as if she could somehow feel the shape of the thing that was growing inside her.

CPSIA information can be obtained
at www.ICGtesting.com
Printed in the USA
BVHW071018181118
533375BV00001B/81/P

9 781612 047225